THE HAWK IS DEAD

Peter James is a *New York Times* and *Sunday Times* bestselling author, best known for his crime thrillers featuring Detective Superintendent Roy Grace, who Queen Camilla recently named as her favourite fictional detective. Praised by critics and much loved by crime and thriller fans for his fast-paced page-turners full of unexpected plot twists, sinister characters and accurate portrayals of modern-day policing, he has won more than forty awards for his work, including the WHSmith Best Crime Author of All Time Award and the Crime Writers' Association Diamond Dagger.

With a total of twenty-one *Sunday Times* number ones, his books have sold more than 23 million copies worldwide and have been translated into thirty-eight languages. The sixth season of the hit drama *Grace*, based on the Roy Grace novels, is currently filming, starring John Simm as the troubled Brighton copper. The series is available to watch on ITVX and BritBox.

Seven of his novels have been adapted into hit stage productions, his most recent being *Picture You Dead*, and his plays have been named 'the most successful stage franchise since Agatha Christie'.

www.peterjames.com
@peterjamesuk
@peterjames.roygrace
@peterjamesuk
@thejerseyhomestead
@mickeymagicandfriends
@PeterJamesPJTV
@peterjamesauthor

The Detective Superintendent Roy Grace books in order:

DEAD SIMPLE

In the first Roy Grace novel, a harmless stag-do prank leads to deadly consequences.

LOOKING GOOD DEAD

It started with an act of kindness and ended in murder.

NOT DEAD ENOUGH

Can a killer be in two places at once? Roy Grace must solve a case of stolen identity.

DEAD MAN'S FOOTSTEPS

The discovery of skeletal remains in Brighton sparks a global investigation.

DEAD TOMORROW

In an evil world, everything's for sale.

DEAD LIKE YOU

After thirteen years, has the notorious 'Shoe Man' killer returned?

DEAD MAN'S GRIP

A trail of death follows a devastating traffic accident.

NOT DEAD YET

Terror on the silver screen; an obsessive stalker on the loose.

DEAD MAN'S TIME

A priceless watch is stolen and the powerful Daly family will do *anything* to get it back.

WANT YOU DEAD

Who knew online dating could be so deadly?

YOU ARE DEAD
Brighton falls victim to its first serial killer in eighty years.

LOVE YOU DEAD
A deadly black widow is on the hunt for
her next husband.

NEED YOU DEAD
Every killer makes a mistake somewhere.
You just have to find it.

DEAD IF YOU DON'T
A kidnapping triggers a parent's worst nightmare
and a race against time for Roy Grace.

DEAD AT FIRST SIGHT
Roy Grace exposes the lethal side
of online identity fraud.

FIND THEM DEAD
A ruthless Brighton gangster is on trial and will
do anything to walk free.

LEFT YOU DEAD
When a woman in Brighton vanishes without a trace,
Roy Grace is called in to investigate.

PICTURE YOU DEAD
Not all windfalls are lucky. Some can
lead to murder.

STOP THEM DEAD
A senseless murder hides a multitude of other crimes.

ONE OF US IS DEAD
Roy Grace is about to find out just how dangerous
a dead man can be.

THE HAWK IS DEAD
Roy Grace never dreamed a murder investigation would take
him deep into Buckingham Palace.

Also by Peter James

DEAD LETTER DROP   ATOM BOMB ANGEL
BILLIONAIRE   POSSESSION   DREAMER
SWEET HEART   TWILIGHT   PROPHECY
HOST   ALCHEMIST   THE TRUTH
DENIAL   FAITH   PERFECT PEOPLE
THE HOUSE ON COLD HILL   ABSOLUTE PROOF
THE SECRET OF COLD HILL   I FOLLOW YOU
THEY THOUGHT I WAS DEAD: SANDY'S STORY

Short Story Collection

A TWIST OF THE KNIFE

Children's Novel

GETTING WIRED!

Novellas

THE PERFECT MURDER
WISH YOU WERE DEAD *(A Roy Grace Quick Read)*

Non-Fiction

DEATH COMES KNOCKING: POLICING ROY GRACE'S BRIGHTON *(with Graham Bartlett)*
BABES IN THE WOOD *(with Graham Bartlett)*

THE HAWK IS DEAD

PETER JAMES

PAN BOOKS

First published 2025 by Macmillan

This paperback edition first published 2026 by Pan Books
an imprint of Pan Macmillan
The Smithson, 6 Briset Street, London EC1M 5NR
EU representative: Macmillan Publishers Ireland Ltd, 1st Floor,
The Liffey Trust Centre, 117–126 Sheriff Street Upper,
Dublin 1 D01 YC43
Associated companies throughout the world

ISBN 978-1-5290-9008-6

Copyright © Really Scary Books / Peter James 2025

Roy Grace®, Grace®, DS Grace®, Detective Superintendent Grace® and DI Grace®
are registered trademarks of Really Scary Books Limited.

The right of Peter James to be identified as the
author of this work has been asserted in accordance
with the Copyright, Designs and Patents Act 1988.

All rights reserved. No part of this publication may be reproduced,
stored in a retrieval system, or transmitted, in any form, or by any means
(including, without limitation, electronic, mechanical, photocopying, recording
or otherwise) without the prior written permission of the publisher.

Pan Macmillan does not have any control over, or any responsibility for,
any author or third-party websites (including, without limitation, URLs, emails and
QR codes) referred to in or on this book.

1 3 5 7 9 8 6 4 2

A CIP catalogue record for this book is available from the British Library.

Map artwork by ML Design
Buckingham Palace illustration © SAHAS2015/Shutterstock.com

Typeset by Palimpsest Book Production Ltd, Falkirk, Stirlingshire
Printed and bound in the UK using 100% Renewable Electricity by CPI Group (UK) Ltd

This book is sold subject to the condition that it shall not, by way of trade or otherwise, be
lent, hired out, or otherwise circulated without the publisher's prior consent in any form of
binding or cover other than that in which it is published and without a similar condition
including this condition being imposed on the subsequent purchaser. The publisher does
not authorize the use or reproduction of any part of this book in any manner for the
purpose of training artificial intelligence technologies or systems. The publisher expressly
reserves this book from the Text and Data Mining exception in accordance with Article
4(3) of the European Union Digital Single Market Directive 2019/790.

Visit **www.panmacmillan.com** to read more about all our books
and to buy them.

THIS NOVEL IS DEDICATED TO HER MAJESTY THE QUEEN'S READING ROOM BOOK CLUB AND LITERARY CHARITY, FOR ALL THE HARD WORK THEY DO IN CHAMPIONING LITERATURE.

AUTHOR'S NOTE

While Their Majesties feature in this novel as themselves, all the words they speak are entirely my own.

The roles of the Royal Household staff are real, but the characters themselves are totally fictitious and my creation.

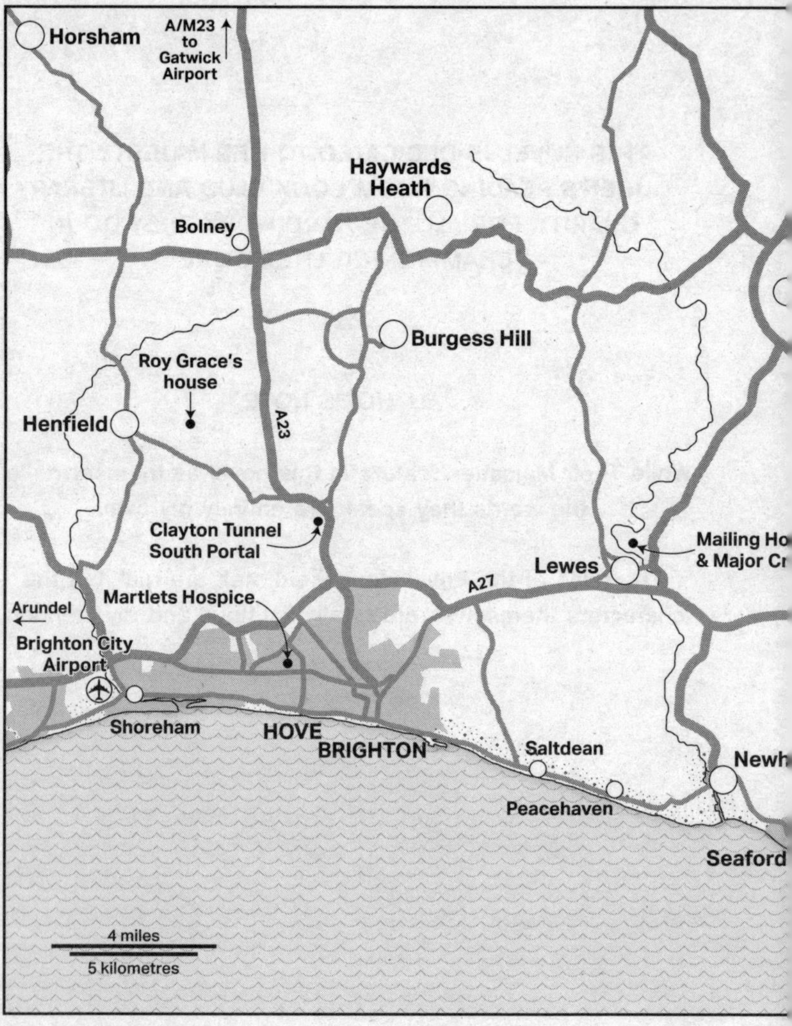
Horsham
A/M23
to
Gatwick
Airport
Haywards
Heath
Bolney
Burgess Hill
Roy Grace's
house
Henfield
A23
Clayton Tunnel
South Portal
Lewes
A27
Martlets Hospice
Arundel
Brighton City
Airport
Shoreham
HOVE
BRIGHTON
Saltdean
Peacehaven
Seaford
4 miles
5 kilometres

SUSSEX

Crowborough
Hawkhurst
Hurst Green
xfield
Heathfield
A22
A21
Battle
Sussex Police HQ
eam
Hailsham
HASTINGS
A259
A27 Polegate
Bexhill
St Wildfrid's Hospice
EASTBOURNE
N

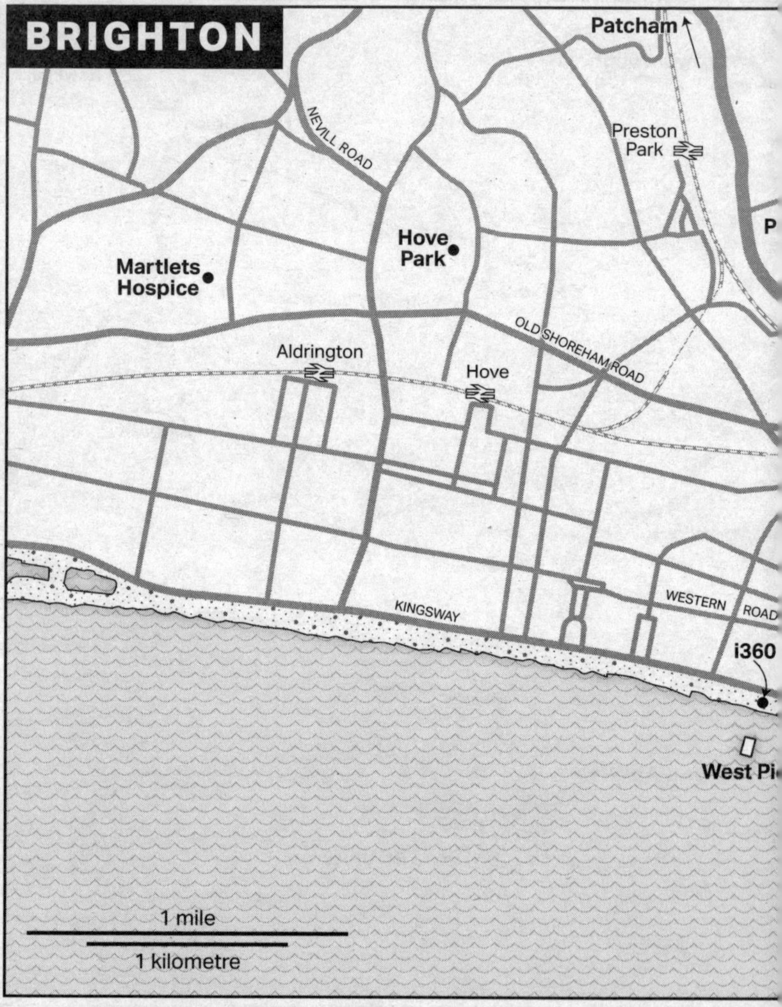

BRIGHTON
Patcham
NEVILL ROAD
Preston Park
Hove Park
Martlets Hospice
P
OLD SHOREHAM ROAD
Aldrington
Hove
WESTERN ROAD
KINGSWAY
i360
West Pi
1 mile
1 kilometre

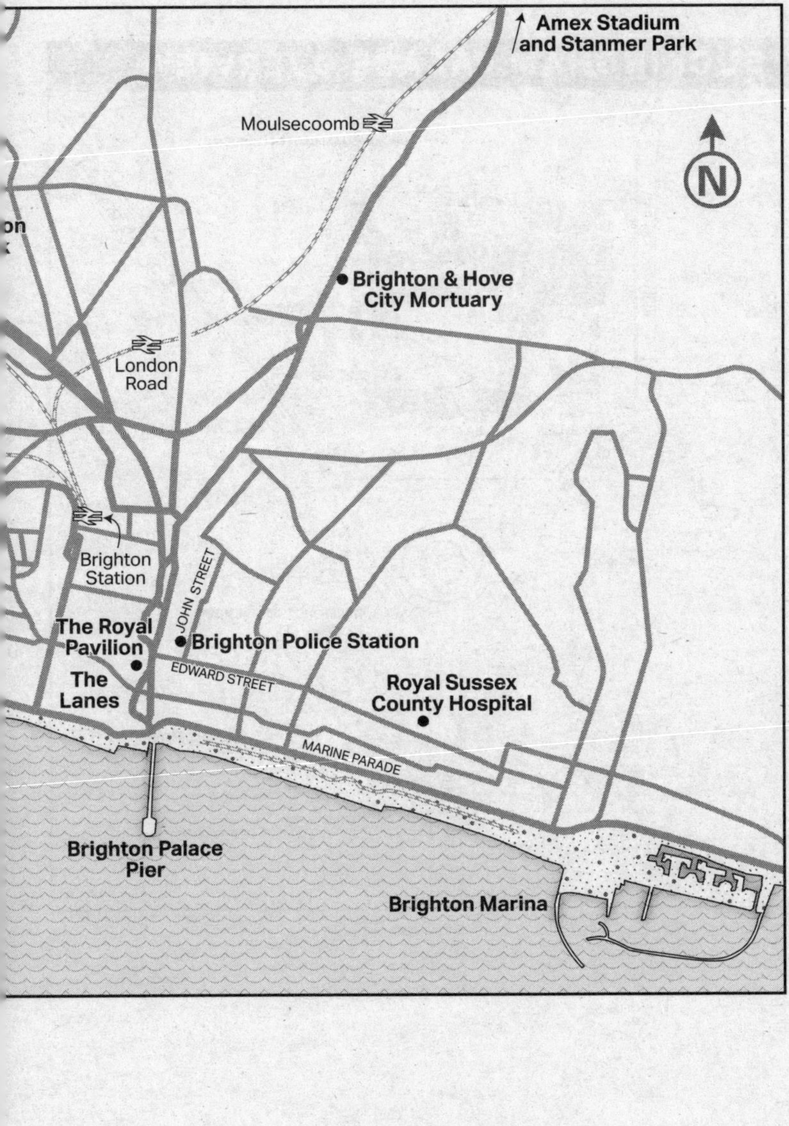
Amex Stadium
and Stanmer Park
Moulsecoomb
Brighton & Hove
City Mortuary
London
Road
Brighton
Station
JOHN STREET
The Royal
Pavilion
Brighton Police Station
The
Lanes
EDWARD STREET
Royal Sussex
County Hospital
MARINE PARADE
Brighton Palace
Pier
Brighton Marina
N

BUCKINGHAM PALACE OVERVIEW

BUCKINGHAM PALACE, NORTH WING

Garden Entrance

Ground Floor

Audience Room

Private Apartments

Private Apartments

Study

Dining Room

First Floor

BUCKINGHAM PALACE, WEST WING

First Floor

- Ball Room
- State Dining Room
- Blue Drawing Room
- Music Room
- White Drawing Room
- Royal Closet
- Picture Gallery
- Green Drawing Room
- Throne Room

Ground Floor

- Offices
- Service Area
- Plate Room
- The Grand Staircase
- The Bow Room
- 1844 Room
- 18th Century Room
- Marble Hall
- Grand Entrance
- Minister's Staircase

BUCKINGHAM PALACE, EAST WING

Yellow Drawing Room — Principal Corridor — Centre Room — Principal Corridor — Chinese Dining Room

Ground Floor

Entrance Archway — Principal Entrance — Entrance Archway

First Floor

BUCKINGHAM PALACE ILLUSTRATION

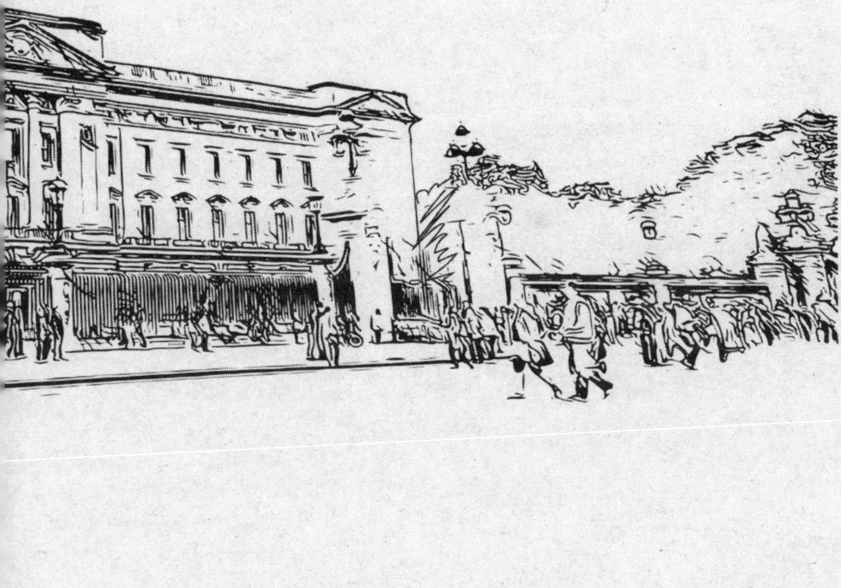

1

Monday 20 November 2023

It was both the southern entrance to the railway tunnel and the southern exit, depending, like so much in life, on your perspective. At this moment, through the crosshairs of the scope of his rifle, it was very definitely the exit. In just under three hours and seven minutes' time, the Royal Train was scheduled to emerge from it, travelling at a steady 70mph, en route south from London to the city of Brighton and Hove.

He smiled. It was the smile of a man who knows something no one else does. Well, just two other people, actually.

The train would be carrying Her Majesty Queen Camilla, and her entourage, on the first leg of a two-day official hospice tour along the south coast of England.

The weather gods had smiled on him. They'd delivered a dense early morning mist, enabling him to arrive unseen beneath its shroud and conceal his motorbike in undergrowth, then be in position by sunrise at 07.25. On his previous early morning recces here, he'd seen no one. No dog walkers or ramblers. This grassy hillock, a bundu of weeds and brambles, was well clear of any of the South Downs footpaths and, lying flat on his stomach on the mat he had brought with him, he was confident he was concealed from view.

As a man whose job involved constant risk assessment, he had calculated that the biggest risk facing him over the coming hours would be a pesky, inquisitive dog. But he had a pocketful of treats, just in case. Preparation was everything, always. As Abraham Lincoln said: *Give me six hours to chop down a tree, and I will spend the first four sharpening my axe.*

The Sako TRG 42 rifle was steady on its bipod stand, the stock cradled into his shoulder. The magazine contained five .338 hollow-point – dum-dum – bullets, which would have a devastating effect on their target by expanding on impact. He would only need one round but he would fire two shots just to misdirect them. And the knowledge he had three spare had a calming effect; to be accurate over this distance of more than 300 metres he needed to be very calm. Very steady.

He peered through the scope again. The grimy red-brick surround to the void of the railway tunnel was cut into the side of the hill, like a scowl. There were steps up to a primitive platform service lift, which could carry maintenance workers up and down from a grassy knoll above, a short distance from the winding driveway to a farm.

He could see all of it through his scope. It was so powerful he could have read the time on anyone's wristwatch.

The mist had risen completely now. He would love to stand and stretch his legs but that would be foolish, camouflage fatigues only concealed you so long as you didn't move, and so much planning had gone into this it was a risk he could not take. He also needed a pee, and had to go through the awkward contortion of removing the empty two-litre bottle of Diet Coke from his rucksack, and directing his urine into it. When he had finished, he screwed the top back on and put it to one side. He would stow it in his rucksack later, along with the weapon that he would break down after he'd used it.

He unscrewed his thermos flask and took another swig of his carefully rationed coffee, as he watched a northbound express, the early train from Brighton carrying commuters to London Victoria, enter the tunnel. In a few minutes the stopping train

THE HAWK IS DEAD

from London Bridge, heading south towards Brighton, would emerge. He got comfortable and practised his aim with the rifle. He had a perfect view into the windows on the left side of each carriage. At the speed these trains were travelling, an accurate shot would be impossible.

But the Royal Train, due at 10.32, wasn't going to be travelling at any speed at all.

The irony hadn't escaped him that he was employed to protect The Queen. That was his day job.

But today was his day off.

2

Monday 20 November 2023

Camilla, casually dressed in a jumper over a blouse and jeans, sat a companionable distance from her smartly suited husband, at the long mahogany table in the breakfast room of Clarence House. Her two Jack Russells, waiting patiently at her feet, were looking at her expectantly while she finished her porridge.

The King, seemingly deep in concentration, had been mouthing words silently to himself throughout breakfast. Between intermittent mouthfuls of muesli, dried fruit and honey he kept jotting down notes, in what looked to her like Arabic, on a pad beside him.

She smiled down at the dogs and whispered, 'Think I've forgotten you?'

Beth and Bluebell's ears twitched. They looked at her even more expectantly.

She adored these two gorgeous creatures, both rescues from Battersea Dogs Home, and the adoration was entirely mutual, though The Queen well knew that was just so long as she remembered to give them their daily treats. She broke off two small pieces from a slice of toast and slipped them under the table. With two quick crunches they were devoured.

'I saw that!' The King chided, raising a faintly disapproving eyebrow, accompanied by a smile that was anything but disapproving.

'It's just a little bit!' She grinned back. 'What are you working on?'

THE HAWK IS DEAD

'I'm addressing a climate change conference at Lancaster House at lunch today. It's a speech on biodiversity to a gathering of world and business leaders. I intend to speak in several languages and I want to do as much of it as possible without referring to my notes.'

She smiled. 'That's brave.'

He glanced up at the wall and seemed momentarily distracted by something. Then he turned back to his wife. 'What's your day looking like?'

'I'm starting my south coast hospice tour. Off to Brighton on the train – visiting Martlets in the morning. Then in the afternoon a children's hospice and in the evening I'm going to see Hugh Bonneville in a play at Chichester Theatre. I'll be overnighting on the train, then on to more hospices tomorrow morning. Then I'm going by helicopter to Bristol to give a talk at a big event SafeLives are hosting.'

'The domestic abuse charity?'

'Yes. Their work is quite remarkable.'

He glanced up at the wall again, frowned and called out loudly, 'Gordon!'

The butler, immaculately dressed as always in his blazer, strode in from the pantry. 'Yes, Sir, Ma'am?' he said.

The King pointed up at a blank space. 'What's happened to that Landseer? I love that picture – why isn't it there any more?'

'I think the Royal Collection may have taken it away for cleaning, but I'll find out, Sir.'

'I almost fell over someone from the Royal Collection as I came down to breakfast,' The Queen said. 'He was lying on the floor at the base of the stairs doing something to the bottom of a picture frame.'

'I'm very sorry, Ma'am, I'll have a word with him.'

She shook her head. 'No, I'm sure he was doing something important.'

As the butler retreated, King Charles said, 'Peregrine's going with you, isn't he, darling?'

Sir Peregrine Greaves, as Private Secretary to Their Majesties, was seen as one of the most senior members of the Royal Household.

'I know you want him on this trip to protect me, don't you?' She gave him a challenging smile.

'Darling, he's concerned about this protest lot – the Not-My-King anti-monarchists, republicans – whatever – threatening to disrupt your arrival in Brighton. He's going along to keep you safe.'

'Perhaps he could be armed with a sword? I'm sure that will be far more effective than the Glocks of the Royal Protection team.'

The King looked at his wife, unsure for a moment if she was joking. 'Darling, you know that Peregrine always has our backs.'

She buttered the other half of the slice of toast she'd given to the dogs. 'I do, but . . .' She hesitated.

'But what?' he pressed.

'Bless him, I know he means well, but sometimes I feel he's over-protective. Yesterday he tried to persuade me to cancel the trip – tried really hard. I told him quite clearly I will not be cancelling. With my schedule as it is, it could take six months to rearrange this tour.'

'I understand,' he said.

'I had a long chat with Tommy last night. He agreed I should stick to my guns. The protestors aren't going away.'

'Tommy' was Major General Sir Tommy Magellan-Lacey, Master of The King's Household, and another senior royal employee. He was someone both The King and Queen adored and trusted totally. The warning about what Queen Camilla might expect on arrival at Brighton Station had come from him, through intelligence from the RaSPs – the Royalty and Specialist Protection team – and from the Scotland Yard Counter Terrorism Command.

THE HAWK IS DEAD

He nodded. 'Whatever you decide, I always want you to be safe.'

She stood up, walked over to him and kissed him on the forehead. 'I'll be safe, I promise you. The train's a lot safer than that damned helicopter.'

3

Monday 20 November 2023

Unlike some of his more sceptical colleagues in the police, Detective Superintendent Roy Grace had no delusions about the reality of global warming. Being a father had made him even more acutely aware of the responsibility of his generation, to be the caretakers of a planet that seemed increasingly endangered – and dangerous – by the day.

He was seated at his desk at 8 a.m. on this glorious, cold but sunny, Monday morning, after a happy weekend with his wife, Cleo, and their children, Noah and Molly. It had been a turbulent few years for his personal life, starting with hearing that his long-missing wife, Sandy, had taken her own life, in Munich, Germany, and that they had a son, Bruno, she had never told him about.

Bruno, a challenging boy of eleven, had come to live with him and Cleo. Then, just when Roy Grace felt he was starting to form a good relationship with the boy, Bruno was killed while crossing a road and looking at his phone.

But Grace was beginning to come to terms with it – at least, as much as he ever would – and there seemed to be some equilibrium in his world right now. And Cleo had found some equilibrium in her world, too, after nearly quitting her job in the mortuary in the aftermath of Bruno's death, finding it too hard to cope with any young children brought in. But now, in addition to Noah and Molly, plus two dogs, Humphrey and Kyla, she'd taken on charity work as well, as local coordinator for the international book donation charity Book Aid, and was loving it. And Grace was loving the satisfaction it was giving her and the total contrast to her grim days in the mortuary.

But although there might be a semblance of equilibrium in Roy's domestic world, there wasn't much in the world beyond the walls of the Sussex Police HQ campus.

Knife crime in the city of Brighton and Hove, and other key hotspots around the county of Sussex, especially Hastings and Crawley, was becoming an epidemic. Whereas a decade ago there'd been an average of twelve murders a year in this county, thanks to the culture of knives, which had begun in London and now spread throughout the nation – partly fuelled by the scourge of youngsters snared into so-called county lines drug dealing – the annual murder rate in Sussex was rising.

And way beyond what, in many ways, was the still relatively safe haven of his home county, there were increasingly dangerous trouble spots, both across England and in almost any direction in the world where you looked. Russia, China, Korea, Africa and even the once dependable USA. Sometimes he wished he had the ability to gather all the leaders of every country in the world, knock their heads together, and tell them to try to appreciate this amazing planet we all inhabited, rather than spreading war and hatred.

An optimist by nature, he always remembered something his late father, Jack, had quoted, stoically, soon after the diagnosis of the cancer that was to kill him. *Life may not be the party we'd hoped for, but while we are here, we may as well dance.*

Roy Grace always held onto that as a mantra for times of adversity. But it would be sorely tested, too often. Especially when in the middle of the night he would answer his job phone to news of yet another horrific crime, and after arriving at the scene would despair of human nature.

A recent case he had just finished working on was a prime

example of this. Operation Spottiswood. A forty-eight-year-old woman, Lisa Dent, who had stabbed to death both her mother, aged seventy-eight, and her sister, Mary, aged fifty-one. She had entombed her dead mother in concrete and walled-up her sister's body in an inglenook fireplace, which she had then plastered over. She told friends and neighbours that they had relocated to New Zealand, to live with Mary and her new husband. It was Financial Investigator Emily Denyer who led the discovery. Lisa Dent, who was employed as a supermarket cashier, had been living a lifestyle well beyond her earnings ever since the demise of her mother and her sister.

Grace sipped his coffee, and called a member of his team, DS Nicholl. When the detective answered, he said, 'Nick, I need to talk to you about a couple of details on Op Spottiswood – can you pop in at some time when you're free?'

'When's good, boss? I know you're pretty tied up at the moment – I am too, I've been seconded to The Queen's visit to Brighton and Hove today. I'm currently with the team sweeping Martlets Hospice – she's due to arrive here at 11.15. You're the Investigations lead for Operation Flagship, aren't you?'

Operation Flagship was the name for the operation to guard The Queen while she was in Sussex.

'I am. Is everything OK at Martlets? No sign of any protestors?'

'Not so far, boss. Let's hope it doesn't all kick off when Her Maj arrives. Do you have any intel on the protestors?'

'I've just come from a briefing with the Chief,' Grace said. 'The intel we have is there'll be a small Not-My-King protest group at Brighton Station and they'll be corralled. But generally it seems there's a lot of positive excitement in the city.' He smiled wryly. 'However, hey, *prepare for trouble, make it double.*'

'I never had you down as a Pokémon fan, boss.'

'When you have young children, you start learning all kinds of stuff you never even knew existed.'

'Tell me about it!'

'So the Royal Train departs from Brighton at 12.30 for Arundel, then Her Majesty's safety becomes the responsibility of the West Division police – do you have any more Royal Protection duties after that, Nick?'

'No, I can come over then, if that works?'

'That's fine, I'm not going anywhere, assuming all goes to plan today.'

'Yeah, and we know what they say about those who assume, don't we, boss!' the DS teased, knowing this was one of his boss's most used phrases.

'Yes, Nick, they make an ass out of U and ME. I'm impressed you remember this. You have clearly been listening and learning!'

'I hang off every word you say!' Nick Nicholl retorted.

4

Monday 20 November 2023

Stan Briggs was a proud man, with much to be genuinely proud about. Balding and bespectacled, he looked like everyone's favourite uncle, but he was sad today. After thirty-seven years as a train driver – the last twenty on the London–Brighton line – he had finally and reluctantly made the decision to retire at Christmas, in just over a month's time.

His wife had repeatedly reminded him that he was already past normal retirement age. And he had repeatedly told her, *choose a job you love and you will never have to work a day in your life.* And he truly loved his job, the thrill of turning his boyhood dream into a reality.

The one consolation about retirement was it would give him more time for his hobby – his passion really – his racing pigeons. It was something he shared with the late Queen Elizabeth, a fellow pigeon fancier, whose train he'd twice had the privilege of travelling on for previous royal visits to Sussex, the last occasion being in 2013.

On the first, in 1988, he'd sat up front in the cab alongside the driver, learning the ropes of driving, or rather *chauffeuring*, this train. Unlike the express trains travelling at 90mph, for the comfort of the royal passengers the speed was generally restricted to 70mph.

The Royal Train was pulled by a Class 67 diesel locomotive, painted in Royal Claret livery, and there was a second locomotive

THE HAWK IS DEAD

behind, in case the train needed to reverse. There were three Royal Train locomotives in total, one being a spare. The regulars were the *Royal Sovereign*, No. 67006, the *Queen's Messenger*, No. 67005 – and No. 67029, the newest, the *Royal Diamond*, named by Queen Elizabeth in celebration of her Diamond Wedding Anniversary in 2007. All three of them, at the instigation of King Charles, ran on environmentally friendly biofuel made from waste vegetable oil.

On this Monday morning, as Briggs had arrived to start what he thought would be a routine shift on the London–Brighton line, he was informed that he would be driving the Royal Train, containing Her Majesty Queen Camilla and her entourage, to Brighton. The front locomotive would be the *Royal Diamond*.

It was for security reasons that none of the pool of drivers who were qualified for the Royal Train ever knew in advance that they would be driving it that day. It was only when they turned up for their shift that they'd be told.

He smiled ruefully as he thought about security and how times had changed, due to financial cuts. Back on that very first trip in the cab, as a trainee driver for the Royal Train, there was a British Transport Police officer on every railway bridge on the entire route from London to Brighton but now there would not be any. But there were cordons both at Victoria Station and the destination, Brighton, as well as a Royal Protection team on the train itself.

A big fan of the new Queen, when Stan was told the news by his manager he was beyond thrilled, if a little nervous. What a great journey to end his career on! Such an honour and privilege. And hopefully, it would all go smoothly.

5

Monday 20 November 2023

The King was supportive of the Royal Train on environmental grounds, and Queen Camilla was even more enthusiastic – particularly as she was never happy in a helicopter.

The back-room bean-counters of the Royal Household had long been advocating scrapping the train. They pointed out the cost of maintaining the three dedicated locomotives and nine carriages, for the very limited occasions the Royal Train was used, was too high compared to air and road travel. They, disdainfully, nicknamed it the *Palace on Wheels*.

But the current train was very far from anyone's definition of a palace. In Edwardian times – then decked out with sumptuous velour upholstery and gold inlay – it had rivalled anything the heyday of the Raj had to offer. But after a major refit for the late Queen's Jubilee in 1977 the interior was far more basic. If in former times the train might have been awarded five stars in any hotel guide, the refurbished one, forty-five years on – with its Formica work surfaces and avocado bathroom suite that wasn't retro cool but just plain old-fashioned – would have struggled to get even three stars on TripAdvisor. Not that any members of the Royal Family who made occasional use of it were in the habit of posting about their accommodation on social media. But at least the actual Royal Carriage itself, with air suspension, a full-width sofa, and beds facing lengthways rather than across the rails, for maximum comfort, gave its passengers a far smoother ride than any commuter train.

THE HAWK IS DEAD

For Queen Camilla, its real value was that it enabled her, travelling around the country for two or more days of public engagements, to stay over in comfort, in total privacy, without having to resort to hotels or return to London. And, parked in a siding, they were secure inside a police cordon.

For Quentin Haig, the Royal Train Officer and Manager of the Royal Train for more than twenty years, this train was his beloved universe, and he was immensely proud of just how immaculate it always was, in advance of any journey. He was particularly happy that it was a favoured method of transport for the current Prince and Princess of Wales, and even more so that Queen Camilla was keen on using it.

A perfectionist, Quentin Haig had arrived at the siding near Milton Keynes at 6 a.m. this morning, as he always did on days the train would be in service. He'd checked that the exteriors of both locomotives, and all the Royal Claret-coloured carriages in which Queen Camilla and her royal party would be travelling, were immaculate. Today they would be using seven carriages. If The King had been accompanying her, with his additional entourage, they would have had eight or, more likely, all nine carriages in use.

Then he had walked along the corridors, through the interior of each carriage. The first behind the front locomotive was the staff sleeper, where he slept, along with three engineers, who looked after the electronics, plumbing and physical hardware, as well as a representative from Network Rail. Then through into the Household Diner, which was effectively the staff canteen. The next carriage was the marginally more ornate and comfortable Royal Diner, followed by The Principals' bedroom carriage with its bathroom suite.

This connected through to the royal sitting room, followed by an office carriage complete with desk. The final two carriages were the sleeping quarters for the Royal Household staff, which on today's journey, along with Peregrine Greaves, The Queen's Private Secretary, comprised: her two Queen's Companions; her dresser; Director of Communications; Equerry to The Queen; the royal doctor; Director of Royal Travel; a valet; a footman; her hairdresser; and a team of Protection Officers.

As he went through the carriages that would be occupied by The Queen herself, he checked every detail, switching on and off the table lamps to ensure the bulbs were working. He ran the taps of Their Majesties' bath, to check the water ran clear and warm, and flushed each of the seven loos.

Finally, at 8 a.m., the train crossed the Thames and then reversed back over it and onto the reserved and heavily guarded Platform 9 at Victoria Station.

The royal party would be arriving at 9.15 for the scheduled departure at exactly 9.30 a.m. Quentin prided himself that not once, in all the years under his watch, had the Royal Train ever arrived at a destination more than fourteen minutes either side of the scheduled time. Today's driver for this leg of the journey, Stanley Briggs, had been made well aware of this. He would nail it, he assured Quentin Haig.

6

Monday 20 November 2023

Queen Camilla had spent much of her childhood in Sussex, at her family's country home in the village of Plumpton, just 12 miles east of Brighton, so it was always a joy for her to return to the county where she had so many happy memories.

As she boarded the train on this glorious November morning she had a spring in her step, although she knew that she faced an emotional couple of days talking to terminally ill people in a series of hospices. But she was buoyed as always by the inner strength she'd inherited from both her parents. Her father, a soldier in the Second World War, was twice decorated for gallantry, and her mother, despite a privileged life, had worked tirelessly for many years for a charity helping children with disabilities.

Breaking with tradition, as part of the modernization of the monarchy, instead of Ladies-in-Waiting, Queen Camilla chose to use the term of Queen's Companions. Their role was similar to that of Ladies-in-Waiting but less formal and more relaxed.

The two Queen's Companions accompanying her on this trip were tall, elegant Baroness Westwood, 'Tiny' to her friends, who was married to one of The King's best friends and who carried The Queen's lunch – comprising a banana and thermos of tomato soup – in her Louis Vuitton holdall, and Lady Elena Trevelyan, a jovial, bespectacled mutual chum of both The King and The Queen. Joining them in the sitting-room carriage of the train, seated closely to The Queen, was the reassuring, smartly dressed figure of Jayne Bennett, her own Private Secretary and trusted source for advice and guidance. Sir Peregrine Greaves and one of the ever-present RaSPs, the tall, burly, quietly unobtrusive, suited and booted Jon Gilhall completed the ensemble. Additional RaSP officers were stationed further down the train.

Camilla, dressed in blue, sat at the Formica-topped desk that had been installed at the request of the late Queen Elizabeth, making some last-minute changes on a speech she was due to deliver tomorrow night in Bristol for her domestic abuse charity, SafeLives.

She and her husband were self-confessed workaholics, even though many of the public wouldn't view them as such. At their time of life, when most people would have been retired for a decade, they both remained utterly motivated, as if aware of the limited time they had to achieve so much.

Out of the corner of her eye she saw the tall, silver-haired figure of Sir Peregrine Greaves approaching, immaculately suited and deferential, as always, but assertive with it. He had a way of walking that made him look as though he was gliding on wheels. She always felt that in part he was like a wise old friend who had her and The King's back, but also in part that he knew more than both of them did. Secrets that he didn't share.

'Your Majesty,' he said, 'I thought before we are rolling that we might have a quick look through today's schedule?'

'Of course, Peregrine,' she said and looked at the sheaf of papers he placed in front of her, skimming down to the first appointment.

10.45: Arrive at Brighton Station.
11.15: Arrive by car at Martlets Hospice. Meet, greet with Director.
11.25–11.55: Tour of hospice. Meet and engage with patients.

THE HAWK IS DEAD

11.55–12.10: Coffee with nursing staff.
12.15: Depart by car for Brighton Station.
12.30: Lunch break on train.
14.00: Arrive at Arundel Station.
14.20: Arrive by car at Chestnut Tree House Hospice.

The schedule at Chestnut Tree House was pretty much identical to Martlets. Then after that she had a relaxing evening to look forward to, watching a play at Chichester Theatre, and drinks with Hugh Bonneville during the intermission. From there, she would travel by road to the train, which would be in a railway siding just outside the city and would remain there for the night. A light supper and then bed.

She glanced at her watch. They would be off very shortly. 'Not too bad a schedule is it, Ma'am?' the Private Secretary asked in a manner that made it both a question and an answer.

During the past twelve months she had attended 233 engagements, and there were times when it felt that half of them were all on the same day. She smiled. 'I think it's very well balanced, both today and tomorrow,' she said, then gave a friendly grimace. 'Well, apart from the helicopter tomorrow afternoon, from Bournemouth to Bristol.'

Greaves was well aware of her dislike of the helicopter, but also that she did accept that often it was the only practical option for most of her tight schedules. 'Ma'am, if I may say, if it is of any comfort, that the safety record of the Royal Helicopter is somewhat better than the safety record of trains – on this particular line at any rate.'

'Really, Peregrine?'

The Private Secretary checked his wristwatch, then nodded. 'I'm absolutely serious, Ma'am. In approximately one hour we will be travelling through Clayton Tunnel, just north of Brighton, where the worst railway crash in British history, at the time, happened.' He gave one of those knowing smiles that always infuriated her.

'What happened?'

'Not wishing to frighten you – apparently, due to a signalling error, a southbound train was halted in the middle of the tunnel. The steam locomotive of the following train smashed into the rear of it. Twenty-three people were scalded to death and a further one hundred and seventy-six were severely injured.'

The Queen shuddered. 'How dreadful. What a horrendous thing to happen. That must be one of everybody's worst nightmares.'

He nodded. 'Indeed. The tunnel is haunted, apparently. Locals say on stormy nights you can sometimes hear the cries of the victims.'

The Queen shuddered again and gave him a quizzical look as if uncertain whether he was teasing.

'One of your predecessors, Ma'am, Queen Victoria, was so disturbed by the disaster that she refused from then on to travel through that tunnel on her regular visits to Brighton. She would alight at Hassocks Station – which was extended to accommodate the then extremely long Royal Train – and travel by coach and horses across the Downs to Brighton.'

'And that's what we'll be doing today, is it, Peregrine?' she teased.

He smiled. 'Well, Ma'am, I think we'll be all right today.'

'Let's hope so!'

Gliding a little closer to The Queen and shooting a wary glance in the direction of her two Queen's Companions, he lowered his voice and looked a little uncomfortable. 'There is an issue I would like to raise with Your Majesty – nothing to do with transport. Perhaps later today we could have a few private minutes?'

She frowned. 'Of course, Peregrine.'

He looked at his watch again, ever the stickler for time. 'Thank you, Ma'am. We should be off any moment now.'

THE HAWK IS DEAD

'Towards the cries of the victims?'

He gave her an uneasy look as if uncertain for a moment whether to smile. When he finally did, it was a smile that did not sit well on the stiff, aristocratic features of his face.

7

Monday 20 November 2023

As the dot of 9.30 a.m. approached, Stanley Briggs stared ahead through the windscreen, past the upright wiper, at the brightly lit and empty platform. The platform to their left was also empty, for security, as were the next two beyond those. He confirmed back on his radio, first to Victoria Railway Station Signalling, and then to Quentin Haig, the Royal Train Manager, that he was good to proceed.

The electronic light box displayed first CD, for *Close Doors*, followed by RA, for *Right Away*. A uniformed member of the platform team, standing by his window, waved a green flag.

Shaking with nerves, with his right foot he pushed the pedal – known as the dead man's pedal – down to the floor. At the same time, with his trembling left hand, selecting forward he eased the accelerator handle gently, very gently, towards him, and released the brakes. The train started to travel forward. So gently it would not have spilled coffee from a mug in front of him; so gently, he hoped, that Her Majesty would not even be aware they were off, unless she looked out of the window.

It seemed, as it always did, for those first moments, not that they were moving but that the rails in front of them were gliding towards them. The platform was slipping past at a steadily increasing rate. Two green lights glowed brightly ahead. And beyond, brilliant daylight.

As the end of the platform receded and they progressed out

THE HAWK IS DEAD

of the station's vast canopy, high-rise and low-rise buildings appeared on the near horizon, along with a tall red crane. They passed under a low, drab concrete bridge, with two green lights for him, which spanned the wide number of tracks feeding into the station's nineteen platforms. On the far side he saw the speck of an airliner out of Heathrow climbing high into the sky. They clattered over a series of points, still going at a gentle pace, and an oncoming red train – the Gatwick Express, passed them to their right at a slow speed, on the up-line.

The four chimneys of the old Battersea Power Station loomed ahead to his left, more high-rises and then they were crossing the Thames, over Grosvenor Bridge. He steadily increased the speed, keeping a watchful eye on his signals. All the ones so far were green, but he was ever mindful that if he saw a red one in the distance he would need to start slowing immediately – careful not to brake too hard with his royal passenger on board, but only too well aware that with seven carriages and a heavy locomotive behind him, it would take him a good mile to bring the train to a halt.

An alert beeped as he crossed another set of points approaching Clapham Junction, setting off a warning klaxon, and he instantly hit the yellow button with his right hand, to silence it. The klaxon, triggered by magnets in the rails before any station or bend or change of speed limit, was one of the two fail-safe systems for the drivers. The other was the pedal he kept firmly pressed to the floor.

If he lifted his right foot off the pedal for more than eight seconds the train would come to a rapid but steady halt and he would get a radio message from the area signaller asking if he was OK. He'd done it on one occasion and, like many of the mistakes he'd made over the years, if you valued your job, you only did it once. He still winced at the memory of the day, with eight full carriages behind him, he'd forgotten to stop at Gatwick Airport.

They rolled through Clapham Junction. It was after rush-hour now and just a handful of people stood on the two platforms – up-line and down-line – they were passing. A few gazed in astonishment, and he saw phone cameras raised.

Then they were out the far side and shortly there were two sets of tracks merging – as an illusion – into just one, at the vanishing point some distance ahead. He stared through the windscreen at the ever-changing view, a privileged one that passengers never saw and one he had never tired of in all his years of driving trains, and suddenly, he had to pinch himself. *I'm driving The Queen! I'm bloody driving The Queen! How good is that?*

He wondered what was happening in those carriages behind him. Was The Queen writing a speech? Or relaxing with a cuppa and talking to some of her travelling entourage? Did she look out at the scenery on her train journeys, or just focus on her paperwork, her computer screen, her phone, like most people these days?

He watched the digital readout as the speed steadily built up. They were approaching the 70mph cruising speed. He adjusted the rate of acceleration: 67mph . . . 68mph . . . 69mph . . . 70mph.

Unlike airline pilots or car and other road vehicle drivers, there was no cruise control equivalent for train drivers, and that was deliberate, for one very simple reason. If a driver had a medical incident and lost concentration for even the briefest period of time and missed a signal, or worse, became unconscious or, God forbid, died, nobody wanted a train to continue hurtling at high speed, with no means to stop it until it hit something. It was for this reason that both the dead man's pedal and the klaxon warning system had been devised.

Stan loved his job on the best of days, and this was truly way beyond the best of days! He was driving the Royal Train, with Queen Camilla on board. This would be something to tell the grandchildren! And to cap it all, the weather was magical.

As he checked the speedometer, holding steady at exactly 70mph, he was mindful that not everyone in Network Rail was happy about the Royal Train. Because of its relatively slow speed of travel compared to the rest of the passenger rolling stock, many of its journeys were made at night to avoid inconveniencing the general public. But, hey, he thought, ardent Royalist that he was, surely anyone delayed by a few minutes today should be happy to know they were being helpful to The Queen, right?

They were approaching the first of the three longest tunnels on the line, Merstham. A railway history buff, Stan knew that back in Victorian days the interiors of railway tunnels were painted with whitewash and illuminated by gas lights, to try to make them less scary for passengers. Eight decades of smut from steam locomotives had long coated the whitewash with a deep patina of soot, turning them grey. Electric lighting had gradually replaced gas, but the lighting in most tunnels today was so feeble as to be almost non-existent.

They burst out of Merstham tunnel into dazzling sunshine. Twenty minutes later, they entered Balcombe tunnel, going beneath the reservoir that all the train drivers joked was the Brighton line car-wash for trains. And, sure enough, water pelted down from the roof and he had to switch the wiper on. The engineers said the tunnel was safe, despite all this leaking water. Yeah, right. One of Stan's colleagues had joked that the last sound anyone would hear, the day the world ended, would be the voice of an engineer explaining how it could not happen.

Exiting from the tunnel they crossed his favourite part of this whole journey. The gorgeous Ouse Valley Viaduct, with its spectacular views to both sides of the magnificent Sussex countryside. Now, ahead, there was only one more tunnel of significance, the one-and-a-half-mile-long one at Clayton, and they would then be close to their destination.

Stan wondered if there was any possibility of meeting Her

Majesty. Just for a few seconds. How amazing would that be? Maybe he could jump down from his cab as soon as they were safely halted at Brighton and wait for her to walk past along the platform. He could try bowing and doffing an imaginary hat, perhaps, to get her attention. It might at least make her smile.

He held that thought as they passed a barren cornfield and he looked at his watch. They were doing fine. They would arrive at Brighton Station well inside those fourteen minutes of leeway. In fact, provided there were no hold-ups, they would be pretty much bang on time. He allowed himself a smile. A rather proud smile. If he gauged it right they might even arrive on the absolute dot!

They passed through Haywards Heath, the northbound and southbound platforms of this major commuter station near-deserted. As they did so an up-line express flashed by to their right, passing just a couple of feet away.

In a moment they would round a curve in a deep cutting, and he would see another of his favourite sights, the magnificent north entrance to Clayton Tunnel, with its striking turrets. It had been designed to resemble a Gothic castle. The intention had been to instil a sense of safety and security for rail travellers, to allay their fears on entering this very long, dark tunnel through the South Downs. And it really did look like a miniature castle, complete with its twin crenellated towers either side of a small dwelling on top. It had originally been created as a signalman's cottage, but for many years it had been a private residence. Occasionally he would see one of the occupants at a window waving, and he would always smile and wave back.

Then Briggs heard a voice he recognized on his radio, sounding very anxious. A signaller from Three Bridges.

'Stan. The up-line driver's reported what he thinks is an obstruction on the southbound line in Clayton Tunnel. Halt your train! Halt your train immediately!'

THE HAWK IS DEAD

Shit.

For a split second, Briggs was torn between slamming the brakes full on and hurtling The Queen and all other passengers forward, potentially causing injuries, or slowing more gradually.

The signaller's words flashed through his brain. *What he* thinks *is an obstruction.*

Not *definitely* an obstruction.

He went for a compromise, braking as hard as he dared as they shot into the entrance, the darkness of the railway tunnel instantly enveloping them, along with the din echoing around them. The speed dropped: 60mph . . . 50mph . . .

Although just 1.5 miles long, for some reason this feebly lit tunnel always felt longer to Stan. The exit was, at this moment, just the faintest distant pinprick of light. He glanced at the cold grey walls, up at the curved roof, then the faint glint from the rails, seemingly unspooling in front of them.

40mph.

Then he saw something.

Jesus.

Something on the track.

It wasn't possible.

Oh no, please no.

He dived for the brake, slamming it full on, but it was already too late. The cab rose up, as if it was on a ramp, then down, but it was no longer on the rails. It was jolting, jarring, jolting, shaking across the sleepers, shaking him out of his seat and throwing him across the cab floor. Sparks were shooting like a lightshow in front of him.

Oh Christ. Oh please, God, no. Not this train, not this train, oh please no.

The walls were hurtling past. The cab rocked from side to side and he was fearful it was about to capsize. The train was slithering, snaking, bumping. Slowing. Stan tried to get to his feet but was thrown sideways. Then, just as he tried again, the train abruptly came to a standstill, hurtling him up and forward, cracking his head fiercely at the top of the windscreen. He fell to the floor, dazed, his head in agony.

All he could hear for a moment was silence. Then a hiss, a crackling sound. The acrid stench of burning electrics.

8

Monday 20 November 2023

Inside the royal sitting-room carriage, which was heeled over at an angle, with the lights flickering, the startled and slightly dazed Queen, flung from her desk, lay on the floor. There were wisps of smoke in the carriage, a loud crackling sound of shorting electrics and someone close by was shouting.

Shaken but unhurt, Queen Camilla's endless training in emergency situations kicked in. She looked around, anxious to see if anyone was injured. For an instant, the lights went out, plunging them into darkness. Then they came back on and she could see what appeared to be the contents of a handbag strewn all over the floor along with a broken teacup and a spreading pool of milk. Lady Elena Trevelyan, a statuesque figure normally unruffled by anything, was also on the floor, looking shocked and missing a shoe. Peregrine Greaves, looking dazed but struggling back onto his feet, had an ugly gash down the right side of his forehead. Tiny, in a rear-facing seat, was one of the few in the carriage who appeared OK.

'I think we should get off the train,' The Queen said, her voice shaky. 'In case it catches fire. Everyone OK to do that? Anyone need help? Where's Jayne?'

'I'm here,' Jayne said firmly from just behind her. 'Your Majesty, we're fine, I think we're all fine!'

The Queen, helped to her feet by her Protection Officer, Jon Gilhall, who seemed unscathed, stood shakily several seconds before Greaves, no longer gliding now but striding like a clockwork toy, reached her.

'You – Your – Your Majesty,' he said, looking totally bewildered. 'I – are you – you?'

He seemed to forget what he wanted to say.

'Sir,' Gilhall said, looking around warily, one hand inside his jacket, where he kept his gun, 'sit down, I'll get someone to bring the royal doctor.' His eyes darted to both of The Queen's Companions. Tiny, on her knees, was helping Lady Trevelyan gather up the contents of her handbag.

Pulling out his phone and stabbing the keypad, Gilhall hurried to the drawer containing the first aid kit. Then he cursed. 'No signal.'

The Queen reached for her handbag, pulled a handkerchief out and dabbed the Private Secretary's badly cut face. 'It's a nasty gash, Perry,' she said. 'Are you OK?'

He gave an uncertain nod. 'I – I don't – don't know – what's happened?'

'There's been an accident, sit down, help will be coming.'

'I'm OK, Your Majesty, Ma'am. I'm fine.' He sounded anything but.

She looked at her two Queen's Companions. 'I can smell burning. We need to evacuate and check on the other carriages, see if anyone is hurt and get them out. Understand?'

The Queen's Companions nodded, Elena shaking badly and looking in shock.

'I'll call for help.' The Queen pulled her phone out of her bag with a trembling hand. Then she saw, too, there was no signal.

'Sorry, Ma'am, I can't get a signal either,' Gilhall said.

Suddenly the carriage door opened, and the bespectacled face of a man in his sixties appeared. He had blood running from a cut on the top of his head and one of his glass lenses was cracked. He was holding a small torch in his hand. 'I'm the train driver,

Your Majesty,' he gasped, 'we must get out, everyone must get out NOW!'

An instant later, the tall, wiry frame of another of The Queen's Protection Officers, PC Dambe, appeared in the carriage, holding a large torch. 'Your Majesty!' he said, the relief on his face palpable as he saw she was on her feet. 'Are you all right?'

'Thank you, Julian, I'm fine. How is everyone else?'

'I'll check, Ma'am.'

'Your Majesty,' the bespectacled man blurted out, louder and even more urgently. 'I'm the driver. We've been derailed by something on the line. Part of this train is now across the northbound line and there's an express from Brighton due in fifteen minutes. I've got no phone or radio signal in here. You've got to get away from the train. God knows what will happen if we can't stop that train.'

'Fifteen minutes?' Dambe said. 'Are you sure we have fifteen minutes?'

'Could be less,' the driver said. 'Unless the Three Bridges signaller has already stopped it. But I don't want to take the risk.'

'I'm a runner. Which is the fastest way out of the tunnel?' Dambe asked.

Stan jerked a thumb. 'South, keep going.'

'What do I do to stop that express?'

'Dial the nines and ask for British Transport Police,' Briggs blurted. 'You might get a signal as you get near the entrance. They've got to speak to the signalling centre at Three Bridges, make sure they know exactly what's happened.' He offered the RaSP officer his torch. 'You're going to need this.'

Dambe shook it away, pulling a small one from his inside pocket and switching on its powerful beam. 'I'm good.'

The two Royal Protection Officers conferred briefly. Then, as Dambe jumped down, the driver said, 'Be really careful, it's dark, don't trip, and just walk on the ballast – don't walk on any wood, it will be slippery, and don't walk on anything metal or go to the centre of the track – the electric rails on both sides are live.'

As if to emphasize this, there was a sudden flurry of loud crackles, and more white sparks visible through the carriage window.

As the RaSP officer squeezed past members of the royal entourage who were climbing down from the carriages and ran off into the darkness, the driver turned to The Queen. 'Your Majesty, you must get away from the train, we need to get everyone away, but you are the priority.'

'I want to know everyone's safe first,' she said. 'What's your name?'

'Stan – Stanley – Briggs, Your Majesty.'

'All right, Stanley, I understand what you're saying, but I'm not leaving until I know all of my team are off the train and heading to safety with me. My life isn't any more important than anyone else's.'

'Beg pardon, Ma'am, but you are the priority.'

Jon Gilhall returned with an open first aid box and went up to the Private Secretary. But Greaves, who seemed to be recovering fast, despite the blood running down his face, brushed him away. 'I'm fine. Go and check on everyone, we've got to get everybody out of this damned tunnel. But our priority is The Queen's safety. Take care of her and I'll sort everyone else out.'

The train driver climbed back down onto the ground, into the narrow space between the carriage and the tunnel, aiming the torch so that Jon Gilhall could see. The officer jumped down onto the uneven ground, then held up a hand to The Queen, as Stanley Briggs illuminated the two steps with his torch. There was minimal natural light emanating from the tunnel's southern opening.

Moments later The Queen, surprising Stanley with her agility, was standing beside him on the large chunks of loose gravel between the train and the tunnel wall.

Briggs was blinking hard, a cold shiver worming through him. If this wasn't the worst nightmare? The Queen of England, with a rip in her dress, her hair dishevelled, standing beside him in a dark, dank tunnel, with electrics fizzing and crackling, a hazardous walk to safety, and an oncoming express train.

'Follow me, Your Majesty, please,' he said. Then he looked at his watch. The express was now due in eleven minutes. If that officer didn't make it in time, if no one was able to stop that express from the Three Bridges signal box, the consequences were unthinkable.

The Protection Officer, with the aid of his torch and a colleague, helped the two Queen's Companions and her Private Secretary, Jayne, down. Then Queen Camilla asked, 'Jon, can you check everyone is safely off the train or if anyone is badly injured?' She could see a growing number of figures standing by the train a little further along.

'Your Majesty,' the driver implored, 'please follow me.'

'We should go, Ma'am,' Peregrine Greaves said, 'you're in danger being here.'

'As I have said, I'm not leaving until I know everyone is safe.' She made her point emphatically. 'I want a head count.'

She could hear voices along the tunnel, as more people clambered down from the train.

'Understood, Your Majesty,' Briggs said. 'But – we are in real danger – I cannot emphasize that enough. Not just from other trains, but also from fire and explosion.'

'Fine, you go,' she said. 'Go!'

He stared at her for a moment as if not understanding. 'I'm not going without you, Ma'am.'

Briggs looked at his watch again. Ten minutes.

Moments later, a bright beam of light fleetingly blinded them, and a distraught Royal Train Manager appeared, holding two torches. 'Your Majesty, oh my God, thank God, you are safe. Are you hurt, Ma'am?' Quentin Haig asked.

'I'm fine, Quentin, everyone in my carriage is fine. Is anyone badly injured?'

He shook his head. 'No, everyone is OK and off the train. We've got to get away from here – there's a northbound express due.'

'We know,' Greaves said tersely.

Haig handed The Queen a torch. 'We're going to have to walk, I'm afraid, Ma'am.'

'Really, Quentin? You mean they can't fly the helicopter in here to get us?'

'No, Ma'am,' he said, totally missing her humour. 'It's too low.'

9

Monday 20 November 2023

Sir Jason Finch was a well-liked member of the Royal Household. In his role as Keeper of the Privy Purse – essentially Comptroller of The King's finances – he had one of the finest offices in Buckingham Palace, a corner ground floor on the east wing, with glorious views of the parade ground from both windows. He loved the views and he loved his work.

His increasingly portly figure attested to his years, post-military, of what he called *proper* lunching and dining. Today he was looking forward to a regular lunch meeting at Wiltons, his favourite fish restaurant, with an art dealer and old school friend, James Mayor. Mayor always knew exactly what was going on in the art world, and he liked to pick his expert's brains.

In particular, today, he was interested in asking Mayor about the recent explosion in value of the paintings of a number of historic artists currently in fashion. In an article in the *Financial Times* he had in front of him, he saw that Gustav Klimt's *Dame mit Fächer* had recently sold for a world record £85.3 million. And that Claude Monet's *Le bassin aux nymphéas* had made nearly £60 million. They had no Klimt works in the Royal Collection, but they did have several Monets. They also had some Fragonards – and one had been sold a few years ago for another world record – £17 million.

He had recently – and discreetly – taken some photographs on his phone of high-value paintings in the Royal Collection, to show the art dealer at lunchtime, over a bottle of Mayor's favourite tipple, Corton Charlemagne.

Using scissors, he carefully cut out the newspaper article, folded it and placed it in a file, which he slipped into one of the drawers of his desk.

10

Monday 20 November 2023

Roy Grace had taken a few minutes out of work, needing a break from the double murder case he was working on. He made a fresh cup of coffee and sat back down, googling 'air fryers'. It seemed that everyone he and Cleo knew had recently bought one of these kitchen appliances and swore by them as both an efficient cooking tool and good for the environment, too.

As he enjoyed cooking, and all the more so cooking healthily with as little fat as possible, he avidly read the food sections of newspapers, curious about any new recipes. He'd recently started using avocado oil to cook with instead of olive oil, after reading that, at frying temperatures, olive oil became unhealthy. But he was struggling to get his head around the concept of air fryers.

They definitely seemed to be energy-efficient, a big tick. But he was still not sure, despite Glenn Branson telling him that he and Siobhan wondered what they'd done before having one.

Just as he clicked on Amazon, to look at what they had to offer, his phone rang.

'Roy Grace,' he answered, and immediately heard the voice of a Control Room operator he recognized, Carol Walker. The Comms operators were normally calm but Carol sounded way more anxious than the norm.

'Sir,' she said. 'We've just been alerted to an incident involving the Royal Train bringing The Queen to Brighton. It's a sketchy report but we understand the train has been derailed inside Clayton Tunnel.'

For a moment, he did not believe his ears. 'Derailed? What information do you have?'

'Just that, sir.'

'When you say *derailed* what exactly do you mean?'

'That's all the information I have, sir.'

'Any report of casualties?'

'No, sir, at least not so far. Oscar One is trying to get more details.'

He thought hard for a moment. Derailed inside a tunnel. Was this the work of terrorists or protestors? But that didn't matter for now. All that mattered was ensuring The Queen was safe. 'Who've you alerted so far?' he asked.

'Fire and Rescue, the Ambulance Service, all Armed Response units and of course British Transport Police. Oscar One has requested NPAS-15 to attend in case it is needed – and the Royalty and Specialist Protection team. The Duty Inspector at Haywards Heath is sending all resources they have to both ends of the tunnel. I thought that, as Silver Investigations, you needed be informed, sir.'

NPAS-15 was the National Police Air Service helicopter for their area.

'Thank you,' Grace said, barely able to believe what he was hearing. 'The Royal Train – you are absolutely sure?'

'Yes, sir.'

'And The Queen is definitely on board?'

'From what I understand, sir.'

'Please update me with any news.'

'Yes I will, sir, either myself or Oscar One.'

Ending the call, Grace, thinking *shit*, speed-dialled his immediate boss, Nigel Downing. 'Sir,' he said, as soon as the Assistant Chief Constable, a calm and pragmatic man, answered. 'In case you haven't already heard, we have a Major Incident.'

THE HAWK IS DEAD

'I've not heard anything, Roy. What's up?'

Grace related what he had just been told. Downing was silent for a moment, then asked, 'Is there any terrorist implication here?'

'I don't know yet, sir.'

'Do you think those anti-monarchists might be behind it?'

'It would be an unconscionable change in tactics for the major groups, sir, but an unknown splinter group could be a possibility.'

'Shit,' Downing said. 'Not great for Sussex, is it?'

Grace raised an eyebrow, a little surprised Downing was more concerned for the PR image of Sussex than Queen Camilla's welfare.

'BTP will have primacy on this, for now, I suppose,' Downing continued.

British Transport Police was a separate national police force, with the same powers as the regular force, but funded independently by the railways. They always had initial command of any incident occurring on railway property.

'I imagine the Scotland Yard Counter Terrorism team will be all over it within the hour,' Grace said.

After a few moments, Downing said, 'I'll inform the Chief – update me as soon as you hear anything more.'

Grace assured him he would, then immediately called Glenn Branson.

'Dull day at the office?' the Detective Inspector answered. 'Need someone to chat to, to relieve the mahogany, as my old teacher would say?'

'We have a major crisis on our hands, mate.'

'I have one, too,' Branson retorted. 'But you go first.'

'How about Queen Camilla's train derailed inside Clayton Tunnel? Would that be more of a crisis?'

There was a brief silence. 'No way?'

'Seriously.'

'Holy crap.'

'That's one way of putting it.'

'Is she hurt?'

'I'm waiting on news. Who do we have available to respond if we need?'

'Norman and Polly are in. I've got a car signed out, we can be on the road in less than five.'

'I'll get back to you,' Grace said.

'You know something, boss – beats me why she'd want to travel on an ancient piece of rolling stock, when she's got a pukka helicopter at her disposal.'

'Apparently Her Majesty believes the train is safer.'

'Does she still think that?'

11

Monday 20 November 2023

Queen Camilla, wishing that she had worn comfortably flat shoes today, shone the torch she'd been given at the lumps of gravel in front of her. Then she led the Private Secretary, with her shocked entourage stumbling raggedly behind. Brenda Warner, her dresser, was lugging two bags of The Queen's clothes as if she was welded to them. Others were guided by their phone torches, as she followed the driver, who was some yards ahead and striding quickly, if a little unsteadily, on the uneven surface, through the cold, musty air. Every few moments, the driver raised his phone high, as if checking for a signal, then would turn and wave the royal party on, anxiously.

Urgently.

'Please hurry, Your Majesty,' he implored.

The Queen stumbled on as fast as she could, feeling it was a bit like walking on a pebble beach. There was an eerie silence, the only soundtrack being the echoes of mass footsteps, the crunch of the stones and the occasional murmured curse, as someone in the single-file line behind her stumbled. The curved walls and roof were a relentless grey, and Queen Camilla saw occasional tiny red dots – the eyes of rodents – ahead. She turned to check on Peregrine Greaves. He gave a bleak nod of reassurance and called out, more in hope than certainty, 'Not far to go, Your Majesty.'

Then he tripped and fell flat on his face.

The Queen turned and, assisted by Jon Gilhall, got the Private Secretary back onto his feet.

'Perry, are you all right?' she asked. 'If you'd prefer we can leave you here with someone, and send for a stretcher.'

'I'm fine, thank you, Ma'am,' he said, a tad huffily, as if he really, seriously, did not need to be asked that question, and briefly examined his hand, which was bleeding.

The Queen shone her torch past Greaves, checking on all the rest of her entourage. As soon as she was satisfied everyone was all right, she soldiered on. As she did so, the words Peregrine had said earlier about the terrible disaster in this railway tunnel came back to her. That the screams of the victims could still be heard on stormy nights.

She'd always had an open mind on the supernatural. Were the ghosts of these poor people still trapped inside? Were they around her and everyone in here now? She shuddered. God, they'd been walking for a good few minutes now, and that distant light only seemed a little closer than it had been when they'd started. She saw the bobbing torchlight of the driver, some way ahead. Watched him check his phone yet again and shake his head. As she walked, shadows jumped out of the dimly lit gloom. But were they shadows, or the spirits of the scalded-to-death victims?

She shuddered again and walked on. Strode on. She was determined to motivate all those of her entourage behind her. Why the train had been derailed – what had caused it – was a question for later. For now her one duty was to lead the royal party out of this godforsaken tunnel to daylight. To safety.

Her Equerry and Jon Gilhall were now striding alongside her. 'Are you all right, Ma'am? Do you need to stop for a moment?' Gilhall asked.

'I'm fine, Jon, how is everyone else?'

'I understand a couple of people are hobbling a bit with minor leg injuries from the accident, but everyone knows we need to get out of here. I've still got no phone signal.'

'Incredible,' she said. 'With all the technology we have today and they can't organize for people to get a bloody mobile phone signal in a railway tunnel? I need to call The King and let him know what is happening before he hears it from someone else. I must call him.'

'Yes, Ma'am.'

She glanced over her shoulder. 'Keep an eye on Sir Peregrine, will you. I'm worried he may have some concussion. Make sure he doesn't fall over again.'

'I will, Ma'am.'

Gilhall dropped back to join the Private Secretary, walking as close to him as he could, ready to catch him if he tripped again. But all the time keeping eyes on the person he was here to protect.

Something was worrying him deeply and had been ever since the disaster had happened. Trains did not derail themselves. They were derailed by *something*.

Someone.

As he walked, he constantly looked ahead and behind him, his right hand close to the holstered Glock pistol nestling inside his suit jacket. As part of his training to become a RaSP officer, he'd been through countless scenarios in which he'd had to both respond to threats, and later account for his responses. Derailment of the Royal Train in a tunnel had never been a part of that curriculum.

And it weighed heavily on him that in this ghastly railway tunnel, with no phone signal, and a potential threat out there, somewhere, his boss's life might depend on him, and on him solely.

No past responsibility had ever weighed so heavily on him.

12

Monday 20 November 2023

No past responsibility had ever weighed so heavily on Stanley Briggs. And he had never felt so scared in his life. This journey, which should have been the proudest moment of his career, had turned into something way beyond his worst nightmare.

He raised his phone up and looked at the screen again. Still no signal. He looked over his shoulder and saw The Queen keeping pace a few yards behind him, with the trail of stumbling, shadowy figures behind her.

The Queen. It was The Queen. He couldn't quite get his head around it. The Queen stumbling through the tunnel behind him. The Queen, who he should have delivered, proudly, to the platform at Brighton Station on the dot of 10.45.

Now instead he was hurrying, as fast as he could, trying to lead her to safety, unsure whether the northbound express had been stopped, or would appear and hurtle past them at any moment. Hurtle into the carriages of the Royal Train, some of which now straddled the northbound line.

Please don't let that happen.

At least they were well clear of the Royal Train now. And nearly out of the tunnel.

Please God.

As he strode on, his mind was a maelstrom of thoughts, going over and over those moments after he saw the obstacle, whatever

THE HAWK IS DEAD

it was, across the tracks. Trying to think what he could possibly have done differently.

Was there anything?

He raised his phone again. And this time he saw a single bar had appeared. Finally! Thank God, thank God! Still striding fast, he hit the button to call the signaller at Three Bridges.

Nothing happened.

Come on, come on, come on!

Then, suddenly, to his joy – and relief – he heard a voice.

'Three Bridges Signalling Centre.'

'This is an emergency call from the driver of the Royal Train,' he blurted. 'Your team rang me earlier. We've been derailed inside Clayton Tunnel and the train is straddling the northbound line. You need to stop all trains in both directions and cut off the electric power. Do you read me?'

'Copy, driver. We had already been alerted. Power has been switched off and all train traffic, northbound and southbound, has been halted. Do you have any casualties?'

'No, no, I don't think so. Some minor injuries, no one seriously hurt.'

He felt so much relief flooding through him that he barely noticed, two minutes later, stepping out of the tunnel into brilliant sunlight, and the smell of grass and hogweed.

He closed his eyes and mouthed a silent prayer.

13

Monday 20 November 2023

Jon Gilhall was at The Queen's side as they emerged from the tunnel into a deep cutting and the very distant cacophony of sirens. The train driver, looking ashen, was waiting for them. 'Your Majesty, I – I don't know what – what to say. There was something on the rail—'

She smiled at him. 'Thank you for leading us out, Stanley. It's a big relief to be back in fresh air.' She turned to check on Sir Peregrine Greaves, and could see the rest of her party straggling some way behind in the tunnel. Then she addressed Gilhall. 'I feel I've walked out of a foul drain. It smells like a stagnant pond – and of soot, but there can't have been steam trains for decades.'

'I agree with you, Ma'am,' he said, his eyes darting everywhere, along both sides of the cutting and up the grassy bank on either side for any sign of anything untoward, then at the tunnel entrance, the old brick surround and the darkness beyond, from which more and more of the passengers were emerging then stopping and standing, looking grateful to be breathing in fresh air. Some of them clearly shaken, others fine.

Jon Gilhall radioed his colleagues; PC Julian Dambe immediately updated him. He confirmed all trains had been halted and the power turned off. A police helicopter would be overhead in approximately five minutes. Vehicles to transport the royal party would be on the scene shortly. 'Can you see a service lift, Jon?' Dambe asked.

'I'm looking at it.'

'There are two BTP officers with a key to operate it on their way, for anyone who is not able to climb the steps. You can see the steps?'

He stared at the steep concrete steps. 'Roger that. I can see the steps, yes, yes.'

'They lead up to a farm track, where the vehicles will be arriving. I'm informed there's also enough space for a helicopter to land, and a royal helicopter has been scrambled – it will be here in twenty minutes.'

'Copy that,' Gilhall said.

Ending the call he turned to The Queen. He was concerned that they were all vulnerable here by the tunnel entrance. Any potential assailant had the height on them. He weighed his options. He could lead his boss back into the relative safety of the tunnel until the whole area was secure, or up the steps. Back into the tunnel was the sensible option. He explained it to her.

The Queen looked at him for a moment as if he was mad. 'I'm damned well not going back into that stinking tunnel, Jon. If you're worried that I can't climb those steps at my age, then think again!' She turned to Greaves. 'Are you up for climbing them, Perry?'

He nodded resolutely.

She turned to check again on the rest of her party. They were some distance behind them, slowly but steadily picking their way along the rough walkway.

'You go ahead, Your Majesty, I'll bring everyone else up,' Briggs said.

She signalled to her Protection Officer. 'Let's go.'

Gilhall suppressed a smile. He admired the fact that, despite the ordeal she had been through, her torn dress and dishevelled hair, she still had poise as she made her way, sure-footed up the big, steep steps. He climbed them beside her, scanning everywhere with his eyes, Peregrine Greaves struggling behind them to keep up.

After several minutes of hard climb, Gilhall and The Queen emerged onto a grassy knoll and into a welcome stiff breeze. He led her away from the steps, looking around warily. Several blocks of concrete were scattered around, as if they were once going to form part of those steps but were then not needed. There was a winding track fifty or so yards away, and an expanse of farmland all around, and in the near distance the gentle wooded and bushy slope of the South Downs.

It was on the hillside that he focused his attention, feeling a deep sense of unease as he scoured it, and then the full 360 degrees around them, hand inside his jacket, close to his Glock. He was looking for any movement, any glint of reflected light. And hoping to hell that backup would be arriving at any moment. He knew his colleagues wouldn't be far behind. Then he heard the voice of Sir Peregrine Greaves and turned.

'I'm so bloody unfit!' the Private Secretary said, gasping from the exertion.

He looked all-in, Gilhall thought. As if the climb had taken everything out of him.

Queen Camilla turned to Greaves. 'Let's sit down for a minute, Peregrine, and get our breath back.' She pointed to one of the concrete blocks.

Just as she did, there was a faint, distant sound, like the crack of a whip, and simultaneously Greaves' hair appeared to lift up from his head.

For an instant.

And for an instant, Gilhall thought that the wind had dislodged Greaves' wig.

Then, fractions of a second later, Greaves' head exploded, spattering blood, bone and brain in all directions.

14

Monday 20 November 2023

Jon Gilhall, momentarily rooted to the spot despite all he had been trained for, tried to process what he was seeing.

The top half of Sir Peregrine Greaves' head literally exploded in a pink cloud. The Queen's clothing was splattered with blood and pale brown particles.

A shooter.

Where?

Then another crack, like a whip. Almost simultaneously splinters of concrete, just inches from The Queen, flew in the air around them.

Christ.

He threw himself at his boss, knocking her to the ground, murmuring, 'I'm sorry, Ma'am,' while at the same time pulling out his Glock and looking all around through the gun sights. He yelled at the top of his voice to the driver. 'Keep everyone down, don't bring them up here.' He was immediately joined by two more Protection Officers, who formed a barrier around The Principal.

The Queen tried to move.

'Please, Ma'am,' he said. 'Please stay still.'

He squinted desperately, trying to keep calm. He pointed the gun up. Around. Down. Where was the shooter? A long way off? His Glock would be useless against a rifle, but he pointed it anyway.

Where was the shooter?

When would the next shot come?

Frantically he shouted into his radio for more backup and for an ambulance.

The distant cacophony of sirens was still too far away. Moments later he heard the *thwock-thwock-thwock* sound of an approaching helicopter.

'Jon, what the hell is happening?'

For once, he ignored his boss and looked up at the sky, listening to the sound of the rotor blades. At this moment it felt like the sweetest sound he had ever heard.

15

Monday 20 November 2023

A train derailment wasn't Roy Grace's jurisdiction – it was on railway property and he knew British Transport Police had primacy on that. But a senior royal in Sussex, regardless of what damned property they were on, very definitely *was* his jurisdiction. His absolute responsibility.

With the full support of the ACC, they were organizing a ring of steel around both entrances to the tunnel as fast as possible. The north entrance was easy, as it was close to the main road, but the southern portal was a lot less accessible, and from the Protection Officer's report, it sounded as if that was the direction in which the royal party were headed. And by his calculation, The Queen and her entourage could be emerging at any moment, if they weren't already out.

And highly vulnerable.

For the past fifteen minutes, since the Control Room operator had informed him of the derailment, Roy Grace had been on the phone. In addition to the cordons around both ends of Clayton Tunnel, he had directed Glenn Branson to request the Air Traffic Control centre at Swanwick and have them implement an immediate no-fly zone for civilian aircraft within a two-mile radius of the tunnel entrances.

Grace had liaised with his team, in turn, key personnel at British Transport Police, the Ambulance and Fire and Rescue services, the Armed Response Unit, the Royalty and Specialist

Protection team, the Scotland Yard Counter Terrorism Unit, the NPAS helicopter, the police drone team and the Duty Inspector at Haywards Heath – the closest police station to Clayton Tunnel. And, finally, he had alerted the Media and Communications Department to prepare for a press and media shit storm.

No phone or radio contact had yet been established with anyone inside the tunnel – it was seemingly a complete dead zone for signals. The only positive so far was that all trains to and from the tunnel had been halted, preventing an even bigger catastrophe.

Was this just a freak accident? The current Royal Train had been in service for almost fifty years. Mechanical failure? Metal fatigue in one of the wheels? Or was it connected to what appeared to have been left on the track? Sabotage, terrorism?

The idea that someone could have deliberately derailed the Royal Train was unthinkable. Except, thinking the unthinkable was what he'd had to do throughout his career.

If it was deliberate, who was behind it? Protestors? Or a group a lot more sinister? A terrorist cell? The anti-monarchists had not, so far, demonstrated with any violence. Derailing the Royal Train was very unlikely to be their work. Which in his view left two options: a genuine accident, or The Queen and the royal party were in very serious danger.

His fists were clenched tight, he realized. As tight as his chest.

He could not recall a moment in his twenty-five-year career more serious on a national scale than this. *If* it was more than just a freak accident, then one half of the monarchy would likely depend on the actions he had put in place.

When he had joined the force he had sworn his allegiance to the now late Queen Elizabeth, and this applied just as much to King Charles and Queen Camilla. He could still remember the words.

I . . . do solemnly and sincerely declare and affirm that I will well and truly serve Our Sovereign Lady . . . without favour or affection, malice or ill will . . . and prevent all offences against the persons and properties of Her Majesty's subjects . . .

His parents had been proud, ardent Royalists, and respect for the monarchy was part of his DNA, as it was for so much of the nation back then. His late father, Jack, had told him how he and his family had watched Queen Elizabeth's coronation on a black and white television screen not much bigger than an iPad, and his late mother had told him how she had camped out with her two sisters in The Mall, in the pouring rain, to catch a glimpse.

One entire shelf of the Welsh dresser in their family kitchen had been full of 1953 Coronation souvenirs. Plates, coins, coasters, Wedgwood mugs and a gilded Coronation coach and horses. Roy Grace still had them all, boxed away among a ton of other memorabilia that he'd divided with his sister after their parents had died, which for sentimental reasons he'd never wanted to part with. They were up in the loft of their cottage. Clutter that Cleo had long urged him to sort out and get rid of what he didn't want.

One day.

That rainy day so many people had in their mind, when they would get around to doing all that stuff they'd been planning to do. That rainy day, which was always, somehow, at least one day or more away. Tomorrow and tomorrow and tomorrow. *Mañana.*

He was about to call the Control Room for an update, when his phone rang. It was the operator Carol Walker again, her voice tight.

'Sir,' she said. 'We've just had a report of a shooter by the south exit to the tunnel. One person is down.'

For an instant her words echoed like a ricochet in his brain.

One person is down.

'Who?' he asked, weakly, his voice constricted, as if for a moment he didn't want to know the answer he feared. 'Her Majesty?'

Please don't tell me it is.

'It is not The Principal, sir. It's one of her entourage. Her Protection Officer has put out an urgent call for—'

Grace barely heard the rest of what she said. He ended the call, stabbing the speed dial for Glenn Branson as he grabbed his jacket and sprinted to the door.

16

Monday 20 November 2023

Jon Gilhall was being blasted by the downdraught from the rotor blades of the black and yellow police helicopter hovering overhead, flattening the grass and weeds all around them. Apologizing yet again to The Queen, three Protection Officers kept their arms folded around her head and body, ready to absorb another bullet from the shooter, should it come.

Happily married, with two children he adored, Gilhall had long reconciled himself to the fact that, in the job he did, the day might come when he would have to put his own life on the line to protect his boss. But, although he had trained rigorously for that day, he'd never seriously imagined it would actually happen.

Now it had. And all his training had kicked in, as if it were muscle memory. The pilot had already overflown the area and the information that they had was that the sniper was likely to have left quickly. Bringing in the helicopter was of course a risk, but to safeguard The Queen it was felt a risk worth taking.

He watched the Eurocopter set down a short distance from them, pleased to see it was between them and where he estimated was the most likely direction of the shooter. NPAS-15, the helicopter shared by Sussex, Kent and Surrey Police, was manned by a crew of three, the pilot, a paramedic and a police officer. The door opened and the police officer jumped down. Head ducked to avoid any risk of contact with the still swirling blades, he sprinted towards them. The paramedic followed and raced over to the body of Sir Peregrine Greaves.

'Is Her Majesty OK?' the officer asked.

'We need to get her to safety, immediately,' Gilhall responded. 'There's a shooter out there somewhere. I'm informed a room's being prepared for her at HQ.'

'What about all the rest of my team?' The Queen asked suddenly.

'They'll follow by road, Ma'am,' Gilhall replied. 'There's a fleet of minibuses on the way. My immediate priority is to get you out of here.' He turned to the officer. 'Did you see anyone up on the hill as you came in? Anyone with a gun?'

'Just a lady dog walker, no one else. We will be flying off in a different direction when we leave to reduce any risk.'

The Protection Officers stood, shielding The Queen from the only other direction the shooter could have fired from. Gilhall then knelt and said, 'Ma'am, let me help you up.'

'I may be old, Jon, but I'm not decrepit. Thank you.' She clambered, agilely, to her feet, as he moved quickly around her, to continue shielding her, for her own safety and to save her from what she might see. But she had already frozen in shock as she looked down at the motionless figure of the Private Secretary.

'Oh God,' she said. Her hand went to her mouth and Gilhall took her arm, afraid she would stumble. 'Oh my God.'

Peregrine Greaves lay on his back, his arms and legs spread out awkwardly. He no longer had a face, it was gone. In its place was a hideous, unrecognizable, misshapen ball of different hues of crimson, blood running from all around it. A couple of teeth were up where his right eye socket should have been. His skull was split open, bone sticking up through his bloodstained white hair, and some of his brain was visible. The paramedic, in green scrubs and orange high-vis jacket, knelt beside him feeling, futilely, for a pulse.

THE HAWK IS DEAD

'Oh my God,' The Queen said again. She stumbled and Gilhall caught her. Shielding her all the way, walking backwards, then sideways, the officers escorted her to the helicopter and, thankfully, into the interior, taking the seat next to her and helping her with her harness.

'Go!' he yelled at the pilot. 'Go!'

The Queen's face was pale with shock. 'Perry. Poor Perry. What – why . . . ?'

'*What happened*, Ma'am?' Gilhall said, supplying the word she was too shaken to say, then offering her a headset, which she declined. He pulled his handkerchief from his pocket and, apologetically, dabbed several tiny bloody spots on her jacket. 'I'm afraid someone's taken a shot at you, Ma'am.'

'And hit Peregrine?'

The police officer who had jumped out of the helicopter and come over to them, now joined them inside and shut the door. Moments later the pilot turned his head and raised his headset off his ears. 'Your Majesty,' he said. 'Are you OK?'

She nodded. 'Thank you,' she said politely and clearly in a state of shock.

He opened the throttle and they rose a few feet off the ground, Gilhall desperately, silently, willing the pilot to get them clear. The pilot went into a vertical climb to clear any obstacles, then dipped the nose of the helicopter and they accelerated away.

Jon Gilhall watched the ground drop rapidly away beneath them, anxiously scouring the hilly, grassy landscape below them for any sign of a moving figure, someone furtive. A killer. A hired assassin. Hit man?

Hired to kill The Queen?

And had botched it?

Which meant he might try again.

17

Monday 20 November 2023

As Branson drove, heading north out of Brighton on the A23 on blue lights, Roy Grace in the passenger seat was wrapped in his thoughts, going through the checklist of everything he needed to put in place. And all the time he was trying to work out what exactly they were dealing with.

As ever his starting point was three questions:
Why him?
Why here?
Why now?

Had Sir Peregrine Greaves actually been the target? To go to all the lengths of derailing the Royal Train in order to shoot one of The Queen's entourage, however senior Greaves had been, made no sense at all. Unless he was overlooking something. But if so, what?

Equally, how realistic was it that The Queen had been the intended target and the shooter had simply missed? Why only two shots?

A third hypothesis was a couple of loose shots from a hunter somewhere out in the fields – aimed at a rabbit? So unlikely as to be barely worth considering. The only hunter with a telescopic sight who was likely to be out there would be someone rough shooting – going for rabbits or birds – with a small-bore rifle. From the brief description he'd had of Sir Peregrine's injury, it had been inflicted by a much more substantial weapon.

THE HAWK IS DEAD

The facts he had to work with at this moment were: firstly, there was known hostile activity anticipated for the royal visit from protestors; secondly, the Royal Train was derailed – accident or deliberate sabotage? Then, twenty or so minutes later, two shots were fired, one of them hitting Greaves.

In Grace's opinion, given these facts, the chances that the derailment and the shooting of the Private Secretary were isolated incidents were very low. So low as to be virtually dismissible. In a nutshell, the simplest explanation was usually the likeliest one. In this case the theory that the derailment of the train and the shooting were linked fitted that exactly.

So, he hypothesized, had one of the protestors derailed the train in the hope of creating a disaster that killed perhaps The Queen and many of her entourage? And as backup they had a sniper waiting, having calculated the party would exit from the south entrance of the tunnel?

That did not sit well with him. The intel on the protestors was that they were harmless, not fanatics prepared – and organized – to kill. His colleagues had got to know some of them in the past few years around the country, and that just did not seem like their work. Added to that, the shooter had only fired two shots. If the intended target had been The Queen, why not fire more?

As Branson continued up the A23, Grace, despite being distracted by his speculations, was fully occupied on his phone, and feeling a deep sense of dread. What should have been a wonderful and proud day for the county of Sussex had turned to tragedy.

Thank God, he thought, The Queen was OK.

For now. The area had been deemed safe by the Strategic Firearms Commander.

The helicopter had passed overhead a few minutes ago. In Grace's comms with the Royal Protection Officer, Jon Gilhall had informed him The Queen was very shaken but unharmed.

NPAS-15 was heading towards the Sussex Police HQ at Lewes, where the secure room Grace had arranged for her was being prepared. She would land in three minutes' time on the adjoining school playing fields, and be greeted by the Chief Constable, Lesley Manning, and a contingent of armed response officers.

Glenn Branson, following the satnav signal, braked and turned off the main road, made a series of manoeuvres, then turned onto a rough, narrow lane that was little more than a rutted, potholed farm track. After several minutes they approached a long, chaotic line of police cars and vans, two fire engines and two ambulances, and beyond them the blue and white police tape of an outer cordon, manned by a young uniformed police constable scene guard who, with his near photographic memory for faces Grace recognized. 'PC Andrew Strong?' he quizzed.

The PC looked proud as punch. 'You remember me, sir?'

'Weren't you the scene guard at that Brighton hotel fire about six months back?'

'I was, sir. Just to let you know a Coroner's Officer will be here soon.'

Grace was pleased to see how quickly the crime scene had been protected and the scene guard put in place. A few minutes later, in their onesie oversuits and signed in on the log, as more and more emergency service vehicles and minibuses were arriving at the RV point, he and Branson walked the quarter of a mile across fields to the inner cordon, signed the second scene guard's log and ducked under the tape.

They strode on up the steep slope of a grassy hillock, where they were greeted at the top by a BTP Inspector, a wiry man in his late forties, also in a protective onesie, looking pale and nervous.

In the far distance behind them were the rolling hills of the South Downs, and the ridge of the Devil's Dyke shimmering beneath the bright sunlight. Much closer behind them were the legs of a pinstripe-suited figure lying on the ground. Grace couldn't see the rest of the man, but he could see a lot of blood on the grass all around.

The Inspector's name was Iain College – Grace and Branson had already been informed by radio. He spoke with a soft Scottish accent.

'Good morning, gentlemen – sir,' he said, deferring to Grace. 'This is one hell of a situation.'

'You could say that,' Grace said, drily. He well knew that British Transport Police were no greenhorns when it came to major crime. They regularly dealt with homicides and other serious offences on railway property, as well as terrorist threats and atrocities. 'What do we have?' he asked.

'We have a body, sir, male, confirmed deceased by a paramedic ten minutes ago.'

'Gunshot wound?'

'I would say it appears so, sir.'

'Do you have a confirmed ID on the deceased?'

'We believe he is the Private Secretary to The King and The Queen.'

Grace shook his head in near disbelief. 'Sir Peregrine Greaves, that's what I've been told.'

As he and Branson moved to step towards the body, College said, 'Just to warn you, it's not pretty.'

'Yep, well when you've been shot dead, no one expects you to look your best,' Branson retorted. He was feeling the same beat of excitement he always got at the start of a major investigation. And this was truly big, the biggest yet of his and Roy's career.

Grace stopped in his tracks as he saw the remains of Greaves' once handsome face.

'Looks like one of my mum's summer puddings,' Branson murmured to him, staring down wide-eyed.

Despite the horror of what he was seeing, Grace found himself suppressing a smile. Good old gallows humour; people sometimes forgot that officers, just like all other human beings, needed their coping mechanisms. Humour had always been his safety net, helping keep him sane in the most horrific of crime scenes. And as those went, this was pretty bad. It looked like the Private Secretary had put on a cheap Halloween mask. Apart from the blood pooled on the ground all around his head.

He turned to the Inspector and asked, 'Is this British Rail property here?'

College shook his head and looked relieved. 'No, sir. British Rail property ends the top of the steps up from the tunnel – this is private farmland – belongs to Pangdean Farm – so this is your jurisdiction. We'll take care of the derailment. But obviously we need to work together, and any help British Transport Police can give you, we will. There's a sergeant and a PC from Haywards Heath down at the tunnel entrance keeping everyone safely just inside the tunnel until the area is declared safe. And a Crime Scene Manager and team of CSIs are on their way.'

As Grace thanked him, his phone rang. It was Nigel Downing.

'Are you at the scene, Roy?' the ACC asked.

'I am, sir.'

'I understand the victim who has died is a senior member of the Royal Household? Is this correct?'

'Unfortunately yes, sir. The Private Secretary. But Her Majesty is safe and should now be at HQ.'

'She is, her helicopter has just landed. She's asking about her dresser.'

'Her dresser?' Grace queried.

'She wants her dresser, she needs to change her clothes, they've blood and – other matter – on them. Her dresser is apparently being rushed over to HQ now. Is anyone else injured?'

'No other casualties reported, so far.'

'No sign of the gunman – shooter?'

THE HAWK IS DEAD

'Not so far, sir. We believe he has fled the area.'
'I'm heading over – where shall I meet you?'
'The outer cordon would be best.'
'I'll radio you when I'm there.'

Roy Grace wasn't entirely sure what the direct-entry, fast-track Superintendent, now ACC, with his past experience in Highways Planning, could bring to the investigation, but if it was even just moral support at this stage, that would be fine by him.

There would likely be officers from the Counter Terrorism Command, and even the Protection hierarchy, under which the Royalty and Specialist Protection team operated, all keen to be involved. Not because they could do the job any better than he and his team, but because being part of this high-profile investigation, and helping to bring it to a successful conclusion, could bring career glory and all kinds of promotion prospects. While this was a murder on his territory, and he was the on-call SIO, he had the feeling competition for ownership of this case might turn ugly, and that senior detectives would be fighting like rats in a sack to get involved in this one.

He was right.

18

Monday 20 November 2023

Five minutes after the police helicopter landed in the playing fields close by, Queen Camilla, along with her Protection Officer, was driven into the safe confines of Police Headquarters, in the middle vehicle of a three-car armed convoy.

The Chief Constable, Lesley Manning, and the Deputy Chief, Gordon Crawford, stood at the entrance to Malling House with a young Inspector to escort Her Majesty to the room that had hastily been prepared for her. It was adjacent to the room to which, on 12 October 1984, Margaret Thatcher had been taken, after the IRA had failed to assassinate her by bombing the Grand Hotel in Brighton, where she had been staying during the Conservative Party Conference.

Two officers from the Armed Response Unit, wielding their semi-automatic rifles, stood a discreet distance away. The Chief Constable, who was forty-nine, her hair clipped into a bun beneath her round hat, stood deathly serious, unsure quite what to expect, her mind considering every option. The Deputy Chief Constable stood beside her. The tall, powerfully built Scot, a no-nonsense down-to-business man, had in the past thirty minutes taken care of all the arrangements under Manning's direction.

Although deeply upset about the death of the Private Secretary – and that the whole incident had occurred on her watch – Manning was relieved beyond words that The Queen was seemingly unharmed. Two Royal Protection vehicles and four motorcycle police outriders were on their way, and would escort her back to London as soon as she was ready.

The Police HQ was locked down, with no one allowed in without her express consent. Two more officers from the Armed Response Team were on guard at the front entrance barrier. Lesley Manning and her team had put in place everything they could think of to protect The Principal. In the aftermath of the assassination attempt, Sussex Police were taking no chances.

Additionally, a Royal Air Force Chinook helicopter carrying armed officers had arrived over the area of the Downs where the shooter was suspected to have been, and was conducting a low-level sweep.

Moments after the police vehicle pulled up, the front passenger door opened. First out was Jon Gilhall. Then The Queen appeared, taking his guiding arm and looking shocked but composed. She gave the two senior police officers a hesitant smile.

'Your Majesty,' Manning said, doing a slightly clumsy version of a curtsy. 'Your Majesty,' DCC Crawford echoed, bowing stiffly.

'Welcome to Sussex – I'm so terribly sorry about the circumstances. Are you all right?' the Chief Constable asked. 'Are you hurt?'

The Queen shook her head, 'No, I'm fine, fortunately, thank you. Although it's not been the morning I'd had in mind – so far. It's been pretty dreadful.'

Neither Lesley Manning nor Gordon Crawford knew quite how to take this, both wondering whether it was a stab at humour.

Then The Queen shot an anxious glance at her small, elegant Cartier Tank wristwatch and looked back at them both with an uncertain smile. 'I need to find somewhere to make some calls – I have to phone The King, he could hardly hear me in the helicopter. Also, my dear secretary, Jayne Bennett. I'll need her to be involved in everything. I would like her to call Martlets Hospice and explain we are running behind schedule and will be a bit late. She already mentioned to me that Perry's late father died at Martlets, so it's even more important that I get there as planned.'

She didn't notice several raised eyebrows.

'Understood, Ma'am,' the Protection Officer said. 'And I've just spoken by phone to your dresser – Brenda – she will be here shortly with a change of clothes. She's requested somewhere for you to retire, change and make your calls.'

All eyes stared at the dark blotches on her dress.

'We have a room all prepared for you, Ma'am,' Lesley Manning responded. 'Your royal doctor will attend to check you over. And a car is on its way to transport you back to London.'

The Queen gave her a look so disapproving it startled Manning. 'Back to London?'

'Yes, Ma'am.'

'I'm sorry, I've come to Sussex to visit terminally ill patients in two hospices – Martlets in Brighton and young children in Chestnut Tree House in Arundel. They're expecting me and I don't intend to let them down.' Her expression softened and she gave Manning a smile.

'But, Ma'am – your safety is paramount,' Gordon Crawford interjected.

She shook her head. 'What is *paramount* is that I visit those two places – and the ones tomorrow further down the coast where they are all expecting me. Someone may have tried to kill me today, but they didn't succeed. I'm very deeply sorry that Sir Peregrine has died – but if whoever shot at me and hit him instead thinks I'm going to scurry back up to the safety of London, they can think again. Jayne, my secretary, agrees. I've come to Sussex to do a job, and that's what we are going to do.'

Manning and Crawford shot each other a glance.

The Queen looked at her watch again. 'I believe I was due at Martlets Hospice about now and Brenda should be here soon. A quick change and we'll be off. It'll be twenty minutes by road from here?'

Manning nodded confirmation. The Queen turned to her Protection Officer. 'Jon, can you check whether Jayne has rung Martlets to let them know we are running late? Please ask her to give them my apologies.'

During the short helicopter ride Gilhall had already tried to persuade his boss to abandon the tour, for her safety. But she'd given him very short shrift and the subject was now closed. He gave a single respectful head-bow. 'Ma'am.' Then he stepped away and pulled out his phone.

'Ma'am,' Manning said. 'I remember your visit to St Wilfrid's Hospice in Eastbourne a few years back, which I oversaw. It's my responsibility to oversee things again here, but now under these more challenging and sad circumstances. I think that after what's happened we should let your doctor, who will be here any moment, check you over before you do anything.'

The Queen peered down at the dark blotches on her dress. 'What will my doctor be looking for – bullet holes?' she asked wryly. 'Or will I be getting trauma counselling?'

Again, neither police officer knew whether or not to smile.

19

Monday 20 November 2023

Roy Grace knew one certainty about every murder victim: the moment of death was like a starting pistol being fired, signalling the race was on between blowflies and the media to get to the victim first.

Today, from the cluster of camera lenses and strobing flashlights at the blue and white tape of the outer cordon, it looked like the media had won, hands – or perhaps proboscises – down. Sometimes, in his darker, angrier moments he struggled to differentiate the media scavengers from the blowflies.

As he strode along the track towards the ACC, who was well inside the cordon and several yards back from the scene guard, he could see familiar faces from the *Argus*, *Sussex Express*, Radio Sussex and ITV Meridian – among the fast-swelling press corps, several of whom were shouting questions at the ACC.

'Sir, is it true The Queen has been shot?'

'ACC Downing, has someone tried to kill The Queen?'

'Nigel, NIGEL!'

'Assistant Chief Constable, is it true there's been an assassination attempt on Camilla?'

Nigel Downing, standing a few yards behind the scene guard, in his full dress uniform, replied loudly, 'I'm sorry, I cannot comment at this stage. There will be a press conference later, probably at Haywards Heath police station.'

'What time will that be, sir?' someone shouted.

THE HAWK IS DEAD

Downing looked extremely relieved to see Grace heading towards him and, distancing himself further from the tape, greeted him with a firm handshake, asking at the same time, 'How's it going?'

'Detective Superintendent Grace!' the reporter from the *Argus* shouted out. 'Is The Queen still alive?'

'ROY!' another shouted. 'Is the rumour true?'

'Her Majesty has not been hurt,' he called back. 'She has been removed to a place of safety. We will be holding a press conference at Haywards Heath police station at 2 p.m. today.'

Then he ushered Downing away, and along the track towards the inner cordon a quarter of a mile away. As they walked, the ACC pointed to Grace's oversuit. 'Should I be putting one on here, Roy?' he asked.

'No, sir, you don't need to go inside the inner cordon.'

'I'd like to see the body.'

'I can assure you, sir, you wouldn't. And with respect, I want the least amount of people walking around the crime scene. It looks like the first bullet pretty much exploded when it struck Sir Peregrine's head and there may be crucial fragments of that bullet, or the second one, that could lead us to the killer. They could easily get trodden into the ground, which is very soft from the recent rain, as you can tell.'

'Understood, of course,' Downing said. 'So can you give me an update?'

'Yes, sir, but firstly, how is The Queen?'

'Being a right royal pain,' he replied with the trace of a grin. 'Can you believe she is insisting on carrying on with her plans for the day?'

'I can believe it, yes.'

'I just spoke to the Chief. She is already on her way to Martlets Hospice.'

'Christ,' Grace said. 'With a proper escort?'

'All police leave in the county has been cancelled for the next twenty-four hours, and all available staff have been called in. She's in a vehicle with bulletproof windows, armed response officers in front and behind and an RAF Chinook helicopter with armed personnel on board, overhead, covering her route. She's determined to continue with her visits and no one is going to dissuade her.'

'I think it's exactly what the late Queen would have done,' Grace said. 'Just carry on.'

'Exactly. But I think the Chief has persuaded her to just do the two hospices, Martlets then the children's one, Chestnut Tree House, but to cancel Chichester Theatre and return to the safety of Clarence House for the night. Going to the theatre would not be a good look.'

'I think that's smart, sir. Not letting patients in a hospice down is one thing. Going to the theatre on the night her Private Secretary has been murdered would not, as you say, be a good look.'

They were approaching the inner cordon and behind the scene guard, they could see several people in oversuits, all busy.

'Right, the update, sir. Currently at the crime scene itself we have Chris Gee, Crime Scene Manager, and CSI photographer James Gartrell, whose work is always top notch, and two more CSIs who have temporarily put a cover over the Private Secretary's body. I'm awaiting the arrival of a ballistics expert to see if they can pinpoint where the shooter was located. We have a drone operator and the machine is currently doing a low-level sweep over the area where we think the shooter may have been.'

Grace pointed at the wide expanse of Downland hills in front of them, a mixture of grass, dense shrubland and trees. 'Whoever it was chose their location well, there's a good 180-degree sweep and the shooter could have been anywhere within that. We've possibly narrowed this down a little – we had some assistance from a local dog walker who told one of the uniformed officers we've got out on the hills searching, that a man on a motocross bike raced past her at speed, approximately five minutes after the shots were fired, carrying a canvas bag – the type that broken-down fishing rods are carried in.'

'Did this person get the licence plate?' Downing asked.

'She got one digit, sir. She sounds a good witness – she's agreed to come in for a cognitive witness interview. But it will very likely be a cloned plate – it looks like our shooter is smart and well-prepped.'

'Well-prepped enough to have the train derailed for him?' Downing suggested. 'All part of an anti-monarchist conspiracy? The Not-My-King lot?'

Grace shook his head. 'I don't think it is necessarily them, sir, no.'

Downing looked at him, astonished. 'What?'

They both heard the whirr of a drone and looked up at the tiny machine with its winking red dot of a light.

'Is that ours?' Downing asked.

Grace frowned. 'I'll ask James Gartrell. But I'm sure it is.'

The ACC looked pensive. 'So you don't think this whole terrible thing is part of an anti-monarchy conspiracy, Roy?'

Grace shook his head. 'The Not-My-King people are part of an anti-monarchy movement, but their issues are around the cost of living crisis in contrast to what they see as the monarchy's opulence. There's nothing in their history to suggest anger at a level where assassination of a monarch could be plausible. Our team have got to know some of them quite well. We will of course check the group out as a line of enquiry to either eliminate or implicate them as suspects.'

Downing nodded. 'I hope you are right. And you are pretty sure the shooter is no longer in the area, Roy?'

'I am, sir. The helicopter did a thorough sweep and our drone hasn't seen anything. The motorbike roaring off five minutes after the shots – and the fact that there were only two shots fired.'

'And the rest of the royal entourage?'

'I initially kept them down in the tunnel, for their own safety and equally importantly to prevent them from coming up and contaminating the crime scene. A second route out of the tunnel and up the embankment has been established, and others are all being transported by minibuses to Haywards Heath police station, where I will arrange officers to interview them. To be honest, it seems the key witnesses we'll need are Her Majesty and her Protection Officer, Jon Gilhall, who were both present on the grass knoll above the tunnel when Greaves was shot. No one else would have been in a position to see anything.'

Downing shook his head. 'This is a terrible day for Sussex, Roy. A terrible day.'

'Why do you say that, sir?'

Downing rounded on him. 'I can't believe you've just said that.'

Grace shrugged.

'Someone tried to assassinate The Queen on our watch, Roy. A terrorist organization or a lone wolf? You don't think that's a terrible day?'

'Sir, even at this early stage I am not yet convinced anyone tried to assassinate her,' he replied. 'We need to consider all the evidence. It's possible she was not the intended target.'

20

Monday 20 November 2023

As Downing gave him a very strange look, Grace heard footsteps approaching behind them, and turned. He saw a short, wiry and energetic-looking man with a bushy beard. He was lugging a large metal box.

'Detective Superintendent Grace?' he asked pleasantly, in a gruff Sussex burr.

'Yes?' He knew the faces and names of just about everyone that the Major Crime Unit engaged with but he could not place this man, especially in his protective clothing. Grace realized it was a mark of how few times in his career that firearms had been involved. The man had clearly been allowed inside the outer cordon for a reason.

'Baz Dyson, Ballistics Scientist, from the Croydon lab, sir.' He held out his identity card. 'What do we have?'

Grace briefed him on what they knew so far. Then Dyson signed the scene guard's log and, momentarily leaving Grace and the ACC on the other side of the tape with his case, walked over to where a light tarpaulin lay across the Private Secretary's body.

The Crime Scene Manager and Dyson had a brief discussion, then two CSIs carefully removed the tarpaulin. Dyson looked down at the body with about as much emotion as he would have looked at a doormat. He studied it carefully for some moments, moved around it a little, only wincing slightly when he saw the back of Greaves' head, then walked back towards Roy Grace.

'You said you want to know two things as a priority, sir – if I can pinpoint the approximate location of the shooter, and establish what the weapon was?'

Grace nodded. 'I want to get search officers looking for evidence around the scene of where the shooter was located. He might well have spent some time in his location.'

'If he's a professional, almost certainly he'd have been there a while. But if he's a pro – a sniper very likely – he'll also know how to cover his tracks pretty efficiently.' He looked up and, squinting against the sun, surveyed the landscape. Then he traced an arc with his right hand. 'Looking at the topography, there are plenty of vantage points with ground cover – the shooter could have been anywhere within, I'd guess, around a mile radius.'

'Can you get any clue from the way the body is lying?' Grace asked.

Dyson shook his head. 'It's not critical whether the body or head are facing the same direction of the impact. In the case of instant death, which this looks like – from the catastrophic head injury – the body is likely to roll or fall in no particular pattern. The question we need to ask is whether this was a targeted head shot.'

'Meaning what exactly?' Grace asked.

'Did the shooter hit at the head deliberately, or was he aiming for a body shot and the bullet went high? If we can work out what he was aiming at, we can estimate the maximum distance he would have been positioned from here.'

Grace frowned. 'Can you explain how you can do that?'

Dyson nodded. 'If we hypothesize the shooter was going for a head shot, and scored a bullseye, it gives us quite a lot of helpful information regarding the location of the shooter.'

'Tell me?'

Dyson nodded and Grace could see the man's expertise and passion shining in his expression. He walked closer to the tape and addressed both Grace and Downing. 'We need to start with what accuracy we'd expect from the rifle we're using, and how distance affects what's capable. From the damage inflicted, I would guess one possible bullet might be a .338 Lap Mag with a ballistic tip, which has a velocity of 900 metres per second. This is supersonic. But at half a mile the bullet will have slowed to subsonic speeds. So from half a mile, say, we'd expect a bullet travel time of around 1.5 seconds. Then we have to factor in the amount of bullet drop – the bullet flies in a parabolic curve. The .338 has an average bullet drop, at half a mile, of around 152 centimetres. At 250 yards it drops to around 22 centimetres. This leads to issues when trying to hit a target the size of a human head at long range. We also have to factor in wind drift, the angle of the shot – downwards or upwards – as this affects the impact point. We'd also have to factor in that a human is a moving target. He might move in that one and a half seconds.'

He paused and Grace nodded, trying to process this, and saw the ACC looking like he was doing the mental maths, also. The ballistics expert continued. 'Now we also have to factor in the skill of the shooter. What calibre of marksman would have the skill level to accomplish a head kill at half a mile? With a .338 or any calibre and rifle combination, in my view the probability for an amateur would be a success level of one in fifty. A trained military sniper would improve those odds to one in ten. A skilled privateer with a long background at winning target-shooting trophies, with home-loaded ammunition and perfect conditions – which they are today – maybe one in five – being generous.'

In the far distance they heard the faint muffled blasts of the twin barrels of a shotgun. A plane, en route to or from Gatwick Airport, flew high overhead. 'So how would our shooter improve his odds of a head shot kill to certainty, Baz?'

'He'd have to shoot from a very maximum range of three hundred yards. At that distance even for only a moderately experienced shooter, your head shot kill ratio would be very high.'

'Three hundred yards?' Grace said, looking up at the hills.

'That's where I'd start,' Dyson said. 'Somewhere in that range with both ground cover and a clear line to the target. I'd look for any cover within that distance that could hide the shooter. Areas or paths of ingress and evacuation. You'd identify the area by indications of ground disturbance – such as a flattened patch where someone may have lain prone for an extended period of time. Depressions where someone may have knelt or had elbows in the ground, and also imprints of bipod legs.'

Dyson knelt, opened his case and removed a compact laser rangefinder. He held it up to his right eye and began, very slowly, to scan an arc of the elevated countryside to the south of them, in a clockwise direction. He stopped to make an adjustment and then remained motionless, studying an area of hilly shrubland. Then he moved on and stopped again, staring intently at another area. He repeated this four more times. 'Interesting,' he murmured.

'Interesting?' Grace quizzed.

Without lowering the rangefinder, Dyson now steadily moved it anticlockwise, pausing a couple of times, before settling on one specific target. He studied it again for some while before he lowered the device. 'I think I've located where the shooter was most likely to have been.' He pointed at a hillock largely covered in bushes. 'If you look at about one o'clock. It's the right distance, with good ground cover from a thicket of gorse bushes. You wouldn't see the shooter from here but he'd have clear line of sight of us. He'd also be able to see the entrance to the tunnel from there.'

He handed Grace the rangefinder and the Detective Superintendent peered through it, taking a moment to adjust the focus. He saw the red dot of the laser and the changing digital readout, in yards, as he moved it around. At 297 yards he thought he could see the small area Dyson was referring to. He lowered the instrument. 'That is a possibility,' he agreed.

'What I'll do is head over there and see if I'm right about the vantage point – by looking back at the body – and see if there are any signs of someone having been there recently.'

'I'll come with you,' Grace said.

'Be my guest,' Dyson replied.

As they strode away from the crime scene, ducking under the far side of the inner cordon tape, the ballistics expert added, 'I've been thinking about the weapon. If your witness is correct about the motorbike and the description of the canvas bag containing what he described as looking like a broken-down fishing rod, there is a weapon that would fit with that description. A Blaser LRS2 – a German-made classic sniper rifle, firing a .300 Win Mag with a ballistic tip. It's got a range of two thousand metres, but as I said, to be accurate enough for a head shot, the distance would need to be three hundred metres or less. The bullet has all the power to inflict the damage we can see, and the reason I'm thinking the Blaser LRS2 is that its takedown ability works well for covert transportation.'

'*Takedown ability?*' Grace quizzed. 'I'm sorry, I'm not familiar with that term.' Despite the time of year, he was feeling increasingly warm and sticky in his new white onesie and clumsy overshoes, as they climbed a steep hillock. They had changed into new protective clothing to avoid contamination issues. The ballistics expert was perspiring too, from the effort of the trek.

'It means you can take the weapon apart, for ease of transport – and covert transportation. The advantage of the Blaser LRS2 is that the scope is attached to the barrel, so its accuracy is never compromised when the weapon is reassembled. It also has a magazine capacity of ten rounds, with a straight pull action making quick second shots while staying on target much easier than a conventional bolt-action weapon. There is possibly another advantage for the sniper, if I'm correct about the weapon, which is that it is not used by any UK law enforcement agency nor by our military – making it harder to trace. There are other weapons it could be that I'm not ruling out yet, a Sako TRG 42 or even possibly an L115A3 sniper rifle.'

They finally reached the location Dyson had identified and Grace halted, signalling for him to stop, too. Ahead was a rectangular area of flattened grass.

Dyson nodded. 'Looks like someone has been here very recently. Unless it's an animal – but unlikely – there's nothing big enough out here to have flattened that area. There's no cows or horses.'

Grace nodded, studying the flattened grass and the area immediately around it, looking for anything that might be a link to the shooter. A discarded cigarette butt, a water bottle top, a scrap of paper. He sniffed the air slowly and deeply to see if he could detect the smell of urine, in the hope the shooter might have had a pee. But the only scents were grass, gorse, bracken and earth.

Dyson raised his rangefinder and focused back on the crime scene. After some moments, handing the device to Grace, the ballistics expert said, 'I could be right, sir.'

Peering through the viewfinder, the range on the digital display veered between 296 and 297 yards. Roy Grace could see the body on the ground and several CSIs on their knees carrying out a fingertip search immediately around the body and a little further away from it.

Keeping clear of the area of flattened grass, Grace squatted down and, mimicking the action of a sniper, prostrated himself, before once again peering through the viewfinder. He could see the old brick surround to the tunnel entrance, down in the cutting below, the lift and the steps.

'Even from this distance of three hundred yards, to be sure of a head shot you'd need the target to be stationary, right?' he asked.

'Yes, correct, sir.'

'You might just have nailed it, Baz,' he said. 'This position is concealed by the gorse bushes but gives a perfect line of sight to the tunnel entrance, the steps and the knoll on top. The shooter would have seen them emerge from the tunnel, and then climb the steep steps, knowing they would almost certainly stop at the top to get their breath back. Would you agree?'

'That's exactly what I would have been counting on,' Dyson agreed.

Grace stood, radioed the Crime Scene Manager, and asked Gee to arrange for some new CSIs to attend this second crime scene to avoid any cross contamination.

After Gee had acknowledged that, Grace turned back to Dyson. 'Another hypothesis, Baz. Could this shooter have possibly been aiming at someone standing alongside this victim and missed, hitting the victim – Peregrine Greaves – in the head instead?'

Dyson considered the question for some moments. 'It's a possibility, but not one I'd subscribe to. Let's look at the facts that we have.' He began a countdown on his fingers. 'First is that only two shots were fired. No sniper is going to rely on only two rounds of ammunition. They've got to have at least some backup shots, and the Blaser's magazine – if I'm right about the weapon – could hold ten. But even if I'm wrong about the gun used here, any sniper rifle will have a magazine with a bare minimum of, say, six rounds. Let's assume our shooter was a pro – or at least a very experienced amateur. If he'd hit the wrong person, when his target was Camilla, he only took a second shot but missed? So let's follow that theory for a moment. You detectives work on hypotheses, right?'

Grace smiled grimly. 'It's a word we prefer to *assumption*.'

'So let's hypothesize. The shooter is up here, concealed by the gorse bushes, with a perfect line of sight on both the south entrance to the tunnel and the grassy area above it. He takes aim at Camilla and his shot goes wide, hitting Greaves in the head.

If the shooter's here to assassinate Camilla and well capable of firing at least another four rounds in rapid succession, why did he only shoot again once?'

Grace nodded. 'Fair point, but don't forget, within a couple of seconds Her Majesty was on the ground covered by her Protection Officers.'

'The sniper could still have got more shots off – he got spooked perhaps?'

Before Grace could respond, he was distracted by a text from Downing.

Roy, we have a problem. Need you back down here asap.

21

Monday 20 November 2023

The unanswered question stayed with Roy Grace as he and Dyson waited for the CSIs to attend and start a forensic search of the possible shooter location. And it stayed with him all the way back down to the activity at the crime scene, the Coroner's Officer having not yet arrived. Suddenly a call came through on his radio. It was a Comms controller.

'Sir, I have Chief Superintendent Carr.'

Grace thanked her and a moment later heard the voice of the Commander for Brighton and Hove Police, who was today also Silver Commander for Operation Flagship.

'Roy,' she said, 'how is it going?'

'I'm at the scene of the shooting now, Rachel,' he said. 'Pretty grim.'

'I've just had a call from the Chief,' she continued. 'The Queen is adamant about continuing with her tour of the hospices, as scheduled for both today and tomorrow. The only difference being she will not attend Chichester Theatre but will return to London overnight. I just wanted to alert you to this.'

'Thanks, Rachel, for confirming, we thought that would be the case.'

'Except now we have to try to protect her, knowing there's a gunman out there somewhere who is maybe intent on killing her.'

Behind the tape he saw a very agitated ACC Downing and he

signalled he'd be with him in a moment. 'Rachel, all we can do is surround her with officers, vehicles in front and behind her car, and a helicopter directly overhead with Armed Response officers on board, plus put a ring of steel around each hospice.'

'That's being done, Roy.'

'OK, keep me posted.' He thanked her and headed straight to Downing.

'Roy,' the ACC said, his normally very confident and assured boss looking uncharacteristically nervous. 'We have a bit of an issue. Just when you thought today could not get any worse, it does.'

'Bet you are wishing right now you were back in your old job of Highways Planning. Just having to worry about potholes.'

'Never! So, this other major problem we now have.' He gave Grace a bemused grin, his arms gesturing he was out of his depth. 'It's the Met.'

Grace wasn't entirely surprised to hear this. Competition between the Met and regional forces frequently arose on major incidents of national importance. The vast Met Police force had around 35,000 officers, compared to the few thousand of most of the country's other forces, and they could be very superior, regarding all other English police forces as less able outfits by comparison. He felt a sudden hollow sensation in the pit of his stomach. 'Tell me, sir?'

The ACC blushed. 'Well, the thing is, Roy, I've just had Sir Mark Peckham, the Commissioner of the Met, on the phone – in person.'

The Commissioner of the Met was, by definition, England's most senior police officer.

Downing waved a hand uselessly in the air, as if trying, unsuccessfully, to indicate it was of no importance, no importance at all. 'Sir Mark feels this might be too big for Sussex Police to handle – that the Met Counter Terrorism Command should have primacy on this case.'

THE HAWK IS DEAD

Grace stared at him for some moments. 'That's typically high-handed of them, sir.' He realized this was where Downing's lack of policing experience was an issue. 'I hope you gave them short shrift.'

Downing grimaced uncertainly, flapping his hand around in the air again. 'Well, I – tried to be tactful, Roy. I – I told them that this had all happened on our – in our – county – and that I was very satisfied you were the right man to handle this. You are a fully trained, accredited SIO. But I'm afraid a group of them have helicoptered down from London and will be here imminently.' He gave Grace an imploring look. 'An attempted assassination of The Queen is a pretty big thing, Roy.'

At that moment, Grace heard the voice of the outer cordon scene guard, PC Andrew Strong. His tone was indignant. 'Sir, I've got a very pushy gentleman, a Superintendent Gregory Mosse from the Met Counter Terrorism Command, demanding to be let through the cordon. Should I allow him through? There are three other men and one woman with him, all from the Met, who are also insisting on coming through. What would you like me to do?'

Tell them to fuck off, was Grace's immediate reaction. Ownership of this murder enquiry was undoubtedly a prized role. Global headlines would be dominated by this incident for days to come. A successful outcome in this tragic case would greatly enhance the investigating officer's profile, as well as the prospects of other forms of recognition.

None of that bothered him, he was very happy in his present role with no ambition to be promoted any higher. He wanted this job now because he genuinely believed he was the best person to do it, and he was damned if he would hand it over without a fight. He turned to the ACC. 'They're here now, sir.' Then he told Strong to let them all through, intending to knock this on the head, here and now.

'I'll fight your corner for you, Roy,' Downing said. 'As best I can.'

'I appreciate that, sir, I'm sure we can take care of this between us.'

It was only moments later that they saw a group of people striding towards them, smartly dressed. Like a posse. The leader, tall, with wavy fair hair and a wispy goatee, striding several feet ahead of the rest, could have been his old arch-enemy Cassian Pewe's younger, less well-groomed brother.

Passing PC Andy Crabb and his police dog, Merlin, who were just about to commence a search of the area, Grace walked to the cordon tape, took a deep breath and headed into the big swinging dick contest by greeting the leader in a formal tone and without a hint of warmth. 'Superintendent Mosse?'

'It's *Detective* Superintendent actually,' he said somewhat smugly, with a big grin on his face.

His demeanour immediately put Grace's back up. All the same, he held out a hand. 'Detective Superintendent Roy Grace. I am the SIO for this investigation.'

'Really? OK.' Mosse's handshake felt as insincere as his reply. 'So, I'd like a rundown of everything you have – if you could kindly brief my team.' He indicated the group behind him.

'Excuse me?' Grace said.

Mosse looked at him, perplexed. He even slowed his words down as if to underline this. 'We will need to be fully *briefed*,' Mosse said. 'And we need to see the body.' He pointed through the inner cordon. 'That OK?'

Grace smiled. 'Well, I appreciate your interest, but this is a Sussex Police Crime Scene. I'll be able to show you photographs and videos of the body later. British Transport Police are dealing with the derailment in the tunnel, where they have primacy. I'm sure they'll be happy to talk to you.' He pointed an arm along the track in the cutting below. 'You can use that access point.'

'Sorry, Roy,' Mosse said. 'This is our crime scene now.'

Grace indicated Downing. 'This is my boss, Assistant Chief Constable Downing. I think you'd better speak to him.'

To Grace's pleasant surprise, Downing rose to the occasion. 'Detective Superintendent Mosse, Detective Superintendent Grace is Head of Major Crime for Surrey and Sussex and both the Chief Constable and I have complete faith in his ability to investigate any crime he is challenged with.'

Mosse gave Roy Grace a strained look then turned his focus on Downing. 'With respect, Assistant Chief Constable Downing, this is no ordinary tinpot murder enquiry. Are you and your colleagues – and your Chief Officers – not aware that someone has just tried to kill Her Majesty The Queen?'

Grace butted in, addressing Mosse. 'We don't know this yet.'

Mosse looked at him in astonishment. 'I'm sorry?'

Grace responded calmly. 'A senior member of Her Majesty's entourage has been shot dead. You are jumping to conclusions, and immediately making dangerous assumptions.'

Mosse glared at him in undisguised fury. 'You're telling me not to make assumptions? Someone's just tried to assassinate The Queen, what part of that don't you understand?' He shook his head and turned to Downing, as if for reassurance. 'Is this officer of yours for real? He sounds barking mad!'

Downing contemplated this for a moment. Then, in a reply that endeared him to Grace for ever, said, frowning, '*Barking mad?* Do you know the origin of this expression?'

'What does that have to do with anything?'

Downing pursed his lips. 'Well, quite a lot actually. The term derives from Victorian days and is used to describe irrational – or *mad* – behaviour akin to the seemingly senseless barking of a dog. I find that a pretty insulting term to use on this well-respected detective, actually.'

Before Mosse could respond, Grace addressed him. 'You're

saying The Queen was obviously the target, and if you hear me out, I'll explain why I think that may be wrong. Firstly, if we hypothesize the derailment and the shooting are connected, which they may well be, then we are looking at an organized, professional hit. I understand at the time the bullet struck Sir Peregrine, he and Her Majesty were just feet apart. I think you'd agree there is negligible wind today that could affect the flight of a bullet, right?'

Mosse stared at him in angry silence. Grace was aware of the Met officer's team behind him also listening.

'According to our ballistics expert, who is currently on site, to be sure of an accurate head shot, the shooter must be within three hundred yards of the target. We are fairly confident we have already established where the shooter was located – within this range. If he aimed at the target's head and was a lousy shooter, he might be a few inches out – right or left, up or down. But four feet off his target? There is no way a professional shooter could be that wide of their mark.' He shrugged. 'But, OK, let's say this person was the worst shot in the world, that he couldn't hit the proverbial barn door at six feet. He aims at The Queen and misses her but hits her Private Secretary, standing close by. He fires a second shot, which misses The Queen. Why doesn't he take more shots? Would you like to tell me your hypothesis? Because I think you are looking in the wrong box.'

The Met officer stared back at him, momentarily stumped.

Grace went on. 'I'll tell you *my* hypothesis. It's a very simple one. The Queen wasn't the target, because Peregrine Greaves was.'

22

Tuesday 21 November 2023

Had John Sheffield, born into nobility, perhaps been a better and more famous poet, his writing might have been his legacy. Instead it was the townhouse he built in 1703, as somewhat more than a mere London pied-à-terre, that was to immortalize his name.

In that same year, Sheffield, a social climber of such scale he was more of a social *mountaineer*, a favourite of Queen Anne, part-time poet and full-time soldier was appointed to the Privy Council, from where he went on to become Lord Chamberlain and eventually Lord Privy Seal. The Queen bestowed on him the joint titles of Duke of Buckingham and Normanby.

On his death the titles passed to his son, upon whose subsequent death, at the early age of nineteen, the titles became extinct. But Sheffield's name lived on into both the history books and the twenty-first century, thanks to his London pad being bought by George III in 1761. George IV started the significant expansion of the Palace between 1820 and 1830 after it became the official royal residence. Queen Victoria and Prince Albert finished the development in 1837, with another expansion: the front East Wing. They financed the project by selling Brighton's Royal Pavilion to the local council.

Positioned east–west, Buckingham Palace has 775 rooms. The east facade with its sternly imposing grey Portland stone, gilded railings, statuesque guards, vast forecourt and solitary flagpole has been, for close to two centuries, the dominant and majestic global icon of Royalty.

The back of the West Wing, out of sight to all but a privileged selection of the public invited to royal garden parties and those visiting on summer-opening tours, is equally imposing but warmer and more welcoming. Constructed from honey-coloured Bath stone, and designed in a neoclassical style with Corinthian columns and pediments and perfectly proportioned windows and doors, it overlooks, at forty acres, the largest private garden in London.

The centrepiece of the west facade, and protruding handsomely from it, is a bow-fronted section. Copper-domed, columned and exquisitely ballustraded, it houses The King's sitting room and private office on the first floor, with a fine view of two trees, and across the gardens to the lake. Directly below is the formal Garden Entrance, with a glass awning covering the four steps up to the doorway, beyond which there is both a staircase and a lift.

In a break with royal tradition, Charles and Camilla currently resided at Clarence House, just a few minutes away. It had been King Charles's London residence since 2003. Before then it was the home of the late Queen Mother. Because of ongoing renovations at Buckingham Palace for the past seven years – which were due to continue for at least another three – they were remaining at Clarence House for the time being.

At 11 a.m. most weekday mornings since acceding to the throne, The King travelled in the State Bentley, driven by the Head Chauffeur, a former Royal Protection Officer, the Royal Standard fluttering from the roof. It was a short journey from Clarence House to Buckingham Palace, where the car pulled up outside the Garden Entrance in the West Wing, at the rear of the Palace.

Normally, the Private Secretary, Sir Peregrine Greaves, would have travelled this short distance in the car with him, and another Royal Protection Officer, using the five-minute journey to discuss the key business of the day. And normally, The King would emerge from the rear left door to be greeted by the charming and ever-ebullient Master of the Royal Household, Major General Sir Thomas Magellan-Lacey, while the Private Secretary would leave by the right-hand door and head into the building.

But today, in the emergency rescheduling that was to affect everything in the coming days, The King arrived at 9 a.m.

Behind Sir Tommy, as normal, stood three liveried footmen, each holding a locked, ancient and very battered leather-bound box. These rectangular boxes were four inches deep, and the dimensions of a small briefcase. Only two people in the world had a key to the Master's boxes – The King and the Master of the Royal Household, and their exchange was a daily routine. Each head of department had a personal box for their correspondence with His Majesty The King. They contained memos and actions required by King Charles, the urgent ones always handwritten in red ink, which Tommy affectionately called his *Red Bombers*, and the responses and follow-ups from the respective head of department.

The fact that the footmen stood as usual, holding the boxes, was the only normal thing about today, Tommy thought.

The chauffeur opened the rear door and The King, wearing a black tie with his dark grey suit, stepped out. Tommy was grateful to his wife, Fiona, for reminding him to put on a black tie, too. The former general had an unerring eye for detail, which had served him well during his past ten years in this post under the late Queen Elizabeth before the new King. Tired this morning after only a couple of hours' sleep, and running on adrenaline and coffee, he'd nearly forgotten about the respectful tie because he'd had so much on his mind in the past twenty-four hours, and so many actions to deal with, which had kept him busy well into the small hours. And from the look on The King's face, he was going to have even more today.

Greeting his boss with his customary single deferential head-bow, he said, 'Good morning, Your Majesty.'

'What the hell's good about it, Tommy?' The King retorted.

23

Tuesday 21 November 2023

Hollywood's legendarily grumpy star W. C. Fields famously said, *Start every day off with a smile and get it over with.* There were occasional days when Tommy Magellan-Lacey felt that his boss, whom he admired and deeply respected, had taken a leaf out of the actor's book. This was going to be one.

The King was immensely hard-working but charming, caring and good fun with it. Normally. The flashes of temper that the press loved to pick up on, such as when a pen he was using didn't work, were in reality few and far between. But when The King did have a mood on him, it always took every ounce of the Master's tact and diplomacy to contain it. Tommy fully understood how it had been possible, in times long past, for a British monarch in a fit of pique to have a loyal subject's head lopped off, on a whim. This was a day for walking on eggshells when around The King, he knew. But at least he had prepared as best he could.

As the chauffeur took the boxes from the footmen and handed them the ones from inside the car, King Charles shook his head at the Master. 'This is unbelievable, Tommy. I mean, poor Peregrine. Terrible, just terrible.'

'It is, Sir. How is Her Majesty?'

Indicating the Master to follow him, The King walked briskly up the steps of the Garden Entrance and, ignoring the lift – he never took one unless he absolutely had to, always preferring the exercise of walking – he strode up the staircase and entered the magnificently ornate bow-fronted room. The room, hung with spectacular paintings and a treasure trove of objets d'art, had doubled as his late mother's sitting room and office and was, as the Master recalled, almost exactly as she had left it. Perhaps in time The King would put his own imprint on it, but it was only a year since Queen Elizabeth had died. Too soon.

Following him in, Tommy waited for the footmen to put the two boxes on a table and retire, then closed the panelled door behind him. The King crossed to his desk, which was still covered in tiny items of silverware and priceless ornaments, and again shook his head. Then, venting anger, he said, 'She's like that bloody James Bond – shaken – very shaken – but not stirred.' He gave him a strange look, half smiling, half angered.

'She's a strong woman, Sir,' the Master replied.

'Too damned strong for her own good. Someone tried to assassinate her, for God's sake! And she's just carried on like nothing happened. This is terrible – Peregrine shot dead.' He shook his head, looking momentarily – and uncharacteristically – bewildered. He sat down at the desk, as if the weight of responsibility was pressing too heavily on his shoulders, then looked up. Softening his tone, he asked, 'What are we doing to support dear Margot and all the staff, Tommy?'

'I have this in hand, Sir, rest assured. I've spoken to the Apothecary, and he's ready to see anyone who's feeling in need of emotional support.'

The *Apothecary* was the traditional name for the Palace doctor, who held a well-staffed medical centre in the Royal Mews.

'And I've had discussions with the Lord Chamberlain, who is addressing all staff in the Ballroom at midday. He will tell them that counselling is available to anyone who feels they need it.'

'Good. But what about Margot?' Margot was Sir Peregrine Greaves' widow.

'I went to see her last night, Sir. Predictably, she's in bits. But she told me all three of her daughters were on their way to Ambassadors' Court to be with her. Just in terms of admin, other staff members have stepped up to cover the Private Secretary's role in the interim.'

King Charles shook his head and gave the Master a wan smile. 'I don't know what I'd do without you, Tommy.'

Magellan-Lacey gave a modest head-bow. 'Thank you, Sir.'

'And what about the investigation – what do we know so far?'

'I've been in regular communication with the Commissioner of the Met, who—'

'Sir Mark Peckham?' The King interrupted.

'Exactly, Sir. He has everything in hand, and is in turn liaising with the Chief Constable of Sussex – her name is Lesley Manning – and her senior team. I understand that she has put her top Major Crime detective in charge of the investigation – a Detective Superintendent Roy Grace. As you know, Her Majesty is now en route by helicopter to Hampshire to the first of two hospice visits today, and where the police are on the highest alert, with all leave cancelled, and additional protection being provided by the Army and the RAF.'

The King stared up at him, looking increasingly agitated. 'My darling wife is being so damned insistent, Tommy! Why can't she understand there is some maniac out there trying to kill her? It's all very well you telling me the police have things in hand. But you are not reassuring me!'

'I'm afraid she is determined to finish her visits to the hospices, Sir.'

The King shook his head again. 'And who is this Grace character? Some provincial copper – why haven't we got the top Met people on it?'

'Officers from the Counter Terrorism Command are going to be on his team. But I understand he's highly experienced, Sir, very well thought of – and the right man for where the incident happened, with a very great deal of local knowledge.'

The King gave him a strange, withering look. '*Incident?* Are you calling the attempted murder of my wife just an *incident*?'

He gave The King a placatory smile. 'I was using police terminology, Sir.'

'Hmmn. If you say so. I want to see this Grace fellow, can you get him here now?'

'He's coming up first thing tomorrow, to talk to Her Majesty.'

'Why can't I see him now?' he said with a growing frustration.

'I spoke to Her Majesty earlier. She is resolved to honour her commitments to the two hospices in Hampshire and will then return to London this evening. She's not actually in his county any more – Grace is only responsible for Sussex and Surrey, not Hampshire. I have a call in to the Chief Constable there.'

The King shook his head in near disbelief. 'Tommy, I don't like her out there, swanning around England, with a gunman on the loose. As I told her last night.'

Major General Sir Tommy Magellan-Lacey said, standing very stiffly, 'I'll do my best, Sir. But you know Her Majesty.' He gave The King another solemn head-bow.

'I do!' King Charles retorted. 'Bloody determined.'

24

Tuesday 21 November 2023

It wasn't just all over the news, it pretty much *was* the news, both in the UK and around the world, eclipsing all other stories.

The pressure on Roy Grace as he sat with his assembled team around the oval conference room table in the Major Crime Suite was immense. It was a few minutes past nine. He had not gone home last night, instead grabbing a couple of hours' kip at around 4 a.m. on the makeshift camp bed he kept in his office cupboard for such purposes, then showering in the gym and changing into the fresh shirt and underwear he also kept in his office.

The only respite he had was the knowledge that Queen Camilla had returned safely to London last night, and today would be visiting, as scheduled, the two hospices in Hampshire – another county, which was not his responsibility.

Despite his lack of sleep, he was energized, thanks partly to a painfully icy shower he had deliberately inflicted on himself, partly to the cocktail of adrenaline and espresso surging through his body, and partly to the fury burning inside him. The fury that some bastard had, in the view of the world's media, attempted to assassinate The Queen.

He felt fully alert and ready to take on everything the day was going to throw at him. And it was going to throw a lot, including showing his presence at the Private Secretary's postmortem, and holding a press conference – scheduled for midday. As he sat, he guided on his screen the very long roll of newspaper headlines, scrolling down the flat video monitor behind him.

TENTATIVE D'ASSASSINAT CONTRE LA REINE D'ANGLETERRE
MORDANSCHLAG AUF DIE KÖNIGIN VON ENGLAND!
MOORDAANSLAG OP DE KONINGIN VAN ENGELAND
ATTENTATO ALLA REGINA D'INGHILTERRA!
INTENTARON ASESINAR A LA REINA DE INGLATERRA
POKUS O ATENTA'T NA ANGLICKOU KRA'LOVNU
رتلجنإ ةكلم لايتغإ ةلواحم
ملہ حم ہنالتاق رپ ہیناطرب ہکلم
ПОКУШЕНИЕ НА КОРОЛЕВУ АНГЛИИ.
SALAMURHAYRITYS KUNINGATAR CAMILLAA VASTAAN!

He continued for some moments scrolling through the local, national and international newspaper headlines. Making sure everyone in this room got the message. That they fully understood what they were dealing with. The biggest crime on their territory since the bombing of the Grand Hotel in Brighton.

He had his regular, trusted team of DI Branson, DSs Norman Potting, Nick Nicholl and Jack Alexander, with Jack acting as Office Manager, as well as Reena Chacko, the Intelligence Manager. Along with Investigators Emma-Jane Boutwood, Velvet Wilde, Polly Sweeney and Will Glover, researcher Luke Stanstead, and a HOLMES2 – Home Office Large Major Enquiry – supervisor. He was also joined this morning by a Detective Inspector from the Metropolitan Police Counter Terrorism Command, a Chief Inspector from the Royal Protection team and a Chief Inspector from British Transport Police. They weren't just there as a peace offering to the Commissioner of the Met, but as officers Grace believed would be able to help in areas beyond his own scope of knowledge and geographical reach.

Checking around the room that everyone he'd wanted was in place, he glanced down at his notes and then back up. 'OK, good morning, team, this is the second briefing meeting of Operation

THE HAWK IS DEAD

Asset, the investigation into the shooting of Sir Peregrine Greaves, Private Secretary to King Charles and Queen Camilla. This shooting occurred at approximately 10.30 a.m. yesterday, November the twentieth, a short distance outside the southern portal to Clayton railway tunnel.'

He pointed to one of the large screens behind him, on which appeared a series of photographs of the south entrance to Clayton Tunnel and the immediate environs. Then he continued by saying, 'You've seen the headlines, there is a lot of shock around this country and the world that someone has tried to assassinate our Queen. We are not for now going to be making any assumptions. We are going to concentrate our energies on the following. Firstly, what caused the derailment of the train? This is something we will be assisted with by Chief Inspector Roy Hodder from British Transport Police, who very helpfully was formerly a Chief Inspector with Sussex Police and so has valuable knowledge of our county. He has some preliminary information which he will be sharing with us shortly.' He nodded at the uniformed officer, a genial man in his early fifties with a balding forehead and almost Victorian side whiskers, who raised a hand in acknowledgement.

'One key line of enquiry,' Grace said, 'is to establish whether there is a link between the derailment and the shooting, or whether what we have are two wholly separate incidents. Another line of enquiry will be, who knew the timetable for the train?' He pointed to another of the screens, which showed a small photograph of Greaves, in a chalk-striped suit with neatly coiffed hair, and a large and very gruesome photograph of the remains of the Private Secretary's head, on the grass, amid blood and other matter. He had chosen to have this image very large for maximum impact on his team.

'I would say that's a no-brainer, chief!' quipped Potting, who, as he often did, began chortling at his own joke.

'That is truly terrible, Norman,' Velvet Wilde chided in her rich Belfast accent.

Several of the team shook their heads, unable to suppress their grins. Grace himself struggled, too. 'Thanks, Norman,' he said. 'Very helpful.' Then he looked back down at his notes. 'We have one hypothesis that the derailment was intentional, with the purpose being to have the royal party leave the train on foot and emerge from the tunnel where any of them would be an easy target for a sniper. A second hypothesis is that, as I just posited, the two events are disconnected and the shooting of Sir Peregrine was accidental – but with what we've seen and know, I am discounting that; it's hardly going to be someone shooting rabbits, is it?'

'Chief,' Potting said. 'I was raised on a farm and used to go shooting rabbits regularly when I was a nipper. We shot them because they were vermin, but they were also good food, and the best weapon for a rabbit is a rifle firing a .22 bullet, which will kill the animal, but leave it intact. A shotgun is another alternative, but you've got the problem of multiple lead pellets inside it.'

'And your point is, Norman?' Grace asked, feeling a tad fractious and with less patience for the old warhorse today than he might normally have had.

Potting turned and pointed at the photograph of Greaves' head. 'Whatever bullet that was, chief – a hollow-nose, dum-dum, ballistic tip – you wouldn't use that for shooting rabbits. You wouldn't use it for any kind of rough shooting, unless you were after moose or buffalo – and there aren't too many of those running wild on the South Downs.'

Grace nodded. 'That's helpful, thank you, Norman. As I said, it's unlikely to be that.'

The Met Counter Terrorism Command DI, Brent Dean, a tall, lean man in his early forties, with a sharp, dark suit and a permanently cynical expression, as if he was bored stiff by all these tedious minions, said in a bland north London accent, 'I think we can do away with all the time-wasting speculations, Detective Superintendent. We all know what has happened. The Not-My-King brigade derailed the train with a steel bar wedged across the rail, in order to get Her Majesty out of the train and make it an easy shot for an accomplice. Fortunately for all of us this accomplice missed – probably because the intended target made him a bag of nerves.'

'Thank you, DI Dean,' Grace replied. 'For the benefit of all us, would you like to expand on your theory – sorry, *hypothesis*?'

'I would say it's obvious, with respect, sir. The shooter missed, hitting the wrong target, took a panicky second shot – then ran to his motorbike and took off. All the hallmarks of an amateur operation.'

Grace nodded. 'To counter that, I would say that for an amateur, the shooter was pretty professional. I went with our ballistics expert to what we believe was the shooter's location, and he – or she – left behind no trace at all. One of our search team spoke to a man out jogging near the suspect location and he said he heard a motorbike close by. He thought it strange for someone to be out there at that time – he has never, in thirty years of jogging there, encountered anyone in that location before. So, between him and the person who clocked the motorbike passing at speed a few minutes after the shots were fired, we have a gap of several hours. Further, if the biker was our shooter, he spent some hours in his location without leaving a trace. No cigarette butts, no urine, no crumbs, no spent shells, nothing other than some flattened grass. We also had PC Andy Crabb and his dog Merlin search the entire area from the shooting location in all directions, but again no potential evidence was found. It could have been a rank amateur, of course. But an amateur waiting that long to take a shot at The Queen? Isn't he going to be nervous? And don't nerves make you want to pee?

To me, it smacks of someone being very forensically aware. Not a rank amateur.'

The Met DI wasn't done. 'So, if you are hypothesizing that it was a professional sniper, and their two shots went wide, one hitting the wrong target, and the other missing completely, why didn't this person shoot again?'

'My point exactly,' Grace said. 'The best hypothesis I can give you is that this person did not shoot a third time, because he had done what he came to do.'

DI Dean frowned. 'With respect, you are making a very dangerous assumption – apologies – hypothesis. If you are wrong, it means someone is still out there looking for another opportunity to shoot our Queen.'

'And if I'm right,' Roy Grace said, 'Sussex Police, the Met and the Royal Protection team are all running round like blue-arsed flies, looking up their own backsides, and missing what is really going on.'

'Which is?' Brent Dean challenged.

'I have no idea,' Grace said. 'But I intend to find out, ASAP.'

25

Tuesday 21 November 2023

In contrast to yesterday's glorious sunshine, overnight the weather had turned back to late autumnal, with an overcast sky and a chill wind. Roy Grace and the ballistics scientist, Baz Dyson, followed by Nick Nicholl and EJ Boutwood, approached the inner cordon. All were in forensic oversuits, and today Grace was grateful for the meagre warmth it was giving him.

And he was grateful to be out in fresh air. Grateful that he'd not had to spend too much time in the mortuary – he'd delegated most of that treat to Glenn Branson. And while the Home Office pathologist, Nadiuska de Sancha, was no doubt feeling the pressure, conducting the most high-profile postmortem of her career, much of it was overkill – on someone who had very definitely been overkilled.

Cause of death wasn't exactly hard to establish. Digging out microscopic fragment after microscopic fragment of the exploded bullet that had caused the catastrophic damage to the victim's head was the laborious task, in the hope that, between the fragments of the two bullets found by the pathologist and the CSIs from their ongoing fingertip search around the crime scene, there would be enough to construct at least part of one whole bullet. Or at least enough to help identify the make and bore of rifle it was fired from, and to start narrowing down the very wide field.

But the postmortem wasn't just about finding microfragments of a bullet. The general health of a murder victim was also a potential factor in any ensuing trial. Grace had once seen a slam-dunk of a murder charge downgraded to manslaughter purely because the victim's health was so poor, it was argued by a QC at the time that it could not be proven it was actually the stab wound that had killed her; it could have been her already badly diseased heart failing from shock.

Although in this case, he thought grimly, as and when this shooter was brought to trial, it would take a somewhat smarter than average brief to convince a jury that cause of death might be down to something other than the victim being short of most of the essential components of his head.

A chill suddenly gusted through him. It wasn't the wind, it was a chill of fear. It blew through his soul every time he let the thought in. What *if* the sniper was still out there, planning their next attempt on The Queen's life?

He'd been informed that she'd arrived safely at the first of the two hospices she was visiting in Hampshire today. The Royal Protection team had greatly increased both the number of their officers guarding her and the thoroughness of their search of the hospices and all surrounding areas. Grace had been told The King had personally intervened and he fully understood.

Regardless of whether he was right or wrong about the intended target, it made no difference to the intensity of the hunt for the identity of the killer. But where it could make a crucial difference was where he put the focus of the investigation. Were they looking for a lone wolf terrorist or someone who was part of a terrorist conspiracy? Someone with a grudge against the Monarchy or The Queen in particular? Or with an axe to grind with the Private Secretary? As with almost all murder enquiries, the answer lay in the motive.

He glanced at his watch: 11.45 a.m. They had an hour and a half before he needed to get back to HQ and spruce up for the 2 p.m. press conference, which he was leading accompanied by

THE HAWK IS DEAD

the Chief Constable, an ACC from British Transport Police, the Commander of the Royal Protection team and the Director of Royal Communications from Buckingham Palace – as well as a member of the Media and Communications department. A press conference at which whatever he said would likely become headlines around the world. He needed a clear head and at least this walk up the hill was helping – probably more than the copious amount of caffeine he'd been downing all morning.

All four of them reached the inner cordon scene guard, where they were met by the Crime Scene Manager, Chris Gee. Nick Nicholl and EJ Boutwood signed the log, then ducked under the tape. Grace produced a sketch created by The Queen's Protection Officer, Jon Gilhall, the only witness to the shooting, marking the approximate positions of The Queen and the Private Secretary when the shots were fired. Grace directed the two officers, here to role-play, to remain in these positions.

Then Grace, Gee and Dyson walked up to the second inner-cordon area, the suspected location where the killer had waited and fired from. Two protectively suited and masked CSIs were on their knees, some distance from the yellow-pegged, flattened area where the shooter had most likely lain.

Gee pointed at it. 'They've cleared that now, sir, you are free to walk or lie on it.'

'And so far you've found nothing at all here?'

Gee shook his head. 'As you know, no cigarette butts – that's a downside of far fewer people smoking these days,' he said almost ruefully. 'So far, no forensic or firearms evidence. There's no trace of anything discarded either and no footprints as yet, but we are still searching.'

'And you are pretty sure this is where he shot from?'

Gee pointed down at the flattened area. 'Someone lay there, for some considerable while, on a mat of some kind.'

'A mat that doesn't shed any fibres?'

Gee, who, Grace always thought, looked impossibly young and fresh-faced to be doing such a grim job, nodded. 'I would say we're dealing with a pro, sir. Someone probably with military training. If we can trust the two witnesses about the timing of the motorbike, the gunman was here for several hours. Only a real pro could be here for that length of time and leave no trace.'

Grace thanked him and then turned and stared across to the knoll, where Nicholl and Boutwood were standing. Dyson was kneeling in the flattened area, attaching a telescopic sight to a small bipod. He looked up at the Detective Superintendent.

'I really am increasingly confident this was the shooter's lair. I went out early this morning and walked in a wide arc, keeping with the approximate range of three hundred yards, and there is nowhere else that gives a line of sight to both the exit to the railway tunnel and the area above it.'

Grace nodded, scanning the surrounding countryside himself. 'We're not of course taking into account the possibility that the shooter could have been a complete amateur who had a go from a much further distance – say half a mile – are we, Baz?'

Dyson shook his head. 'If you like, after this I can take you to a point half a mile away, but you'd see immediately, looking through the scope, that the chances of hitting either of them with a single shot are pretty small – and that is for a professional. At the risk of sounding like a cracked record, I go back to my hypothesis. If we had a complete amateur, lone wolf, at say half a mile, he'd never have fired just a couple of shots if he'd missed his target. He'd have fired a volley.'

'Unless his gun jammed?' Grace questioned.

'Guns don't jam very often – not the kind that snipers use.'

'Your view remains that the shooter fired only two shots, because they hit their intended target? But if the shooter had hit the intended target with the first shot, why the second shot?'

Ignoring the question, Dyson said, 'I've made a checklist of relevant factors, starting with a meteorological data search of wind conditions at the time of the shooting. The biggest effect on a bullet is a cross-wind. But at 10 a.m. yesterday there was just a light breeze, making the wind factor negligible. Heat haze can also affect the visibility of the target, but at 10 a.m. yesterday there was none. The sun was behind the shooter – which it would be now if we could see it – so he didn't have to contend with it in his eyes and worry about silhouetting of the target.'

Grace nodded. 'Sounds like he chose his day and location well.'

'Or got lucky.'

'Or unlucky?' Grace tested.

The ballistics scientist shook his head. 'Another factor is whether there could possibly have been any confusion between how Camilla and the victim were dressed? That needs to be ruled out.' He prostrated himself and made some adjustments to the bipod.

Grace smiled. 'I don't think so. Her Majesty was wearing a royal blue dress. The Private Secretary was in a dark suit. The shooter would need to have had seriously impaired vision.'

'Another factor could be the gun not zeroed properly. But if we are considering a professional, that is highly unlikely.' He paused for a moment and squinted through the scope, adjusting the focus carefully. 'Interesting,' he said. 'Are you confident that the position your two detectives are standing in is exactly where Camilla and Greaves were standing at the time he was shot?'

'That's what Her Majesty's Protection Officer gave me, and he was very sure,' Grace said.

Dyson nodded. 'Because that could make a very significant difference. If The Queen had been standing four feet behind the Private Secretary – by that I mean in line – that would make her a much harder target. But if, as we have here, she is four feet to the side, then it's very different.'

'I'm confident we have the right position for the two of them,' Grace said.

Dyson paused for a moment, thinking. 'OK, we don't yet know the calibre of the bullet, but as I've said, I have a pretty good idea, and the range we have is no issue – strike one. Wind conditions would need to have been in excess of 20mph to make enough drift for a four-foot error from this distance – which we know they weren't yesterday. Strike two. Come and have a look through the scope.'

Grace lay down on the grass and pressed his right eye up to the rubber surround of the scope lens. Then he lined the crosshairs up on EJ's head. It was a big target, filling the scope. He moved it across to Nick's head until that filled the scope. It was a considerable distance, one that would need a deliberate switch of target, not an accidental flinch or a twitch.

'See what I mean?' Dyson asked.

Grace turned and looked at him, nodding.

'Are you interested in history at all, sir?'

'History?' Grace frowned.

'I like famous last words. One of my favourites is Major General Sedgwick, the highest-ranking Union officer killed during the American Civil War. Seconds before he was shot, one of his officers warned he was too close to the front line. He responded, "Nonsense, they couldn't hit an elephant at this dist—"'

Grace grinned, then gave him a questioning look. 'Your point being?'

'The head you can see through the scope. Whether it's your male or your female officer. It's pretty big, right?'

'It is,' Grace agreed. 'Both.'

'So, imagine you are the shooter. You are highly forensically aware and you've taken the greatest care to ensure that you leave no trace, other than the flattened grass. You've come with a weapon that will deliver a catastrophic wound wherever your bullet strikes. If you want to be one hundred per cent sure of killing your target, then a bullet with a ballistic tip, straight through the forehead, is going to do the business, every time. Take another look through the scope and tell me how easy you think it would be to miss?'

Grace looked through the scope again. Then turned back to Dyson. And shook his head. 'You couldn't, could you?'

'My mother couldn't have missed from here,' he replied. 'And she has advanced macular degeneration.'

26

Wednesday 22 November 2023

'Best behaviour, eh?' Glenn Branson said. 'Like, *proper* best behaviour?'

Roy Grace, in the back of the taxi with his colleague, nodded solemnly, as they glided away from London's Victoria Station. Normally they would have driven, but time was too tight this morning.

The very pungent smell of new-car polish of the interior was adding to the faintly queasy feeling in his stomach. And he felt butterflies, which wasn't like him. But then this case wasn't like anything he'd ever previously experienced. He smiled at the DI, relieved to see that, for once, he was dressed discreetly in plain charcoal, rather than in one of his trademark loud suits. 'Proper best behaviour,' he echoed, his voice tight with anxiety, and glanced at his watch: 9.05.

He had no idea how the morning ahead was going to unfold. But then again there wasn't any precedent for a detective interviewing The Queen of England as a witness to a murder. At least he'd gone home last night and slept in his bed, rather than in his office, but he'd been too wired to get any decent quality of sleep, waking constantly and jotting down additional notes of questions to ask today, worried he might forget them otherwise. He read through them on his phone now.

'It's times like this that make me wish more than anything that my mum was alive,' Branson said.

THE HAWK IS DEAD

'Yes?' Grace remembered that Glenn had hardly known his father: he'd once told him he'd left home months before he'd been born.

'If she could have lived to see this, she'd have been so proud,' he said with a wistful smile. 'Little me, going off to interview The Queen!'

Grace smiled, glad for his friend's happiness. 'So don't screw it up!'

Branson feigned an aloof look, and tapped his own chest. 'I'm now a certified Tier 5 interviewer. That's a higher qualification than you.' He narrowed his eyes, but was unable to mask his grin. 'Just remember that – boss.'

'Don't worry, I spent some time with Alec Butler, who is also a Tier 5, to plan today's interview,' Grace retorted.

Branson gave him a big smile.

They were passing Buckingham Palace to their left. The taxi rounded the Victoria Monument, then headed along The Mall, passing the handsome white stucco facade of Clarence House, before halting at lights. They turned left, along the east side of St James's Palace, with its Tudor red-brick facade, then after a few moments, left again into Pall Mall.

'You seem in high spirits,' Grace said.

Branson shrugged. 'Things are good at the moment – you know – with me and Siobhan. We think she might be . . .' He tapped his tummy.

Grace's face lit up. 'Seriously?'

'Uh-huh!'

At that moment the taxi halted at a barrier. Beyond it, to the left, was a further part of St James's Palace, with a black Range Rover parked outside. Two heavily armed police officers stepped out of a hut beside the barrier and the cabbie lowered his window. He repeated part of the instructions Roy Grace had given him. 'Dropping off Detective Superintendent Grace and DI Branson.'

'To see Sir Tommy Magellan-Lacey,' Grace added, lowering his window and holding out his warrant card.

It did not immediately impress either of the two Royal Protection guards. But moments later a door to their left opened, and out stepped an exuberant-looking man – in his early sixties, Grace guessed. He was smartly suited, with elegant wavy hair and wearing a black tie, making Roy Grace very glad he'd had the presence of mind to wear one himself, as had Branson.

The guards acknowledged the new arrival with a friendly greeting, and moments later, tension over, Grace paid the driver and they climbed out of the cab.

'Detective Superintendent Grace? I'm Tommy!' The Master of the Royal Household held out his hand, with a warm smile.

'Very good to meet you, Sir Tommy. This is my colleague, Detective Inspector Glenn Branson.'

Magellan-Lacey pumped Branson's hand, still smiling warmly, and with a very posh voice said, 'You've both come up from Brighton?'

'We have, Sir Tommy,' Grace said.

'It's a wonderful city! Fiona and I went to a wedding there a few years ago, loved it. We had fish and chips on the pier. Best fish and chips ever! Come in – coffee? Tea? Probably not appropriate to suggest something stronger?'

'Probably not!' Grace agreed, pleasantly surprised at how down-to-earth this eminent man was. 'A coffee would be very welcome.'

Branson nodded. 'Same for me.'

The two detectives walked through the narrow front door into an instantly warm and friendly-feeling environment. The hallway walls were hung with photographs, paintings and cartoons, and there was a large cuckoo clock that chimed on the half-hour as they walked past. It felt more like being in a farmhouse than a palace, Grace thought, narrowly avoiding tripping over a dark brown cat.

THE HAWK IS DEAD

They were ushered into a kitchen-dining room with cream walls and black marble worktops that felt even more cosy farmhouse than formal grand. There was a cream Aga oven, a dining table with a green and white polka-dot cover and wooden chairs. All around were framed family photographs, with a strong emphasis on the armed forces. There was a much younger, beaming Tommy in uniform, a round cutting board engraved with 'Tommy & Fiona', photographic collages of young people wearing army berets and, pinned to a door, a printed wall-hanging of a helicopter. And there were books everywhere. The whole effect was warm, disarming, homely.

'I can't believe we are in the middle of London!' Glenn Branson said.

'Is this your house, sir, or what they call grace-and-favour accommodation?' Roy Grace asked.

The Master of the Royal Household smiled a tad wistfully at them, busily filling a kettle. 'I'm afraid these days it is more grace than favour, we have to pay rent.'

Grace clocked the faint shadow of a frown as he said this.

'But, hey, we get to live in the centre of London with free parking, and those chaps outside are a damned sight better than any burglar alarm!'

'Or guard dog,' Grace said.

'Indeed.' The Master looked up with a warm smile and began spooning coffee into a cafetière.

Glenn Branson peered at a silver-framed wedding photograph on a shelf. It was a dashing young Tommy Magellan-Lacey in his army uniform with a beautiful woman, with flowing brown hair, in a bridal dress, standing outside a church. 'Lovely photograph,' he said.

'Thank you!'

'Does your wife work in the Royal Household too, Sir Tommy?'

The Master shook his head. 'No, Fiona works in the art world.

She has a job with a private gallery.' He poured boiling water into the cafetière and indicated for them to sit at the kitchen table. 'So, gentlemen, what progress in your enquiries?' He tipped a packet of chocolate digestive biscuits onto a plate and placed it on the table.

Grace gave a courteous smile. 'I'm afraid we don't have as much as I would like to report, so far,' Grace said. 'I'll bring you up to speed. But, first, may I ask how Her Majesty is?'

'She's deeply saddened by the death of Sir Peregrine, and very shaken, of course, but she is a remarkable lady. She has so many of the qualities of resilience of the late Queen and the same sense of duty. As you know, she insisted on continuing with her tour, much to the consternation of The King, who is understandably extremely worried about her safety. He's asked to see you while you are here – I hope you can give him some reassurance?'

'I'll do my best, sir,' Grace said.

Tommy Magellan-Lacey looked at his watch. 'We'll head over to the Palace in twenty minutes – Her Majesty is expecting you at 10 a.m.'

'Thank you. The other members of my team should be there now.'

The Master glanced at a printed sheet of paper. 'Detectives Norman Potting, Velvet Wilde, Jon Exton, Alec Butler and Polly Sweeney from the Major Crime Team?'

'Yes, sir. Polly Sweeney will be the Family Liaison Officer for Sir Peregrine Greaves' widow. I'll accompany her there later this morning. The others will be interviewing all members of the Household staff who had contact with the late Private Secretary.'

'Good,' the Master said. 'Margot Greaves is pretty shaken up, as you might imagine.'

As he and Branson helped the Master of the Royal Household bring mugs and milk over to the table, Grace felt charmed by the man, liking the fact that no doubt he could have had some palace servant make and serve the coffee but chose to do it himself.

THE HAWK IS DEAD

When they were seated at the table, Sir Tommy facing them, with just a glass of water in front of him, Grace brought him up to speed with the investigation.

'So you're pretty confident you've located the shooter's lair?' he said.

'We are,' Grace replied. 'Yes. Something I want to ask you is whether Sir Peregrine might have had any enemies?'

The Master gave him a dubious look. 'You are not thinking he was the target, surely?' But there was a flicker of something in his expression.

'It's my job to keep an open mind.'

'An open mind?'

'Was Her Majesty the intended victim? That's a very important question.'

The Master stared at him with a look of utter disbelief. 'Of course she was. The entire world knows she was, Detective Superintendent Grace.'

Grace shook his head. 'They don't *know* she was the target. They've been *told* she was. That's a very big difference. And, of course, that's the story they want to believe. But they don't have the information that I do.'

'Which is?'

27

Wednesday 22 November 2023

She wasn't supposed to have the key. Only a handful of people in Buckingham Palace did. They included the Master of the Royal Household, Sir Tommy Magellan-Lacey, the Head of Security, Will Treadwell, and the Director of the Royal Collection Trust, Lorraine McKnight. She wasn't even sure if The King himself had one. Or The Queen.

It was a great big, ancient metal affair that was more like a museum piece, or something out of a dungeon, than a functioning master key that could unlock every single door in the Palace. But then, of course, this place was a museum really, in so many ways, she thought. A living, lived-in museum. There were sixty-four thousand ornaments and objets d'art in the North Wing alone, quite apart from all the paintings hung on the walls.

Every piece was valuable and some were priceless. Many were gifts to Kings and Queens down the ages, others bought or commissioned by the Royal Family. She was walking along a red-carpeted corridor, past a display cabinet crammed full of small jade ornaments; collecting these had been a passion of the late Queen Mary, who died in 1953.

So much stuff in here, she thought. The Director of the Royal Collection did have a full inventory of all four wings in this palace, along with thousands more ornaments and pieces of furniture, as well as everything in Windsor Castle, Sandringham, the Palace of Holyroodhouse, Balmoral, Birkhall and all the other royal residences. How could anyone keep track of it all, or place a value on it?

All of it was quality. If you were a monarch or at least heir to the throne, no one would be giving you a humble spice rack as a wedding present. Unlike the three grotty ones she and her now divorced husband had been gifted at their own wedding. Including one that had a tag stuck to the bottom, from someone else gifting it to the 'friends' who had given it to them.

How nice to be Royal. Royally rich. How nice to have so much stuff that you didn't even know how much you had.

She glanced at her watch: 9.20 a.m. She had plenty of time to complete her assigned task this morning. Using the master key, she unlocked a magnificent wood-panelled door and slipped through into a bare, grimy white corridor that smelled of freshly sawn wood. Buckingham Palace was undergoing major renovations, one wing at a time, and this wing was now being started on.

She stepped around a hazard warning triangle, ignoring a notice that read, *HARD HAT AREA*, and climbed a narrow, steep staircase. The top few stairs were sealed off by a strip of red and yellow tape and a large sign:

EXTREME DANGER – KEEP OUT!

She checked behind her. No one, she was alone. She ducked under the tape and continued to the top, then stopped and stood on bare floorboards, getting her breath back for a moment. Ahead of her was a ten-foot high by five-foot wide jagged opening, which had been bashed through the wall that went up to the flat, grimy ceiling above her. A cold draught blew on her face, which became even colder the closer she stepped, increasingly cautiously, towards the opening.

When this wing had been constructed, during George IV's reign, massive light shafts were put in by the architect, John Nash, to bring light into the interior of all four floors above ground, and the basement. With modern, inexpensive lighting systems, and in addition The King's own plans for the Palace to produce much of its energy requirements by natural, sustainable means, these light shafts were redundant, and this one was in the process of being converted into a lift to provide access to the other floors in the Palace.

She stepped forward increasingly gingerly, putting out her arms and pressing her hands against the wall either side of the gap as she drew even closer. She'd never been good with unguarded heights.

Finally reaching the very edge, she peered down. Work was progressing well, she could see. At the very bottom of the shaft were six fierce-looking vertical spikes, rising several feet. The lift engineer had explained their purpose a couple of weeks ago, when they'd begun work on them. They were to form a seating-guide for the base of the lift car.

They could of course also serve a very different purpose, she thought. And that was the reason she was here. Conducting a recce of all the sites in the Palace where an accident might occur. A fatal accident.

28

Wednesday 22 November 2023

Grace told Magellan-Lacey the opinion of the ballistics expert.

'But he could be wrong about the shooter's lair, right?' the Master replied. 'Other than the flattened grass – which could have been done by a trainspotter, or a bird watcher, or a courting couple, just about anyone – you found no hard evidence that anyone had fired a gun from that spot.'

'We didn't, no,' Grace said.

'So it is possible the shooter was much further away, which could account for them hitting the wrong person?'

'I'm not ruling anything out at this stage, Sir Tommy,' he replied, slightly distracted – as well as cringingly embarrassed – by Branson, who had unsuccessfully dunked a biscuit in his coffee and was now trying to spoon out the soggy, broken-off mess. 'But if we look at the situation as a whole we have two events – the derailment of the train and the shooting of the Private Secretary. In my view they are very likely linked.'

Magellan-Lacey looked alarmed. 'You've had it confirmed the derailment was not an accident?'

Both detectives nodded, although Branson was still preoccupied salvaging his coffee – or his biscuit. Grace answered. 'British Transport Police have not yet completed their investigations, but they believe the derailment was caused by a length of spare rail being placed across the path of the Royal Train.'

'By the anti-monarchy protestors?'

Grace looked dubious. 'There are two factors here. The first is that our intelligence on the anti-monarchist movement tells us they are non-violent. Derailing the train is a whole different league.'

'Do you think these people were trying to assassinate Her Majesty by derailing the train?' the Master asked.

'I'm told we were very fortunate that the driver was able to slow down from 70mph to 40mph after receiving a warning of an obstruction on the track. Had the train derailed at the higher speed, there would likely have been multiple casualties – and by that I mean fatalities.'

The Master's face blanched. 'Do you think we're dealing with a terrorist organization?'

'It's a possibility we can't rule out, sir, but I don't think so. I believe we are dealing with someone who knows about trains, because of the way this was handled. I've been informed that if a metal object is put across the track and touches the live rail, the signalling centre – in this case at Three Bridges – gets an immediate alert. The signaller responsible for that section of line would then warn the driver of an obstruction ahead, which is what happened in this case. Only the warning wasn't soon enough for the driver to stop.'

'But at least he managed to slow down a fair bit, thank heavens,' the Master said. 'But what makes you think whoever carried out this sabotage knows about trains?'

'It's not easy to derail a rain,' Glenn Branson said. 'I spoke to the senior instructor on Network Rail yesterday: the weight of a train would crush most objects put across the rail – scaffold poles, corrugated iron, the sort of thing that idiotic vandals often put on the rails. The one thing that would stand up to the weight of a train is a length of actual rail – but it is extremely heavy.'

'How many would it need to lift it?'

'I did the maths,' Branson replied, frowning glumly at his

coffee, which now looked like a disaster zone. 'A metre of track weighs about fifty kilograms. It was a length of almost two metres that was used.'

Sir Tommy looked like he was doing a mental calculation. 'That's a hundred kilograms – about sixteen stone – the weight of a pretty hefty human being.'

'But if it had been placed upright against the tunnel wall – which is only a few feet from the track, one strong person could easily topple it, making it fall onto the track.'

The Master frowned again. 'So it would have taken only one person in the tunnel to push it over to cause the derailment?'

'Yes, sir,' Branson said. 'I spoke to a manager – a Christopher New – at Three Bridges who told me there was a fifteen-minute gap between a southbound express train exiting the south entrance to Clayton Tunnel and the Royal Train entering the north entrance. Yet the line fault signal was triggered only three minutes before the Royal Train entered. Either whoever was in the tunnel struggled to topple the rail,' Branson posited, 'or it was deliberate timing.'

'Which is my hypothesis,' Grace said. 'They wanted to derail the train but they wanted to slow it down enough to avoid casualties.'

The Master looked baffled. 'Why on earth – I mean – this is not making any sense to me.'

Grace shrugged. 'You're a former general and you were in combat many times in your career, in war zones, both on land and in helicopters. I read your background – it is extremely impressive.'

'Thank you, but what's your point?'

'My point is you must have used many different strategies, sir. Did you ever use the one called "strategic ambiguity"?'

'Of course. It's a tactic to confuse or mislead an opponent, by keeping intentions ambiguous.'

'I would say that's what was in play with the derailment. It had an apparent purpose and a hidden purpose. The apparent was to stop The Queen's visit to Sussex. But I think the hidden purpose wasn't that at all. It was to get everyone off the train and out into the open, where the Private Secretary could then be shot, while everyone would think, as with the derailment, that Her Majesty was the target.'

29

Wednesday 22 November 2023

The Master frowned and shook his head as he absorbed this. He looked quite bewildered. 'Astonishing,' he said. 'This is quite astonishing. Was anyone seen entering or leaving the tunnel prior to the derailment?'

'No, sir,' Grace replied. 'There is no CCTV and so far we have no witnesses who actually saw anyone near the tunnel.'

'Something we wanted to ask you again, Sir Tommy,' Branson said, seemingly abandoning his coffee. 'If you can really think hard: might the Private Secretary have had any enemies? He was in a pretty influential position in the Royal Household, we understand.'

'He was indeed in a very senior and influential position.' He frowned. 'But did he have any enemies? By which I presume you mean someone who might have wanted him dead?' He eyed the two detectives and received their nods of affirmation. 'No, absolutely not – well – I can't imagine so for a moment.' He reflected for a few seconds. 'He was a very decent man and always played with a straight bat. Although of course there are plenty of undercurrents in the Household – you are always going to get them in any sizeable organization. Used to happen all the time in the units under my command.' He smiled. 'I suppose if you wanted to list the Private Secretary's enemies, you'd have to take a look at the following three groups.'

He raised one finger, a second, then a third. 'Those former staff members who have been sacked; staff bitter that they've not received a medal they felt they were due; then staff who are feeling passed over for promotion.' He frowned. 'You never know who might have a screw loose, do you?'

'Do many of the Royal Household staff come from the armed forces, like yourself, Sir Tommy? Quite apart from those who are of course current serving members of the armed forces?'

Magellan-Lacey nodded. 'Quite a percentage – at all pay grades.'

'How many staff in total are working in the Royal Household?' Grace asked.

'There are five hundred people on the Royal Household staff paid for by Sovereign Grant – in other words from public funds. The Household comprises five departments. First is the Private Secretary's Office, which deals with policy, handles The King and Queen's correspondence, speeches, engagement with Government, the Realms and Commonwealth. Then we have the Lord Chamberlain's Office, which deals with all ceremonial aspects, the military, horses and carriages as well as the medical and ecclesiastical households. The Master of The King's Household, which is responsible for all entertaining and events for The King and Queen and all the other members of the Royal Family. And, very importantly, the Privy Purse and Treasurer's Office, which handles all financial affairs. The final department, the Royal Collection Trust, is a self-funding charity, which does not draw on public funds.'

'Wow!' Branson exclaimed.

'We have seven hundred people employed by the Royal Collection Trust. They are essentially the curators of more than a million highly valuable works of art.' The Master paused. 'I can tell you, with very rare exceptions, they are all good people, proud to be in royal service and aware of the privilege. Of course they have their foibles and one of them is that they are mostly traditionalists, so any changes can stir up a hornets' nest.' He smiled and raised his hands in a gesture of mock despair.

Continuing, he said, 'I do get a fair amount of resentment, jealousy, that sort of thing. The footmen you'll see around in the Palace wear magnificent uniforms, they get noticed by people, whereas the cleaning staff and the maintenance staff, who do just as important a job, are all but invisible because they're in civvies. That creates resentment. But most of all, the staff here do not like change. I'd be a very rich man if I got a pound for every time I heard the grumble, *but this is how we've always done it.*'

'Didn't Einstein say the definition of insanity was doing the same thing over and over and expecting a different result?' Branson said.

The Master smiled and nodded. 'Exactly. And we've had a lot of changes to the status quo, recently. We've had a new King and Queen, and now part of my role is to oversee the major renovations at Buckingham Palace. We have 775 rooms and a budget of £369 million, we need both to modernize and to become more energy efficient and environmentally friendly.' As he sipped some water, Grace's eyes went from the Master's face to Glenn's coffee disaster. The Master didn't appear to have noticed it.

'In some people's eyes,' Magellan-Lacey said, 'I'm the bad guy. I've stopped a lot of people from having their own credit cards and I've been moving individuals out of their coveted, grandly furnished private offices, with magnificent art on the walls, into new open-plan areas I'm creating – which a lot of them don't like.' He smiled and raised his arms in another despairing gesture. 'I get people moaning at me all the time. "Oh, Sir Tommy, but there's no room for that Canaletto from the Royal Collection on my wall now." That kind of stuff.' He smiled again and continued.

'I even have to contend with The King not liking the whole concept of open-plan – he feels people should have more privacy. But I'm afraid it's all about delivering on a budget that's coming from the public purse.' He gave a rueful smile and tapped his own chest. 'If anyone would be a target for assassination in this

Household it should be me, not poor Peregrine.' Then he looked at his watch. 'Right, gentlemen, we'll head over to Buckingham Palace – it's just five minutes' walk. As I mentioned, The Queen is expecting you at 10 a.m. and she's a stickler for punctuality – as I know most police officers are too,' he said, looking at them pointedly. 'And after that The King would like a private word with just you, Detective Superintendent. I assume that will be all right?'

'Of course,' he replied.

The Master stood up with a breezy smile, walked into the hallway and checked the knot of his tie in the mirror. Then he turned back and looked briefly at each detective, his tone turning both cutting and slightly imperious. 'No disrespect, gentlemen, but I sincerely hope you're going to make a better fist of this operation than DI Branson just did of dunking his biscuit in a mug of coffee.'

30

Wednesday 22 November 2023

Glenn Branson gave Roy Grace a look that said it all.

I can't believe this!

Grace nodded in acknowledgement. Nor could he. Not really.

Accompanied by the Master of the Royal Household, they had just walked past Clarence House, crossed Green Park and Constitution Hill, with the gleaming gold Victoria Monument to their left, and were now walking through a gawping crowd of several thousand tourists from around the world towards the gates of Buckingham Palace.

Moments later, after cursory inspection of their IDs, they were nodded through by two heavily armed officers who greeted the Master with respectful familiarity, and then they were striding across the hallowed quadrangle.

'Are we seriously *here*?' Branson murmured, rhetorically.

Close up, the facade of Buckingham Palace was even more beautiful and imposing than when he had seen it in the past, driving by or on television, Grace thought. Branson, who was rarely quiet, was rendered mute.

Tommy Magellan-Lacey walked at a brisk pace and both of them had to step on it to keep up with him. They strode past a guard in a bearskin, motionless as a statue, at the entrance to the famous archway through the building into the inner courtyard. The guard only acknowledged the Master's breezy greeting with a brief *friend-or-foe* swivel of his eyes.

On the far side of the archway the Master made a right turn and headed for a door. The warm yellow colour of the stone in this vast courtyard was quite different from the coldly imperious white Portland stone exterior of the public-facing front of the Palace. Ahead was the famous covered courtyard where the royal cars – and on state occasions, carriages – pulled up to collect or disgorge royalty and significant dignitaries.

Magellan-Lacey was holding a huge, ancient key that looked like it could unlock a dungeon. He plunged it into the door, opened it and ushered them into a hallway. There was a short flight of stairs with shiny mahogany banister rails, which led them up into a long, red-carpeted corridor with a magnificently arched ceiling.

Grace stared around in awe. Everything was spotless. Polished to a gleam, and the carpet immaculate. It felt a little as if they had boarded a flagship that was awaiting imminent inspection by the Admiral of the Fleet.

The walls were lined with paintings, one, of Westminster Abbey, filled with extraordinarily realistic faces, Grace thought. Another they passed was of a grand outdoors event, with two regal ladies arriving in a horse-drawn carriage, the faces of everyone present painted in such detail, it looked to Grace, as he tried to spot the artist's name, more like a gilt-framed photograph.

The magnificence of the art sent a thrill through him, further making him feel the weight of responsibility that rested on his shoulders. The stakes were far higher than anything he'd ever encountered in his career.

Was The Queen in very real danger from a terrorist group – homeland or foreign – out there and planning their next move?

He thought back to his battle two days ago, with the smug Met Detective Superintendent Gregory Mosse, over whose crime scene this should be. A battle he had won. But he was now thinking of the words of the late Duke of Wellington after the Battle of Waterloo: *The only thing worse than losing a battle is winning one.*

Would it have been more sensible – or at least less stressful – to have abdicated responsibility to Mosse? Had he been stupid, greedy – just plain crazy even – to insist on taking the case? Something far too big for him to chew?

And now he was in it up to his neck. Thanks to his hubris?

Last night he'd confessed his fears to Cleo. She'd reminded him that in over ten years in his roles as both a Senior Investigating Officer and more recently also as Head of Major Crime for Surrey and Sussex Police, his clear-up rate for murders on which he had been the SIO was one hundred per cent. Cleo told him to forget that The Queen was involved, and all that went with that, and just think of it as a murder like any other.

That thought sustained him now as they continued along the corridor of the North Wing of one of the most famous buildings in the world. *Just another murder.*

Yeah, right.

Ahead of him, the Master, who had greeted several people walking along the corridor, including a woman in a smart suit, two workmen and a liveried footman, had stopped. 'Detective Superintendent Grace and Detective Inspector Branson, this is Matthew Corbin – Deputy Master of the Royal Household.'

A very tall man with rimless glasses, a light beard and a thick head of brown hair stepped out of an open office door to the left. He wore a dark suit and today's obligatory black tie.

'Matthew, this is Detective Superintendent Grace and his colleague Detective Inspector Branson. Detective Superintendent Grace is the Senior Investigating Officer on Sir Peregrine's murder.'

'Nice to meet you, gentlemen,' Corbin said. He had a friendly but reserved demeanour, and spoke with an accent that sounded

South African, Grace thought, shaking his large, firm hand. 'Some of your colleagues are already here, Detective Superintendent, and established in the Billiards Room.'

Grace nodded. 'Yes, I have detectives talking to everyone who worked with Sir Peregrine – to see if we can find any reason someone might have wanted to kill him.'

Corbin looked surprised. 'Are you saying he was the target and not Her Majesty?'

'I'm keeping all my options open at the moment,' Grace replied. 'Perhaps we could arrange a time later this morning to talk to you?'

'Of course.' He hesitated. 'Yes, I'll be here at my desk. Any time – except midday for fifteen minutes, when I have a meeting with The King.'

Grace looked past him at the interior of his long, narrow office, which reminded him of his own, except this was a lot less cluttered. There was a small round meeting table, with four chairs, a workstation beyond, and a view across the interior courtyard of the Palace. Then he thanked him and the Master continued leading the way along the corridor.

'I'm afraid this corridor is a bit like the M25!' he said, opening an internal door and looking over his shoulder at Grace and Branson. 'Goes all the way around the Palace – we're in the North Wing at the moment, this is where the royal apartments are, up on the second floor, and we're currently heading for The Queen's Sitting Room. We could just keep turning left at the end of each corridor, into the West Wing, South Wing, East Wing – which is the front of the Palace everyone sees, and then we'd end up back here again.'

'Sir Tommy, how long did it take you to learn to navigate your way around the Palace?' Branson asked.

'Well, I was given a jolly useful tip by one of the royals just after I took up this post – for the late Queen. He said, "*Navigate by the paintings, Tommy."* But then they moved the paintings!' He gave his jovial laugh.

A short distance further on they went down a few steps and the Master stopped outside an ornate door. Just as he was about to open it, Grace noticed an elaborately gilded clock, with a yellow and red tag attached to it marked *SALVAGE*. 'Salvage, Sir Tommy?' he questioned. 'What is that for?'

'Ah, right, it's while we have the builders here doing all the renovations, the Royal Collection team have tagged all the most valuable portable items – in the event of a fire they're the ones everyone must try to save first.'

Then he opened the door, and in an almost hushed voice he said, 'This is the Regency Room – which The Queen likes to use for meetings. Come in and make yourselves comfortable and I will go and bring her in. She'll be accompanied by her own Private Secretary, Jayne Bennett. No objection to that, gentlemen?' He looked at each of them in turn with a disarming smile that Grace felt could turn, in a flash, to chilling hostility if he received the wrong answer.

The room was cold and smelled of polish. Grace shook his head. 'Not at all. She is very welcome to have anyone present she would like.'

'Excellent!' the Master said, and pointed at an embroidered and tasselled gold-coloured sofa, with two almost matching armchairs facing. 'The Queen likes to sit on the sofa.'

It was an instruction, not a statement.

Then he was gone, closing the door behind him.

31

Wednesday 22 November 2023

Grace and Branson exchanged a glance, both feeling for a moment like schoolboys in the headmaster's study, then looked around the emerald-carpeted room. It was finely furnished in a regal rather than homely way, and could have comfortably swallowed the entire footprint of his cottage, Grace thought. And yet, at the same time, here in the context of this palace, it didn't really feel large at all.

High-ceilinged, with an imposing crystal chandelier, the wallpaper was a fern-coloured fleur-de-lis pattern. French windows with swagged gold-coloured curtains looked out onto balustrading and the gardens beyond. An ornate clock sat on the mantelpiece, framed by black marble statuettes holding lampshades. Below, a fire screen stood in front of an unlit wood-burning stove. Beautiful but dark and sombre paintings were hung from chains around the walls, and there was a handsome bookcase, each shelf tightly packed with leather-bound volumes. A round, antique wooden table, polished to a mirror shine, with four matching chairs, filled one of the window bays.

'Cleo would go crazy if she saw this,' Grace said. 'She loves antiques.'

'That why she likes you, is it?' Branson quipped, getting in a dig at the ten-year age gap between Roy Grace and his wife.

'Yeah, right, I—'

He stopped in mid-sentence as a polished, conservatively

THE HAWK IS DEAD

dressed woman in her forties came into the room, followed by the unmistakable figure of Queen Camilla.

Right behind her was Magellan-Lacey, who spoke in a brisk, businesslike manner. 'Your Majesty, Detective Superintendent Roy Grace and Detective Inspector Glenn Branson from Surrey and Sussex Major Crime Team. And, gentlemen, if I may also introduce Her Majesty's Private Secretary, Jayne Bennett.'

The Queen looked at each of the detectives for a moment, as if sizing them up. Grace forgot for a second to bow. It was Branson who did so first with almost theatrical exaggeration. Grace gave a more restrained and rather awkward lowering of his head.

The Queen was dressed in a black two-piece with a matching scarf around her neck. He was, momentarily, at a loss for words.

Fortunately, The Queen wasn't. 'Good morning, gentlemen. May we offer you some refreshments – I gather you've come up from Sussex. Some tea or coffee?'

'Thank you, but we're fine, Your Majesty,' Grace said.

The Queen gestured them to the armchairs, then sat down on the edge of the sofa, facing them. The Master left the room and The Queen's Private Secretary sat at the round table in the window and produced a notebook followed by a pen.

There was a brief silence, which Grace hastily broke, immediately aware as he spoke that, uncharacteristically, his voice was probably an octave higher than normal and had a nervous quaver.

'Your Majesty, I believe you have quite a strong connection to Sussex?'

'I do indeed,' she replied. 'My family home throughout my childhood was in Plumpton – only a few miles from Brighton, I'm sure you know it. I have great affection for the county. Are you from Sussex?'

'Born and bred,' Grace said.

'And me,' Branson added.

'It's a beautiful county.' The Queen smiled briefly, then stiffened, signalling small talk was over and stared directly at Grace. 'Detective Superintendent, I had been under the impression that someone had taken a pot-shot at me and missed, hitting poor Perry instead – which is just . . . simply dreadful – but I'm informed you have a different opinion, is this the case?'

'I am considering all options, but I do have a different opinion, Ma'am,' he said. 'And I will explain my reasons to you fully. I would like to start at the beginning before we get to them, if I may?'

'Please do.'

'I appreciate this may be distressing, but it is important for the investigation that we go into detail. If you can cast your mind back to Monday morning, can you tell us in your own words exactly what happened?'

'Yes, of course – from what point?'

'Starting from the moment you boarded the train. Did everything seem normal to you?'

'A bit too normal,' she said. 'To be honest, I didn't notice much, I was making some amendments to a speech I was planning to deliver last night – which I did. It wasn't until the train suddenly began slowing down really quite sharply, and then the carriage started shaking and people – including me – were being flung out of their seats, that I realized obviously something was seriously wrong.' She paused to reflect for a moment then continued.

'It was all happening so quickly. In a flash it was over and we were stationary, and I heard screaming. I was lying on the floor and smelled something burning – like an electrical fire. I got onto my feet – with some difficulty as the carriage was at an angle, and one of my shoes had come off. The driver and Peregrine as well as my Protection Officer were urging everyone to get off the train. I felt I had to make sure everyone was all right. Tiny and Elena – my two Queen's Companions – were a bit shaken but fine, as was my dresser and dear Jayne, here.' She looked across at Jayne, who nodded reassuringly. 'The Train Manager looked as if he might be in shock, and I saw the Director of Comms had blood running from his nose. It was all very traumatic.'

She paused for a moment and interlocked the fingers of both hands. 'Is this enough detail for you?'

'It's very helpful, Your Majesty,' Grace said.

'Did you have any observations at the time or in the immediate aftermath, Your Majesty?' Branson asked. 'One thing we need to do is to rule out any members of your Household staff being involved in whatever was really going on. After the derailment, did you notice anything unusual in the behaviour of any of them?'

'Anything unusual? What exactly do you mean by that, Detective Inspector? To be frank, it was an unusual event and the normality of people's behaviour at that moment was the very last thing on my mind. We were all very shaken. I wanted to see if everyone was all right, and the driver was extremely anxious to get us off the train.'

'Ma'am, what I mean is,' Branson explained, 'like, for instance, one of your members of staff not being as shocked as you might have expected?'

The Queen gave him a look that stopped short of being totally withering. 'How shocked, exactly, do you mean?' She gave a fleeting smile as if trying to signal she wasn't beating up on him, she just wanted to understand. 'Do you have a slide-rule, marked one to ten, Detective Inspector, like some kind of Richter scale that you use to test victims of train derailments?'

Grace, seeing his colleague struggling in deep water, waded to his rescue. 'Ma'am, what DI Branson is asking is if Your Majesty felt anyone's behaviour indicated, in any way at all, that they might have known the derailment was going to happen? Perhaps someone looking unusually anxious during the journey, anything of that nature?'

'Absolutely not!' she said, emphatically. 'One moment

everything was absolutely normal, and the next, everyone was in a state of total shock and bewilderment, as I was. The driver seemed to be very distressed, poor man. He was concerned about an express train coming towards the tunnel and wanted us to get out as quickly as we could. It was quite horrid in there, and trying to walk across those stones – ballast, I think they call it – in court shoes, was something I wouldn't recommend.'

32

Wednesday 22 November 2023

Grace responded. 'I'm afraid we do have to be rather pedantic with our questions, Ma'am.'

The Queen nodded and smiled warmly. 'I understand, Detective Superintendent. I read a lot of crime fiction so I do have some idea how your lines of enquiry all work. I just wish I could give you some brilliantly sharp observation, perhaps a Miss Marple moment, that could give you a lead but, to be honest, throughout that train journey south from London towards Brighton, everything and everyone could not have seemed more normal.'

Grace smiled back, starting to feel a tiny bit more relaxed in her presence now. He glanced at Branson before turning back to her. 'Your Majesty, today I just wanted to have a very informal chat with you about the events, but it may be helpful to our enquiries at some point soon to do what we call a formal cognitive witness interview, in a controlled environment. I appreciate that you are extremely busy, though.'

She frowned. '*Cognitive witness* interview?'

Branson explained. 'It's a very structured technique for helping a witness to remember key details – some of which are often buried in their subconscious. If I can give you an example, there are questions we put to witnesses of a car crash. In the first we ask, "*Did you see much glass on the road after the collision?*" In the second we ask, "*Did you see much glass on the road after the smash?*"'

She gave him a wry smile. 'And the answer to the second will always be *much more glass*. So you are going to hypnotize me, are you?'

'Not remotely, Ma'am,' Branson replied. 'But it would take about two hours of your time.'

'I'll do whatever you need me to do,' she said. 'Of course.' She frowned again. 'One thing I want to ask you, which no one has told me yet, is how the train was derailed. Assuming you – we all – are very clear it wasn't an accident.'

'It was derailed by a piece of rail, Your Majesty,' Grace said. 'A length of spare rail laid across the track. I understand that Network Rail, who are responsible for the track, keep varying lengths of these at intervals along all the main routes, so they can do a quick repair if ever needed. One of our primary lines of enquiry is around any persons seen entering either the north or south portals of Clayton railway tunnel in the preceding days, or on Monday.'

'Maybe Queen Victoria was quite sensible getting out of the train and going by horse-drawn carriage across the Downs to Brighton,' she said drily and shot a glance at her watch. Then she looked at each detective in turn. 'Do you think you are going to find these people quickly?'

'I wish I could say yes, Ma'am,' Grace replied. 'It is helpful in many ways that we are looking for more than one offender – from what we understand it is probably two people at least, rather than just a lone wolf.'

'One of them who is either a very good shot or a very bad one.' She raised her eyebrows at him.

'I believe the person was a very good shot, Ma'am.'

'Otherwise I might not be here – is that what you are implying?'

Grace locked eyes with her. 'Ma'am, if he was a good shot, then he hit his intended target. There is always the possibility that the shooter was much further away than we believe, in which case his margin of error could be as much as four feet – the approximate distance between you and Sir Peregrine at the moment he was shot.'

'What about we just *hypothesize* for a moment, as I believe you detectives like to say. Let's *hypothesize* that this gunman – shooter – was indeed a very bad shot. And that he missed his real target. And did the same again with his second shot. That would mean he might try again.'

'We are acutely aware of this being a possibility,' Grace said. 'Until we find and arrest the offenders, your personal security – and that of His Majesty The King's – needs to be at the highest level of alert. We are working closely with both your Royal Protection team and with the Met's Counter Terrorism Command, and updating them twice daily.'

'That's very reassuring,' The Queen replied, not looking at all reassured.

'One final question I have for you today, is whether, to your knowledge, Sir Peregrine Greaves had any enemies?'

She frowned. 'Enemies?'

'Someone who, for whatever reason, might have wanted him dead?'

She was silent for some while before responding. 'Well, there is quite a hornets' nest of jealousies, rivalries, jostling for position and favours within the Royal Household. I'm sure Tommy can elaborate on this. It's probably no different in many ways to what goes on in any large corporate structure. Some people get a bit frustrated, some people get angry. But angry enough to commit murder? Managing to engage co-conspirators?' She shook her head. 'I don't think so – we are getting into very far-fetched territory here, don't you think?'

Grace waited for a few moments after she had finished speaking, then replied, 'I'm afraid the facts do take us into the realm of the far-fetched. I don't want to sound insensitive or in any way disrespectful, but could there have been any other reason someone might have wanted Sir Peregrine dead? If we are right – and we may not be – but if we are, the people behind this went to a great deal of trouble to kill him. And we need to understand why.'

The Queen shook her head, very slowly, from side to side. 'Perry was universally popular. The only thing I can think of is that he did like the trappings that went with his job, and had been upset over one issue recently – he was so upset he spoke to The King about it.'

'Which was, Your Majesty?' Grace asked.

'Well, Tommy was trying to move his team, along with all the others in the Royal Household, into open-plan offices. Perry always had a beautiful office in St James's Palace, with some very fine paintings on the wall. He was extremely upset because there was nowhere for these to be hung in the proposed new offices.'

'That doesn't seem like much of a motive for killing him, Your Majesty,' Branson said.

'I think I would agree with you.' The Queen looked at her watch, then back at each detective in turn, before levelling on Grace. 'Perry did say to me he had an issue he wanted to speak to me about when we were on the train.' She paused for a moment. 'But he was always wanting to tell me something or other. They all do, Detective Superintendent, I don't get a moment's peace. I doubt it was anything significant. Now, I'm afraid I have to attend another meeting in a quarter of an hour. The King wants to speak to you, and on this occasion, I'll take you to his office.' She turned to Branson. 'If you come with us, Jayne will show you the Billiards Room, where your colleagues are conducting their interviews with my staff. Then I understand Tommy is taking you and another member of your team to see Peregrine's widow, Margot, Lady Greaves?'

'That is correct, Ma'am,' Grace replied.

THE HAWK IS DEAD

She stood and both of them immediately followed, a respectful step or two behind.

'Please don't think, Detective Superintendent Grace and Detective Inspector Branson, that I want to be anything other than helpful to your enquiries. Don't look at me as anyone special. Just treat me as you would any other witness to a murder. Neither I nor The King are above the due process of the law.'

33

Wednesday 22 November 2023

Grace held the door for The Queen and her Private Secretary, then followed Glenn Branson out into the corridor. His eye was immediately taken by an ancient and very lifelike portrait of a nobleman with a massive beard, staring imperiously out of the canvas.

'You have some wonderful art in the Palace, Ma'am,' he said.

She turned towards him, now with a very big smile, as if he had touched on a favourite subject. 'Is it an interest of yours?' she asked.

'Both my wife and I, Ma'am,' he replied.

'Well, in that case we'll take the slightly long way round, and go via the Marble Corridor and up to the Picture Gallery, where we have some of our finest paintings – and some wonderful statues.' Then, as if she was assuming the role of Palace tour guide, The Queen said, 'Did you know we have the largest private collection of Canalettos in the world here in Buckingham Palace?'

He shook his head, wishing he could be videoing this for Cleo. The Queen herself giving him a tour!

'I'll show you some, as well as our very magnificent Rembrandts.'

Along the way, Glenn and Jayne peeled off, but Grace barely noticed, he was so mesmerized by all the paintings Queen Camilla was pointing out. As well as the display cabinet after display cabinet of fine ornaments and jewellery they passed.

THE HAWK IS DEAD

'Do you have a favourite painting, Ma'am?' he asked.

'Yes, I do. I'll show it to you. It's in the Picture Gallery.'

After a few minutes, with Grace awkwardly tongue-tied, they climbed a wide staircase and entered a long gallery with rose-pink walls and a vaulted glass ceiling. Gilded sofas with grey satin coverings, as if there for viewing purposes, were arranged along either side of white marble fireplaces. There was a hush about the room, an almost cathedral-like sense of awe. Grace couldn't help it, he had to just stop and stare for a second at the paintings on both sides.

'Some of the very best Canalettos are on the left,' The Queen pointed out. 'It was George III who was responsible – and rather unintentionally – for acquiring these, as well as my favourite painting.'

'Really?' Grace said.

'George III loved books. He bought a collection from the British Consul in Venice in 1762 – a fellow called Joseph Smith. Apparently Smith was short of money and offered The King a deal on fifty-three Canalettos, and threw in another picture by a then relatively unknown Dutch artist called Vermeer.'

'Amazing!'

'Indeed,' she said. 'And over on the right, just over there, we have our best Rembrandts.'

Grace was torn between the stunning landscapes of Canaletto's Venice and the sombre but incredibly detailed and lifelike Rembrandts, hardly knowing which way to look and wishing he could stop and linger.

'But this,' Queen Camilla said, really animated now, 'this coming up is my absolute favourite painting in the entire Royal Collection – this simply gorgeous Vermeer – it—'

She stopped in mid-sentence and stared, puzzled, at a landscape featuring a couple together in an idyllic woodland setting. There were two Doric columns behind them and a lake in a forest further back, surrounded by an array of beautiful people in beautiful period clothes.

She turned to Grace. 'I'm so sorry,' she said. 'The Royal Collection team are constantly doing this – taking away paintings and other works of art to clean them and replacing them with something else, like this Fragonard. Jewellery too. There's a particularly beautiful coronet I just adore, with a quite magnificent diamond, which has been removed from a display cabinet and gone ages. I keep asking the Director of the Royal Collection when it's coming back. I'm afraid the Royal Collection team really are a law unto themselves!'

'With the best of intentions, Ma'am?' Grace questioned.

'I'd like to think so,' she said. 'Although they are sometimes a bit too possessive – they seem to think they own these works. The Monarchy, in fact, hold them all in trust for the Nation as their guardians.'

He followed her up a flight of stairs, impressed by her agility as she raced ahead.

Then she knocked on an ornate door in front of them. From the other side, Grace heard a familiar voice from radio and television. Posh, commanding, a little strained but above all warm. 'Come in!'

He took a deep breath. Was this really happening?

But at the same time a cog had started turning inside his head. Just slowly. That old familiar sense of unease. Something he could not immediately lay a finger on. But it was there. Unsettling him.

34

Wednesday 22 November 2023

The room, as Grace closed the door behind him, almost took his breath away. It was on a different level of splendour to everything he had seen so far in this Aladdin's Cave of a palace. Gold walls, lined with mostly oval-framed period portraits, beneath an intricately stuccoed gold ceiling. There was a large bay window, giving a view out across the lawns to the lake beyond. A group of chairs arranged around a gold-inlaid coffee table formed a seating area. Candelabras, fine porcelain ornaments and busts on columns were everywhere he glanced.

King Charles rose from behind a very small but beautiful leather-topped desk, on which lay a memo pad and two red felt-tipped pens. He could not have been dressed or presented more immaculately, Grace thought. His silver hair gave him a distinguished air, and his dark navy suit fitted him as if it had been sculpted rather than sewn. Against his white shirt, his black tie was perfectly knotted. Far better than Grace could ever manage himself.

The King was a tiny bit shorter in real life than he had imagined, but Grace was reminded of a quote about the late legend Greta Garbo, which he had heard but never really understood before: *Greta Garbo's understudy does everything that Greta Garbo does, except what it is that Greta Garbo does.*

He understood it now.

This was no understudy holding out his hand. Over seventy

years of joy, stress and the burden of duty etched into his features in equal measures.

'Detective Superintendent Roy Grace?'

'Your Majesty.' Grace shook his hand then gave a head-bow. 'If I may say, Sir, this is one of the most beautiful rooms I've ever seen.'

The King looked pleased. 'Thank you.' He stood ramrod straight and put a hand into one of his jacket's side pockets, gesticulating with the other hand. 'This was my dear Mama's sitting room. It's barely been touched since her death,' he said. Then his demeanour became much more serious. 'But you're not here for a guided tour, Detective Superintendent, are you?'

Grace smiled. 'No, Sir.'

The King gestured at the cluster of chairs for him to sit, then sat back down himself. 'Thank you for coming, I appreciate how busy you must be at the moment. I wanted a private word, because I need to understand exactly what you know at this stage. Where are you at with your investigation? Do you have a suspect – even if you can't tell the press about it? I appreciate you have an excellent reputation, Detective Superintendent, but this is my darling wife they've tried to kill, and there are ramifications of national significance. What have you learned so far from the postmortem, from the derailment, from the bullets used and from your general Intelligence sources?'

'Your Majesty, it's what we call *early doors* so far in the investigation. I can assure you that we have more resources on this case than ever before in the history of the Surrey and Sussex Major Crime Team.'

The King gave him an odd, almost desperate stare. 'And is that enough? If someone had tried to kill your wife, the woman you love, wouldn't you be throwing every resource in the nation at it?'

Grace hesitated before replying. Three years ago, someone

had tried and very nearly succeeded in killing Cleo, but he wasn't going to go there now. The King looked deeply worried – and no wonder.

Taking a deep breath Grace replied, 'Your Majesty, let me give you some important reassurance. I do not believe Her Majesty was the target of the shooter. I have discussed this with both the Met Police and the Royal Protection team, both of which have officers on my team.'

'I'm sorry, Detective Superintendent, I don't quite understand,' The King said sharply.

'Sir, Your Majesty, please allow me to explain my thought process.'

The King, glaring at him now as if Grace were an imbecile, gestured impatiently for him to continue. Grace told him his findings to date.

When he had finished, The King was a little calmer but seemed only partially reassured. 'But why – why on earth would anyone want to kill poor Peregrine? He was an extremely decent and loyal man – I'd never heard a bad word about him from any of my staff. Ever.'

'Might he have had any enemies, Your Majesty? It's a question we are asking all who knew him. Perhaps someone he was holding back from promotion by staying too long in office?'

'Enemies? Good Lord, I can't think of anyone less likely to have had enemies. Peregrine's deputy is a thoroughly decent chap, and well aware he has several years to wait for that promotion – if indeed he made it through the selection process. I've a horrible feeling, Detective Superintendent, that if you are looking for the murderer inside the walls of the Royal Household, you are very much looking in the wrong place – however credible what you've told me might be. And all the time you are looking in the wrong place, the killer is out there, preparing to strike again. I need reassurance that my wife is safe. Can you give me that?'

Grace stared The King back in the eye. 'Queen Camilla is safe, Your Majesty,' he said. 'I can assure you.'

The King looked doubtful, still. 'If you say so, but God help us if you are wrong.'

35

Wednesday 22 November 2023

'God help us if you are wrong.'

The King's voice was loud and clear through Jon Smoke's headphones. Just as The Queen's voice had been a short while earlier. And the voices of the detectives.

He would collect the tiny radio mics later after the bosses had departed the Palace for the day. The mic in the royal sitting room was concealed behind one of the 160 volumes of Prince Albert's books on French history – in French – on the bookcase shelves. The one in the former Queen's sitting room, now The King's office, was inside the grate of the fireplace, which was never lit.

What he had heard made him angry. So angry.

That clever dick detective. Convincing first Camilla and then Charles that Her Maj had not been the target. How the hell had that happened? Well, he knew, he'd listened to the explanations – hypotheses – the detectives had given. He'd not considered this, not seriously. He – they – all had made the assumption that with the Royal Train derailed, and a Private Secretary shot dead as they emerged from the tunnel, the shooter had missed his target, panicked and fled. Surely that was blindingly obvious. Blindingly obvious The Queen had been the target. Blindingly obvious to everyone.

Everyone except one stubborn detective.

And Camilla seemed to have swallowed it. Charles, too – perhaps a little less so, but he'd accepted the detective's very persuasive argument.

And what he had just heard underpinned the detective's comments in his press conference yesterday. About not jumping to conclusions, or whatever the phrase he used.

The police investigation was no longer going to be the hunt for a gunman and his Not-My-King cohorts, which they'd prepared for and laid the trail for.

Instead it would be a far deeper and more dangerous dig into *Why Sir Peregrine Greaves?*

And just how far would they have to delve?

It was a dangerously shallow grave. There was a lot that needed to be taken care of, and very fast.

'Sod it!' he said aloud. It came out as a rasp of anger, he thought to himself, appropriate, since he actually was a RaSP officer. A trusted member of the team who guarded the cluster of Royal Palaces, including Buckingham Palace itself as well as Clarence House and St James's Palace, where the bosses and all the senior royals, including the Prince and Princess of Wales and the Princess Royal, had London residential bases.

Not that Jon Smoke had anything against the members of the Royal Family he was paid to protect. Good luck to them, he thought. Make the most of whatever privilege you'd been born into, because he was born into a shit life that just kept on getting more shit.

His dad was a drunk and a wifebeater who, when Jon was seven, hit his mother too hard one night, and she died. His dad was put away for a long sentence and Jon was taken into care, never seeing his father again – he died in a prison brawl. He moved away from his Newcastle birthplace and, for the next nine years, went from crap foster home to even crapper foster home. When he was sixteen, he walked out of the last one, in south London, and past a shabby-looking theatre, with a sign in the window advertising for stagehands. He didn't know what a stagehand was but went in, and got taken on.

A stagehand in this theatre was basically a skivvy and he was fine with that, and with the wage he got. He was less fine with the lecherous old wardrobe master trying to snog him in the pub around the corner, after the last night of a particularly weird and not well-attended play.

A year on, attracted by a TV commercial recruiting for the Army, he applied, and was accepted. After enlisting, for the first time in his life, he discovered he was actually good at something.

Shooting.

He had a real talent – or *aptitude*, as they called it – for target shooting.

Within two years he was on the Army shooting squad, competing – and winning silver – at the National Shooting Centre at Bisley.

Two weeks after, just turning nineteen, he was invited to an interview where he was told he had been selected to train for the elite sniper course, provided he passed the psychological evaluation. He passed and was elated that he had an ability – talent, whatever it was called – that meant he was actually valued. He spent five months at the Infantry Battle School in Brecon, in Wales, undergoing rigorous training under the British Army's Sniper Wing. He learned precision shooting accuracy at long range, camouflage and fieldcraft.

The most important thing he took away was how to remain stationary in a concealed position for, if necessary, days on end. This was to stand him in good stead after he joined the Paras – and save his life. And bring him to where he was now, facing a very golden future.

36

Helmand Province, Afghanistan, 2007

Three miles north-east from Camp Bastion, with its 20-mile-long perimeter wall and 2.2-mile runway. It was late afternoon going into early evening, and the searing sun was starting to power down. Jon Smoke had read that Australia has more creatures that can kill you than any other country. That might well be the case, he thought, but nowhere on earth had more creatures that could bite you than right here.

He'd spent two solitary days perched twenty feet up this dense tree, uncomfortably hot in his ghillie suit, but glad of the camouflage the gear afforded him – as well as grateful for the shade of the leaves. He might be concealed from the Taliban but not from the damned critter population of Afghanistan. No one ever told you that you had to fight two different enemies and that the Taliban was the lesser of the two. His camouflage concealed him from them. But not from the plague of vicious and eerily translucent camel spiders the size of saucers, which could and did regularly jump four feet straight at him, scaring the hell out of him. Until Scottie told him to relax, they weren't attacking him, they just liked the shade that humans provided and wanted to be in it before anything else got there.

There were equally large and gross centipedes with a vicious and painful bite, as well as scorpions, sandflies, mosquitoes and ticks, all of which alternated between viewing him as Public Enemy Number One – and plat du jour.

THE HAWK IS DEAD

'The theatre of war,' he reflected. It was a weird description. Or perhaps not. There was no proscenium arch to define the stage. It was simply everything he could see that stretched out ahead into the far distance. The set was an arid desert landscape, with steep escarpments, patches of scrub and occasional clusters of trees like the ones he and Scottie were concealed in now. If you removed some props and just added a few cacti, Clint Eastwood might have ridden by on horseback with a cigar in his mouth, to the soundtrack of *The Good, the Bad and the Ugly*.

The set was decorated – dressed, they called it in the theatre world – with props: a burnt-out tank, a half-track detonated by a landmine, lying on its side. Skeletal vehicles from both sides haphazardly scattered by the roadside and away into the distance. Along with clouds of flies and other scavengers of the desert feasting on the corpses and scattered limbs and entrails of fallen fighters. Not fake props these, any more than the rotting cadavers inside the vehicles were, either. Certainly, not the kind you'd rent from a theatrical costumier, to take to a fancy-dress party.

Every few minutes, when what passed for a breeze wafted in their direction, he could smell it. The stench of death. It was like no other smell on earth. Heavy, rancid, cloying. Cigarette smoke masked it. He craved one now, but his supply of fags was running low. He'd had to ration himself to one every six hours. Three hours and ten minutes to go.

Breathing just through your mouth worked, also.

The light was definitely starting to fail now. Maybe the offensive would begin tonight. He had his night vision scope ready.

'Curtain up in ten minutes,' he whispered to himself and smiled. His mind went to strange places when he spent hours in solitude. He let it create scenarios. It especially helped get him through the long hours of darkness – which would be here imminently.

Occasionally he exchanged words – friendly insults mostly – with his fellow sniper and buddy Stuart Macdonald, Scottie, who was ensconced in another tree a short distance away. The banter helped keep up their spirits.

'How you doing, wanker?' Macdonald shouted in his thick accent.

'Better than you, tosser! I'm in the jacuzzi with three naked ladies and a bottle of Champers!' he retaliated.

Macdonald was a gung-ho, instantly likeable, Scotsman from Aberdeen. They'd passed out of the sniper course together, and two weeks later, seconded to the elite Parachute Regiment, found themselves both on the same military transport plane bound for Kabul, Afghanistan. And still together, helicoptered into the hotspot, Helmand Province.

Scottie ribbed Smoke incessantly about what wankers all Sassenachs were. Jon didn't mind, he didn't feel any loyalty to England. Being English – British – meant nothing to him. Scottie also told irreverent jokes, many of which crossed the line, which Jon Smoke liked, and they helped take his mind off what might lie ahead.

Not that he was afraid of dying, he was a fatalist. And, in truth, right now at twenty years old, with no family and no girlfriend, he didn't actually have anything in particular to live for. Unlike his new buddy, who was crazily in lust and love.

Soon after they'd first met, Scottie had showed him photographs over a pint or two in a local pub of a beautiful nineteen-year-old woman, Effie, who was his fiancée. Smoke hadn't been able to resist telling this short, stocky, pugnacious-faced man that he appeared to be punching above his weight.

'Always, my friend! *Ah, but a man's reach should exceed his grasp, or what's a heaven for?*' Scottie had retorted.

'What?'

'Robert Browning.'

'Who's he? A politician?'

Scottie had shaken his head. 'I always knew you Sassenachs

THE HAWK IS DEAD

were wankers – didn't realize you were illiterate, too. He was a poet – only one of your most famous poets ever.'

He went on to tell Smoke that Effie was a beautician and that when he came home from this tour, with the money he had saved he was going to invest with her to set up her own salon, quit the Army and become her business partner. Oh, and that she was four months pregnant.

Smoke envied him his plan as much as he envied him his fiancée. He didn't have any plan beyond what he was here to do right now.

They'd both been here for more than forty-eight hours now, in position to give cover to their platoon when it made its next advance towards a Taliban encampment 10 miles ahead. And also in a position to watch, and if necessary neutralize, any Taliban attempting to further mine the road ahead with Improvised Explosive Devices (IEDs) – homemade bombs.

The advance should have happened last night, but it hadn't, and there'd been no word all day on his radio from his commanding officer, Brigadier Jason Finch. Now dusk was falling again. Falling fast. His supply of water was getting low and the artificial bladder he urinated into, painfully, via a catheter he'd inserted himself, was getting increasingly swollen. He needed a shit badly, but that was going to have to wait until—

He stiffened.

Voices. Faint.

But not coming from the right direction.

Peering through the dense leaves and the falling twilight, through his spotting scope, he saw – *Jesus* – a ragbag group of ten, maybe a dozen, heavily armed Taliban soldiers, some turbaned, marching straight towards them. Maybe a mile off. They would be here in about twenty minutes.

Keeping his voice low, Scottie told him he'd seen them too.

This wasn't supposed to be happening.

Smoke did a quick calculation. He had three weapons. His L115A3 sniper rifle, fitted with a night-sight, his L85A2 semi-automatic rifle and his Glock 17 pistol. He had fifty rounds of .338 Lapua Magnum ammunition for his sniper rifle. But the bolt action was slow – he'd only pick a handful of them off before they began to return fire. And, as the AK47s the Taliban were armed with were capable of firing 650 rounds a minute, he and Scottie would be cut to ribbons in seconds.

He had a better chance with the semi-automatic, L85A2 rifle, strapped to his back. He had five magazines, each holding thirty rounds of 5.56 NATO ammo. That gave him a total of 150 rounds. The gun was capable of firing at a similar rate to the AK47 in automatic mode. But he and Scottie would need to make every bullet count. If not, they would both be in very big trouble.

He turned down the volume on his radio to its lowest setting, then radioed his lieutenant, and when he heard his calm, re-assuring voice he said, 'Sir, a group of estimated ten, maybe twelve Terry Taliban heading towards us. ETA twenty minutes. Do you want us to engage?'

'Are you and Scottie well concealed?' he asked.

'We are, sir,' he replied, then immediately regretted it. If they could have blasted the bastards to pieces, which they could have done with their combined firepower, they could have been back at base in an hour for a shit, a shower and some decent grub. And kip.

'Hold station. I don't want you to reveal your presence.'

Jon Smoke was to reflect, as he stalked the corridors of Buckingham Palace all these years later, on the impact that brief radio comms, which he shared with Scottie, was to have on his life.

When, fifteen minutes later, as both snipers held their breath, and the Taliban marched directly beneath them, Jon heard a loud crack. Then a yell. Followed by a yelp of pain.

Then a lot of shouting in a language he did not understand.

THE HAWK IS DEAD

And despite the now poor light, he could see what had happened. He had a ringside view he would never want again for the rest of his life. One of the key branches Scottie had been perched on had broken and he'd plummeted to the ground. Straight into the middle of nearer fifteen – not ten – ragbag and angry enemy soldiers.

At first they began yelling at his colleague, and that was sort of understandable, sort of fine. And grabbing poor, helpless Scottie's weapons, that was understandable too.

But not what happened next.

37

Helmand Province, Afghanistan, 2007

Smoke could not see clearly but he could hear, louder than he had ever wanted to, screams of terror and agonizing pain. Then more screaming. Then he heard his name, howled in desperation. 'Jon! Jon!'

Jesus Christ.

He reached for his semi-automatic and pointed down. But between the leaves obscuring his view and the dark and the sea of people beneath him he couldn't tell where Scottie was exactly and did not dare fire for fear of hitting him.

Then he heard the worst, most ear-piercing scream he had ever heard in his life. It was a scream that rose from the very pit of hell.

And a desperate cry again. 'Jon! Jon!' But weaker this time.

Immediately followed by another scream that was even worse.

Smoke felt physically sick. He just wanted to fire. To shoot every bastard, but still he did not dare and then –

'Ahhh a hahhhhhhh – a hahhhhhhh! No – NO! NO! NO! PLEEEEASE. JONNNNNN!'

A final terrible shriek.

Then silence.

A moment of utter silence that was even more terrible than the screams. It was followed by shouting in the same language he did not understand, but which sounded like a command. Then the ragbag platoon moved on, towards his base. And he couldn't contain himself any more. He clamped on the night scope, set the switch to automatic and took aim.

Squeezed the trigger.

And mowed every one of them down before any had the chance to return fire. He kept on shooting, methodically, until every damned one of them was on the ground.

Then he climbed down from his tree, and as soon as his boots hit the sand he sank into a crouch, pulling out his Glock. He saw several people moving, writhing, and heard moans of pain. Removing the night scope from his rifle, he raised it to his eyes, checking no one was aiming a gun at him. Then he looked for Scottie. And saw his motionless body.

'*Fucking bastards,*' he murmured, very deeply shocked and upset. Then, still crouching, he moved forward. He passed three dead Taliban. Then one who was still moving. He put a bullet in the back of his head and he stopped moving. Smoke had three magazines for the Glock, each holding seventeen bullets. He used thirty-six bullets. Not one of the group was moving now.

Finally, he stood upright and walked back to Scottie's body. And fought back the bile that rose in his throat, shaking his head, and also fighting back tears at the sight of the remains of his friend.

They had poked his eyes out, then cut him open down his midriff and pulled out his entrails in some weird replication of the old British method of hanging, drawing and quartering traitors and other miscreants.

His blood was boiling.

Then he went to Scottie and, somehow, after hauling him onto his back, managed to carry this deadweight 3 miles to Camp Bastion, keeping up his own morale by shouting out, constantly, 'Scottie, I'm bringing you home. I'm bringing you to your pregnant fiancée! Hang on in there, just hang on in there!'

Although of course he knew his buddy was dead.

He'd never expected a hero's welcome when he finally arrived back, shattered, at Camp Bastion. His commanding officer, Jason Finch, had been very supportive on his arrival. But not so Colonel Roland Miles, who accused him of deserting his post, and threatened him with a court martial. It was Jason Finch, in overall command of the division, who had intervened and prevented any further action.

Neither Smoke nor Finch had ever received recognition for their service during this time. Jon Smoke, thanks to Finch's intervention, had avoided a court martial. But, he was aware, it had cost Finch to do so. He had been grateful to him since. On leaving the Army he had joined the Metropolitan Police and then a few years later he had been very pleasantly surprised to be contacted by the now knighted Sir Jason Finch, recently appointed Keeper of the Privy Purse, and offered a coveted position on Her Majesty's Royal Protection team.

The colonel who had wanted him court-martialled had been killed a few months later in a helicopter crash in Helmand Province – shot down by a Taliban surface-to-air missile.

As Sun Tzu said in *The Art of War*: 'If you stand by the river bank for long enough, the bodies of all your enemies will float past.'

Jon Smoke lived by that quote. Although sometimes your enemies needed a helping hand on their way.

38

Wednesday 22 November 2023

'And this is The King's current pride and joy!' Sir Tommy Magellan-Lacey announced, with a flourish.

The Master of the Royal Household was escorting Roy Grace from his meeting with The King to Sir Peregrine Greaves' widow. Polly Sweeney was due to meet him at the entrance to the St James's Palace apartment the Greaveses had shared until his untimely death on Monday. But the Master, clearly devoted to his two bosses but also passionate about this royal palace he was in charge of renovating, seemed keen to take the opportunity to give Grace a little bit of a tour en route.

They were in the garden outside the North Wing, directly beneath the royal apartments. In front of them were two majestic plane trees, which Tommy had just told him were called Albert and Victoria. They had been planted soon after Queen Victoria had acceded to the throne and had witnessed so much, Grace thought. He loved ancient trees, and sometimes wondered if they weren't a lot more intelligent than we gave them credit for.

Magellan-Lacey was pointing at what looked like a very large and enclosed Japanese-style gazebo adjoining the outside wall of the wing. Looking closer, Grace saw it was a very cleverly disguised dark green cylinder, ten feet tall and about the same across. It had a small side window, that was more of a porthole, a door in a rivetted panel that looked like it belonged on a submarine, and pipework running out of the side and in through the Palace wall. Just beyond it was a skip, smartly painted in a matching dark green, which was stuffed full of branches of vegetation, leaves and other plants and dead flowers.

'This is part of His Majesty's plan for a sustainable future,' he said, continuing in his hushed voice and boyish enthusiasm. 'An anaerobic digester!' He walked over to it and gestured proudly.

Grace frowned. 'What is that?'

'A bit more than it says on the tin, actually.'

Grace followed him over to it. Through the porthole he could see a bubbling mass of glutinous gunk.

'All the household waste goes into here, some piped and some by hand, where it is compressed. It is highly corrosive and alive with bacteria. This breaks down all organic material and releases methane for burning to heat up the Palace boilers. Very smart.'

'Extremely,' Grace said, looking at the gunk inside.

The Master then explained. 'There are five departments within the Royal Household, all based in this palace. One thousand, two hundred and fifty staff. The King hates any kind of waste, so he designed this, for food, garden, and horse waste.'

'Excellent,' Grace said. But all the time, much though he was loving this tour, he kept his focus on the job. On the grim and incredibly responsible reason that he – and many of the key members of his team – were all here.

As Magellan-Lacey steered Grace back indoors, and again led him along the labyrinth of corridors to his office, he asked, 'Is there anything else you can tell me, Detective Superintendent? I know you chaps always have to keep everything close to your vest, so it's Chatham House Rules in here – anything you tell me goes no further.'

'Understood,' Grace replied. 'Very confidentially, what we have to work on so far is that a local resident, name of Sarah, who was walking her dog, was startled by a motorbike roaring past her, at a time we've calculated was around ten minutes after the shooting.'

'A reliable witness would you say, Detective Superintendent?'

He smiled thinly. 'It's normally bodies that dog walkers discover – this is a rare bonus to get one who is a witness to an actual suspect.'

'Could she identify him?' the Master asked.

'Well, what I know so far is she did manage to remember part of the licence number – just one digit – and she will be interviewed by an Advanced Interviewer to see if she can remember any more – and, in particular, the man's features. We are also running a check on all the ANPR cameras in the area to see what, if anything, they have picked up.'

'ANPR – Automatic Number-Plate Recognition?' Magellan-Lacey asked.

'Correct.'

'You have a lot of those cameras?'

'They cover all main arteries, but not the back lanes. If this was a professional hit targeting Sir Peregrine Greaves, as we suspect, and it was the shooter on the motorbike, he may well have taken a country route. But at some point he may have gone on a main road and been picked up by a camera. We've done a plot of all the main roads he might have ended up on, and the estimated times, and are collating information from all the cameras. Another key line of enquiry we're following at this time is the information from the ballistics expert who is advising us, as you already know. If he is correct in his hypothesis, he believes the shooter was a trained military sniper.'

'Interesting – what does he base that on?'

'The bullet type – from the fragments assembled so far – appears to be a .338 Lap Mag with a ballistic tip. That is standard British Army issue for the L115A3 sniper rifle, I think it is, that was in use in Afghanistan. He thinks it is possible the shooter was a veteran of the war in Afghanistan.'

The Master of the Royal Household looked at him levelly.

'Detective Superintendent, you have quite a reputation for solving homicides. Do you get gut feelings when you are on a case?'

Grace shrugged. 'Sometimes. Not always.'

He nodded. 'Do you have one on this case?'

Grace thought carefully before responding. 'As I've already told you, sir, I do not think Her Majesty was the target. My hypothesis is that the offender either had a grudge against Sir Peregrine Greaves, or that he wanted to send a message – some kind of very warped message – to Their Majesties.'

'Can you elaborate?'

'I wish I could, but at this stage, I can't. It's certainly not a priority.'

Two floors and one corridor away, Jon Smoke was listening to every word.

I wish I could, but at this stage, I can't.

Since his time in Afghanistan, Smoke rarely smiled. But what he heard now made him smile. For the first time in a long time. This idiot detective was in thrall to the Royal Palace and to the royals themselves. Just like everyone who came here.

He might need eliminating. He'd be one of his team's easier targets.

Much easier than Sir Peregrine had been.

39

Wednesday 22 November 2023

Polly Sweeney was a smartly dressed and very personable colleague in her early fifties. She was chatting to the two Royal Protection Officers by the security barrier at the entrance to the St James's Palace complex, as Roy Grace and Sir Tommy Magellan-Lacey approached.

After she'd shown her ID and received a pass, the three of them walked past Sir Tommy's residence, then made a left turn through an archway and into an inner courtyard, with a green and white sign on the wall: *AMBASSADORS' COURT*.

Discreetly, continuing in his temporary role as tour guide, the Master of the Royal Household pointed out the buildings where other royals had their London residences. Walking further along the courtyard he stopped at an imposing front door in the equally imposing ancient red-brick building and rang the bell.

There was a burst of deep barking from the other side of the door, followed by a stern but faint command to sit that instantly quietened it. The door was opened a few moments later by a tall and clearly very distressed woman in her mid-fifties, flanked by two shiny-coated black Labradors, now sitting obediently. Her tear-stained face lit up a fraction as she saw Sir Tommy but immediately turned to a frown as she clocked Grace and Sweeney.

'Margot, Lady Greaves,' Magellan-Lacey said gently. 'May I introduce Detective Superintendent Roy Grace and Polly Sweeney, from the Surrey and Sussex Major Crime Team.'

'Yes, ah, yes, you told me about them coming.' A handsome woman, her grey hair coiffed in a conservative but understated style, she was wearing a dark dress with a white ruff collar and black suede pumps. 'Good morning, officers,' she said in a voice that might, under other circumstances, have been commanding, but now sounded broken, and as bewildered as she looked.

Grace felt for her. On Monday morning her husband had set off for work, as normal. A few hours later he was on a mortuary table, with his head blown to smithereens, awaiting a post-mortem. It didn't matter whether you led a gilded life in a palace or struggled to make ends meet in a council dwelling, grief was a leveller. It stripped away all the trappings you'd ever surrounded yourself with.

'Do please come in,' she said, holding the door with one hand and signalling to the dogs to stay still with the other.

The apartment, Grace noticed immediately, was very different in feel to the warm family farmhouse atmosphere of Sir Tommy's residence. This was more formal, more structured. Grand paintings were hung on the walls. The bust of a man he recognized as the late Sir Peregrine stood on a columned plinth. She led them through into a grand drawing room, clearly designed and decorated to impress. It was hung with fine paintings, several of them Venetian scenes. In one corner was an antique roll-top desk, the lid shut, with a matching chair. 'May I offer you tea or coffee?' she asked.

'We are fine, thank you, Lady Greaves,' Grace said as the two dogs now sniffed at his trousers, no doubt picking up on his own dogs' scent, he thought. 'And may I say how very sorry I am for your loss.'

'You may,' she said glumly. 'But probably not as sorry as I am. I trust you are going to tell me who murdered my husband and what you are doing to catch them?'

Grace and Sweeney sat on one large sofa, facing Lady Greaves and Sir Tommy across a glass-topped coffee table that doubled as a display cabinet, filled with what looked like regimental badges.

'If I can take one crumb of comfort from this nightmare,' Lady Greaves continued, 'it's the knowledge that my husband at least saved the life of our Queen.' She looked down, her voice cracking now, tears rolling down her face. The two dogs sat either side of her, as if sensing her distress. She stroked both of them, light sparkling off the stones on a large ring on her finger, and said, 'What's that thing they say about "taking one for the team"?' She looked at Grace then Sweeney, shaking her head slightly. 'That's the only thing getting me through this right now. The knowledge that my husband saved The Queen's life. Thanks to a gunman who didn't have a bloody clue how to shoot.'

Grace exchanged an awkward glance with his colleague. Then he caught the Master's eye, before speaking. 'Lady Greaves, firstly may I offer you my very deepest sympathy. My colleagues and I can only begin to imagine what you and your family must be going through,' he said. Phrases he had used on far too many tragic occasions in the past. Sometimes the simple words helped break the ice, but not today.

'Really?' she retorted. 'In which case, you must all have very vivid imaginations.'

Grace thought carefully for some moments, then asked, as gently as he could, 'This is a difficult question, Lady Greaves, but is it possible your husband might have had any enemies?'

She jerked upright, as if she had just been plugged into an electrical socket and switched on. 'Enemies? He was very much liked by both The King and The Queen. Everyone who met him adored him and held him in high esteem. He wouldn't have held such an elevated position in the Royal Household if he had enemies.' She sniffed and dabbed her eyes with a tiny handkerchief she pulled from her sleeve.

Grace opened his arms in a pacifying gesture. 'Lady Greaves, at this stage we have a completely open mind on the circumstances around your husband's death. But we have to eliminate everything we can from our enquiries. One possibility is that it was your husband who was the target and not The Queen.'

'How ridiculous!' she replied, her face suddenly reddening. 'How do you come to such a conclusion?'

'It's a hypothesis, ma'am. As I said, we need to rule out all possible alternatives. This may be hard for you to accept, but from the evidence we have to date, there is a good possibility that your husband may have been the intended target and not Her Majesty.'

She was silent, gathering her thoughts, then burst out, 'This is nonsense, surely, Tommy?' She gazed across at the Master, looking really upset.

'The police need to keep an open mind, Margot,' Magellan-Lacey replied, giving her a reassuring smile.

'But, Tommy, you know how popular Peregrine was. Everyone loved him. He was the kindest man in the world – and he totally worshipped both Their Majesties. He was so proud to serve them.'

Grace nodded. 'I'm sure he was, Lady Greaves. But did he ever express any concerns to you?'

'What do you mean? What kind of concerns?'

Polly Sweeney interjected. 'Concerns about some individual – or some organization – anyone involved in criminal activity who might have wanted to silence him?'

'I'm sorry,' Lady Greaves said. Her voice cracked. 'I really don't think I can take much more of this.' She dabbed her eyes again.

Grace and Sweeney exchanged a silent signal with their eyes. Then Grace said, 'Lady Greaves, I appreciate your seeing us today.' He gestured towards his colleague. 'Polly is going to act as your Family Liaison Officer – she will keep you constantly informed and updated on all aspects of our enquiry into your husband's death. You can feel free to contact her at any time of the day or night, if you want information or think of anything that might be helpful – or just feel you want to chat, to talk to someone.'

Lady Greaves gave Polly Sweeney a sceptical look. 'So you are not only a detective, you are a mine of information, a grief counsellor and my twenty-four-seven new best friend?'

Polly Sweeney blushed at the sarcasm. 'Well – not exactly all of that, but I am indeed here for you around the clock. And please feel free to talk to me any time.' She passed Lady Greaves her card. The widow took it and put it in her pocket.

'Thank you, officer,' she said. 'But the only person I really want to talk to is my husband. And that's a little tricky now.'

40

Wednesday 22 November 2023

'I'm afraid, as you can see, poor Lady Greaves is not in a good place,' Sir Tommy Magellan-Lacey said, as they walked back across Ambassadors' Court. 'But –' he glanced over his shoulder, as if to ensure she wasn't still within earshot and lowered his voice – 'she's not entirely correct about her husband having no enemies, as I told you earlier.'

'Disgruntled enough for someone to want to kill him, Sir Tommy?' Polly Sweeney asked.

It took a few moments for him to answer. 'We do have quite a high percentage of personnel on the Household staff who have been through some pretty traumatic experiences. I suppose it's always possible that being rejected could have pushed someone over the edge.'

'Well, regardless of Lady Greaves' protestations – which are fully understandable, given the shock and grief she must be experiencing – someone clearly did want to kill him. That is the reality we seem to be faced with,' Grace replied.

They were all silent for a moment, mulling over that reality.

'May I ask you both what your plans are now?' the Master asked.

'I have to get back down to Sussex – my team will continue their interviews in your Billiards Room for as long as that takes, if that is all right with you, Sir Tommy?' Grace replied.

'Absolutely!'

THE HAWK IS DEAD

'And I'll hang around in London for a few hours,' Sweeney said. 'Maybe Lady Greaves would be more comfortable with a private chat, woman to woman.'

Magellan-Lacey looked dubious. 'Maybe. I'll suggest it. Look, you must both be gasping for a drink. Come back and have a quick coffee?'

Grace and Sweeney exchanged a glance. 'I won't say no,' Grace replied.

'Nor me!' added Sweeney.

They were approaching the front of the Master's residence, and the police barrier just beyond. Grace said, 'Sir Tommy, can I ask you something? Just from what I've seen today, there are a vast number of paintings and sculptures and beautiful ornaments on display within Buckingham Palace. It must be hard to keep track of everything, surely?'

'It is a massive task for the Royal Collection team,' he conceded. 'There are sixty-four thousand items in the North Wing of Buckingham Palace alone. And then there are all the other Royal Palaces, filled with stuff members of the Royal Family have been gifted over the years, and continue to be – birthdays, anniversaries, gifts from visiting dignitaries. I don't think Their Majesties could possibly know everything they have – I doubt they've even seen a lot of it. It's just not physically possible.' He unlocked his front door and let them through to the kitchen, stopping and stooping to address the dark brown Burmese cat. 'Hello, George!' He stroked it for a moment, before the cat glanced at the visitors, arched its back and shot up the stairs.

Grace and Sweeney sat down at the wooden table, while the Master fussed around with the cafetière and kettle. Then he brought over a plate laden with biscuits and tore away the cellophane wrapper. 'These are Florentines, they were given to us by the Chief Rabbi's wife who made them herself – they're delicious! Help yourselves.'

Grace looked at them, tempted as he was hungry now, but restrained himself. 'Have you ever had a thief or been aware of items being stolen within the Royal Household?' Grace asked.

'We have indeed, Roy – all right if I call you Roy?'

'Of course.'

'And I'm Tommy. Cut the *Sir Tommy* crap! Understood, officers – sorry – detectives?'

'Understood!' they both acknowledged.

'There's a chappie in jail right now – a former footman, dim-witted fellow – who started nicking ornaments and other bits and pieces from Clarence House and Buckingham Palace and flogging them on eBay – under his own name!' The Master scratched the back of his head. 'The fellow laid the stolen items out on his bed to photograph them for eBay, with the pattern of his bedsheets clearly visible in the background!'

'A lot of criminals aren't that bright, fortunately,' Grace said.

Magellan-Lacey nodded ruefully. 'There used to be complete trust in here – and we all left our lockers unlocked. That silly footman stole my CBE and flogged it on eBay to a Hong Kong student. He confessed after he was arrested and even gave me the name of the student, but he'd gone home and I wasn't able to track him down. So there's now some youngster strutting around Hong Kong with my CBE hanging around his neck.' He gave a short laugh. 'I had to buy a replacement – it was bloody expensive!'

'When was this?' Grace asked.

'About five years ago. I can get you a more precise timeline if that would be helpful?'

'It would,' Grace said. 'No other thieving, or valuables going missing, that you are aware of?'

'Certainly nothing that's been brought to my attention.'

'When I was with Her Majesty a short while ago, she seemed eager to show me her favourite painting, a Vermeer, I think she said.'

THE HAWK IS DEAD

The Master nodded and said quietly, 'Yes, that's right. She loves that painting. It's magnificent. A lot of people think it's the finest piece in the entire Royal Collection.'

'She seemed surprised – and quite annoyed – that it wasn't on display and had been replaced by something else.'

'I'm afraid the Royal Collection team are a bit of a law unto themselves.'

'That's exactly what Her Majesty said to me,' Grace said.

'Yes, well, they decide when something needs cleaning, or they simply feel has had too much exposure to light and needs to rest for a period of time. I think they are a little over-protective, personally. But they do a fine job and always have done, and the Royal Collection is in very safe hands with them. I wish I could say the same about some other aspects of the Palace.'

'Really?' Polly Sweeney said and took a bite of a Florentine.

He nodded. 'There have been decades of cost-cutting and shoddy workmanship, which we are only just beginning to discover, thanks to all the renovation work. And I mean not just shoddy but jolly dangerous.'

Grace was surprised. 'Really?'

'Roy, I took you along the East Wing corridor, where the royal apartments are. The late Queen and the Duke of Edinburgh walked along it every day, many times a day. When we lifted the carpet up last year, we discovered a whole section of the corridor floor had been removed, probably decades ago, when new pipework was put in, and was never properly replaced. There were just some very thin planks that had been partially sawn through. If anyone had jumped up and down on them hard enough, that section of the floor would have collapsed and the late Queen would have plunged through, like something out of *Monty Python*.'

'Could that have been done by some disgruntled workman?' Sweeney questioned. 'Someone actually hoping The Queen or Prince Philip would fall through?'

'Entirely possible, although I'd say more likely it was down to the cost-cutting and poor craftmanship.'

'Tommy,' Grace said. 'It would be helpful to have a list of any disgruntled former employees who have military or police backgrounds – and, for belt and braces' sake, any current employees who you think might have some kind of grudge or resentment over being passed over for promotion.'

'Or medals, too,' the Master said. 'Not getting a medal when someone else does, that can be a big source of resentment. Over what time period do you want?'

'If you can go back ten years – I would think anyone harbouring a grudge who's planning some kind of revenge would act within a decade. How long had Sir Peregrine worked for the Royal Household?'

'Gosh, I can check – but around twelve years.'

'He was in the Royal Navy?'

'Correct. He was a good and brave man. Terrible loss.'

They were interrupted by Grace's job phone ringing. Raising an apologetic hand he answered. 'Roy Grace.'

It was EJ Boutwood. 'Sir, we've just had a call from the witness who saw the motorcyclist on the Downs. She's just remembered the second digit of the motorbike's licence plate.'

'Brilliant!' Grace said. 'That will greatly help with narrowing the field on the ANPR search. Have we got a time agreed with her for her cognitive interview?'

'We have, sir: 2.30 p.m. tomorrow. Alec Butler and Velvet Wilde will be conducting it.'

Grace thanked the DC and ended the call. Then he updated the Master. 'Good news, potentially. It seems like our key witness has remembered further information.'

'Your key witness? This lady who saw the motorcyclist? Sarah – was that her name?'

Grace nodded. 'It's not much, but it's a second digit of the

THE HAWK IS DEAD

motorbike's licence plate. Hopefully in the cognitive witness environment she might remember more.'

'Maybe the entire plate?' Magellan-Lacey asked, hopefully.

'I've known that happen,' Grace said.

The Master clapped his hands together in a sudden flash of exuberance. 'Here's to Sarah!'

41

Thursday 23 November 2023

Even though they'd crammed extra chairs into the Major Crime Suite conference room, there weren't enough for all the rapidly expanding team, some of whom had to stand.

Roy Grace normally held his morning briefing meetings much earlier, but today he'd delayed proceedings, waiting for two detectives from the Scotland Yard Counter Terrorism Command, who had been stuck in a jam on their way down from London. Also, unusually, because of the high profile of this investigation, he was joined by ACC Downing, and a PIP4 Strategic Adviser who would be with him to answer questions at the next press conference, straight after this briefing.

Behind Grace was a large screen, headed *OP ASSET*. A photograph of the dead man in situ at the scene, as well as photographs of the area where the shooter had lain were shown. On another screen, an association chart of Sir Peregrine's family, friends and work colleagues – so many it needed multiple images – was shown. Finally, there were photographs of the derailed train, the inside of the tunnel, and the topography around the south exit.

'Good morning, everyone,' Grace said. 'For the record, the time is 11 a.m., this is the sixth briefing meeting of Operation Asset, the investigation into the shooting of Sir Peregrine Greaves, Private Secretary to Their Majesties, and the investigation into the derailment of the Royal Train in Clayton Tunnel, which we believe to be linked. We welcome to the investigation DCI

THE HAWK IS DEAD

Jacqueline Crawley from Counter Terrorism Command, Sergeant Sam Frost and Security Coordinator DS Russ Lewis from the Royalty and Special Protection unit – RaSP.'

He updated the team on his meetings yesterday with both The King and The Queen, the murder victim's widow and the Master of the Royal Household, along with the information provided by, to date, the only witness who saw anything, whose full name was Sarah Stratten.

Then he continued, 'The team conducted interviews yesterday at Buckingham Palace with members of the Royal Household who had had any association with the deceased during the past ten years. You were joined part-way through by DI Branson. Have you anything significant to report from this?'

'Jack has something of interest, chief,' Potting said. 'To get through everyone we divided the workload initially between us and then with DI Branson when he joined us. Jack had the only real odd note of the day.'

Grace looked at the tall young DS. 'Tell me, Jack.'

'It was one of the footmen, sir,' Jack Alexander informed him. 'Wearing his full livery. Name of Geoffrey Bailey. His body language seemed wrong. It was like he used the opportunity of the interview to air a personal grievance. He said nothing about the deceased, he was just bitter that he'd been ignored – left out of – Sir Peregrine's recent recommendations for awards of medals by The King to Royal Household staff. Bailey also told me he was gay, and I got the sense he was implying some kind of discrimination was at play, but he didn't explicitly make any allegation of that sort.'

'Was he any more specific about the medal he'd hoped for?' Grace asked.

'Apparently there's a whole hierarchy of medals within the Royal Household, sir – they are handed out for long service or for special work – he didn't state which particular medal he felt he should have received, but I'll find out.'

'Is there anything in his past record to indicate any familiarity with firearms?' Grace asked.

Sam Frost, the Royal Protection Officer, raised a hand and Grace signalled to her to go ahead.

'We have had concerns about this person, Geoffrey Bailey, for some time and have been keeping a watch on him. The late Queen was advised by us that he was a bit of a loose cannon, but she said she liked him and so he was kept on. After her death, we did advise Their Majesties to let him go and they agreed – initially. But when he was served a termination notice, he went running to them. One issue we have with both Their Majesties is that they can be very supportive of their staff. It's a nice trait, but it does mean our hands are a little bit tied when we feel someone is a potential problem.'

'Are you suggesting this Geoffrey Bailey might have been the offender, Jack?' Grace quizzed.

'No, boss, he has a cast-iron alibi – he was working in Buckingham Palace all day on Monday, from 7 a.m. until after 5 p.m.'

Grace nodded, thinking. 'OK, let me understand your concerns about this footman a little better. When you interviewed him, he aired a grievance about being passed over for a medal. But does that have a relevance to our murder enquiry?'

'I can't say it does, sir, but there's something about him that made me very uneasy. I think he was hiding something.' He tapped the side of his nose. 'I intend to find out more.'

Grace smiled.

'Everyone else I interviewed – and I think every single person the whole team interviewed – expressed some emotion about Sir Peregrine's death, except Geoffrey Bailey. It was all about him – and I just had the feeling that he might know something more than he was telling us, and was using his exasperation over the medals to mask it.'

THE HAWK IS DEAD

'OK, I think you're quite right to raise a flag with this man, Jack,' Grace said. 'He definitely needs to be interviewed in more depth. I agreed with Sir Tommy Magellan-Lacey that we would give him a list of anyone we were dubious about and wanted a second interview with. Polly is going to be up in London quite a bit over the coming weeks, in her FLO role with Sir Peregrine's widow – I'll ask Sir Tommy when would be a good time and then you could go up and interview him with Polly.'

'Yes, sir.'

Grace turned to the BTP officer. 'Steve, welcome to your first briefing. Do you have your initial findings on the derailment to share with us?'

Steve Butcher, a jovial, balding and lightly bearded man in his late thirties, nodded vigorously and held up a laser pen. 'I do, sir. I can now confirm the cause of the derailment. I also have something I think will be of interest to you and the team, boss. It would be helpful first to take a look at the inside of Clayton railway tunnel.'

He pointed his cursor at the large photograph of the tunnel entrance, on the screen, and it danced around, just inside the south portal. 'The tunnel is pretty narrow – just wide enough for two sets of tracks, the up and down lines, but not allowing much space at all for anyone working inside the tunnel. That's why these recesses were created, approximately every twenty yards, along the entire length of the tunnel on both sides, so that workers could slip into these for safety whenever a train was entering the tunnel.' The cursor circled around what looked like the entrance to a cave, and then along further ones into the distance.

'Now, something of real significance is that ten of these recesses go further back and connect to the air shafts built into the tunnel roof – their purpose was to enable the steam from the old locomotives to escape. There is a room in each of these ten recesses for the railway workers to have a break and rest, where in the old days they could light a fire to keep warm.' He gave a knowing smile. 'I'm sure some of you are wondering what this has to do with the derailment of the Royal Train, and I can tell you – it appears to have quite a lot to do with it.'

He moved the cursor onto another photograph, which showed a rope ladder hanging down a dimly lit circular brick structure. 'We conducted a search of the tunnel while the rescue operation to remove the wrecked train was under way, and found this ladder, which when examined turned out to be brand new, clamped to the top of one of the air vents. We think this particular vent was chosen very carefully – it comes out through the roof of the tunnel on the hillside above, in dense scrubland, and is pretty much concealed from view to anyone walking on the nearby fields.' He paused to check a note, then continued.

'I can confirm the cause of the derailment was a six-foot length of rail that had fallen onto – or more likely been toppled onto – the down-line section of track, across both rails and the third, live rail. This sent an alert to the signalling centre at Three Bridges that there was an obstruction on the line, and the Ops Manager there, Christopher New, immediately contacted the driver of the Royal Train, which was at that time approaching the entrance to the tunnel, warning him and telling him to halt the train.'

'So why didn't he, Steve?' Glenn Branson jumped in.

'The driver was pulling seven carriages as well as an additional locomotive at the rear, travelling at 70 miles an hour. It takes the best part of a mile to bring a train safely to a halt at that speed. He was already approaching the entrance to the tunnel when he got the obstruction ahead alert. He'd managed to reduce the speed to forty at the time of impact with the rail – if he hadn't, there would have very likely been serious casualties, if not fatalities.'

'Which gives us a number of unanswered questions,' Grace said. 'The first being what injuries the offender – or offenders – had intended for everyone on the train? Or would whoever had put that rail across the track have timed it deliberately and exactly,

THE HAWK IS DEAD

knowing the train wouldn't be able to slow down enough to prevent it being derailed, but that it would slow down sufficiently to avoid any serious injuries?'

'Good question, sir,' the BTP officer said.

'Chief,' Norman Potting said. 'We had a railway line that went across our land where I grew up, dividing our two main fields. It became disused back in the 1960s when Lord Beeching axed a lot of rural railways. I had to help my dad shift the rails – and they are bloody heavy, I can tell you.'

'They are,' Branson agreed. 'A six-foot length of track weighs about sixteen stone. That would take a strong person to lift.'

'But if balanced against a wall of the tunnel,' Grace asked, 'we know that just one person could push it and topple it over onto the track.'

'Yes, sir,' Butcher replied.

Grace considered this for some moments. 'The signaller at Three Bridges notified the driver of the Royal Train of an obstruction on the line, just before the train entered the north portal of Clayton Tunnel. And Sir Peregrine was shot as he exited the tunnel – perhaps twenty minutes later. There's no way the shooter and the person who caused the obstruction on the line could be the same person, if those timings are correct. Pretty much impossible for that person to have climbed the rope ladder and run to the shooter's location all within roughly twenty minutes.'

'I'd have to agree with you, sir,' Butcher said.

'Which confirms we are looking for two people. At least.'

They were interrupted by a phone ringing. The James Bond theme. A flustered Norman Potting, the delegated point person for any urgent calls that came into the Incident Room during the briefing, answered it, raising an apologetic hand.

The room was silent as Potting listened, then said, 'Thank you, I'll inform him right away.' Then he turned to Grace.

'Chief, you need to hear this. You really need to hear this.'

42

Thursday 23 November 2023

Roy Grace left Glenn Branson to continue with the briefing meeting and to attend today's press conference along with ACC Downing and a senior member of the Media and Communications Team. Branson would be making a media appeal, asking people to come forward if they had seen anyone in the surrounding area acting suspiciously or with a firearm on the days prior to or on the day of the shooting. Sometimes, Grace knew, these appeals could result in fresh information.

Twenty minutes later he was driving, with Norman Potting in the passenger seat, past the magnificently bizarre Gothic north portal of Clayton Tunnel, towards the small town of Hurstpierpoint.

Ordinarily, Grace would have left this task to more junior members of his team. But right now nothing was ordinary about this murder investigation. And, secretly, he was loving being a proper detective again himself. Too often in his work these days, the nature of his position kept him deskbound, leaving the outside enquiries to others on his team.

After a short distance, he turned left onto Hautboys Lane, a narrow, winding country road that ran around the bottom of this area of the South Downs, along which were isolated cottages and a few larger houses.

'Coming up on the left, chief, three hundred yards,' Potting said, peering hard at the satnav screen.

THE HAWK IS DEAD

Grace slowed down and saw a picture-postcard thatched cottage ahead, with a pink Fiat 500 parked on the driveway in front of an adjoining thatched garage.

'*Dunroamin*,' Potting said, reading the cottage's name board with a faintly cynical tone, as Grace pulled the car to a halt. 'Would you want to live in a pun, chief?'

'If it was as pretty as this, I could probably get used to it,' Grace replied with a grin, and opened the car door. From inside the house they could hear a dog barking. As they walked up the path to the front door, past an American-style cylindrical metal mailbox, with its flag raised, the barking grew even louder. Entering the porch, Grace looked for the bell. He could only see a brass knocker, and gave several sharp raps on it, which sent the dog on the far side into a yappy frenzy.

Moments later the door was opened, just a few inches against a safety chain. He could see wary eyes behind oval tortoiseshell glasses, and little else. The dog carried on barking. 'Yes?' It was a question, not a greeting.

Grace, followed by Potting, showed his warrant card and introduced both of them, having to speak loudly above the barking.

All the same, the eyes still studied them suspiciously for some moments and then she asked to see their warrant cards again. Finally she seemed satisfied enough to close the door, unlatch the chain and open it again, kneeling and restraining the livid, small grey schnauzer by its collar. 'It's OK, Bonzo! These are police officers, it's OK!'

The dog did not think they were OK at all. It curled its lips, baring sharp, rusty-looking incisors, glared at them then snarled. As Potting followed Grace over the threshold, he knelt and held out a hand to the dog. He had learned a long time ago that, for some reason, dogs liked him. After a moment of seeming standoffish, the dog cocked its head. Then, smiling, and saying, 'Good boy, good boy!' the detective was stroking its chest with his knuckles.

The dog followed Potting along the narrow hallway, the walls lined with photographs of species of butterflies, and an ancient map of Sussex, into a chintzy sitting room with framed family photographs, many in black and white, on almost every shelf.

'Please have a seat, officers,' Sarah Stratten said in quite a plummy voice, directing them to the sofa in front of a very old-fashioned television. She was extremely tall, so much so she had to stoop to avoid bashing her head on the door frame. Her silver hair cropped short, combined with her large oval glasses gave her a rather arty air, enhanced by the massive purple cable-knit jumper that enveloped her, a large pendant on a chain, blue jeans, and trainers that would not have looked out of place on a drug dealer. And she herself looked out of place here, Grace thought. The cottage felt like it belonged to an old lady, with antimacassars on the sofa and armchair, and lace doylies under the ornaments, yet Sarah Stratten could not have been more than sixty, tops, he thought.

'Can I offer you any tea or coffee?'

'A coffee would be very welcome,' Grace said.

'Tea for me,' Potting said. 'Builders', please – no sugar.' Then he stroked the dog, now his new best friend, sitting at his feet.

Grace looked around at the photographs, seeing what he could learn about the woman from them. There was a traditional church porch wedding one, her and her husband – late husband, perhaps? A series of a young man, starting as a small boy on a tricycle, and progressing up to a tall thin youth in a mortar board and graduation gown.

He pulled out his notebook from his inside pocket, and a pen, aware that most officers these days took notes on a tablet, but he didn't care.

'So I suppose I should be honoured. I get a Detective

Superintendent – and a *Detective Sergeant*, too,' she added, as she carried in a laden tray.

Grace smiled. 'How long have you lived here, Mrs Stratten?'

'In this cottage? Just six months. It belonged to my late mother. My husband and I had been renting it out on Airbnb since she died, four years ago. I was born in Hurstpierpoint, but my husband was a barrister with chambers in Birmingham, where we lived. We'd always planned to move down here when he retired. But I'm afraid he died suddenly a year ago. So I decided to move down anyway and do a renovation job, which I haven't yet started, as you can probably tell.'

'It's very charming,' Potting said.

Sarah Stratten grimaced. 'That's how we marketed it – country cottage with "ye olde worlde charm". All that's going to change.' She touched her very modern-looking and stylish beaten-silver pendant, as if signalling where she was going.

'So, Mrs Stratten, we understand you had a very unpleasant and threatening phone call – late last night?' Grace said.

'It was jolly late – about one in the morning.'

'What can you tell us about it?'

'Well, I answered because I thought it might be my son, Hugo – he lives in Auckland, New Zealand. He split up with his wife and has rather hit the sauce.' She tipped an imaginary glass towards her mouth. 'If you see what I'm getting at? Often when he's had too much he forgets the time difference and calls me at all hours. But it wasn't Hugo, it was a man with a very blunt voice. He said he understood I was a witness who had come forward saying I had seen a motorcyclist on the Downs, shortly after the terrible assassination attempt on Camilla.' Her confidence suddenly evaporated and she stared at both of them with those worried eyes again.

'It was very good of you to come forward,' Grace said, encouraging her.

She looked dubious. 'He then said – and God, this sounds

corny – he said that if I knew what was good for me – and my dog – I should keep my trap shut and not agree to a cognitive witness interview – I think he called it.' She shrugged, giving an involuntary smile. 'Those were his words. He told me my phone was bugged and he would know if I called you.'

Grace frowned. How the hell did whoever had called her know she was going to be put through a *cognitive witness* interview? That wasn't something the public generally knew about.

'But you did call us,' Potting said.

'We are very grateful to you,' Grace said.

'Do you think I could be at any risk for contacting you?'

'To be honest, Mrs Stratten, we don't yet know what we are dealing with. I think it's unlikely your house or phone are bugged, but I'll get a bug sweep of the house done as soon as possible today, and if you can be without your mobile phone for a short while, I'll get it checked by Digital Forensics. We'll inform the local police to keep an extra eye on your property and put an alert for them should you call 999. If you are very concerned we could arrange for you to move into protective custody in a safe house – but I don't get the impression you'd want that.'

'No one is going to frighten me out of my home!'

'Good. Normally threats like this are just bluff, so let's hope this is the case. Can I ask you: this man who called, what do you remember about his voice? For instance, did he have an accent?'

'To be honest, I was in a deep sleep when he rang. I did even wonder when he hung up if I had imagined it.'

'British Telecom have confirmed you received a call at 1.07 a.m.,' Potting said. 'The duration was two minutes and eleven seconds. It was from a mobile phone with the number withheld – almost certainly a burner, which means untraceable.'

Sarah Stratten nodded. 'I'm familiar with that term. The man was definitely British. A northerner. A trace of Geordie, perhaps – Newcastle?'

'Is there anything else you can remember about the call?' Grace asked, and sipped his coffee. It was strong and hit the spot.

'Not really,' she said. 'I wish I could tell you more.'

'And the motorcyclist you saw when you were walking Bonzo – I know you went to the exact location with one of my detectives on Tuesday. Is there anything more you can remember about this motorcyclist?'

'To be quite honest, no. I was startled out of my wits. I'd been walking Bonzo every morning since I moved into the cottage, on more or less the same route, and never saw a soul. Then this bloody thing came blattering out of nowhere, scaring poor Bonzo and passing literally inches from my face. I think I actually startled him, too. But I really couldn't see much of him – he wore one of those helmets with a dark visor and was in full motorcycling leathers.'

'It was definitely a *him*?'

'Well, I can't be one hundred per cent certain of that.'

'Can you remember any details about the motorbike?' Potting asked. 'What kind was it – I mean the style of machine rather than make, and the colour?'

Sarah Stratten smiled. 'Actually, yes, I can. Both my husband and Hugo were into motocross and used to do it together from the time Hugo was in his early teens. They had those cross-country motorbikes with raised mudguards. It was one of those that this person was riding. I think it was black, but there may have been a splash of red.'

Grace made some notes. 'Despite the threat you've had, are you still up for doing an in-depth interview – to see if we can jog your mind any further?'

'My husband defended – and prosecuted – criminals,' she said. 'He regularly had death threats when he prosecuted. None of them came to anything. No one is going to silence me.'

43

Thursday 23 November 2023

As they left the cottage, Grace asked Potting to drive, so he could focus on making a series of urgent phone calls. As the DS started the car, he said, 'Chief, whoever this was who rang Mrs Stratten, has police knowledge. *Cognitive witness interview*?'

'My thoughts exactly, Norman.'

For a good two minutes Grace had a frustratingly poor signal, then finally he got his phone to connect. As soon as one of the Incident Room team answered, Grace asked to be put through to Luke Stanstead.

He instructed the researcher to speak to the two London detectives on the Op Asset team and see if they could establish from the profiles that they had on the individual Not-My-King protestors, a number of key facts. The first was the names of any Geordies or people from the Newcastle region. Second, to check with the DVLA – the Driver and Vehicle Licensing Agency – for any who had a motorcycle licence. And, third, to check if any were former – or even serving – police officers. He wanted as much information as he could gather about this protest group to rule them in or out of his investigation. This was an important line of enquiry.

Next, Grace checked his watch. It was 12.15 p.m. He knew from what Sir Tommy Magellan-Lacey had told him that his daily audience with The King was normally between 11 a.m. and

THE HAWK IS DEAD

12 p.m. He dialled Sir Tommy's mobile number. After a few rings he heard his familiar, upbeat voice.

'Roy, good morning – sorry – good afternoon! Are you calling with good news? You've arrested the killer?'

'I wish I could tell you that, Sir Tommy.'

'Well you certainly worked your charm on Their Majesties yesterday!'

'I did?'

'You impressed The Queen. She thought you were very different from the stereotypical detectives in crime fiction novels – and on the screen.'

Grace was fleetingly lost for words. 'I'm very happy to hear that, sir.'

'And The King, too, was very taken with you.'

'Really? I wasn't sure how that went.'

'It went well. He called me in later yesterday and told me he has complete confidence in you. So, no pressure, eh?' He gave one of his characteristic bursts of laughter.

'No pressure,' Grace echoed.

'HMTK is a very astute man, Roy. If you have his approval, I can tell you that is very significant.'

'So now I have to live up to it,' Grace said.

'What I learned in the military, which may give you something to think about: *We don't rise to the level of our expectations, we fall to the level of our training*. My opinion, in the short time I've known you, is that you have damned good training. I don't think you are going to let us down.'

'I appreciate your confidence, Sir Tommy. And I appreciate what you've told me about Their Majesties. Perhaps you could relay to them that being the SIO on this case is a great honour. And I will do whatever it takes to find the man who shot Sir Peregrine and any accomplices he may have had.'

'Absolutely will do!'

'Something I need your help on,' Grace said, 'is one of my lines of enquiry. Do you know how many officers there are on the Royal Protection team?'

'Yes, about six hundred.'

'All of them carry firearms. Quite a number come from Armed Response backgrounds in the police and many have military service?'

'Yes, absolutely, Roy.'

'There are two things I need to know, Sir Tommy. Firstly, the names of every Royal Protection Officer who has a motorcycle licence, and secondly if any of those have a northern accent – especially a Geordie one.'

'Are you saying you think this might be an inside job, so to speak, Roy? This is very deeply alarming if that's the case.'

'I'm not ruling anything out at this stage,' Grace replied.

'But what could be the motive?'

'You told me there are a lot of undercurrents within the Royal Household staff – is there something more serious we don't know about yet?'

'That's possible – but there is also a great deal of respect and loyalty to both the bosses. I'll find out what I can.'

Grace sat in silence a few minutes after he ended the call. Never in his entire career, up until now, had he felt so out of his depth. The enormity of what he was dealing with was sinking in and seemed immense. Perhaps it would have been easier if Sir Tommy had told him that Their Majesties had thought he was a lightweight and wanted someone from the Met, who really knew what they were doing, to take over the case.

He felt deeply honoured that he had the trust of both The King and The Queen. But what if he was wrong in his hypothesis and it actually was The Queen who had been the target?

He was scared as hell.

44

Thursday 23 November 2023

The huge vault, formerly used as a cold store in the days before fridges and freezers, was accessed past a wall of fuse boxes, and through a series of whitewashed interconnected arches, deep in the basement of Buckingham Palace. Now, instead of being kept cold it was being kept dry, by a battery of dehumidifiers.

It was temporary home to a different kind of perishable from the food that would once have been stored here: oil paintings, some of which were here for safe keeping while the rooms where they normally hung were being renovated and redecorated. And others that were particularly old and delicate were occasionally rested here to protect them from too much exposure to light.

In addition to paintings, a large number of ornaments and items of glassware were also being stored down here for safety during the renovations.

But it was a picture that Sir Jason Finch, dressed as always in his three-piece chalk-stripes, had come down here to find. A black and white dog – a Newfoundland – painted by Sir Edwin Landseer in 1867. A similar size and subject had recently sold at auction for £1.1 million.

He looked around with greedy eyes, bewildered, at the racks and racks of paintings, all in protective wrapping. Every single package worth tens or hundreds of thousands, or millions.

'Sir Jason!'

Startled, he turned at the sound of the haughty voice, to see the tall, elegant Director of the Royal Collection Trust, Lorraine McKnight, standing right behind him.

'Lorraine – ah – hello – yes.'

'Can I help you with anything, Sir Jason?'

'Well – actually – ah – I was wondering – about – a Landseer – black and white – a Newfoundland dog – I – I wanted – to have a look at it.'

She was giving him a strange look. 'He was a fine painter,' she said. 'So talented with animals. Dogs, horses, stags.' She was still looking at him oddly.

'Yes, gosh yes, indeed. Animals. Landseer. Terrific painter.'

'It's rather coincidental,' she said. 'The Landseer Newfoundland dog – that's the reason I've come down here – to try to locate it.'

45

Friday 24 November 2023

Polly Sweeney rang the bell at the St James's Palace residence of Lady Greaves and wondered what lay in store for her here today. She knew from long experience as a Family Liaison Officer that there were generally five stages of grief that a bereaved person went through – the times between each stage varying considerably, from days to weeks to months.

The stages, although not necessarily linear, were defined as: denial; anger; bargaining; depression; acceptance.

After the reception she and Roy Grace had had from Lady Greaves just two days ago, Sweeney was surprised when the door opened and she was greeted as if the very recent widow was actually pleased to see her. As if she had fast-tracked all the stages to reach *acceptance*.

Lady Greaves was similarly dressed to before, in black: 'widow's weeds', Sweeney thought, the old phrase sounding a bit irreverent in her mind. But it was often these little snippets of gallows humour that helped get her through the grim tasks her role demanded.

Lady Greaves' grey hair was styled as the last time, as if she had just come from the hairdresser, and she wore make-up that was heavily applied. But Sweeney took it as a positive sign she was taking care of her appearance. She followed her through into the drawing room they had been in two days earlier. The roll-top desk in the corner was now opened up and she saw a pile of letters, all, judging by the ones she could see from the opened envelopes, handwritten. Letters of condolence.

After instructing the maid to get coffee for two, when they were settled on facing sofas, Lady Greaves quizzed Sweeney on the police progress in the investigation.

'We have one very good witness, Lady Greaves,' she answered.

'I hope your team are not pursuing the theory of Peregrine being the target?'

'Well, the thing is, a murder enquiry is partly a process of elimination,' Polly Sweeney said with her usual tact.

The maid appeared with the coffee and they waited in silence until she had departed. Then Lady Greaves said, 'Quite so.'

Sweeney, remaining pleasant, said, 'I'd like you to help me in every way you can. I plan to interview you now and will record the details on my laptop on a statement form, which I will ask you to read and sign as an accurate record. This information needs to be accurate to the best of your knowledge as you may be asked to give evidence at any subsequent trial.'

After a moment's hesitation, the widow nodded.

Polly gave her a reassuring smile before continuing. 'Lady Greaves, what I need to know from you is more about your husband's background. He was in the Navy, correct?'

'He was, on a Short Service Commission. He spent much of his career there in Navy Intelligence.'

'Could he ever in his service career have fallen out badly with someone? For instance, was he ever involved in any courts martial where someone might have held a grudge against him?'

She shook her head vigorously. 'No – absolutely not – nothing of that—'

Then she stopped in mid-sentence. And for the first time Sweeney spotted a chink of self-doubt.

'He did spend some time on attachment with the Government Communications HQ. Would that make him a spy?' she asked, jokingly. 'Perry loved codes – and cryptic puzzles. He would do the *Times* crossword every day and got annoyed if it took him more than ten minutes.' She laughed, drily. 'He kept a notebook – well, more of a diary – and he wrote everything in that in code – codes were a bit of a hobby of his.' She fell silent for a moment, as though she was struggling with a thought she couldn't process. Then she said, 'I don't know if I should even tell you this as it is only going to feed your misplaced theory.'

Sweeney said nothing. Lady Greaves picked up her dainty bone china coffee cup and sipped. Then she said, 'It was about two weeks ago, Peregrine came home in a very disturbed frame of mind. He told me that he'd heard something astonishing. Utterly astonishing. So astonishing he just did not want to believe it – could not believe it.' She fell silent again.

After some moments, Sweeney prompted her. 'Did he tell you anything more?'

'He said he was going to his study to write it up in his diary. In code, of course. I asked him to tell me what it was, but he said that if it was true, it would be utterly explosive. Then he said he could not believe it was true and he didn't want to set off any kind of rumour mill.'

'And he still wouldn't tell you?'

'You need to understand that Peregrine was a principled man, honoured to serve the late Queen and now their current Majesties. As well as being a very private man. He'd often get a bee in his bonnet about one thing or another in the Royal Household, but he never liked to talk about issues until after they were resolved. I used to beg him to share things with me, but it simply wasn't his nature. He always used to quote that old Royal Navy maxim: *Loose lips sink ships.*'

'You have his diary?' Sweeney asked.

'It's in his study.'

'Would you let us borrow it?'

Margot Greaves shrugged. 'I don't see why not. But you'd need a damned good code-breaker to read it. I've had a go – I enjoy a bit of Sudoku, all that stuff. But I've never been able to finish a *Times* crossword, let alone decipher a page of his diary.' She gave a wry smile. 'He could have recorded all kinds of affairs in it. And I wouldn't have had a clue!'

'Let's hope he didn't,' Polly Sweeney said, and smiled back as she continued the interview.

'He wasn't that kind of a man,' Margot Greaves retorted. 'Trust me. All he cared about was his duty to The King and The Queen. He was that rarest of people – a truly good human being.'

46

Friday 24 November 2023

There was a game Lorraine McKnight played some nights, when she lay awake in the small hours, worried, her brain whirring, unable to get back to sleep. These sleepless episodes were happening more and more just recently, and they had started, she supposed, soon after the renovations to Buckingham Palace had commenced.

A trustee of the National Gallery and the former Head of Fine Art at Sotheby's, she had been the Director of the Royal Collection for the past eight years. In this role she was responsible for all the paintings and miniatures, prints, drawings, sculptures, furniture, ceramics, glass, silver, gold, jewels, books, manuscripts, textiles, photographs and historic weapons and armour held by the Royal Family and curated by the Royal Collection Trust. There were well over one million items, spread over thirteen palaces and houses, and it was one of the most important art collections in the world.

Her game, rather than counting sheep, was to try to tot up the combined value of everything she was responsible for in her current role. And she was responsible for every single item. After just a few minutes it usually did work and she would be fast asleep. But not last night. She'd lain awake for a long time thinking back to some hours earlier when she'd discovered Sir Jason Finch down in the vaults where some of the Royal Collection's most valuable works of art and pieces of jewellery were being stored for safety during the renovations.

He'd seemed embarrassed by her presence, almost like a schoolboy caught in the act of doing something furtive. And, she had reflected repeatedly during the long night, he seemed to have gone to unnecessary lengths to explain – almost as if he had a pre-prepared excuse for being down there. But as, effectively, the Chief Finance Officer, the completely trusted Keeper of the Privy Purse did not need an excuse – he was entitled to go anywhere in the damned Palace that he chose.

Now, at 8.55 a.m., after having walked their boys to school, the statuesque forty-seven-year-old was on her morning commute, pedalling the ancient sit-up-and-beg bike she loved, in breezy sunshine across Hyde Park.

It took her twenty minutes from their home in the less fashionable part of Notting Hill she shared with her husband, the boys and a dachshund called Tilly (who was recovering from slipped disc surgery), towards where she would take her life in her hands, and cycle around a section of Marble Arch rather than use the underpass. From there she would whizz down the Constitution Hill cycle path towards the entrance – and sanctuary – of Buckingham Palace, or a short distance on to her office in St James's Palace.

It was funny, she was thinking today, how you could both love and hate your job at the same time. She loved that she got to work with so many stunning paintings, the Vermeer and the Canalettos being among her favourites, as well as so many truly extraordinary objets d'art, many gifted to the Royal Family over countless generations – wedding presents, state visit cultural gifts, and in the past, noblemen seeking favours.

But she hated that the renovations, which had started seven years ago and were part of a ten-year programme – albeit under the very able control of the highly respected, and fun, Master of the Royal Household – had made a nightmare of her inventory.

When she had first joined, she could have stated with confidence, if she'd been required to, exactly where every single one of those million-plus items were. Now it had become a logistical nightmare, with stuff being moved all over the place – sometimes by the craftsmen in the Palace – and frequently without her authorizing it. And, in addition to that, wherever renovations were taking place, the ever-present risk of fire increased, especially in such an old building as the Palace. And she was the one who had to make the decisions about which items should be saved first in – God forbid – the event of such a calamity. All of these had to be listed and labelled with a Salvage sticker. Memories of the fire at Windsor Castle in 1992, which destroyed one hundred rooms and countless treasured items, still haunted the Royal Collection team.

On Monday she'd at least been able to respond competently to Sir Tommy Magellan-Lacey, when he had called her to say that The King was wondering where his beloved Landseer, which normally hung in the breakfast room at Clarence House, had gone. She was able to inform him that the painting had been taken down – as it was routinely – to be checked for condition, to ensure it wasn't suffering any damage from light or humidity in its current location.

But she had been on a lot shakier ground when, on Wednesday, The Queen had called her to ask why the Vermeer that was normally in the Picture Gallery had been replaced with a Fragonard. Not only was she unable to tell Her Majesty why the painting had been taken down, but in her subsequent enquiries, Lorraine was unable to even locate it.

It would turn up, she knew, as would several other high-value items that had gone on the missing list recently – dismissing the fleeting thought that Jason Finch could possibly have had anything to do with that. She just hoped that Tommy didn't suddenly go on the warpath, and come to her demanding to know where they were. Hopefully he had enough on his plate right now in the aftermath of Monday's nightmare events.

PETER JAMES

But she would make it her very first task today to locate the missing Vermeer from the Picture Gallery and get that Landseer back on the wall in Clarence House as an absolute priority.

47

Friday 24 November 2023

'Oh yes,' the diamond cutter muttered and nodded, peering through his monocular loupe at the magnificent oval diamond on the small velvet pad.

He laid down the loupe and put his glasses back on. They were tiny, round and black, reminding her of the kind that might have been worn by a 1930s university professor.

The cutter was in his early seventies, slight and bald, dapperly dressed in a grey suit and knitted tie, and very self-assured. A force of nature, crackling with energy despite his years, just like the diamond, way older than both of them combined, which sparkled so intensely it looked almost alive and moving. He was lord of his small but rich domain, the narrow office with long viewing shelves – *diamonds did not need a big office*, he always said. It felt an oasis of calm here, two floors above London's Hatton Garden, the epicentre of the UK gem trade in the heart of busy, lunchtime-traffic-snarled Holborn.

'Oh yes,' he muttered again. And then a third time, nodding increasingly enthusiastically. His name was Gary van Damm, scion of a diamond trading and cutting dynasty. He only knew her as Mrs Smith. He didn't know her real name, never had and never asked, despite the fact they had been doing business for over a year – extremely good business!

Secrecy and trust, two of the platforms on which the global diamond trade was founded. All their communications were via the dark web and all his payments to her were in Bitcoin. Payments in the tens of thousands, hundreds of thousands and very occasionally even higher. As today would be.

'So nice to see one of these again,' he said. 'Granny's Chips! Or rather, to be strictly accurate, one of Granny's *Personal* Chips! Do you know the story?'

'I don't think I know the full story, no,' she replied.

'You are familiar with the legendary Cullinan diamond – the largest rough diamond ever found?'

'Of course. It was cut up and the two largest stones – known as Cullinan I and Cullinan II – are part of the Crown Jewels.'

'Correct. In 1905 the diamond came out of a mine in Cullinan, South Africa – it weighed 3,106 carats. And its colour was perfect. In today's money it would have been worth about thirty-seven million pounds.'

She raised her eyebrows.

'At that time the most famous diamond cutter in the world was a Dutchman called Joseph Asscher – actually a rival to my great-grandfather. His cutting process produced nine major stones from the Cullinan diamond, as well as ninety-six smaller ones, most of which are now part of the British Crown Jewels – such as that big stone you'll have seen in the Sceptre. But . . .' He raised a finger, giving a knowing smile. 'Some of the stones, of a very nice size indeed – this being one – fell between the cracks.'

'How did that happen?'

'No one is quite sure. The late Queen Elizabeth loved diamonds, as did her mother, and it's quite possible either of them – or indeed Queen Mary before them – held them back for personal use. And why not!'

'If you've got it, flaunt it!'

'But save the receipts!' he retorted with a grin.

In response to her puzzled frown, he explained, 'It's a Yiddish expression.'

'Ah!' She smiled. 'The two biggest remaining stones, Cullinan III and Cullinan IV, were made into a brooch by Queen Mary, and then handed down to her granddaughter Elizabeth – our late Queen.'

'Correct,' van Damm said. 'Hence the jokey moniker "Granny's Chips". Its value today is around sixty-five million pounds, if not more. The last time I saw it was in 1981. The late Queen, God bless her, wanted to wear it at the marriage of Prince Charles to Diana, but it had some slight damage – I was asked to polish the damage out. Which of course I did. But there's something that not many people know.' He smiled, raised a finger, and winked conspiratorially.

He looked down at the diamond and nodded again. 'This is truly something. To see this – Number 7 of Granny's Personal Chips – I can't even put a value on it yet.'

She smiled. 'So we will make a lot of money out of it?'

'Oh yes. A very nice amount indeed. On current prices, one carat today varies from two to twelve thousand pounds depending on the colour of the stone. And this is perfect. And it is close to three hundred and fifty carats!' He seemed in an uncharacteristically elated mood. 'You know the origin of the word "carat"?'

She shook her head. 'No, I should, but jewellery has always been my weaker area of knowledge.'

'Carob beans! The Greek name for the carob pod was *keration*. They discovered every carob seed weighed almost exactly the same – a fairly consistent 0.197 grams. The traders were able to use them as counterweights when buying diamonds, gold or gemstones.'

'Not a lot of people know that,' she said, mimicking Michael Caine. 'You're a mine of information today. So you have one of your oligarch or Far Eastern clients lined up for it?'

He shook his head, with an expression of mock horror. 'Dear lady, this stone is far too identifiable. Yes, one of my oligarchs would buy it, but he wouldn't pay top dollar because he knows he would struggle to sell it, without risking rather too many questions. Considering all the trouble you've gone to purloin it, and the potential earnings from it, we need to have it very subtly altered – re-cut it. Cosmetic surgery on an old lady, shall we call it?'

'And you can get that done?'

'Oh yes, but not here – we wouldn't want to take that risk. We need a – shall we say – *friendly* diamond cutter safely tucked away abroad. I have the right man in Mumbai. I'll just pop it in my jacket pocket and hop on a plane. Then we'll have to get it shipped to the Gemological Institute of America for assay – that has to be done on every stone above half a carat. After that, we're good to go. Put it out to auction to my network of private buyers. Magnificent diamond with possible royal provenance. What's not to love?'

'Your expenses, perhaps? Flights to Mumbai? New York?'

Gary van Damm shrugged. 'Small beer. And I'm afraid here's another expense, and this does not come cheap.' He reached down under his desk and produced what looked, for an instant, the identical twin of the diamond on the velvet pad. It was in a small black box. 'A very fine replica of the stone you've brought in, don't you think?'

He placed them side by side and then performed a magician's sleight of hand trick, switching them so fast, so many times, that she lost track of which was which. And when he removed his hands she could not tell, at first look, which was the real one and which the fake.

He gave her a questioning look.

'It's good! An amazing job just from those close-up images I sent you,' she said.

'Good enough, right?'

It was good enough. It would go into the box of Granny's Personal Chips, and perhaps lie there for decades, if not centuries, so long as no one had any reason to question the authenticity. Just like so many of the paintings and precious objects in Buckingham Palace they had taken and replaced with forgeries in recent times. 'I'm honestly not sure which is which!'

He picked up one with his fingers and laid it back on the velvet pad. 'This one.'

She could see it now, the full magnificence of it: an individual presence even, an almost magical quality. It looked brighter, *truer* than its pale imposter. 'Awesome!' she said. 'It really is quite awesome and fitting for our retirement plan!'

He nodded and interlocked his hands, as if he himself was locked in thought. A faraway expression on his face faded after some moments into a dreamy smile. 'Yes. Yes it is. I'll tell you something: you've brought me some very fine diamonds in the past, but this – this is the one to die for.'

48

Friday 24 November 2023

Jon Smoke's mobile rang. The caller's number was withheld – which indicated it was probably one of his team or a member of the Royal Household. On the rare occasions when either gave out their number, it would be to someone trusted and on a strictly need-to-know basis. For everyone else on the outside, the starting point would be a landline call to the main Buckingham Palace switchboard.

He was seated on a wooden chair in the white wooden kiosk outside the Garden Entrance to the West Wing, where he had gone for his lunch break, and was swigging lukewarm coffee from a flask. It was a place the RaSPs sometimes used for their rest periods instead of their common room in the Royal Mews. Through the window he had a magnificent view over the Palace lawns towards the lake. One of the gardeners was grinding across on a very old-fashioned ride-on gang mower, carving beautiful stripes.

One thing for sure, this palace, with its well-tended grounds, wasn't exactly a shithole. And he should know, he'd worked in some real shitholes after leaving the Army. After joining the Met Police, he'd ended up on the Armed Response Unit attached to the Violent Crimes Task Force, dealing with knife and gun crime in the worst parts of East Croydon and environs. A few words in the right ears from his old army commanding officer, Jason Finch, had seen him transferred to the Royalty and Specialist Protection team. And with it, the opportunity for a very cushy future had presented itself. But that was how life worked, wasn't it? One day you got a smack in the mouth. Another day, you got a box of chocolates. Or a beautiful oval diamond on a velvet pad.

It had taken him a long time in therapy, after returning from Afghanistan, to even consider the idea of a relationship. But Chloe, an estate agent, who he'd first met in the local pub, understood and had his back. Maybe she had it too much, he worried. She thought he was a better person than he really was. But, hey. Pick your battles, right?

She knew him just as a copper who protected the royals. She didn't know that he was part of a very small group of people within the Royal Household who had recently become extremely wealthy. She was aware he intended to move permanently away from England to a life in the sun, and she was happy about that, and about the prospect of a new start in Dubai. She liked the idea of setting up her own estate agency in a country that was always warm – with potentially a large supply of wealthy clients.

But for some months now he had begun to tire of her. Nothing he could put a finger on, just the spark had gone. Time to move on.

Besides, he liked Dubai for an altogether different reason – one he couldn't tell her about. Dubai was one of the few places in the world that had both sunshine and a pleasant lifestyle, if you have the means – but, even more importantly, a little neglectful in their extradition treaty with the UK.

He took a suck on his tobacco-flavoured vape, inhaled deeply, then blew the smoke out as he answered the phone with a curt, 'Yes?'

A petulant voice said, 'I know what you've done.'

He recognized the voice immediately. The caller had made no attempt to disguise it. And Jon Smoke was in no hurry to respond. Instead, he took another drag on his vape while contemplating this curve ball that had come at him out of the blue.

Another smack in the face.

Back in Afghanistan, after Scottie's horrific death, he'd had his own way of dealing with further smacks in the mouth. From then on while on patrol he took no prisoners. There'd been a night when they'd confronted five Taliban fighters. Still crazed with fury over Scottie, he'd made sure none of them had survived. He'd had help from another soldier who also had skin in that game. Her name was Rose Cadoret. She had killed two of them herself.

'I know what all of you have done and I know who all of you are.'

'Is that so, Geoffrey?' Smoke replied.

'I'm owed a Royal Victorian Medal. I've been passed over for it three times now. It was awarded to a *woman* last week, for God's sake! She's done nothing compared to the service to Their Majesties that I've given. Claire Tavender. I mean, really?'

'You feel you're owed a medal?'

'I don't *feel* I'm owed a medal,' Geoffrey Bailey said. 'I *am* owed a medal. Fifteen years. I'm absolutely fed up seeing just about everyone else in the Royal Household get one award or another, and yet me, I get nothing. I'm due to retire in six months – and I bloody well want a medal. I deserve it, surely? I was Page of the Backstairs to the late Queen for ten years. Now I'm serving Their Majesties in the role of footman, and yet I'm feeling ignored. You have the ability to make it happen, and don't try to deny it!'

'Geoffrey, I'm just a humble Royal Protection Officer. I don't have any sway.'

'And I'm a banana, Jon Smoke. The choice is yours. Use your influence to get me that medal or I'll blow your whole nasty scam wide open. I know all about "Granny's Personal Chips". Just in case you're wondering how I know, let me explain. The *late* Sir Peregrine and I were *very* good friends – if you understand what I'm saying?'

THE HAWK IS DEAD

Smoke did understand. He'd heard from a very good source – too good a source – that Sir Peregrine enjoyed the company of both sexes. But really, with this toxic little man?

And yet, now he was hearing this, he was remembering. Peregrine's office was directly opposite his St James's Palace residence. Sir Tommy had informed him some months ago that both he and his wife had noticed the light on in Sir Peregrine's office at strange, late and irregular hours, and were a little concerned. Sir Peregrine had never been one for working one hour more than was absolutely necessary. One of his team had gone to the office to investigate and had been met by a very flushed and angry Sir Peregrine giving him short shrift and a story about working on an urgent speech for The King.

He thought fast, needing to buy time to think this through further. A big red flag was waving in his face. 'If I can get you that medal, would you be happy?'

'Get me that and I would be delirious!'

'OK,' Smoke said. 'I know who to talk to.'

'Of course you do.'

'Tomorrow night, meet me by the Garden Entrance at 7 p.m., sharp. I'll have the medal.'

'Of course you will!'

49

Friday 24 November 2023

'OK,' Roy Grace asked, 'anyone here good at puzzles?'

It was 5.30 p.m. He stared around the conference room at the thirty members of his team crammed in here for the evening briefing. Behind him were three large screens showing the crime scene photographs of Sir Peregrine, his family tree, and the association chart listing Buckingham Palace staff and all others with whom the dead man had had dealings.

With his team expanding to over fifty people by the end of the weekend, future briefings would have to take place in a bigger venue, and he'd taken steps for that to happen.

A few people raised their hands, including Norman Potting, Polly Sweeney, Luke Stanstead, EJ Boutwood and DI Brent Dean from the Met Police.

'How about cryptic crosswords?' Grace asked.

All five raised their hands again as well as a few more.

Grace held up a sheaf of papers. 'What I have here are photocopies of a number of pages from Sir Peregrine's diary, which are written in code. From the date, we can establish this is the last entry he made very shortly prior to his death.'

He had their full attention.

'Polly has told us his widow, Lady Greaves, believes he wrote these recent entries in code because he had real concerns – which he wouldn't share with her – about someone in the Royal Household who was up to something suspicious. Someone who

THE HAWK IS DEAD

might therefore also be behind Sir Peregrine's murder. Maybe more than one person. I want you all to take a look and see if anything pops into your mind on how to figure this code out. I've tried my damnedest for the past hour but I can't make head or tail of it.'

He pointed at one of the screens on the wall, clicked the remote and an image of the first page came up. Maths had never been his strong point, and he had no real clue where to start with the blocks of numbers and letters that appeared.

A row of numbers ran across the page finishing with two letters, as they did on every page he had looked at in Sir Peregrine's diary. The ones they all saw now were:

2 3 4 5 6 /7/ 0 0 1 2 3 4 5 6 7 8 9 CH

Underneath were twenty-three rows of letters, in blocks and in columns. The top line was:

L Q C K P /H/ UR KX ES FJ TD AM CI WL VP QY ON BH ZG

Below that was another row of figures, separated by a divide.

8 3 0 2 7 4 / 0 1 2 3 4 5 7 8 9

Below them were five columns of rows of letters and numbers. The top one read:

7 / W U C H A 1 49 64 83 28 36 07 01 99 48 39

There were further columns with combinations of letters of the alphabet and numbers after those.

Desperate though Grace was to get the code cracked, he did take a certain perverse pleasure in seeing the baffled looks on all his team member's faces. Maybe he wasn't as rubbish at maths as he feared, after all?

The Met Detective Inspector, Brent Dean, raised a hand. 'Boss, the Army might be a good place to get help if we're stuck; Sir Peregrine was a military man – in Naval Intelligence, I understand – this could well be a code he was familiar with back in the time of his service. Although I would suggest the first port of call be the National Crime Agency – their Major Crime Investigative

Support Team will have contacts. They keep a register of expert witnesses.'

Grace looked at the sharply suited, shorn-headed and confident – borderline arrogant – detective. 'I've dealt with them before, but thank you, Brent. I can't go through a load of bureaucracy from them. You know what will happen if we ask them? Some time next week we'll be sent a bunch of CVs of people from the private sector – academics, practitioners, former cops, you name it, who might be able to help. The stakes are too high. We haven't got the luxury of time, we can't wait until next week in the vague hope we may find a code-breaker – we need to know right now what Sir Peregrine said.'

The DI nodded, looking pensive rather than chastened. 'Maybe GCHQ would be a better bet, sir.'

'Have you ever had dealings with GCHQ?'

The DI shook his head. 'No, boss.'

'I'll tell you how it works,' Grace said. 'The protocol is that we'd have to put our request to them through Counter Terrorism Policing South East – CTPSE for *long*.'

There was a titter of laughter. Acronyms in the police force had pretty much become a language in themselves – and because they were constantly changing, they were a bane of life for everyone. He paused for a brief moment, then continued.

'They might or might not send us back a code and an inbox address. We'd then have to send our request using that code – and CTPSE would transfer it onto the National Secure Network, from where it would then go on to its trusted partners. It's just possible, if you are very lucky, that sometime afterwards – days, weeks, maybe months – you might get an intelligence log disseminated to you from an unknown source with the code partially or totally cracked. In view of this being top-level national importance, we might get a response in weeks rather than months,' Grace said.

Dean nodded. 'Sounds like you've been there before, boss. I do appreciate that standard territorial policing doesn't have easy access to GCHQ or MI5 – but this is, as we all know, a very exceptional situation. I believe you would find them more co-operative than you think.'

'Maybe,' Grace said acerbically. 'But I'm not prepared to take that risk.'

'Chief,' Norman Potting cut in. 'Might be worth a word with DCI Westinghouse.' The detective was one of the four SIOs, along with Grace, on his Major Crime Team.

'Detective *Superintendent*,' Grace corrected him. 'Andy Westinghouse has just been promoted.'

'And very well deserved it is too,' Glenn Branson commented.

There was a general murmur of assent.

'I think you'll be working for him soon, and not the other way round, boss,' Branson quipped, 'the way he's been rising through the ranks.'

'I can think of worse people to have as a boss,' Grace said with a grin, then turned to Potting. 'Why do you think Andy Westinghouse can help us, Norman?'

'He used to be in the Army,' Potting said. 'He and I worked together some years back. He told me one day that he came top in the Signals exam when he was at the officer training course in Sandhurst. He said that he was very good at cracking codes.'

'Seriously?' Grace asked.

'Scout's honour, chief!' Potting held up his right arm and gave the signal, covering the nail of his little finger and raising the middle three fingers.

Grace thanked him, telling him he would call the newly promoted Detective Superintendent as soon as the briefing meeting was finished.

50

Friday 24 November 2023

Andy Westinghouse answered his phone on the first ring. Grace began by congratulating him on his promotion.

'That's good of you, sir, but I suspect you had a little to do with it?'

'You did it on pure merit, Andy!'

'Hmmmn! Well, I'm very grateful, and I appreciate you calling.'

'Actually, there's something else. I've just learned that you know a bit about codes?'

'Well yes, but probably a bit rusty. Have you got a map of buried treasure?' he jested.

'Nothing quite so much fun, Andy.' Grace explained about the diary, and the urgency – as well as the options the Met detective, Brent Dean, had suggested.

'Well, I've always loved codes, Roy – when I joined the Army and graduated from Sandhurst I was intending to join the Royal Signals, until I realized that the infantry was where I really wanted to be. So this is an ex-Naval officer who has written the code. Quite possibly he uses a military one. I wonder if it's in BATCO.'

'Batco?' Grace queried.

Westinghouse spelled it out. 'B-A-T-C-O. It stands for Battle Code. That was what we used for encrypting any military messages on the Clansman net – the radio comms system up to the early 2000s before Bowman took over. What time period did Sir Peregrine serve in the Forces?'

'He was there in the early 2000s.'

'That fits. BATCO – if that's what you have – is cumbersome and time consuming. If you can ping a page of it over, I'll be able to tell you.'

Grace sent it while they were still talking. Moments later, Westinghouse said, 'Got it! Give me a moment.'

Less than a minute later, Westinghouse said, 'Yes, it is BATCO but a variation – and it'll be a bugger to decipher.'

'Could you do that for us?' Grace asked.

'How many pages of it do you have?'

'Eight.'

'I'm pretty confident I could crack it – I'm one of those sad people who's a hobbyist cryptographer – but it would take me a good couple of days, if not longer.'

'That's quicker than any of our other options. I could live with that, Andy.'

'The problem is, sir, I wouldn't be able to start until at least Sunday – I'm Silver on Op Archer. We're about to raid and probably seize a container ship in Newhaven Harbour with fifteen million pounds' worth of cocaine on board – in two hours' time.'

'I'm sorry, yes, I'd forgotten, Andy. I've been somewhat absorbed in Op Asset. Can you think of someone who could start right away – tonight? A cryptologist? Anyone from your Army days, someone retired perhaps who'd be up for a challenge – and protecting the Royal Family?'

'That would take time too, sir. I could put you in touch with the Army Intel Corps – they have people who could have a good run out at the code – but . . .' He fell momentarily silent.

'But?' Grace prompted.

'There would be issues. The Army will want to know the reasons you want the code deciphered – and then they might want to cover up or minimize a former member of the Armed Forces' behaviour. There's a bit of a fraternal loyalty in the Forces that's similar to the posh British school system. You know what they say about public schools?'

'No, tell me?'

'They might throw you out, but they'll never let you down. The Armed Forces are a bit like that too. If there's an issue with a former officer, their regiment will be the first to close ranks. If there's a whiff of the notion of corruption, the Army, Navy and Air Force will want to cover up, or at the least minimize their former member's behaviour.'

'I don't think there's any suggestion of Sir Peregrine being corrupt,' Grace replied. 'We think he may have stumbled across something – the thing that led to him being murdered.'

'I completely understand, sir. But just knowing how the Army works – I'm worried that going down their Intel Corps route won't give you the speed you need. But I have just had a thought. Remember DC Scroope?'

'Denton Scroope?'

'That's him – a Surrey detective from Godalming, near Guildford, but I think he moved to Ringmer a couple of years ago when he retired. He was on the Major Crime Team before being transferred to Professional Standards.'

'I remember him,' Grace said. And he did remember the man, very clearly.

Denton Scroope, a pedantic DC, who had been born – as Norman Potting had described it – with a brain the size of Google, and an equally massive sense-of-humour bypass. He would finish the *Telegraph* crossword in under ten minutes, daily without fail, during whatever tea or lunch break he had. Grace knew also that Scroope had at one time during his police career been seconded to GCHQ. In a rare unguarded moment, Scroope had let it slip that he had been on a team that intercepted and decoded terrorist communications.

Scroope had been fond of telling everyone that it was one of

THE HAWK IS DEAD

his ancestors who had signed Charles I's death warrant. Although he was always quick to say he was a very distant and remote relative – and in a rare display of something approaching humour would add that he was on more of a twig than a branch of that particular family tree.

'I'm still in touch with him,' Westinghouse said. 'We exchange the occasional puzzle – I'll give you his home and mobile numbers.'

Thanking Westinghouse and ending the call, Grace immediately dialled Scroope's mobile. As he did so, he had a mental image of an imperious aardvark with spectacles. Scroope's pompous, precise voice as he answered matched the image perfectly.

After Grace explained what he needed, Scroope responded, deadly serious and with no hint of irony. He spoke slowly, as he always had, in a dry, pedantic manner, leaving a gap between words that was a fraction longer than necessary, as if addressing a simpleton. 'I think I could be your man for this. I think you've come to the right person, Roy. Very fortuitously, for you, less so for me, due to the vagaries of the mind of *She-Who-Must-Be-Obeyed*, my weekend plans have been rescheduled, so I will be able to get straight on to it.'

Grace put the phone down, silently detesting the demeaning way Scroope talked about his wife, something he still heard way too often these days. He emailed the diary pages to him straight away, asking him to call as soon as he'd had a look. Less than five minutes later, Scroope called him back.

'Interesting, Roy. Challenging. This is definitely a bastardization of BATCO. I will do what I can. But I need you to know I will only be able to proceed at the speed of a tortoise.'

'I'd prefer a cheetah or a gazelle, Denton.'

'I don't do either of those animals. Just tortoises,' he retorted, somewhat cryptically.

PETER JAMES

'The tortoise and the hare,' Grace said. 'Got it!'

'No, Roy,' Scroope's humourless voice responded, the *pedantic* dial turned up to maximum. 'Only tortoises.'

51

Saturday 25 November 2023

A few years ago, after being shot by a criminal he was chasing through a network of underground tunnels, Roy Grace had been to see a psychotherapist. It was at Cleo's insistence because she feared, after he had woken night after night from terrible nightmares, that he might be suffering post-traumatic stress. It was the second time in his career he had been shot. The first, in his very early days, chasing a bank robber. Fortunately, both times he had only received a leg wound but therapy had helped him on each occasion.

The one thing he had taken away from the more recent course of sessions he had attended was something the therapist had said: *Almost everything will work again if you unplug it – including you.*

Downtime. Everyone needed it. But in those first few crucial weeks of a murder enquiry, that was never an option – at least not for him as the Senior Investigating Officer, although he always tried to ensure that members of his team got enough rest and crucial days off.

Glenn Branson had told him, after the briefing last night, that he looked shattered and he should try to get a good night's sleep. Have a lie-in, he'd urged, and spend some time with his family in the morning – even if just a few hours – and he would cover for him. Grace had agreed, reluctantly, and on the condition that he reciprocated on Sunday, and Glenn took some time out to spend with his wife, Siobhan.

But, attractive as the notion of a *good night's sleep* had been to the exhausted Detective Superintendent, reality had other ideas. He'd fallen asleep within minutes of climbing into bed, before the opening credits of a new television series Cleo had heard was brilliant had finished rolling. But a few hours later, at 1.30 a.m., he was wide awake, his brain churning. So he reached for his phone to check his email, in case there was anything back from Denton Scroope. There wasn't.

The enormity of the responsibility on his shoulders was affecting him in a way that no previous case had. He'd always prided himself on being non-judgemental. Every victim he encountered had once been someone's child, and perhaps someone's lover. He treated every case equally.

Or had done until now.

It was impossible to pretend to himself this was just another job, that it was a case like any other. Quite apart from the media frenzy that was showing no signs of abating, with shouty headlines around the globe still proclaiming the assassination attempt on The Queen, he had twice-daily phone calls with Magellan-Lacey, enabling the Master to update both The King and The Queen, as well as a daily call with the Chief Constable to update her. The daily press briefings were held with the largest turnouts he had ever experienced. In addition he felt the hot breath of Nigel Downing on his neck, the ACC hovering like the proverbial cat on a hot tin roof, desperate for any development, any scrap of news, any bone he could throw to the Chief Constable.

He'd lain awake during the small hours of every night this week, fretting over what he might be overlooking. And at the same time, feeling torn. Part of him still wondering if he would have been more sensible not to have fought for primacy on this enquiry, and let the Met get on with it. But deep down he knew he wanted the job.

Passing the buck just wasn't in his DNA. He was all too well aware that just like there were good and bad lawyers and doctors, there were good and bad detectives. And the Met Detective Superintendent Greg Mosse, who had argued that it was he who should be the SIO, was a classic example of a bad one. An arrogant one, with tunnel vision. And the condescending Met DI he'd had foisted on him, Brent Dean, further convinced him he'd made the right decision.

But Grace knew he needed to be careful not to fall into that very same trap himself. It was vital to constantly re-examine his own hypothesis and ask himself that question: *What if he was wrong, and The Queen really had been the intended target?* With the consequence that her would-be assassin was still out there and preparing their next attempt?

It was normal on all major investigations where a prime suspect was not identified quickly for the SIOs to have another detective review the case at regular intervals. Some SIOs resented the intrusion but Grace welcomed it – and more than ever on this case. He knew he wasn't infallible and with so much at stake he dreaded the thought that he had missed something.

The first review of Op Asset had been yesterday, and it had been carried out by Detective Superintendent John Smith. After a day of diligently reading Grace's Policy Book, checking the lines of enquiry and looking at all the actions, he'd concluded that Grace was covering every possible angle.

Lying awake now, his brain was churning again through what he and the team knew so far, trying to reassure himself that his assumptions were valid, repeatedly going back over everything he had to date.

The assurance from the ballistics expert that there was no way the shooter could have missed The Queen – if she had been the target – by such a wide margin was extremely significant.

The understanding of how the Royal Train came to be derailed – by a deliberate act, involving at least one accomplice, of pushing a length of rail across the tracks. That combined with the shooter bore all the hallmarks of a carefully planned conspiracy.

The anti-monarchy protestors had been under the Met Police Counter Terrorism team microscope since the shooting, and the Met's report delivered to him yesterday concluded it was highly unlikely they would have been involved in such a well-planned operation – but it was impossible to rule out that a splinter group or some extremist faction might have been involved.

Separate intelligence from a specialist Surrey and Sussex Counter Terrorism branch had concluded there was nothing on this particular group of protestors to suggest that there was a faction among them violent enough to commit murder and they had found no connections with any of them who rode motorbikes and had a service background.

But Grace knew that they weren't the only people who could be a threat to either of Their Majesties. The footman, Geoffrey Bailey, whom Jack Alexander had raised a flag about, might be one potential lead. Someone with a grievance who felt he'd been passed over for a medal. Undervalued. It seemed unlikely, but he looked forward to hearing the result of Jack's interview with him on Monday.

One of his many actions had been to draft in extra resources across the Sussex Force. The Chief Constable of Surrey had done the same. Outside Enquiry Teams were deployed across both counties, interviewing everyone who had posted anything on social media that the Digital Support Unit thought might be of concern.

Following Sarah Stratten's sighting of the motocross bike and rider, footage from all speed cameras, ANPR and motorway cameras was being examined for any sightings of a motorcycle containing the two digits of the licence plate she had so far recalled. That information had been given out at the press conference yesterday.

THE HAWK IS DEAD

Grace hoped the woman might remember more, during her further interview, which had been arranged for Monday. He suspected the plates would be false, but if they could identify the make of motorcycle, that would narrow the field significantly. Many Roads Policing officers were petrol-heads, and often keen motorcyclists, and the description Sarah Stratten had given of the type of bike and the colour, black with a splash of red, had already resulted in some informed suggestions of the possible make coming from RPU officers. Yamaha and Honda were top of the list. That was too broad to be of immediate help, but it might be useful information later.

He derived his strongest comfort from Polly Sweeney's report from her meeting with Lady Greaves.

'It was about two weeks ago, Peregrine came home in a very disturbed frame of mind. He told me that he'd heard something astonishing. Utterly astonishing. So incredible he just did not want to believe it – could not believe it. He said he was going to his study to write it up in his diary. In code, of course. I asked him to tell me what it was, but he said that if it was true, it would be utterly explosive. Then he said he could not believe it was true and he didn't want to set off any kind of rumour mill.'

Shortly after 3 a.m., while Cleo slept soundly beside him – something he really envied about her, she truly slept the sleep of the innocent – feeling totally wired, he slipped out of bed, as carefully as he could not to wake her, pulled on his dressing gown, and padded downstairs to the kitchen.

Neither Humphrey nor Kyla – an adorable golden doodle, their recent acquisition from the Brighton RSPCA – in their respective baskets, batted an eyelid as he switched on the lights, turning the dimmer down as low as possible. He filled the kettle, hit the switch, and perched at the breakfast bar, alongside Molly's high chair. Then he leaned forward with his head in his hands, toying with the thought that had woken him for the second time tonight.

The very positive thought.

The more he went over what Lady Greaves had said, the more certain he was that his hypothesis was correct.

The Private Secretary, by all accounts, was an honourable man and a loyal servant to both his bosses. If Sir Peregrine had had even the slightest suspicion that there was something as massive as a plot to kill The Queen, surely he could not have contained himself? He would have had to tell people – and his wife, for sure. Grace knew that he would have told Cleo in the same circumstances. With something as big as that knowledge, he would have had to unburden himself – anyone would.

He was desperate to know what Sir Peregrine had written in his diary, and wondered if he had made the right decision trusting the deciphering to the strange, quirky Scroope. But, he convinced himself, he trusted Andy Westinghouse's judgement.

The kettle flicked off. Grace brewed himself a mug of tea, then sat back down, staring for some moments at the blackness of the window in front of him. The blackness of the night beyond. But inside the blackness of his mind, it felt like the clarity of dawn was finally breaking. If Sir Peregrine had known there was going to be an attempt on The Queen's life on that train journey to Brighton, he would have alerted everyone, immediately, and no way would he have allowed her to make that journey. Surely? None of this would have happened. No way. The whole trip would have been cancelled.

So it had to be something else. But what?

Had Sir Peregrine stumbled across something going on within the Palace that had made him a target? Something he was about to expose? Something that required him to be silenced – eliminated?

Might he have been aware that what he had learned had put his life in grave danger? Was that why he had written it all down in code and not simply told someone about it?

THE HAWK IS DEAD

Or could it be that he had something to hide, himself? Was he compromised in some way? Could someone have been blackmailing him?

Polly had reported that Lady Greaves said her husband did not seem scared, more outraged and concerned about the political ramifications within the Royal Household – which did not sound like the behaviour of a blackmail victim.

If Sir Peregrine had discovered something, then whatever that was, the scale of it had to be massive – so big as to warrant his killers going to great lengths to cover up that he was the intended victim? An elaborate plan to derail the Royal Train and make it look like Queen Camilla was the target?

The notion might seem absurd. And yet it was the only thing that actually made sense to Roy Grace about the events of Monday.

He carried his mug upstairs to his den, opened his laptop and made a series of notes to enter into his Policy Book when he was back in the office later in the day.

Elaborate plan to derail the train and shoot Sir Peregrine – suggesting something very big at stake. What? A scandal that could damage the Monarchy? Sexual or something financial? Involving who? Could it be as high as the Lord Chamberlain or the Keeper of the Privy Purse?

He was so tired, he realized, he was going round in circles. Closing his laptop he walked along the landing and crawled, totally spent, back into bed. And fell asleep instantly again.

It wasn't the crowing of their rooster, Billy Big Balls, as Cleo had named the strutting grey and red arrogant little bastard, nor the noise of the dawn chorus outside their window, that woke him just a couple of hours later. It was the buzzing of the thoughts inside his head that sprang him wide awake with the absolute certainty that he was right about Sir Peregrine being the target, and had been from the start.

But at the same time he was mindful of the fact that he needed to find evidence that would speak for itself. Thanks to Polly having worked her charm on Sir Peregrine's widow and obtaining the diary, he was hopeful he would find at least some pieces of that jigsaw puzzle before the end of the weekend. It wasn't just his immediate boss, ACC Downing, who was waiting for answers. Nor the Chief Constable of Sussex or the Police and Crime Commissioner. It wasn't even The King of England or The Queen.

From the newsfeed that poured in relentlessly, it was much of the entire world.

Waiting for answers from him.

52

Saturday 25 November 2023

Grace eased himself up in bed gently, trying not to disturb Cleo. Feeling barely refreshed at all, but well aware that any further sleep was not going to happen, he reached for his phone. Still nothing from Denton Scroope. Then, out of dutiful habit, he checked the daily Chief Officer's Briefing Sheet. There was nothing to trouble him on it, and he said a silent prayer to the god of Senior Investigating Officers' Downtime that there were no major incidents or developments overnight to distract him, or call on his already stretched resources.

Outside, Billy Big Balls crowed. There were mornings when he loved the sound of that rooster, and there were mornings when he could have cheerfully strangled him. Today was one of the latter.

He slipped out of bed, and five minutes later, dressed in his running kit, holding Kyla on her lead and with Humphrey alongside, went out into the garden and opened the rear gate. As Humphrey bounded off ahead a short distance up the hill, then stopped to do a dump, Grace, keeping Kyla on her lead, did his leg swings and a short programme of stretches.

Then, with an excited Kyla running beside him, he headed off up the steadily increasing gradient, chasing after Humphrey. As he ran he was thinking again. What was he missing, overlooking, not getting in the mix? The name Geoffrey Bailey popped up again. The footman who Jack was concerned about, and the only

Person of Interest they had from their interviews of the Buckingham Palace staff so far, was due to be formally interviewed on Monday morning by two of his team – Sir Tommy had made the arrangements.

Jack, still very young, was rapidly proving himself to be a smart detective with good instincts. Maybe Geoffrey Bailey would turn out to be a significant witness. Or more? But right now Grace was pinning most of his hopes of a breakthrough on the contents of the diary.

As he ran on up the hill, feeling increasingly exhilarated, he smiled. For the first time since the start of this investigation, he felt really positive. And he'd really hit the jackpot with the weather this morning. It was going to be a glorious autumn day and he was damn well going to take Glenn's advice and enjoy a few hours of it at least.

He and Cleo had planned to take Noah and Molly for a walk along Noah's favourite beach, behind Hove Lagoon. Although he suspected the only reason it was Noah's favourite was because of the range of ice creams served even out of season in the Big Beach Cafe, owned by superstar DJ and Brighton legend Fatboy Slim.

Still smiling, he ran on up to the top of the hill and along the ridge, through a huge field of sheep, with Humphrey trained to ignore them and obediently doing so, staying close to his heels. Kyla, kept on a tight leash, tugged away, as if wondering why she couldn't meet all these new playmates. They were running along part of the South Downs National Park, which stretched 100 miles from Eastbourne to Winchester. Just a few miles from the village of Plumpton, where Camilla's family home had been and where she had spent much of her childhood. And as a bonus, the village had always boasted a particularly good pub, he thought.

The sun was tracking its way into a cloudless sky and he was starting to sweat. God, he needed this, he thought. For the past

THE HAWK IS DEAD

few days, his brains had felt as though they were being steamed inside a pressure cooker, or rather – what were those new things called? – a Thermomix? No . . . Then he remembered. *Air fryers!*

Arriving back home, with Kyla off the lead now that they were out of the field of sheep, he collected five eggs from the hen coop, warding off Billy, with his exotic plumage and razor-sharp spurs, who was particularly aggressive to anyone who came near his girls, and carried his booty triumphantly into the kitchen, placing them in the rack along with the other nine eggs that Cleo had collected in the past few days.

'Eggs for breakfast!' he announced. 'I am the Eggman!'

'Yayyy, Eggman!' Noah responded.

Molly raised her hands and squealed in solidarity with her brother, even if she didn't quite get it.

He showered and then changed ready for a few hours on the beach this morning before returning to work. As he went back down into the kitchen, Cleo was sitting at the breakfast bar, leafing through the pages of the *Argus*, with Molly on her chair beside her, eating scrambled egg from a bowl. Noah lay on the floor, with Kyla beside him, his arms wrapped around her neck. Radio 4 news was on in the background.

'Who else is still hungry?' Roy Grace asked.

Noah and Cleo announced they both were.

Grace felt a sudden, almost overwhelming burst of happiness. Everyone he loved in the world, really and truly *loved*, including the two dogs, was here in this room right now with him – this beautiful kitchen with its view across to the rolling hills of the South Downs and the tiny white pieces of cotton-ball fluff that populated them.

'OK!' he said, removing a tub of butter from the fridge. He placed a frying pan on the hob, turned the heat up and shook in several drops of avocado oil. Next he took a plastic container of maple syrup from one of the cupboards, and a loaf of sliced sourdough bread. 'Who'd like French toast and who'd like an omelette, or—'

His work phone rang, interrupting him.

He hesitated for a moment, so very tempted to ignore it. But that wasn't an option.

'Roy Grace,' he answered.

Instantly, he recognized the intensely serious, earnest voice of Denton Scroope. 'Roy, I believe I'm making progress deciphering the code. It's a slow process – whoever wrote this knew what they were doing.'

Feeling a beat of excitement, Grace said, 'Tell me? What have you learned so far?'

'This document is real, and not just an exercise, Roy?'

'It's real,' Grace assured him.

'And the author of it is dead?'

'Correct.'

'Then I do not think it would be wise to tell you over the phone what I have deciphered so far, Roy. I really do not. I need to do it in person. If you want to make the best use of time and allow me to keep working on the pages, perhaps you could come over here?'

Yet again, Roy Grace was faced with a horribly familiar choice. Work or family? In his former life with his wife Sandy, he'd destroyed his marriage by choosing work too many times – not that he had any option. And he had no option now. A morning on a beach in Hove with his wife and kids, or protecting the lives of his King and Queen?

At least in this marriage, second time around, he had a wife who understood.

53

Saturday 25 November 2023

It seemed to Rose Cadoret that it was a rite of passage for every tourist in London to pose for a selfie somewhere in front of Buckingham Palace. They descended in their masses, individuals or in groups with guides holding up coloured sticks, sometimes in cagoules and rain hats, sometimes in baseball caps and T-shirts. Why did some tourists think it was OK to stand in The Mall, one of the world's most beautiful avenues, wearing the most ludicrously shapeless and gaudy outfits?

The magnificent edifice of the East Wing, three storeys high and topped with a tall flagpole from which the Royal Standard flies whenever the monarch is in residence, is iconic. To many its presence is a serene constant and a reassurance of order that rises above whatever troubles currently ail the world.

But what Joe Public never saw, Rose Cadoret thought, was the dingy labyrinth of corridors and rooms one floor below. It could have been the basement of any institution in the world – a grand hotel, a hospital, a residential skyscraper. Down here was a never-ending, artificially lit warren of low ceilings filled with pipework, some wrapped in insulation, hazard warning signs, green baize notice boards screwed to the cream-painted walls, with the usual institutional posters pinned on them: *CATCH IT! BIN IT! KILL IT!* or, *GERMY PLACES IN YOUR OFFICE YOU SHOULD CLEAN!* along with diagrams showing hand-cleaning techniques.

With all the Palace renovations going on, the basement

smelled variously of recently sawn wood or fresh paint. There were hoardings everywhere, plastic gates and building materials, as well as huge gaps in the walls and floors where exploratory drilling had taken place. As a result, there were so many places where an object – even quite a large object – could be concealed.

Conveniently.

Rose Cadoret passed a door due for updating, on which a sign read, *QUEEN'S LUGGAGE LIFT STAIRS*. It was next to another that read, *BASEMENT FLOOR RED ROUTE* – with a large red arrow pointing to a sign. *YOU ARE HERE*.

I am indeed! Rose thought, seating herself at the Formica table in the Cleaning Staff Office. *I am very much here.*

And she was, happily, very much alone.

Few members of the Household staff worked weekends, other than those guarding the Palace, and she knew she wasn't going to be bothered down here late on a Saturday morning.

Opening her Waitrose carrier bag, she took out the five exquisite miniature jade figurines she had removed from a cabinet up on the first floor – part of a collection that had been one of Queen Mary's passions – and for which there was already a keen buyer waiting. Then she began encasing them in bubble wrap, for their protection. When she had done that, she would take them home. In her plastic Waitrose bag of course. None of the Palace guards would raise an eyebrow at a senior member of the Royal Collection walking around with a painting under their arm, let alone carrying a bag of groceries. Which was how she had smuggled out many dozens of objects over the past months.

With these jade figurines, as with most objets d'art and paintings catalogued in the Royal Collection, it was impossible to know their true value, but some jade was worth more than diamonds, and the recent world record price for a piece of jade was a staggering $27.4 million.

Their buyer, who was paying just £100,000 each, was getting

an absolute bargain. But the three of them weren't greedy and at this price they had a very happy, discreet and reliable middleman, with whom they dealt through the dark web. These jade figurines would be despatched to private museums in the Middle East, or Eastern Europe or the Russian bloc – and sometimes even the US – to collectors who would have no scruples about obtaining a piece of another nation's heritage at a knock-down price, and might well take extra pleasure in that knowledge. And it would likely be many decades before any of them came back on the market, their provenance long vanished in the mists of time.

Just like the three of them, she thought with a wry smile. The gravy train was coming to a halt. About to hit the buffers. Although – she hesitated – maybe *train* wasn't such a great analogy, bearing in mind what had happened. Could anything they'd done have backfired on them more than the Royal Train derailment?

But, hey, always look on the bright side, as the Pythons' song went. And go with the positives. They'd had a good run over this past year, since they'd come up with their plan. And they all knew it was the opportunity of a lifetime for the three of them. They'd all served their country, risked their lives, and for what?

To be dumped on from a great height.

Potentially court-martialled, for what exactly? For doing what they signed up for. To fight the enemy and protect their nation. So, OK, they'd lost their rag out in Afghanistan, after Jon had witnessed the torture and killing of his mate, and she'd seen what atrocities had been done to the corpse. And a very decent senior officer had nearly been stripped of his rank for standing up for them.

She didn't believe in God. Certainly not a god who had let that happen to her friend, Scottie. But maybe there was another rival god. One who said, *Life sucks. So fill your boots whenever you get the opportunity!*

It was either fate, or that other, rival god, who had fixed for the three of them to all end up in varying roles within the Royal Household. Jon on the Royal Protection team and herself, Deputy Director of the Royal Collection. Initially, with her art school background, she had decided what she really wanted was excitement – and got far more than she had bargained for in joining the Army. But she had loved her time as a soldier. At first, anyway.

And that officer who had stood up for them – how could fate have arranged, years later, for him to have ended up in such a powerful position within the staff of Buckingham Palace?

The plan had been a simple one. The knowledge that there would never be an opportunity like this again, after the renovations had finished. The Palace in disarray. Priceless valuables all over the place.

It had always been an inventory nightmare for the trustees of the Royal Collection. But never more so during the ten-year renovation programme of the Palace. Paintings and statues and ornaments were constantly being moved around at the request of the builders, making it impossible for the Royal Collection team to know precisely where everything was at any given moment.

Creating a wonderful window of opportunity.

But now time was running out. Each of them – dividing the spoils equally – had already amassed considerable fortunes in untraceable Bitcoin accounts. There was an even bigger fortune in items they had stolen and safely stashed in a storage unit in Hounslow, near Heathrow Airport. A treasure trove worth tens of millions of pounds. To be drip-fed out to buyers over the next few years.

They should cut and run now, Rose knew, while they were still ahead, and not under any suspicion. But there were so many tempting rich pickings to grab while the going was still good – like these jade items. Rose knew there had probably never been an opportunity like this and there never would be again. By the time the discrepancies in the Royal Collection inventory started to be noticed, all three of the trusted Palace employees (well, four, if you included the wife of one of them, who was invaluable) would be long gone. And very rich indeed.

They were already richer than their wildest dreams. And if Jon Smoke hadn't fucked up, they would all be even richer still.

She worried about him, because he was the liability in this trio. She was angry, too. Angry because even though they'd had an on-off relationship, she was starting to feel he did not deserve an equal share. He was a danger to them. More of a danger than an asset?

54

Saturday 25 November 2023

The drive from his home, near Henfield, across to Ringmer took Roy Grace along the foot of the South Downs, past Lewes where the Police HQ was, and through beautiful countryside, with the hills of the Downs to his right. Views he never tired of.

He had considered swinging by HQ to pick up Branson and bring him along, too, but decided he could do without the chiding his colleague would give him for not heeding his instructions to at least take the morning off.

Cleo understood, although he could see the disappointment on her face and the even bigger disappointment on Noah's and Molly's. He felt terrible. The same guilt that always enveloped him like a cloud whenever he had to let his family down. And to make it even worse, right now, at 10.30 a.m., it was promising to be chilly but perfect sunny weather.

Following the satnav he turned off the main road that ran through the village of Ringmer and briefly headed back towards the Downs, before then making a right turn into a pleasant, modern close of identical, three-bedroom detached houses, each with a small front garden, a car port and a garage. A minute or so later he pulled his Alfa Romeo saloon to a halt outside No. 31, which had definitely the most immaculate garden in the entire close. The front lawn looked like it had been trimmed with nail scissors and the two vehicles in front of the garage, a Ford Explorer and a Nissan Micra, gleamed as if they were on a showroom forecourt.

THE HAWK IS DEAD

Denton Scroope greeted him at the front door, in a baggy sweater, even baggier jeans and horrible slippers. 'Good morning, Roy, it is very good to see you again. I trust it is all right to call you Roy, rather than *sir*, now I'm retired?'

'Of course, *Roy* is absolutely fine.'

'I just like to establish the protocol.' Scroope spoke as slowly and pedantically as ever, and looking even more like a bespectacled aardvark than Grace remembered. 'Please, come in, but if you wouldn't mind removing your shoes – the boss . . .' He gave a small shrug.

Grace, casually dressed, complied, stooping to remove his trainers, then went inside, stepping onto a pristine mustard-coloured carpet, and was immediately hit by the clammy, airless warmth and a rank, sour reek. Pets of some kind, he guessed, wrinkling his nose. Hamsters? Snakes? Guinea pigs?

The centrepiece of the tiny hallway was a bust of an arrogant-looking man with long, flowing hair and a pointy beard, set into a niche.

'Charles I,' Scroope said, as Grace stared at it.

'Ah.'

'Did I ever tell you, Roy, that it was one of my ancestors who signed his death warrant?'

'Yes, yes you did, Denton.' Politely, he didn't add, *quite a number of times*.

'Not really a close relative – more a distant cousin, many times removed – I'm not so much a branch of his family tree, more a twig, haha!'

'I think you told me that, too,' he said.

'Ah yes. Did I tell you also that very fortunately I was free last night and today, due to the vagaries of the mind of *She-Who-Must-Be-Obeyed*?'

'You did, Denton, yes.' He was beginning to wonder for how long he could stand this sour reek – which was totally at odds with the pristine condition of the hallway with its immaculate carpet and rose-pink paintwork.

'Yes!' Scroope said, suddenly becoming very animated. 'She saw it on the Testudines chat group on WhatsApp, and felt she had to go for them immediately – so she literally jumped in a taxi to Lewes Station to catch a train to Newcastle.'

Looking again at the sinister glare from the bust, Grace responded distractedly, 'I'm sorry – Testudines?'

'Ah yes, Roy. Astrochelys – they're a critically endangered genus of the tortoise family Testudinidae. Kelly was so very excited to discover that a pair in England had successfully mated and produced offspring.'

'Your wife has gone to Newcastle to buy tortoises?'

Scroope nodded animatedly.

And now Grace understood the smell. And to his chagrin understood it even more when Scroope ushered him into the stiflingly warm sitting room, one wall of which was entirely taken up with tiers of glass-fronted cages, each containing tortoises of varying sizes and patterned shells. There was a three-piece suite filling most of the room, a large television and a glass-topped coffee table, with a number of – he hoped just stuffed – tortoises displayed beneath.

The smell was even more unbearable.

'In the absence of Her Ladyship it falls to me to offer my former boss light refreshments. Tea or coffee?'

Grace cringed inwardly at this crass remark. He could have murdered a coffee but he didn't want to do anything that would prolong his stay in this stinking steam-bath of a room one second longer than necessary. 'I'm fine, Denton, but thank you for offering.' He smiled. 'Tortoises?'

'Kelly breeds them.'

'OK.'

'We actually met on a Testudinophiles dating website.'

THE HAWK IS DEAD

In response to his frown, Scroope said, 'Tortoise lovers.'

And suddenly Grace realized what it was about Scroope's face. It actually wasn't so much an aardvark he reminded him of, it was a tortoise. The long nose, sagacious eyes, slow and measured movements.

Grace momentarily lost focus on the reason he was here, as he tried to conjure up the image of a woman who might search out a life partner on a tortoise lovers' website. Then he saw the answer on a shelf above the fake coal fireplace on the wall opposite him.

It was a framed wedding photograph of Scroope and a woman who was far more attractive than he had imagined, striking eyes and long fair hair. The photo reminded him of something Cleo was fond of saying, when she'd returned home after a particularly mismatched couple had come for the viewing of a deceased loved one at the mortuary. *There's someone out there for everyone.*

But how in God's name, Grace wondered, had this guy Scroope netted such a nice-looking wife? And, equally mystifying at this moment, why tortoises?

He asked the question. And Scroope raised a finger in the air, looking very animated, as if someone had just plugged him in and switched him on. 'Well, I can tell you that, Roy. Most people go for dogs – or cats. But dogs have a lifespan of what – nine years for a Great Dane, twelve for a mid-size dog like a Labrador and fifteen, seventeen at the outside, for most smaller dogs – with the vet bills to accompany that great age. What this means is the heartbreak you are going to experience. Tortoises, by contrast, live to between one hundred and one hundred and fifty years.'

Grace nodded, unsure whether he was starting to get acclimatized to the smell or was about to throw up. 'And do tortoises give you the same kind of unconditional love that dogs do? Or the affection of cats?'

'Well, sir, that would depend on which side of the despatch

box you rest your feet. Tortoises are engaging creatures – if you allow yourself to become immersed in their world. And of course they don't moult and give you hay fever.' He raised a finger in the air, with a look of triumph.

Grace nodded.

Scroope continued, almost evangelically. 'Tortoises won't of course give you the affection that dogs will. But they are low-maintenance – they don't need walking, they won't break your heart by dying after too short a life. Their long lifespan gives you both a sense of continuity and a connection to the past. And they have a wonderfully calming demeanour. Personally, I like to think that long after I'm gone, these creatures will still be here.' He shrugged. 'But you haven't come here to talk about tortoises, Roy. You want to know what I've managed to decipher so far.'

Grace nodded again. 'Yes. Maybe we can talk more about tortoises some other time.'

55

Saturday 25 November 2023

Geoffrey Bailey, small, reedy, immaculately dressed, stood in freezing cold wind, in the darkness outside the Garden Entrance to the West Wing of Buckingham Palace. There was just the faintest glow of light from a handful of windows – The King's energy-saving policies were being scrupulously implemented.

As forecast, the sunny weather had ended abruptly this afternoon. The temperature had plunged further, and the rain was chucking it down as if it had been saving up to do this for days. It felt and sounded like the blasts of shotgun pellets on his umbrella, which he was struggling with in the fierce, gusting wind – and the rain also came sideways at him beneath it, drenching his trousers.

He looked at his watch, the very showy Bulgari that one of his lovers had bought him recently, and cursed, because fancy though it was, he couldn't see the dial to tell the time in the dark. Instead, he checked his phone. Ten minutes late. His Gucci loafers were sodden.

Was this going to be a no-show?

A sudden gust, stronger than all the others, turned his umbrella inside out.

'Shit!' he yelled, as the rain pelted his head and he struggled to get the damned thing working again.

'Y'all right?' A Geordie voice spoke out of the darkness.

'Where have you been? You said 7 p.m. sharp.' Bailey's voice was petulant, but he knew he held all four aces in his hand. 'I'm bloody freezing.'

'Yeah, well at least you got a brolly. I'm on lates tonight – I've got to patrol the grounds without one and I'll be freezing and sodden all evening. I'll get you out of the cold in a few minutes. So just keep your hair on, sweet cheeks, don't want your wig flying off in this hooley, do we?'

'I do NOT wear a wig.'

'Oh right, it just looks like one, does it?'

Ignoring the comment, too cold and wet to banter, Geoffrey Bailey said, 'You've got my medal?'

'Yeah,' Smoke said. 'I've got your medal. Sir Tommy felt bad you'd been overlooked and got it sanctioned. Because he respects you, like all the Royal Household does.'

'I've done over fifteen years of loyal and faithful service. It's no more than I deserve,' Geoffrey Bailey opined.

'Oh no, you deserve much more. So much more! Everyone knows that.'

'Really?' He preened at the unexpected compliment.

'Oh yes,' Jon Smoke replied. The rain was drenching him, plastering his close-cropped hair to his head. But his police uniform with its heavy attachments of torch, taser, baton and phone, in addition to the weight of his stab vest, kept some of it at bay. However, the rain wasn't his problem. This little shit of a footman, Geoffrey Bailey, was.

He wouldn't be for much longer.

'Let's see it then!'

Smoke pulled it out of one of the pouches in his uniform, and held the round silver medal up in the darkness, dangling it from the ribbon.

Geoffrey Bailey hit the torch button on his phone and stepped forward. Attached to the blue and red striped ribbon was a round silver medal bearing the legend EIIR and the late Queen Elizabeth's face.

Disappointed, Bailey said, 'But this is an old one. The King has a new one out, I've seen it.'

'They're using up the old ones on useless twats like you,' Smoke said.

Then, before Bailey could respond, Smoke shot a karate ridge hand strike into Bailey's throat with such force it shattered his larynx. The footman reeled, dropping his phone and letting go of his umbrella as he fell backwards. Smoke was kneeling over him an instant later, and still dangling the medal.

Bailey tried to speak, but all that came out was a gasping crackle and a few partially formed words that sounded like an alien language.

'It may be old but it's still a nice medal, you should learn to be grateful. You should be choked to receive it, and you will be,' Smoke said, briefly illuminating it with the beam of Bailey's phone torch. Then with his gloved right hand, he shoved his fingers into Bailey's mouth and prised it open, at the same time, with his left hand, ramming the medal and ribbon as far down the footman's gullet as he could. And then held it there.

And continued holding it as Bailey struggled for breath. Fighting desperately, flailing his arms at him. Growing weaker by the second.

And weaker.

'I'm sorry you don't like your medal, Geoffrey,' Smoke said. 'It's a nice one. A lot of people would give their life for a medal like that.'

He kept the pressure on, holding that medal deep. And kept holding until the footman was totally limp.

Then he slipped his arms around his waist and lifted him up. 'You said you were cold. Let's get you out of this nasty weather.'

56

Sunday 26 November 2023

To accommodate Roy Grace's expanded team, the briefings on Operation Asset were now being held in a screened-off section of the canteen at Sussex Police HQ that also doubled as the press conference room.

Although he had originally wanted Glenn Branson to take at least part of today off, what he had learned from Denton Scroope was of such significance he needed his Deputy SIO to be present to hear it.

Grace, addressing the fifty-one team members seated on the rows of chairs in front of him, opened the meeting by referring to the chart on one of the screens behind him. 'OK, there's an important reason I'm telling you this, so please bear with me and take careful note.' He paused as everyone looked at him, and some nodded.

'As you'll see if you take a close look at the chart, the Royal Household comprises five departments. At the top is the Lord Chamberlain, who's the head of the Royal Household. You could think of the Lord Chamberlain as a part-time non-executive chairman. The five departments comprise the Lord Chamberlain's Office, which has overall responsibility for the Ceremonial, Military, the Royal Mews, Horses and Royal Carriages, Medical and Ecclesiastical.' He paused again, as several of the team made notes.

'Next is the Privy Purse and Treasurer's Office, headed by the

Keeper of the Privy Purse, Sir Jason Finch – he is effectively the Chief Financial Officer, responsible for all financial matters relating to The King and Queen and for the entire Royal Household. Then we have the Private Secretary's Office, which is the conduit between Their Majesties and the outside world. This was the role carried out by the deceased, Sir Peregrine Greaves. He acted as an adviser on constitutional duties, briefing Their Majesties on any issue they needed to be aware of, managing their correspondence, their diaries, media, travel and of course crisis management whenever an issue has arisen. You may have noticed there have been a few in recent times . . .' He paused for a ripple of laughter that was more enthusiastic than he had anticipated.

'Then we have Master of the Royal Household's Office, headed by Sir Tommy Magellan-Lacey, who is currently our principal contact within the Royal Household and is assisting us. His department's role is the management of all staff as well as the many contractors working on the Buckingham Palace renovation.' He paused to sip some bitter machine coffee from a paper cup.

'And, lastly, the final department is the Royal Collection Trust. This is headed by a lady called Lorraine McKnight. The Trust, which employs seven hundred people, is different to the other Royal divisions in that it is a charity, responsible for looking after the Royal Collection – which I understand from Sir Tommy is one of the most important art collections in the world. It comprises paintings, sculptures, furniture and other decorative items that are housed in the royal residences across the UK.'

Grace then ran through the list of the current lines of enquiry. First was a report from the Digital Investigations Support Unit. The team of computer, phone and IT experts had carried out an exhaustive search of social media and online search engines, including the dark web, and using AI, to see if any connection could be made between the derailment of the train, the subsequent shooting and the Not-My-King protest movement. But all their findings to date indicated that beyond aggression during some protests the protestors were not fanatics, and so far no group or individual among them had been flagged up. In fact it was almost the reverse, with many social media posts from members of the movement condemning what had happened.

He had reports back from team members on the number of Royal Protection Officers who had motorbike licences – it was seventy-two and the names and whereabouts of each officer on last Monday was being checked.

The index of the motorbike, of which Sarah Stratten had remembered the first two digits, had thrown up a number of ANPR hits around the country, but so far none of the motorbikes matched her description of a motocross bike.

Another line of enquiry, a list of all members of the Royal Household staff who had not been at work last Monday – and their alibis – was still being worked through. Reports from the house-to-house enquiry team on all properties they had visited within a quarter of a mile of the crime scene had so far yielded nothing.

One development of potential significance was a report from the ballistics scientist that gunshot residue had been identified from scrapings taken from the grasses in front of the suspected shooter's location. This was now being analysed to see if the type of bullet fired could be identified.

British Transport Police had so far not come up with anything beyond the discovery of the rope ladder down the air vent. Calls were being made to shops and garden centres that supplied this brand in the area, as well as to Amazon, but while a couple of leads had been followed up, there were currently no live ones. And there was no CCTV of anyone entering or leaving Clayton railway tunnel.

It seemed to Grace, at this moment, that the aggrieved

footman, Geoffrey Bailey, was potentially their best lead, as well as working on the entries in the encrypted diary.

'Some of you will remember retired DC Denton Scroope.'

'Mr Pedantic himself,' Norman Potting said.

'Indeed, but Mr Pedantic has a particular skill – an ability to break codes. He worked until late last night and has made some progress but there is still a way to go on the encrypted pages of Greaves' diary.' He held up a sheaf of notes, all clipped together, then looked slowly around the room. Like a fine actor on a stage, he had them all gripped. A sea of attentive faces stared back.

'What I have here,' he said, 'is potential dynamite for our investigation. I hope very soon we will have the complete picture of the diary, which I will then share. I don't need to say this, but this information is politically sensitive. Everything you hear stays in this room and you will be asked to sign non-disclosure orders. Is that clearly understood?'

He scanned the faces in the room, letting them all know just how serious he was. And saw the acknowledgement on each of them.

'Our next briefing will be here at 8.30 a.m. tomorrow morning. In the meantime, I want all those of you who don't have specific actions to take a little downtime. Come back tomorrow morning ready to brainstorm ideas. OK?'

Taking on an even more serious demeanour, he then signalled to Glenn Branson and some of the team that he wanted to see them in his office.

57

Sunday 26 November 2023

Crammed around Grace's small office table were Glenn Branson, Polly Sweeney, Jack Alexander, Nick Nicholl, Norman Potting and the Intelligence Manager, Reena Chacko.

'From what we've just heard in the briefing, this Sir Tommy – he's quite a busy fellow, boss!' Nick Nicholl quipped. 'Does he have to run around the shops, too?' Mimicking King Charles's voice he said, 'Eww, Tommy, one has run out of mustard, be a good chap and nip along to Tesco for a jar of jolly old Colman's English.'

There was a roar of laughter and Grace himself smiled, before quickly raising a silencing hand.

Then Branson cut in. 'I can tell you one thing about Sir Tommy, he's not a fan of biscuit dunking.'

'Neither of them allowed by protocol or etiquette perhaps, Glenn?' Norman Potting queried, supplying his two-penn'orth to the discussion.

'Right,' Grace said. 'I was absent yesterday, not having a nice lie-in, as a few of you wags have suggested, but gagging for fresh air in a house full of tortoises.'

'Nick any for speeding, boss?' Potting asked.

'I sure didn't nick the man I had gone to see for speeding – he moved even more slowly than the tortoises,' Grace replied with a brief smile. 'Right, let's be serious now and move onto the diary. I've called you in here because I know absolutely I can trust you six not to leak anything. I didn't want to share this with the wider team at this stage – what I say must remain very strictly confidential, any leak could potentially destroy our investigation. You need to hear it because it will impact and influence the enquiries that you are undertaking – but what I'm about to tell you must remain within these four walls. Understood?'

From their nods and expressions it clearly was.

'OK, I do actually have quite a bit of the diary decoded already, and I'm going to share these decoded words from Sir Peregrine with you now.'

There was complete silence, other than the beep-beep-beep of a reversing van somewhere close outside, as Grace began to read aloud:

> 'Information has come to my attention from a trusted source that I cannot reveal, for his own protection – and perhaps for mine, too. His providing this information is not entirely altruistic, he has an axe to grind about his contribution at work being overlooked. He is also something of a loose cannon – I suspect I'm not the only person he has told. I also cannot be sure if he is exaggerating any of what he has said. In my opinion he is not the most reliable of people, but I do believe the essence of what he has told me is correct.
>
> Which is that we have a group of conspirators – let's call them thieves, for that is what they are – who are taking advantage of the temporary disruptions to normal procedures caused by the renovation works currently being carried out at Buckingham Palace.
>
> My source has discovered they are stealing high-value items belonging to the Royal Collection, which have been housed in the Palace. These items include ornaments, sculptures, paintings, small but rare pieces of furniture, and

significant jewellery. An item on the target list is a priceless diamond of great historical significance from a collection known as "Granny's Personal Chips". My source told me they are planning to replace it with a fake that would be undetectable to the naked eye.

I cannot conclude for certain from this one instance that what my source tells me is correct. The "Granny's Personal Chips" diamonds have been around for more than eighty years and the theft and switch could possibly have happened a very long time ago. So in the meantime I have continued to make my own very discreet enquiries with people in whom I have absolute trust, across the divisions of the Royal Household.

If you are deciphering this, it can mean only one thing, which is that The Hawk is dead. Maybe from natural causes, but more likely he has been killed in order to silence him by the very people he is in the middle of trying to investigate. Which would mean they are even more dangerous than I have realized.

And which would make The Hawk a whistle-blower from beyond the grave.'

'Hawk?' Norman Potting interrupted. 'Who's The Hawk? A cryptic clue?'

'Sir Peregrine himself?' Grace suggested. 'There's a peregrine falcon – that's a kind of hawk, isn't it? You're the one who grew up on a farm, Norman! What do you think?'

Potting nodded. 'People often see them as the same, but falcons are smaller than hawks. In North America falcons get nicknamed "duck hawks", so it could be cryptic, I suppose.'

Grace picked up his phone. 'I know the person to ask.' He started the call and moments later the Master of the Royal Household answered.

THE HAWK IS DEAD

'Sir Tommy, I'm sorry to bother you.'

'Not at all,' Magellan-Lacey replied breezily. 'How are you doing? Have you got some good news? Close to an arrest?'

'We're making progress,' Grace replied.

'Good, splendid, super!'

'Just a very quick question, hopefully: is anyone in the Royal Household nicknamed The Hawk?' Grace asked.

'Yes, absolutely, poor Perry – Sir Peregrine.'

'That was his nickname?'

'Indeed. Peregrine falcon – often mistaken for a hawk. He picked up the moniker while on secondment in Washington, DC. It was sort of behind his back, but he knew about it and I think secretly he actually rather liked it. Even HMTK and HMQ sometimes referred to him as that, affectionately.'

Grace thanked him and ended the call. Making sure the line was disconnected, he returned to the decoded text:

'So why is this written in code, I hear you ask?

Well, my source is an employee whom I have become fond of and with whom I have had occasional meetings in private, which I should not have agreed to. I hope that my dear wife, Margot, can be shielded from this particular detail, as she has no idea of my proclivities. My feelings for this person never meant I did not love Margot and our children as much as any husband and father could.

Ordinarily, I would never have disclosed any of this, but this is not an ordinary situation. I'm getting close to having sufficient evidence to expose it, and I'm fully aware that in doing so it will have massive repercussions within the Royal Household, which I have faithfully served for many years.

And, in particular, I want to expose the ringleader of this sordid little group. Someone who is high up in Royal

Service, whom I have respected for very many years, and who I know is valued and trusted by both His Majesty King Charles and Her Majesty Queen Camilla.

My source has given me this person's name, but I'm frightened to reveal it, in case I am pointing a finger at the wrong person – and I would hate to destroy their career through a false accusation. So what I am doing is making all the discreet enquiries I can to establish beyond reasonable doubt – as a jury is required to do in a court of law – that my source has the right person.'

Grace paused and looked around at his team. 'Does anyone have any comments at this stage?'

Jack Alexander spoke. 'Boss, surely a lot of these items in the Royal Collection are extremely well known, how on earth could buyers have been found for them? I mean, it's just not feasible?'

Grace took great pleasure in replying. 'I think you'll find your answer in a moment.'

Alexander looked nonplussed. Grace read on:

'I told my source that surely the thieves would have problems in disposing of a number of the items because they are so well known. But he informed me that many valuable works have been sold via the so-called "dark web", making the transactions virtually untraceable, with them mostly going to unscrupulous collectors in Eastern Europe and Asia. Additionally, some pieces are melted down and sold for the value of their precious metals. And stones, such as diamonds, are re-cut to alter their identity completely. Utter sacrilege to our heritage! They must be stopped!'

Grace looked at Jack. 'Does that answer your question?'
He received a nod.

THE HAWK IS DEAD

Norman Potting raised a hand. 'Chief, do you have any sense of who this person *high up in Royal Service* might be?'

'I don't, Norman, no. Not yet.'

DS Alexander raised a hand again. 'Boss, the footman I interviewed on Thursday, Geoffrey Bailey, may fit the description of "the source" in the diary, especially if Sir Peregrine wanted to keep their relationship a secret.'

'He does,' Grace acknowledged. 'You and Polly are interviewing him formally – has a time been arranged?'

'Yes, sir,' Polly Sweeney interjected. 'Tomorrow at 3 p.m.'

'Good.' Then he addressed the entire team. 'OK, I appreciate you all being here on a Sunday. I'm sure there'll be a lot of vicars and priests unhappy not to see some of you in their churches today.'

There was a ripple of laughter.

'There's something further that Denton Scroope has found and as yet has not been able to decode. Five groups of letters. He doesn't know their meaning but he believes they are very significant. They are as follows:

R I S K K

E J N W

R S Z K Y Z N K Z K S

N X W K X Z X W K X

And the final one: J F K Y.'

Grace looked at each of his inner circle. 'Any clues, anyone?'

'Above my pay grade, chief,' Norman Potting grumbled in his rural burr.

'Well, there's your homework, everyone!'

He turned to Branson. 'Glenn, stay on, I need a word.'

58

Sunday 26 November 2023

In his office, minutes after the briefing had ended, Roy Grace sat with his back to the less-than-glorious view of the upper car park.

'I can't reiterate enough, keeping confidential what you've just heard. We can't have any of this getting out,' Roy said.

'What the fuck, man?' Branson exploded.

'Glenn, we're at work. You call me sir, or boss. Understand?' Grace chided him, more harshly than he'd intended. Grace's voice was so uncharacteristically imperious, it startled Branson into compliance.

Branson shook his head.

'What's this all about?'

Facing him across the desk, Grace said, 'You know exactly what this is about.'

Early in their relationship, Grace had concerns about Glenn Branson marrying the senior crime reporter of the local newspaper, the *Argus*. His concerns were as much for his friend's future promotion chances within the police as they were about the risk of leaks. Since the couple had started dating, there had been far too many confidential stories appearing in the paper about cases the Major Crime Team had been working on.

'She knows the importance of this case, Roy – sorry – *SIR*.'

Grace smiled at Branson's exaggerated deference. 'Walls have ears, mate.'

THE HAWK IS DEAD

'Siobhan's zipped,' he assured him. 'Proper zipped.' He mimed the motion across his lips.

Grace nodded. 'I just know how it is. Sandy used to get mad at me for not telling her about stuff that was going on – really mad – and she'd try every trick in the book to coerce information out of me. But there's nothing in the marriage vows – well at least in the Anglican ones – that says you have to share secrets. Worldly goods, maybe. And with Sandy it was just pure curiosity, she wasn't after information from me to advance her career.'

'And you're saying Siobhan is? *SIR?*' Branson said, tightly, still clearly mad at him.

'We both know how much Siobhan's job means to her. You know damn well in the past she's inveigled information from you. Right?' He stared at the DI pointedly.

Branson had the good grace to lower his eyes and nod. He remembered. Two incidents when he and Siobhan had been dating, one of which got him perilously close to being investigated by Professional Standards – and it was only Roy Grace's intervention that calmed that situation. And then another instance when a key piece of information about a crime scene had appeared in the *Argus*. Grace had deliberately withheld it from becoming public knowledge, to help them weed out the numerous timewasters who delighted in calling the Incident Room on any major crime investigation with their crackpot theories.

'Glenn,' Grace said, softening his tone. 'I'm not having a go at you and I know you've laid the ground rules down with Siobhan – and that she is a person of integrity – but maybe I'm just being paranoid.' He smiled. 'OK?'

Branson nodded. 'OK.'

'The stakes have rarely been higher. Any newspaper would kill for a scoop on this investigation, and it would blast their circulation into orbit – for a day or two anyway.' He smiled more widely. 'Enough said. I've something I want to discuss with you privately, away from the team – a thought I want to run by you.'

'Is it about what I told you about Siobhan wanting to get a pet? You're going to suggest me and her get a tortoise?'

'No, you're both too quick off the mark.' He winked. 'And anyhow, with the baby on the way, perhaps that's enough to be getting on with for now?'

'Yeah, it sure is,' he said, smiling.

Grace leaned forward, placing his elbows on his cluttered desk and interlocking his fingers. 'If what Greaves says in his diary is correct and, acting on it, we go blundering into Buckingham Palace asking questions about missing artwork and other valuables, we are just going to drive these conspirators – thieves – underground—' Then he stopped abruptly. 'Shit!'

Branson frowned.

'I've just realized something. Last Wednesday, when The Queen was giving me a tour, en route to The King's office—'

Branson raised an interrupting hand. 'Sorry, boss. *"When The Queen was giving me a tour, en route to The King's office . . ."*' He grinned. 'I don't imagine that's a line many SIOs ever get to say in their careers. And it just rolled off your tongue so naturally.'

Grace returned the grin.

'Just make sure that goes into your Policy Book – for posterity.'

'I'll make sure, Glenn.' He emphasized this by pointing his index finger upwards. 'OK, so The Queen wanted to show me one of her favourite and most valuable paintings in the Royal Collection, a Vermeer that was hung on a wall in the Picture Gallery, I think that room was called. But the Vermeer wasn't there, there was another – apparently much lesser – painting in its place. She seemed surprised – actually more annoyed than surprised – and she then explained that the Royal Collection team were often moving works of art about or taking them to be cleaned. So I didn't think any more of it – until now.'

THE HAWK IS DEAD

'Now you're wondering if it might have been nicked?'

'Yes. I'm thinking we need to make discreet enquiries as to its whereabouts. There might be a perfectly innocent explanation – as Her Majesty . . . implied.' He paused for a moment. 'But what I wanted to discuss with you, privately away from the team, is an idea I've had for a line of enquiry that might help in avoiding alerting too many people in the Royal Household to our suspicions. If it succeeds, it might also help recover at least some of the stolen items.'

Branson looked at him. 'I'm all ears.'

'OK, if Denton Scroope has accurately deciphered Greaves' diary – and I believe he has so far – then we have a group – ring – of trusted people in the employ of the Royal Household who are stealing from their employers, and selling the valuable items through contacts made in the dark web. Would you agree?'

'If Scroope's deciphering is correct, then yes, boss.'

'He still has to decipher one more page that consists of five seemingly cryptic entries that might be connected to the group. He thinks they may give us either names, locations or a list of objects. And meantime we need to be looking hard at the dark web. My thinking is we need someone to carry out a deep dive into the dark web, firstly to see what dealers or dealings they can find for the kind of works being stolen from the Palace. Also, and I think this will prove harder, to see if they can find any evidence trail of transactions involving stolen Royal Collection works.'

Branson nodded. 'That makes a lot of sense.' He hesitated for a moment. 'Are you going tell Magellan-Lacey what we've learned from the diary – and our next plan of action?'

'I've asked him to let me have a list of everyone who could be considered *high up in Royal Service* and anyone – in any of the five Royal Household departments – who might have reason to be disgruntled. I've not yet heard back. I've a meeting scheduled with him tomorrow so he can update both The King and The

Queen, but I've not decided yet what to tell him. I'm not sure I want to take the risk, however helpful he is, of us losing the advantage we currently have from what we've got from the diary. At the moment we have control and I want to keep it that way.'

'That's good thinking.'

'But I have a further idea. What if we could have someone create a false identity, setting themselves up as a dealer who is acting for a wealthy overseas collector – an oligarch or some such – looking for highly unique items around the world that have some kind of historical provenance.'

'Entrapment – is that what you are saying?'

'That's exactly what I'm saying.'

'We can't do that. The police setting up a sting? That wouldn't play well in a court of law. It rarely does.'

'It doesn't – which is why we need a person who's not connected to us in any way, and ideally someone who's been involved in criminal activity on the dark web and would know their way around. The dark web isn't just one layer below the normal web everyone uses for legitimate purposes – it's multiple layers, which is why one of the networks to access it is called The Onion Router, because it's like peeling back the layers of an onion. We can be pretty sure these thieves are smart enough to have their sales activity buried very deep down in the dark web – unlike that idiot footman Sir Tommy told us about who was nicking stuff and flogging it on eBay.'

'Including one of his own medals.'

'I think he was more pissed off about that than anything,' Grace said.

'Yeah.' Glenn Branson frowned. 'Do you have someone in mind? Someone not connected to us in any way.'

Grace looked deadly serious. 'I do. Someone we nicked last year. I did a pretty good job behind the scenes, talking to the CPS and the judge, in getting her the minimum sentence possible.

THE HAWK IS DEAD

She knows her way around the dark web like nobody does. And she owes me a big favour – although she might not see it that way.'

'Are you talking about a certain Shannon Kendall?'

A year ago, Shannon Kendall, a computer expert with a background in cybersecurity and an authority on the dark web, had been the lover of a killer for hire, for whom she ran a business selling handguns on the internet. Grace and Branson had secured her arrest and conviction for the firearms offences.

'I am indeed talking about a certain Shannon Kendall. She's currently enjoying His Majesty's hospitality in HMP Downview – just an hour's drive from here – so surely she'd be only too happy to reciprocate some of that hospitality in helping avoid any more theft of The King's valuables?'

Branson cocked his head. 'I'm thinking, good luck with that one.'

'Got a better idea?'

'Nope, not right at this moment.'

59

Monday 27 November 2023

One of Arthur Lambourne's colleagues joked that an English summer consisted of three fine days followed by a thunderstorm. Not far off the mark, the elderly groundsman thought. You could apply the same to the Indian summers that used to reach into October but now seemed to extend as far as November and December. Three days and then, boom!

He'd seen the changes in the weather pattern all right, during his fifty-five years of maintaining the Buckingham Palace lawns – his particular responsibility, and passion. Changes in pretty much everything. Who'd have thought when he entered royal service all those decades back, proud as Punch, that one day the head of the twelve-strong gardening team would be female – and a darned knowledgeable woman at that.

A few years back when he'd first told his daughter, Nel, about the appointment of his new boss, she had responded, only partly in jest, *Girl Power!* Then again, of course, up until a year ago, the boss of not just the entire Palace but the entire nation had been a female too.

He had been deeply saddened by the death of Queen Elizabeth, and had fond memories of the many times they had conversed when she was out walking across the lawn, her corgis running free. But he was enjoying very much just how keen a gardener King Charles was – his wife also. Lots of new ideas, new plans. You had to move with the times, Arthur knew, even though it

THE HAWK IS DEAD

often felt in the sanctuary here, behind the walls that kept the outside world at bay, that in many ways time stood still. He just wished the weather would stay still sometimes, too.

The back end of last week had been glorious, enabling him to get out on the ancient Atco gang mower – which, through loving care, he'd kept in service for over a quarter of a century – and create those perfect stripes that he knew The King liked so much. Almost as much as he loved the acers, which were in abundance along the borders of the huge area of lawn. Then fierce rain had come in late on Saturday. And the even more torrential downpour that accompanied the thunderstorm came next, followed by yet another glorious day yesterday. All of which meant the grass had grown to the point where it needed cutting again today.

The one positive about the rain was that it had cleared away all the droppings from the pesky – albeit beautiful – Canada geese that descended annually on the Palace lake, terrorizing the ducks, moorhens, coots and swans, and crapping all over the lawns like they were a public toilet for wildlife.

If he'd had his way, he'd have sorted them out with a twelve-bore. But, and he could understand the reasons, the sound of gunshots ringing out within the Palace grounds was probably not a great idea.

Mind you, some of the late Queen Elizabeth's corgis were a problem too. Not the female ones – although they also did their business on the grass – but Vulcan, the little bugger, had had particularly acid wee. His urine was like a vial of sulphuric acid being poured onto his precious lawn. Small, horrible and ugly brown patches all over the place.

Her Majesty's passing had been a terrible time for him. He had admired her and liked her so much, but if there had been one positive it was that the two newest corgis to survive her had gone to live with Sarah Ferguson and no longer signed their names on his precious forty acres of greensward. Camilla's Jack Russells were much better – because they at least pooped in the flowerbeds – which weren't his problem.

Arthur smiled at the memory of an encounter with an American at a Garden Party, some years ago – later, he discovered he was the US Ambassador to the UK – who had approached him while he was tending to a damaged area of grass well away from the proceedings and asked him, 'Hey, tell me, how do you get a lawn so amazing, so perfect as this?'

Something about the man's demeanour had really irritated Arthur – he couldn't say what exactly, but the man had really rubbed him up the wrong way. He'd replied in his native rural Hampshire burr: 'Oh that's easy, sir. What yer needs to do is aerate the soil, plant yer grass seeds, making sure the birds don't eat 'em all. Then you wait for the grass to take root and grow. Once that's happened, all you need to do is cut it, weed it, water it and roll it – for about one hundred and fifty years.'

He still chuckled to himself sometimes, if he was having a bad day, at the Ambassador's expression.

But he wasn't chuckling today. The assassination attempt on Her Majesty last Monday had left him and all the Palace staff in a state of shock. But if there was one thing he had learned in all these years it was that no matter what, the show must go on. Tomorrow there was a state visit scheduled for the ruler of the United Arab Emirates. The Master of the Royal Household had already briefed him – albeit unnecessarily – that the lawns needed to look immaculate. *Even more immaculate than ever, eh, Arthur?*

When he'd informed Sir Tommy that they would indeed look even more immaculate than ever, he'd been rewarded with a, *Good chap – super!*

Which meant having finished mowing them he had to go over them again with the grass collector – which he was now doing – not such an easy task with sodden cuttings. And looking over his shoulder, he could see the grass bags were almost full. Mowing the lawns in November, incredible. Who'd have ever thought he'd be doing that? Whether it was global warming or something else altogether, Mother Nature was out of kilter, all right.

He steered the mower over towards the West Wing of the Palace, towards the skip behind the large, dark green cylinder, which was ten foot tall and the same wide, and connected to the Palace wall by a series of pipes, like a mutant insect feeding off it. The anaerobic digester – the initiative of The King that helped run the Palace hot water and central heating.

Before emptying the grass bags into the skip, he needed to use the pitchfork in the skip to load some of the current contents into the digester, through a hatch in the side, to top it up. He opened the hatch, dug the pitchfork into the mulch, then as he tipped it in, he froze.

Oh no. Oh shit. No. No!

Was he hallucinating?

Within the bubbling mass there appeared to be a human body, on its back.

60

Monday 27 November 2023

The large sign in big blue letters on a white background greeted visitors as if they were arriving for a jolly at a holiday camp.

WELCOME TO HMP DOWNVIEW

The sign was planted on a narrow verge of lawn, partially covered with brown leaves, in front of a tall, handsome oak tree. Behind it rose a fortress-like steel wall, with wire mesh making it even taller, and topped with razor wire. It wasn't there to keep people out.

As Glenn Branson pulled the car into a bay, Roy Grace checked his watch. It was 9 a.m. They'd arrived early for their 10 a.m. appointment because, Grace knew, it was always a faff getting into a prison. And anyway, they were both cops, and cops always arrived early – something Grace's dad had taught him. It showed respect, Jack Grace had said. If you arrived late, your message, loud and clear was, *My time is more important than yours.*

No police officer ever felt comfortable entering a prison. You were always acutely aware that if for any reason you were unfortunate enough to be there when things kicked off, and it turned into a full-scale riot, the inmates would like nothing better than to give any coppers on the premises a good kicking. But at least, Grace consoled himself, this was a female prison – and most riots occurred in male prisons.

THE HAWK IS DEAD

He signed in at the reception desk, sliding his warrant card under the Perspex shield, and clipped the pass he received in turn to his jacket. Then, hesitantly, after switching his phone off he placed it in the locker he'd been allocated and turned the key. Immediately, he felt very vulnerable. And he could see from Glenn's expression that he did too. It felt like being separated from their umbilical cords. Whatever authority they had in the outside world, they had now surrendered to the prison's governor.

Five minutes later they were led by a short but reassuringly confident female officer, with keys jangling from her belt, through a maze of double doors, unlocking one, entering, locking it behind them, then unlocking the one in front, until finally they were shown into a bare-walled interview room, with twin chairs – screwed to the floor – either side of a steel table, also fixed to the floor.

'Think I'd prefer a room at a Premier Inn,' Branson quipped. 'Or maybe a Travelodge.'

Grace was about to reply when a rotund male officer led in a woman they both instantly recognized, a waif-like figure in a red velour jumpsuit and trainers. Her fair hair was cropped short, unevenly, as if she had done it herself. They'd arrested her a year ago, when she was twenty-four, and they'd last seen her about three months ago when they'd given evidence at her trial – and when Grace had addressed the judge in Chambers with an impassioned plea for a lenient sentence due to her cooperation with the police.

But her demeanour right now was anything but grateful. Anything but pleased to see them. Anything but wanting to be here, in this horrible room, with *them*.

Since they had last seen her, she had lost some weight and her skin was pale. Her elfin looks reminded him of a young Mia Farrow, Branson thought.

'I'll be just outside, gentlemen,' the officer said in a tone that implied he'd be straight in to their rescue if this fragile, vulnerable creature suddenly became an existential threat to them.

As the door closed, Shannon Kendall stood glaring at the two detectives. At Roy Grace in particular. 'Thanks,' she said in her bald, classless accent. 'Thanks a billion, Detective Superintendent Grace. Thanks a billion for nothing.'

'Whoa!' he said. He indicated for her to sit.

'You lied to me, didn't you?' She narrowed her eyes in fury.

'I never lied to you, Shannon. You agreed to give evidence against Rufus Rorke on my assurance that I would do all I could to get you the minimum sentence possible,' he replied calmly. 'I told you very clearly that I had no powers as a police officer to grant you immunity from prosecution – and that was how it works in this country. What I did tell you was that I would do all I could – within the law – to tell the judge how much you had helped our enquiry. I spoke to the judge privately in her Chambers. Do you understand?'

'No,' she said, defiantly, still on her feet.

'Then let me explain. You were charged with serious offences to which you could have been sentenced to a long term in prison. What were you actually sentenced to?'

There was a long silence. Then Shannon said, weakly, 'Three years.'

'Are you aware how lenient a sentence that is?'

There was another long silence. Finally she sat down. Grace and Branson sat opposite her.

'Why are you here?' she asked.

Grace leaned a little towards her. 'I've spoken to the relevant authorities to see if I could get special dispensation to grant you an early release on licence if you agree to cooperate with us.'

She sat back in her chair, her face tight. 'Meaning?'

'You have a lot of knowledge about the dark web, Shannon, right?'

'So what if I do?'

'We are currently running an investigation of national importance. We need someone on the team with extensive knowledge of the criminal wheeling and dealing on the dark web.'

'I thought you have your own Digital Forensics people.'

'We do,' Grace said. 'But they work with the police, looking in from the outside. We need someone who has been inside the labyrinth as a criminal, who's prepared to work with us. I thought of you.'

'And what would be in it for me?'

Grace looked at her levelly. 'I've got agreement that you would be released tomorrow, subject to certain conditions.'

'Which are?' She looked suspiciously at each detective in turn. Branson attempted and failed a reassuring nod.

'That you work from home for as long as we need you on this investigation – and for which you will be paid the going rate. Do you still own a property?'

'I've got a small flat in Hove, in Westbourne Villas.'

'You could stay there?'

'Of course.'

'Any reasonable expenses would be covered, and the only restriction is you would need to be visited by a probation officer monthly.'

She was silent for a while. She stared at Branson then again at Grace before speaking. 'How can I trust you? How do I know I won't get banged up in here again once I've served whatever purpose it is?'

'There'll be a legal document,' Branson said. 'Your release terms and your terms of temporary assignment to the Sussex Police. If you agree it'll be drafted and signed by late afternoon. We'll arrange someone to collect you from the prison entrance and take you straight to your flat to start work.'

She touched her mouth with a finger, and scraped between

two teeth with the nail, her eyes darting wildly, almost like a hunted creature, Grace thought.

'And what if I say no?'

Grace shrugged. 'Why would you?'

61

Monday 27 November 2023

Grace and Branson were led back to the reception area by the same officer. Grace wondered again, as he did each time he visited a prison, how much of a chore the officers found it to be constantly unlocking and locking two sets of doors to move from one area to another. Or did your mind just switch off to it? Or, his mind wandered mischievously for a moment, did prison officers have double doors in their homes that they had to constantly lock and unlock, to keep their hand in?

They collected their phones from their respective lockers, handed over their passes and locker keys and went back out into the blustery morning.

'Well?' Branson asked as they walked towards the car.

'She'll do it. For King and Country. Once she's considered her options.'

'You smooth-talking salesman,' he retorted, grinning.

Grace concentrated on powering his phone up and entering the code, as Branson was doing the same with his. Then he frowned. There were two texts from Magellan-Lacey, one from Jack Alexander, and one from ACC Downing. All of them said pretty much the same thing, that they couldn't get through to him and please call them back extremely urgently.

The second text from Sir Tommy read:

Roy, don't know if you've heard the news about Geoffrey Bailey. Please call me as soon as you can.

Grace called him back first, and the Master of the Royal Household answered almost immediately, sounding very relieved to hear the detective's voice. 'Roy, thank goodness. Have you heard?' His voice was calm but urgent.

'No, I'm sorry. I've been in a meeting – with my phone off.'

'Right, well, we've got a bit of a shit show going on here. The footman – Geoffrey Bailey – who a couple of your chaps were coming to interview later today – has been found dead.'

Grace stopped in his tracks. He felt a strange sensation, as if something heavy had just sunk all the way through his body. He wasn't sure if it was his imagination but the sky seemed to have darkened suddenly, too. 'Dead?' he echoed, and saw Branson glance quizzically at him. 'Under what circumstances, exactly? Suspicious?'

'Well, I don't imagine he climbed into the anaerobic digester by himself,' Magellan-Lacey responded.

'The anaerobic digester – that you showed us – which converts waste into heat?'

'Exactly.'

Grace hit mute on his phone and turned to Branson. 'That footman Polly and Jack were going to interview this afternoon has been found dead – sounds like he's been murdered.'

Branson frowned. 'Geoffrey Bailey?'

Grace nodded, unmuting the phone. 'What can you tell me about the situation?'

'Well to be frank it's bloody awful. We've got a sealed-off crime scene right outside the Garden Entrance to the West Wing, right below The King and The Queen's offices, with a whole caravan of Met Police vehicles arriving and parking on the gravel. Bailey was discovered by an elderly gardener, a super chap.'

'What's his name?'

'Arthur Lambourne. He's completely distraught, as are both Their Majesties – The King would like to see you as soon as you can get here.'

THE HAWK IS DEAD

'I'm very happy to talk to him, but the Met will have primacy on this – and the investigation will be under one of their SIOs.'

'I know, Roy – the SIO's already here and throwing his weight around.'

'Don't tell me his name,' Grace said. 'Greg Mosse?'

'How did you guess?'

Grace decided to save for later the explanation that Greg Mosse was the Met Detective Superintendent who'd tried to take primacy on the shooting of Sir Peregrine Greaves. 'I can come straight up now. I'm currently in Sutton – I could be with you in an hour or so.'

'I think that would be a very good idea, Roy. I think you'd be a calming influence.'

Ending the call, Grace turned to Branson. 'You're always going on to me about your driving skills. I'm authorizing you to do a blue light run to the Palace. Fill your boots – and try not to kill us both. Just remember how many times you've scared the shit out of me.'

'Yeah, and just remember how many times you've survived!'

Grace gave him a sideways look. 'Who was it who said, "*Live every day as if it's your last, because one day it will be*"?'

'I think,' Branson said with a wicked grin, 'it was someone who isn't around any more.'

62

Monday 27 November 2023

Ask any young, fresh-out-of-probation police officer what the big bangs of the job were, Grace thought, and they were likely to tell you it was driving on blue lights and getting into a bundle – a roll-up – a good old full-on brawl. Totally legally. He knew, he'd loved all that stuff when he'd first joined.

After officers matured a bit – at least most of them – they would realize that the real bang of their chosen career was making a difference to people's lives, in a way that few other jobs could. That was true for Roy Grace, but being something of a petrol head, the thrill of driving on blue lights had remained. And although his focus at this moment was fully on the case, and he was nervous about what The King might confront him with, cutting through the London traffic with the blue lights on and the siren wailing was quite the thrill.

During the journey he'd been thinking back to what Jack Alexander had raised as his concerns about the footman. Over the phone on the way here Jack was unable to add any more to what he had already related. Which was that Bailey's body language had seemed wrong, and the perceptive DS had felt Bailey was using the opportunity of the interview to air a personal grievance. That grievance was, apparently, that he felt he'd been passed over by Sir Peregrine Greaves when he'd recently awarded coveted Special Service medals to Royal Household staff.

Enough of a motive to murder Sir Peregrine? And so elaborately?

Grace didn't think so. The shooting had been carefully planned and staged. If Geoffrey Bailey had been behind it, he would never have been stupid enough to have kicked off about his grievance to a detective. And, Grace figured, because he had been stupid in doing that, it indicated that no way was he smart enough to have planned the shooting of last Monday.

And yet, all his instincts told him there was a connection. But what? The deciphering of Sir Peregrine's diary had revealed a confession about the Private Secretary's inappropriate relationship with an employee.

They arrived at the front gates of Buckingham Palace, which were swarming with press, shortly before midday – five minutes earlier than Grace had predicted to Sir Tommy. Dapper as ever in a suit and tie, black shoes honed to a mirror shine, he was there to guide them into the inner courtyard, and then directed them to a parking spot by the internal entrance to the West Wing.

'Good show!' he said as the two detectives climbed out of the car. The smell of hot engine oil and burnt brake pads rose from it. 'You must have driven like the wind!'

'I had a good pilot.' Grace threw a glance at Glenn Branson, who was beaming – despite the very tragic reason they were here. He'd reminded Branson in the car not to say a word to anyone about the diary, not even to the Master.

'Excellent!' Sir Tommy said, seeming as enthusiastic as ever. 'So, Sir Peregrine's Deputy Private Secretary will look after you, Detective Inspector Branson, while I take you, Detective Superintendent Grace, to see His Majesty. After that, we'll convene in my office for a debrief. All right with you chaps?'

'What about Her Majesty?' Grace asked. 'How is she?'

'HMQ is out of town at the moment – quite fortunately for her – on a number of long-standing engagements. Although HMTK's not happy, he'd rather she be wrapped in cotton wool until this whole situation is sorted.'

Five minutes later, Roy Grace entered King Charles's magnificent office, accompanied by Sir Tommy. As immaculately dressed as before, but looking drawn and worried, The King rose and greeted Grace, shaking him firmly by the hand.

'It's good to see you again, Detective Superintendent, but not under circumstances I would have chosen.' There was a faintly droll tone to his rich voice, but no hint of humour in his expression.

Grace gave a small head-bow. 'Your Majesty, I completely understand.'

The King walked over to the bay window, passed a small desk on which lay two red felt-tipped pens and a memo pad, and beckoned Grace to accompany him. Down in the garden below, in front of the two magnificent plane trees, Albert and Victoria, was the sight of a full-on crime scene in action. Two tents, a small grey van and a much larger forensic unit van, and half a dozen people in white oversuits, overshoes, hoods and gloves. Two of them were on their hands and knees conducting a fingertip search, and one was videoing all and everything.

'I have never, in all my life, had to see this, Detective Superintendent.' His tone, as he turned towards him, was pained, not accusatory. Grace saw a look of almost despair on his face and suddenly felt deeply sad for the man. And, irrationally, a sense of guilt, as if this was somehow all his fault.

The King turned back and pointed down at the lawn. 'I mean, we've had the occasional incursion into the Palace grounds, but a dead body? A crime scene like something out of – out of one of those crime dramas my wife loves? One of my Household staff murdered here, within the Palace walls – and just a week after poor Peregrine. I feel as if I'm in the middle of a nightmare – my whole world turned upside down. Poor Geoffrey Bailey, he'd served my dear mama so diligently. Please tell me what is going on – and how is my wife being protected, as she insists on being out and about all over the country again?'

THE HAWK IS DEAD

Grace glanced at Sir Tommy, who gave him a nod of reassurance, then he addressed The King.

'Your Majesty, horrific though the two events are, we don't know at this stage that they are definitely connected.'

The King's eyes narrowed. 'Sometimes, Detective Superintendent, the simplest explanation is often the correct one?'

'Yes, indeed, sir.'

'So two members of the Royal Household have been murdered, within one week of each other.' He tilted his head slightly and gave a penetrating stare. 'Is it not more than probable they may be connected?'

Grace desperately wanted to give The King some reassurance. He did not like, apart from anything else, to see him looking so sad and worried. He thought hard for a moment before replying, trying to be as diplomatic as possible. 'Sir, one of the things we learn as detectives is to be very careful about making assumptions. We can hypothesize, and yes without doubt there is a credible hypothesis that the two deaths may well be connected. On the surface it looks that way. But we also need to hypothesize that they may not be. The most dangerous thing any police officer leading an enquiry can do is to lead it down a blind alley because they are determined to make their facts fit the hypothesis, rather than the other way around. I need to make that clear, sir.'

The King looked at him respectfully for a moment. 'I understand. Go on, please.'

'I'm a Sussex detective and I'm the Senior Investigating Officer on the investigation into the death of Sir Peregrine Greaves. But I have no standing in Metropolitan London, which is a completely different jurisdiction. I understand a Met Police officer, Detective Superintendent Greg Mosse, is the SIO investigating the death of your footman, Geoffrey Bailey. We will of course collaborate and exchange information to see if there is a link between the two – or, equally importantly, if there is not.'

The King nodded. 'You are a very experienced detective, I understand. What is your gut feeling?'

'Sir, I don't yet have enough information on the deceased footman. I'd be lying to you if I said I had a *gut feeling* at this stage. If you'll allow me the time to find out more, then I will be very happy to then let you know all my thoughts.'

The King gave him a thin smile of approval, then looked at the Master. 'Tommy, will you ensure that Detective Superintendent Grace gets all the cooperation he needs from the Met team? Especially from Detective Superintendent Mosse?'

'Absolutely, Your Majesty.'

Roy Grace gave a thin smile, too. The King was smart and perceptive. He'd clearly already met – and seen through – the condescending Greg Mosse.

In this brief meeting he felt he had created an ally. This was reflected in the smile on Sir Tommy Magellan-Lacey's face. And the very warm handshake The King gave him as he departed.

63

Monday 27 November 2023

'Excellent,' Sir Tommy said as they walked along the corridor away from The King's office. 'I'm impressed, Roy, you handled that extremely well. I think HMTK likes you!'

'I'm glad to hear that,' Grace replied. 'Understandably he's deeply concerned about The Queen. But I'm more and more certain she wasn't the intended target – and that it was Sir Peregrine.'

'Because of that gap between them when the shooter fired?'

'I've talked again at length with the ballistics expert, and also a member of our Sussex Police Armed Response Team. Four feet,' Grace said. 'Four feet and just two shots. If Her Majesty had been the target he would've fired again – and maybe multiple times, until he hit her. Although her Protection Officers shielded her, I still don't think she was the target. I think the shooter was trying to give the impression she was the target to misdirect the investigation.'

They were joined by Glenn Branson.

Grace continued. 'I'd like to have a chat with Detective Superintendent Mosse and then the three of us here can convene for a debrief on everything we have so far.'

'Yes, that's a good plan.' Tommy hesitated. 'Have you managed to make any progress on deciphering Sir Peregrine's diary? I'd be surprised if that doesn't reveal something of significance.'

'It's with someone who is working on it as a matter of extreme urgency,' Grace replied, evasively. He was feeling very relieved how his short meeting with The King had gone. Now, crucially, should he need it, he had an ally to get Mosse to cooperate with him.

'Excellent. Super.'

They went downstairs to the Garden Door Entrance, and Sir Tommy ushered them both outside. They descended the steps beneath the large glass canopy directly below The King's office, and stopped as they reached the blue and white outer cordon crime scene tape stretched across the gravel a couple of yards in front of them. Grace took in the activity of the crime scene for a moment, while he heard the Master, on his phone, giving a request for Detective Superintendent Mosse to come and meet them.

The anaerobic digester, over to their left, was partially masked by tenting. A length of hose lay near it. 'When was the body removed and identified?' he asked as soon as Sir Tommy was off the phone.

'About two hours ago, Roy. I saw it – him – myself – pretty horrible, but no question it's Geoffrey Bailey.'

'And where is the body now?'

'It's been taken to the Westminster Mortuary.'

For someone who had just witnessed a partially digested corpse – and of someone he knew – the Master seemed, on the surface, to be coping well. But then again, Grace knew something of his background in fighting in Afghanistan. Maybe, he wondered, if you were strong enough to come back from that without suffering PTSD, you could cope with anything?

Then he heard his name being called. Approaching on the other side of the tape was a tall figure in a white forensic onesie, the hood pulled back to reveal wavy fair hair in disarray.

'What are you doing here, Detective Superintendent Grace?' Greg Mosse asked.

THE HAWK IS DEAD

Grace folded his arms and looked back at him. 'I thought we should compare notes. I'm also curious,' he added, 'about which Savile Row tailor made that onesie you're wearing. Because, you know, it really doesn't fit you that well around the shoulders. I could recommend an excellent tailor in Brighton.' He spoke with the hint of a smile that contained no hint of warmth.

Placing his hands on his hips, Mosse startled Grace by replying, 'Thank you, Roy, when I move down to Brighton I'll take you up on that.' Grace gave him a strange look. 'Compare notes?' Mosse added.

'I just popped along because I figured you might need some help.'

Mosse looked at the Master for support. 'I think we are managing very well, thank you, wouldn't you say, Sir Tommy?'

'I'm afraid I'm not qualified to comment, Detective Superintendent. Handling of crime scenes is way above my pay grade, as the expression goes.'

'I wanted to ask you,' Grace said, 'if, in your humble opinion at this stage, you believe there might possibly be a connection between the shooting of Sir Peregrine last Monday and the death of this footman, Geoffrey Bailey? And shouldn't we compare notes?'

'It's far too early to tell. Surely you would know that?' Mosse replied.

'Even as a possible hypothesis?'

'We have our own way of carrying out investigations in the Met. I imagine they are a lot more thorough than how you do things out in the sticks. Besides, we have a Met detective on your team – he is capable of reporting back anything I need to know.'

'But I don't have anyone on your team to reciprocate the exchange of information.'

'I really don't consider that necessary.'

Grace pointed at the hose lying near the tent. 'Is that what you used to wash the body before removing it from the contraption?'

'Preservation of the crime scene is the first priority,' Mosse said, a tad too quickly and too sharply. And too defensively.

'The body is only part of the crime scene. You hosed him down, which could have destroyed crucial evidence around it,' Grace said.

'And what would you have done different?'

'I'd have had officers in protective suits remove the body and lay it on a sheet on the ground and then asked the Home Office pathologist to carry out an inspection in situ.'

Out of the corner of his eye, Grace saw Sir Tommy stifle a smirk.

'Well, we do things differently here in London,' Mosse said. But his tone was a tad less confident.

Knowing he had scored a point, Grace pressed home his advantage. 'So you authorized the removal of the body from the place where it was found, to the mortuary – with the approval of a Home Office pathologist – or without?'

'Detective Superintendent Grace, I'm far too busy dealing with everything here to start answering your questions. I'm the SIO, this is my crime scene and I make the decisions. Is there anything you need from me, or can I return to the task I'm here to do, which is to run this murder investigation?' Then in a withering tone he added, 'I'm sure you have things to do, too.'

'I think, actually, there's probably more you need from me than I need from you, Greg. But you just carry on, screwing everything up in your own brilliant way.'

For a moment, Grace actually thought he was going to be punched in the face. Greg Mosse raised his gloved fists in the air. Then he turned and strode away without another word.

'A bit harsh, Roy, don't you think?' Sir Tommy said as they climbed back up the stairs, followed by a further four flights of

THE HAWK IS DEAD

stairs up to the former footmen's quarters, which, under the Master's renovation plans, had been converted into open-plan offices for the entire Royal Household staff.

'People like him make me furious,' Grace replied. 'You don't solve crimes by being arrogant, you solve them by cooperating.'

Tommy opened his arms expansively, gesturing to the huge and airy space they had just entered, in which sat rows of white desks, many of them occupied. Each had an identical neat black mat, black keyboard and black mouse, and low partition walls in a rich, dark green. It had a modern, inviting feel. 'I think I told you Sir Peregrine fought tooth and nail to avoid being moved from his very large office to here, and the rest of his team, too.'

Another possible motive for Sir Peregrine's death? Hardly.

'That won't be so much of an issue now, sadly, will it?' Grace reflected.

'No, I guess that issue has been, er . . . blown away, as it were,' Tommy said, looking a little embarrassed at his inappropriate joke.

'Am I allowed to swear in your presence, Sir Tommy?' Grace asked, changing the subject and still stewing about Mosse's attitude.

'Swear away! To your heart's content. But just not in front of Their Majesties,' he cautioned.

Grace nodded. 'Detective Superintendent Mosse is a classic old-school detective, a bloody dinosaur, who should have been put out to pasture a long time ago, even though he isn't that old.'

The Master nodded. 'I know that, Roy, and The King knows it too. Which is why we're placing our faith in you. One hundred per cent.'

64

Monday 27 November 2023

'I'm not sure about this,' he said.

They stood at the top of the narrow, steep staircase, below the top few stairs, which were sealed off by a strip of red and yellow tape and a large sign:

EXTREME DANGER – KEEP OUT!

'I'm not sure about you,' Rose Cadoret retorted tartly. She was wearing a dark blue dress a little shorter than dictated by the unspoken rules of standard Palace decorum. She ducked under the tape, and continued to the top, then stopped and stood on bare floorboards, getting her breath back for a moment while Jon Smoke caught up with her. Unlike last Monday, today was not his day off – all leave had been cancelled.

They stood in front of the jagged, unguarded opening that had been bashed through the wall, the flat, grimy ceiling above them. A cold draught blew on their faces.

'You are a bloody fool,' she said suddenly, with genuine fury in her voice. 'You fucked up last Monday, and now you've fucked up again.'

'Hey!' he said. 'Last Monday I had no choice. That was the closest together that they stood. If I hadn't taken that shot, the opportunity would have been missed – and all our careful planning down the khazi.'

THE HAWK IS DEAD

'They walked out of the tunnel, all the way up those steep steps to the top, and there wasn't one moment when they were closer together?'

'Firstly you've got to understand that from that distance it's very hard to hit a moving target with precision. I'm a sniper – I know.'

'So why weren't you closer?'

'I was close enough.'

'Clearly not.'

'We hadn't accounted for that Royal Protection Officer getting in the way.'

'You're a bloody RaSP too, for God's sake. Didn't you think he would get in the way?'

'I did the best job I could. Greaves was on to us and we needed him dead. I seriously believe I made the right call at the tunnel.'

'Then you went and threatened the witness, the woman walking her dog – why did you do that? No one else saw you, and your number plates were false. Other than that she saw a man on a motorbike, what was she going to be able to tell the police? Nothing. So why did you threaten her – just for sadistic fun?'

'My bike is recognizable, Rose,' he said, defensively.

'Really? How many thousands of identical ones are there? And what do you think threatening her was going to achieve?'

'We have to cover our backs.'

'And Geoffrey Bailey? We all agreed you were going to put the frighteners on the little twat. We didn't tell you to toss him in the gobbler and turn the whole Palace into a crime scene.'

'You told me to silence him. He's not talking much now.'

'No? He's bloody shouting now, at the top of his voice.'

'Just calm down. Greaves and Bailey were our two immediate threats. Both have been eliminated. We just need to keep our shit together.'

She looked at him. There was both amusement and anger in her expression. And something else, he could read. Hunger.

'So why've you brought me up here, Rose?'

'You need to see this, because I've had an idea. This was a light shaft, going back to Georgian times, to allow light down into the lower levels of the Palace. Tommy is now converting it into a lift running from the basement up to the top floor – the former footmen's floor, that's now housing the Royal Household admin team. Take a look.'

Smoke suddenly felt very wary of this woman who, until this moment, he'd considered an ally and his partner in crime. And more.

To any stranger she appeared an attractive, demure and cultured lady. But he had seen a different side. The one he'd been privy to when they'd served together in Kabul, the brutal monster that resided inside her when she was on patrol. The one that had turned her into a killing machine more savage than even he had been.

And now she was looking at him in a very strange way.

Reaching the very edge, but keeping an anchoring arm firmly on the wall, and a wary eye on her, he leaned forward and peered down into the deep, draughty shaft. In the weak light at the very bottom he could see six thin, fierce-looking steel spikes rising vertically several feet. Retreating back to safety by stepping away from the opening, he turned to her. 'How the hell is this open like this? Health and Safety would go nuts if they saw it.'

'I opened it,' she said with a smile that creeped him out. 'And they won't go nuts, because they won't notice it. I'm going to cover it back up with plastic sheeting – which will be fine so long as no one leans against it.'

He looked at her. 'And who are you planning to have lean against it?'

'You know exactly who. Two's company, three's a crowd, right?'

'Are you saying what I think you are saying? About a warehouse full of a lot of loot?'

Her eyes were smiling at him. 'A very great deal of loot.'

'And you think we could eliminate our third party?'

'An unnecessary appendage? And do you think he'd hesitate for one moment about throwing us both under a bus if it came to the crunch? He's never got his hands dirty, has he? He's Mr Clever. Eliminate him and all our worries are over.' She looked deadly serious.

He smiled. 'There's something about you,' he said. 'About your mind. How it works.' He smiled again. 'It turns me on.'

She stared back at him. Their eyes locking. Then, seconds later, their lips locked. Their tongues swirling crazily. She pressed the flat of her right hand against his right thigh and moved it up, suggestively, to his groin.

He slid up her dress, found the top of her underwear with his fingers, slipped two of them inside and down into her short, smooth hair, and down.

Pulling her mouth away from his for a second, she gasped, 'God, you drive me crazy!' Then she kissed him wildly again, this time her hands working his belt buckle, then his trouser zip.

'Not here, we can't!' he said, breathless now.

'Oh we can!' she said. 'Oh yes we can.'

Her eyes were glazed with lust – mad lust.

'No!' he hissed.

She pulled down his baggy, heavy trousers, then his boxer shorts, and took him in her mouth.

'Shit! Oh God! You are—'

He was unable to resist now. She pulled down her own knickers and straddled him, on the bare wooden staircase. 'Oh yes, Jon Smoke. I love it.' She was gasping. 'You know what you are? You know? You are the fuck at the end of the universe!'

'You're not so bad yourself,' he said.

'Bastard!' She slapped him hard across the face, then kissed him again, even harder.

65

Monday 27 November 2023

'I thought we could talk more privately here – safer,' Sir Tommy said, dishing up coffees, and keeping his voice low even though they were now in his home in St James's Palace. 'Until we get to the bottom of all that's going on – and who is involved – we need to be very guarded.'

Grace and Branson, seated opposite him at the kitchen table, both nodded. 'We do,' Grace said. He glanced around the spacious room then back at Magellan-Lacey and asked, 'Out of interest, how long have you been Master of the Royal Household?'

Sir Tommy looked thoughtful for a moment. 'Ten years!' He beamed.

'And you enjoy it?' Branson chipped in. He sipped his coffee but ignored the plate of chocolate digestive biscuits in front of him, still smarting from Sir Tommy's remark about his dunking capabilities last time he was here.

'Best job in the world – absolutely. Apart from –' he shrugged – 'you know – the terrible events of last Monday and now today. And of course the late Queen's passing. That was an immensely sad time for me – and everyone.'

'It was,' Grace said. Through the window he saw two sentries, rifles shouldered, march in step across the courtyard.

Narrowing his eyes and addressing Grace, Magellan-Lacey asked, 'When do you think you might have the deciphered pages from Sir Peregrine's diary?'

'I would hope within a few days, at most,' he replied, shooting a wary glance at Branson.

'Good,' he said. 'Excellent. Hopefully that will reveal something significant.'

'You told us before, that you knew Sir Peregrine pretty well? Friends as well as work colleagues? That the four of you – with his wife and yours – would have dinner together quite often.'

'Yes, Roy, we got on pretty well, poor chap.'

Grace nodded in acknowledgement. 'Did you notice anything different about him – about his demeanour – in the days – weeks – before his death? Did he seem worried about anything?'

Magellan-Lacey shook his head. 'To be honest he was always a bit of a closed book – you know – one of those people who never really lets you get near the real them. But having said that he could be great company – great fun when he did let his hair down. He was a brilliant mimic – he could do a wonderfully irreverent impression of both The King and The Queen – and quite a few other members of the Royal Household.' He smiled. 'The King's actually a damned good mimic himself, when he chooses to be. He could have had a very successful career on the stage, had circumstances been different. But in answer to your question, no, I didn't see any change in Peregrine – I last saw him on the Friday before he died and he was very much his usual self, but I can ask around and see if others noticed anything.'

'Have you managed to think of any reason someone might have wanted him dead?' Branson asked.

The Master took some moments before responding. 'I can't.' Then he shrugged. 'But who knows? Doing his job is not always easy – the same with mine. People jokingly nickname the Royal Family "The Firm", but in many ways that's what it is. One thousand, two hundred and fifty employees just here in the Buckingham Palace, Clarence House, St James's Palace complex is more than many medium-size firms employ.' He raised his eyebrows before continuing. 'There is always going to be the odd disgruntled employee.'

'Angry or bitter enough to kill someone over their grievance?' Branson pushed.

The Master hesitated. 'Well, I think I said to you chaps before, many of our Household staff have military backgrounds – perhaps that makes for more likelihood of outbursts of violence than with people from civilian backgrounds.' He shrugged. 'I'm purely speculating.'

'Speculate away!' Grace encouraged. 'We need ideas. And actually there is something I wanted to ask you about – your own military service background. You were in Kabul, I believe.'

'I was – not the best place in the world.'

'You were out there at the same time as a current Household staff employee, Rosemary Cadoret – then a corporal, I believe?'

'Yes – well, Rose is technically employed by the Royal Collection Trust – an excellent person, tremendously wide knowledge of art.'

'There's also a member of the Royal Protection team – Jon Smoke – who was in Afghanistan, too?'

'Jon Smoke, yes, indeed.'

'From what we have found out about Smoke and Cadoret's records, they came close to being court-martialled over the shooting of a group of Afghan terrorist prisoners of war? It was only the intervention of Sir Jason Finch that prevented that court-martial from happening – is that correct?'

Magellan-Lacey looked around furtively, as if to ensure no one was eavesdropping. Again he spoke quietly. 'To be honest, their commanding officer, a colonel, was a complete buffoon. About on the same level as that detective from the Met, Greg Mosse.' He grinned like a naughty schoolboy. 'Of course I shouldn't really say that!'

'Feel free,' Grace said, grinning back.

'He put Jon Smoke and another soldier, an excellent fellow called Stuart Macdonald, who was a good friend of both Smoke and Cadoret, into a highly dangerous position behind enemy lines – completely against advice. There was no tactical advantage to be gained from putting them at risk like that. Yes, they did shoot some Taliban insurgents dead, and here on a fine November morning in the middle of London, sixteen years later, it does sound a terrible thing. But being on stage in the theatre of war is a very different place – different world.' He paused.

'In what sense?' Branson asked.

'It's something civilians simply don't understand. In war, the normal rules of moral conduct become suspended. Dehumanization of the enemy becomes part of the psychology – enemy soldiers become targets rather than human beings. It's something you have to try to instil in your troops. I'll tell you an interesting statistic: analysis of battles fought in wars around the world throughout the past century reveals that on average only twenty per cent of soldiers ever fire their weapons. And some of those who do just shoot in the air, over the heads of the enemy.'

'Twenty per cent?' Grace said, astonished. 'You're saying that eighty per cent of soldiers in battles never fire their guns at all – or don't shoot to kill?'

'It's a fact,' Magellan-Lacey said calmly. 'Most people don't want to kill anyone – and when the chips are down they can't – even when their own life might depend on it. So part of the job of a commanding officer was to make damned sure as many of your troops use their guns as possible. Dehumanizing and ramping up hatred of the enemy is one of the ways. But that's not a tap you can just turn on and off at will, if you understand what I'm saying?'

They nodded, they understood. Grace studied the man's face

closely. He was shocked by what the Master had just said, but he admired his humanity. 'Sir Tommy, are you aware of any particular issue between Sir Peregrine and Geoffrey Bailey?'

He frowned. 'Issue? What do you mean, exactly?'

'Was there any animosity?' Grace responded. 'Under questioning on Wednesday, Geoffrey Bailey gave one of my detectives, DS Alexander, the opinion that he had a grievance over not being granted a medal. DS Alexander was due to interview Bailey for a second time, this afternoon.'

'I know, I arranged a room for them.' He grimaced. 'I'm afraid Geoffrey Bailey was one of those employees – you get them in every organization – who constantly finds grievances in everything he has to do.'

Grace smiled thinly. 'Tell me about it.'

Magellan-Lacey looked at his watch. 'I'm going to have to shoot to a meeting in a minute, I've got an appointment with HMTK, he wants an update on everything. There is just one other thing I've thought of – it may be nothing.' He turned and pointed out of the rear window. 'See that room, that's Sir Peregrine's office.'

'The one he didn't want to leave?' Branson said.

'Exactly. My wife noticed something strange a while ago, a good year or so back and it happened more than once, always late at night – around 11 p.m. or so. She'd see what appeared to be a torch flashing in the window.'

'Like a signal?' Grace said.

'Exactly. Like a signal. Just a few seconds then gone. The first time she said nothing as she thought she'd imagined it – that maybe it was a reflection of a vehicle's headlights or something, or one of the RaSPs checking around with a flashlight. But when it happened again she told me.'

'Was it some kind of code?' Branson suggested.

'Three long flashes each time. Could be the O in SOS – but she only saw it a couple more times. Once we both sat in darkness around that hour and waited, but nothing happened.'

Grace was silent for a moment, thinking. Remembering the deciphered lines from the diary.

I hope my dear wife Margot could be shielded from this particular detail, as she has no idea of my proclivities.

Proclivities.

Was Sir Peregrine signalling to someone? A late-night assignation?

Geoffrey Bailey?

'Before we wrap up for today,' the Master said, 'I just want to give you a quick update on a couple of bits of detective work your team has charged me with. The first was a list of all Royal Protection Officers who are in possession of a motorbike licence – as well as those who actually own a motorbike. My deputy, Matthew Corbin, has completed that task and handed over the list to your chap in Sussex, Luke Stanstead.'

'Excellent,' Grace said.

'And secondly, Matthew has also sent Stanstead a list of all Household staff and RaSPs who had a day off last Monday. He will set up interviews with any of the names on either list for your team.'

'That's very helpful.'

'Good. Right, anything else?'

'Two things, quickly, Sir Tommy,' Grace said. 'The first is the press – as soon as they get hold of this second murder, whether connected or not, the world's media is going to go crazy.'

The Master put his right hand to his mouth and momentarily, with a thoughtful expression, tore at his thumbnail. 'Yes – Buckingham Palace Comms have already had their first calls. Until we have drafted a statement, in conjunction with the police, they are fending them off.'

THE HAWK IS DEAD

'What are you intending the statement to say?' Grace said.

'It will be along the lines that the Palace believes at this stage there is no apparent link between the shooting of Sir Peregrine and the death of this footman.'

'And you think the world press will accept that?' Branson asked.

'Nope!' Sir Tommy gave a defiant beam. 'Not a chance, not for one second.' He shrugged. 'When it comes to the British Royal Family, the world media invent their own stories.'

'Indeed. I can't imagine how frustrating that must be for everyone.'

He waved a hand, as if swatting away a cluster of flies. 'They've all grown up with it. They've mostly developed pretty tough hides.' He glanced at his watch. 'And the second thing?'

'Well, it's not connected with this enquiry at all,' Grace said. 'Out of interest I've been googling Buckingham Palace and the Royal Household, to learn as much about its history as I can – and I came across something that really intrigued me. "Granny's Personal Chips". I'd be fascinated to see them some time – is that a possibility?'

'Yes, I'm sure that could be arranged. I'll speak to Lorraine McKnight, the Director of the Royal Collection. I'm sure she'll be very happy to arrange for someone to show you them. But you know, if you are interested in jewellery, I can ask her to find you some things on your next visit that I think are even more beautiful.'

'Thank you,' he replied. 'I'd like that. I would also like to interview her at some point this week, as well as Sir Jason Finch.'

'Of course, I can arrange that very easily.' The Master looked like he was frowning. 'But actually Jason's away for some time this week on annual leave – I believe to Amsterdam. I'll speak to his secretary and get something in the diary for as soon as he's back.'

Sir Tommy walked with them back over to Buckingham Palace, to their car. Grace tapped Sussex Police HQ into the satnav, and Glenn drove them out through the gates. He turned left up Constitution Hill, now obeying the speed limit.

As they approached the queue of traffic going into Hyde Park Corner, Branson turned to Grace. 'Jewellery? Since when have you been interested in jewellery?'

66

Monday 27 November 2023

I would also like to interview her at some point this week, as well as Sir Jason Finch.

That fleeting frown across Sir Tommy's face, when he'd said this, was what had been bugging Roy Grace most of all since they'd left the Palace. It was bugging him even more than Detective Superintendent Mosse's refusal to engage or cooperate.

'You're very quiet,' Glenn Branson said. 'Are you still alive?'

They were in south London, crawling in heavy traffic through the urban sprawl of Streatham, but Grace had been so submerged in thought he'd barely noticed where they were. Part of it was unpacking the meeting they'd just had with the Master of the Royal Household. But it wasn't just that, he had a very bad feeling deep inside him. When he tried to analyse it he realized it wasn't just because the shooting of Sir Peregrine had happened on his manor, on his watch. Or now the murder of the footman.

It was because the world had changed in so many ways in these past few years. And not in a way he liked. It kept him awake at night worrying. Worrying about so much. About the future his kids, Noah and Molly, had in front of them. A weird, crazy world, where every day when you opened the newspaper you'd read of more violence, more of man's inhumanity to man, and of yet another new war in a country you'd never heard of, full of deprived and starving people and atrocities perpetrated on them.

'Tell me something – are you an optimist or a pessimist?' he asked Branson.

'You know the definition of a pessimist?' Branson replied after some moments.

Grace shook his head. 'Go on?'

'A pessimist is an optimist with experience.'

Grace, smiling thinly, reflected for a moment. Then he retorted, 'You could say the same about a *defeatist*. Is that you?'

'Never!' Branson replied, halting at traffic lights.

Grace nodded. 'That's what I saw in you when we first met. An optimist. I saw a bit of me in you. That you were someone who not only genuinely cared but had the passion in your heart. The belief that as a copper you could make things better for people. We have right now the highest profile case of our careers so far – maybe the highest we will ever face. And all we have to go on, so far, is a description of a motorbike – which fits thousands of machines – a list of Royal Protection Officers with motorbike licences, a list of Household staff, including RaSPs, who had last Monday off, a rope ladder in a tunnel air vent and forensic analysis of gunpowder residue, which we're waiting on and might confirm a bullet type – but that probably won't take us anywhere – plus a part-decoded diary. And you know the biggest irony of all? That our best hope lies with a convicted criminal who you and I put behind bars. Ain't life grand?'

Branson smiled. 'That witness, Sarah Stratten, might remember more in time?'

'Maybe, but I'm not sure she has more to give that will take us anywhere. The telephone analysis shows the call was made from a burner that could have been bought in a million shops or online.' He shook his head and looked down at his lap, as if he was expecting to find some answers printed in the creases in his charcoal suit trousers. 'We have, as I've said before, a dinosaur running the enquiry into the footman's death. A dinosaur angry

THE HAWK IS DEAD

he didn't get to be SIO on Sir Peregrine's investigation, who's made it clear he's not interested in cooperating with us. Which is just plain nuts.'

'The two deaths might not be connected,' Branson said, trying to be placatory.

'They are connected,' Grace retorted emphatically. 'One hundred per cent. We just have to figure out how.'

'Where do we start?'

Grace frowned. 'Everything comes back to Sir Peregrine's cryptic – and coded – message, *Someone high up in Royal Service*, and the entries that we believe now relate to five potential leads. What do we always do when investigating a financial crime?'

Branson gave him a long, thoughtful look. 'Follow the money?'

'Exactly,' Grace replied. 'We start by looking more closely at Sir Jason Finch, Keeper of the Privy Purse – the financial comptroller – and if and where he might fit into all of this. I get the impression Sir Tommy may be protecting someone – to avoid a scandal. I can't forget that look. It would be good to eliminate Finch.'

67

Monday 27 November 2023

Glenn Branson drove perilously close to the back of a double-decker bus, which had pulled out in front of them. As they screeched to a halt, inches from an advertisement on its rear for the lowest interest mortgages in the UK, he turned to Grace and said, 'Sir Tommy?'

'I'm not happy with his body language,' Grace said. 'A question I put to him about Sir Peregrine – I asked him if he'd noticed anything different about him – his demeanour – whatever – in the days before his death. Whether the deceased Private Secretary had seemed worried about anything. Sir Tommy said he hadn't but would ask around. And you saw his reaction when we asked about Finch?'

'You think he might be covering Sir Jason Finch's backside?' Branson suggested.

'Well, he seemed a little uncomfortable when I asked him if he could think of any reason someone might have wanted the Private Secretary dead. Was he trying to cover for his friend to avoid the – seemingly inevitable – discovery by Lady Greaves of her late husband's "proclivities"?'

'Old boys' network, maybe?' Branson suggested.

'Perhaps. And perhaps the same reason he's not really mentioned Sir Jason Finch in all our conversations with him or that Finch had been involved with Cadoret and Smoke back in Afghanistan.'

THE HAWK IS DEAD

As Branson drove on, Grace was thinking hard about the deciphered code, which he had on his phone.

An item on the target list is a priceless diamond of great historical significance from a collection known as 'Granny's Personal Chips'. My source told me they are planning to replace it with a fake that would be undetectable to the naked eye.

It was around the time he had mentioned Granny's Personal Chips and the interviews he wanted to do that he'd thought he had seen a slight reservation from Sir Tommy.

What was that about, if it was anything at all? Had Sir Tommy discovered something his friend, Sir Peregrine, was up to, and was trying to cover up for him?

But if so, why tell them about the strange torchlight flashes his wife, Fiona, had seen?

His phone rang, interrupting his thoughts. It was ACC Downing. He sounded anxious. 'Where are you at the moment, Roy?'

'On our way back down from Buckingham Palace, sir.' It wouldn't be often in his career that he would say that, he thought. 'I'll be back at HQ in about an hour.'

'Can you come and see me the moment you're back. Meantime, any updates? Comms are under siege, everyone wants to know about the connection between the two murders.'

'I have no evidence at this stage to link the deaths of the two men, sir.' He hesitated. 'But I might need a bit of diplomacy with you and the Met, to get more information on this.'

'What do you mean exactly, Roy?'

'I'll explain when I see you, sir. But basically I need a baseball bat – to hit a big swinging dick.'

68

Monday 27 November 2023

'Come in!' the regal voice called out in response to the bold knock on his office door.

The Master entered, closing the door behind him, gave his usual single stiff head-bow and said a solemn, 'Your Majesty.'

King Charles stood up from behind his desk and slipped one hand in his jacket pocket.

'Tommy, yes, I – I wanted to have a word about this Detective Grace.'

'Sir?' the Master responded.

'I spoke to Detective Superintendent Mosse, down in the garden, who told me he has doubts about him. He has had quite a lot of troubles of his own apparently, including a missing wife. And Mosse says he feels he's probably out of his depth – most of the stuff he deals with are small-time provincial crimes and he can't understand why someone of his minimal experience was put in charge of the investigation into Peregrine's murder and the attempted murder of my wife.'

The King strode over to the window and looked down at the crime scene below for some moments, before turning back to the Master. 'Tommy, let me ask you a very delicate question: do *you* really think Grace is up to the job? Because having met him, I think he is.'

'I'm not aware of the details of Detective Superintendent Grace's personal life, Sir, but over this past week I've done some

THE HAWK IS DEAD

checking on him, and so has the Lord Chamberlain. He appears to be extremely highly thought of within both Surrey and Sussex Police. His track record in investigating major crime is exemplary, and he is a very highly experienced homicide investigator. Perhaps you don't recall, because you see so many people, but you awarded him a Bravery medal when you were the Prince of Wales.'

'Good God. I'm sure you're right. He must think me very rude that I didn't mention it.'

'I don't think so, Sir, not at all. But if I may say so, I agree with you. Detective Superintendent Mosse is being somewhat disingenuous. I wouldn't say that arresting and securing a conviction on a serial killer fits the description "small-time provincial crime". He's also broken and put behind bars several members of a major Albanian crime ring, an international online scamming group that murdered two people, along with countless other very major and nasty criminals. If I may add also, Sir, to his credentials, after a six-month stint with the Major Crime Task Force here in the Met, he was offered a Commander's role in London, two years ago, but turned it down because he wanted to remain hands-on in fighting major crime in Surrey and Sussex.'

'I see.' The King looked reassured.

'If I could say something else that might put your mind at ease, Sir?'

The King gestured for him to go ahead.

'If I was unfortunate enough to have a member of my family murdered, and I had to choose between Detective Superintendent Grace and Detective Superintendent Mosse to head the investigation, from what I have seen of the two men, and with all my past military experience, I can assure you there would be no contest. It would be Detective Superintendent Grace, without a moment's hesitation. And if I was going into battle, I would feel very confident knowing he had my back.'

The King smiled. 'Thank you, Tommy. You know how much I trust your judgement. I'm relieved to hear you say this, and I completely agree.'

'Thank you, Sir.'

'Just one more thing.' He frowned. 'I can't remember what time The Queen will be back this afternoon. I believe she's opening a hospital in the Midlands, somewhere.'

'She is, Sir. She'll be back here by 5 p.m. – she has her Silver Swans this afternoon.'

'Ah, right, yes. Of course, it's Monday. Indeed.' He smiled. 'Ballet – she loves it and what a marvellous way to keep fit and supple. She has a lot more fun with that than I have with my ruddy one-man morning boot camp, doing my Canadian Air Force exercises.'

'I can't really see you doing ballet, Sir,' Magellan-Lacey said.

'Nor you, Tommy. Although your job involves you doing an awful lot of tap-dancing. I think you're very good at that.' The King gave him a wry smile, then turned towards his desk, a cue that the meeting was over.

'Sir,' the Master said, gave another respectful single head-bow and retreated out of the door.

69

Monday 27 November 2023

As soon as they arrived back at the Sussex Police Headquarters, shortly after 4 p.m., Branson dropped Roy Grace off outside the Queen Anne building that had for decades housed the top brass of both Sussex Police and, more recently, the East Sussex Fire and Rescue Service. Then he drove on up the hill, through the campus to the Major Crime parking area.

Nigel Downing occupied the same office, with its huge desk and fine view south across the hills of the South Downs, as his three ACC predecessors, Alison Vosper, Peter Rigg and Cassian Pewe, who had all intimidated Grace in some way. But ever since Downing had become ACC responsible for Major Crime – and therefore his direct boss – the atmosphere in this beautiful office felt different. Downing felt like a colleague who wanted to work with him, rather than a superior looking to catch him out.

Although the solid-framed, crew-cut ACC, in his white short-sleeved shirt with his rank badge of crossed tipstaves on a laurel wreath on his epaulettes, was looking considerably more testy than usual as Grace was ushered into his office by his PA.

As Downing indicated for him to take a chair in front of his desk, his PA asked if he wanted tea or coffee. Grace asked for tea and some water. As she left the room, the ACC shook his head, looking almost bewildered. 'What is going on, Roy?'

He had prepared detailed notes for Downing on his phone,

on the journey down here, but before he could say anything, the ACC pointed at his computer monitor. Grace could only see the back of it. 'There is only one news item today, Roy – pretty much around the world. *The Queen's would-be assassin strikes again.*'

Grace rolled his eyes. 'I'm afraid that's only to be expected, sir. On top of that we have an SIO on the case who is certain he's the bee's knees – you had the pleasure of meeting him last week at Clayton Tunnel.'

Downing nodded. 'Yes, Detective Superintendent Greg Mosse.' He paused. 'So, two members of the Royal Household murdered within a week of each other. Do you think there's a connection?'

'I do, sir, yes. But Mosse is not someone I can work with. I'm going to need you to help go over his head. Perhaps to approach Deputy Assistant Commissioner of the Met Police, Laurence Taylor. I worked with him when he was a Superintendent in Sussex and he's one of the smartest coppers I've ever met – present company excepted, sir!'

'No need for flattery, Roy. I'll message him.' Finally, Downing smiled. 'So can you give me an update on the murder enquiry that *is* in your control, Op Asset?'

Grace filled him in on all that the team had come up with to date, plus the release of Shannon Kendall from prison, which was to take place tomorrow, and that she would start working immediately.

Downing nodded. 'And you remain convinced that the shooting of Sir Peregrine was not an assassination attempt on Queen Camilla that went wrong?'

'One hundred per cent, sir. I would stake my career on it.'

Downing gave him a strange look. 'You do know, don't you, Roy, that there have been several attempts on the lives of British monarchs over the centuries?'

THE HAWK IS DEAD

Grace had forgotten that Downing had told him, soon after they had first met, that his passion was for history. He shook his head. 'I wasn't aware of that, sir, no – well, I was aware of the Gunpowder Plot assassination attempt on King James I. I didn't know of any others.'

Downing's eyes widened. 'The first was an attempt to kill Henry IV and restore Richard II to the throne. The plot was foiled and the conspirators were executed – hanged, drawn and quartered – not a pleasant death.'

'I imagine not.'

'They'd be hanged until they were just semi-conscious, then disembowelled and dragged around the streets behind a horse-drawn carriage, with their innards hanging out and some other delicate bits cut off.' Downing smiled, as if he was enjoying this description.

'The history of man's inhumanity to man doesn't make pleasant reading, does it?' Grace said.

'Nope! Then we had Elizabeth I. There were several assassination attempts against her. The most famous was the Babington Plot in 1586, aiming to replace her with Mary, Queen of Scots. That did not end well for Mary. Then we had George III. Several attempts against him. One was by a fellow called James Hadfield who fired a pistol at The King in the Drury Lane Theatre in 1800. He was acquitted on the grounds of insanity.'

'I didn't realize you were quite such a walking encyclopaedia, sir!'

Downing smiled at the compliment. 'Queen Victoria had multiple attempts on her life. The first was in 1840 by a man called Edward Oxford, who fired several shots at her carriage and fortunately missed. During the Second World War, the IRA devised a plan to assassinate King George VI, but that was foiled. In 1970, a log was placed in front of the royal train in the Blue Mountains. In June 1981, a teenager fired blanks at The Queen at the Trooping of the Colour in London. Another teenager tried again four months later with a rifle in Dunedin, New Zealand, but he missed. And there have been other subsequent threats, thankfully none successful.' He was silent for a moment then he said, 'Including now.'

70

Monday 27 November 2023

At a few minutes to 7 p.m., Roy Grace sat at the kitchen table, across from Cleo. They were surrounded by the detritus of Noah and Molly's playthings that were strewn around the floor, along with several ragged, chewed dog treats and toys, including a hedgehog from which Humphrey had pulled out most of the fluffy innards. Grace didn't mind, he found the sight comforting, a reassurance of normality in a world that seemed to be losing its grip.

Or was it he who was losing his grip?

The weather certainly had lost its grip, with rain pelting down outside, interspersed with hail.

'You OK, my love?' Cleo asked, and dug her fork into her steaming, microwaved Keralan cod curry that came with black rice and broccoli. Neither of them were into convenience food but they'd found an online company that made products that actually seemed healthy, and on evenings when both of them had had busy days, quick meals like this were a good and inexpensive option.

'Sorry, I'm not being very chatty, am I?'

'You've spoken to the dogs more than me since you got home, but that's fine. I'm not jealous, I know where I sit in the pecking order!' She smiled.

Humphrey and Kyla were both slumped in their adjoining baskets. Noah had abandoned what looked like the Lego interpretation of a city that had just suffered an earthquake of some magnitude on the Richter scale. Molly's upturned red plastic food bowl was lying under her high chair.

'*Love does not consist of gazing at each other, but of looking outward together in the same direction.* Do you know who said that?'

'Someone very wise,' he replied. 'It's true.'

'Indeed.'

'Do you think we do it?' she asked with a teasing look.

'Stare into each other's eyes or in the same direction?'

'I suppose that depends on whether we're sitting opposite each other eating a meal – or driving somewhere in a car.'

He gave her an uncertain smile, picked up his fork and speared the rice, turning some of it over and releasing steam. 'I'm sorry – I had a rather mixed day.'

'At Buckingham Palace?'

'Some of the time, yes. I had another meeting with The King.'

She smiled again. This time it was the kind of warm, interested, gorgeous smile he'd fallen in love with soon after he'd first met this amazing, beautiful woman.

Then she quizzed, 'How many couples in the world, at this moment, are having their evening meal and one of them tells the other, so casually, *Oh, I had another meeting with The King today*?'

He gave a bemused look. 'It is extraordinary, surreal. It's an immense privilege, I know but – hell . . .' He shook his head. 'The responsibility of this whole thing.'

She looked at him sympathetically. 'I know.'

'It might be easier if I felt the top brass had my back. But I had a meeting with Downing this afternoon and he went and read out a litany of past assassination attempts on British monarchs – giving me the clear impression he feels I may not be right in my hypothesis that The Queen was not the intended target.'

'But you *are* certain she wasn't, right?'

He shrugged. 'I'm as certain as it's possible to be.'

'And Glenn? He has good instincts.'

THE HAWK IS DEAD

He nodded. 'Glenn's with me. But until we arrest the shooter we can't be one hundred per cent sure.'

'Are you getting closer to that?'

'I think we could be if . . .' He shook his head. 'If I hadn't run into a detective who thinks one day soon he will be my boss.'

'Oh God, not another Cassian Pewe type?'

'Not exactly, but he does rather fancy himself and thinks he's a comedian.' He shrugged. 'The one positive is the progress Scroope's made with the coded entries in the diary. There's only a few bits of it that are currently baffling him. He thinks they may be names – but they could be items, locations – we really don't know at this stage. There are five altogether. They're different to the rest of the code – in that they appear to be cryptic clues.'

She smiled. 'My grandad on my mum's side would have had fun with those – he used to give us all cryptic puzzles inside our Christmas crackers every year.'

'Is that where you got your love of crosswords, Sudoku and puzzles from?'

'Yes, I'm sure it was him who started me off. Can I have a look at them or are they classified?'

'I'll have to get you to sign under the Official Secrets Act if you succeed in deciphering them!'

'Deal!'

He unlocked his phone, then turned it round to face her.

'R I S K K?' Cleo read the letters aloud from the screen.

'Scroll down,' he urged.

She ate another mouthful, then read out: 'E J N W.'

She looked up at him and he just nodded, then she scrolled down again. 'R S Z K Y Z N K Z K S. These are what the tortoise man can't decipher?'

'He'll get there. He's working on the key but time is critical.'

She read out the next: 'N X W K X Z X W K X .' Then the final one, 'J F K Y.'

She studied them for a moment, frowning. Then she jumped up and went over to the Welsh dresser, returning with a lined notepad and a pen. She wrote in large letters, R I S K K, then chewed another mouthful of her food, deep in thought.

Grace watched her as she started jotting down numbers, then tapped the pen against her teeth before jotting down some more. An instant later she seemed distracted and was looking past him, over his shoulder. Then he heard Noah's voice. He turned to see his son, in his *Ghostbusters* pyjamas, walking barefoot into the room. 'Mummy, Daddy, I can't sleep.'

Cleo and Roy both jumped up. As they did so, his job phone rang.

'Roy Grace,' he answered.

Cleo signalled that she would take care of Noah.

Grace heard a voice at the other end that he recognized and did not fill him with any kind of joy. At all.

71

Monday 27 November 2023

'Roy, it's Greg Mosse – I hope I'm not disturbing you from anything important?'

'I'm actually in the middle of eating.'

'Oh, I'm so sorry – I can call back – when would be convenient?' His attempt at trying to sound apologetic reminded Grace of an expression he'd once heard. *If you can fake sincerity, the rest is easy.*

'It's OK, if this is quick. My wife's just had to go up and deal with one of our kids.'

'Look, two things. First is, I think you and I got off to a bad start and I just want to hold out an olive branch and say I'm sorry that happened – we need to work together – and it is indeed possible that our two investigations are linked. There's too much at stake for us not to cooperate.'

'I'd agree with that,' Grace replied.

'Good. Excellent. We need to share information – on what you have to date on the shooting of Sir Peregrine, and what I have to date on the death of Geoffrey Bailey. I do of course get daily updates from my Met officer on your team, but I think it would be far better if we could bury the hatchet and work together.'

Warily, Grace said, 'I would be very happy to do that.'

'That's great. Great. The second thing is there's something very strange that's been discovered during the postmortem on Geoffrey Bailey.'

'Which is?'

'I don't want to keep you from your dinner but I've been allocated a room to use for interviews at Buckingham Palace. Would you be free to meet me there some time tomorrow – the sooner the better?'

'I've got a briefing meeting at 8 a.m. I could be there by 11 a.m.'

'Excellent. I'll inform the guards at the front entrance. We'll have a good talk and make a plan of action. We all need to sharpen our pencils, right?'

'My team use ball-point pens,' Grace replied. 'They don't need sharpening.'

72

Monday 27 November 2023

Her boss had been in a strange mood all day. Normally, the Director of the Royal Collection would leave the office in St James's Palace sharply at 5 p.m. every day, in order to get home in time to bathe her young children, put them to bed and read them a story.

Which was Rose Cadoret's idea of hell. Dogs, yes, cats, yes, children, no thanks. She was with Woody Allen, who called having children, *Aimless reproduction*.

But the reason they were both still at work at 8 p.m. on this wet Monday night, was because Lorraine McKnight was suddenly, today, on a mission to get to grips with the Royal Collection inventory. She'd had a flea in her ear from Tommy, she told Rose. The King's favourite painting in the Breakfast Room at Clarence House had gone missing, and now no one knew where the hell The Queen's beloved Vermeer had been moved to from the Picture Gallery.

Well, no one except herself, Rose thought, who was feeling increasingly pissed off with her boss. And very concerned. She was tired, hungry and facing the prospect of a thirty-minute bike ride through the darkness and rain to her flat in Putney.

She could take the bus tonight, except she couldn't. Nor a taxi. She had a full rucksack, and none of the Palace guards had ever raised an eyebrow as she gaily pedalled past them, every evening, smuggling out art treasures. But that wasn't the main reason that she had to cycle tonight.

Lorraine pointed at the computer screen. At the rows of columns of RCINs – Royal Collection Inventory Numbers – by which every item of the one million and fifty-seven thousand items in the Royal Collection was identified. 'I don't know what's going on, Rose,' she said, sounding exasperated. 'There are around two hundred items I can't account for at the moment. Tommy might blame me for that damned Vermeer going missing, but all of this is his fault. Those bloody builders all over the place have no respect for art of any kind. Instead of informing me of every object they have to move, so we can agree a temporary new location and log it there, I think the lazy buggers just shove stuff anywhere they think is out of harm's way.'

'It's disgraceful,' Rose said. 'Perhaps we should try to have a meeting with Sir Tommy tomorrow and tell him the issues his builders are causing. They probably have no idea of the value of some of the items they're moving around.'

Lorraine McKnight nodded thoughtfully, then jabbed a finger at the screen. 'Look, this has been driving me insane. There are twelve jade statuettes unaccounted for. Twelve! Well over one million pounds in value lying around somewhere – and no one can tell me where!'

I could, Rose thought. *I could tell you exactly. Two are in a Russian Oligarch's mansion in Surrey. One is in a fierce Royalist's collection in Minnesota. Four are in our warehouse in Hounslow. And five are in my rucksack.*

'If the Keeper of the Privy Purse suddenly decided to do one of his spot checks, we'd be in the soup – well, I would.'

'Does Sir Jason do that – spot checks?' Rose asked, trying to mask the concern in her voice.

'He's a very sharp man and he's always had a particular interest in the Royal Collection. It's an important part of the nation's wealth – valued at over £10 billion back in 2010, held in trust by the Sovereign – now King Charles. Finch sprang an inventory check on us for the entire Collection not long after he'd been appointed to the post. As you can imagine it was a pretty massive task, tying us all up for weeks. Happily, nothing was missing.'

'Everything accounted for?'

'Every single item.' She shook her head. 'But at this moment there are paintings, miniatures, jewellery, statuettes – pretty much across the entire Royal Collection spectrum – that I can't account for. I honestly think it would scare me if I attempted to put a value on them.'

Rose said nothing.

Lorraine McKnight yawned. 'OK, let's pack it in for today.' She looked at Rose, who saw the worried flutter in her eyes. 'I'm seriously beginning to wonder if we should bring the police in.'

'Police?' Rose echoed.

'We're making the assumption that all these items have been temporarily misplaced. But what if that's not the case? What if some or all have been stolen and we're blind to the fact?'

Rose hesitated before replying, thinking hard. 'Well, it's a possibility, Lorraine – but I think pretty unlikely.'

'I'd like to think so.'

'All the workers have been vetted carefully,' she added.

Lorraine McKnight suddenly tapped her keyboard, clicking out of the inventory. Then she clapped her hands together. 'OK, tomorrow we are going to get everyone on the Trust here in the Palace to drop everything, and hunt for the missing items. Prepare to stay late again tomorrow, to work through the night if necessary. We're going to find every damned one of these items. If we don't, I'm going to contact the police. Does that sound a plan?'

'It sounds a plan,' Rose replied.

But not one you're going to be alive to execute, she thought.

The Director stood up and walked across to the row of hooks on the wall by the door, and unhooked her bicycle helmet from one. Then she wrinkled her nose, looking at the window and the rain that was pelting against it. 'It's a pretty shitty night – are you cycling home or taking a taxi – or an Uber or something, Rose?'

'You're cycling?'

'Always.'

Rose smiled. 'I'm cycling, too.'

73

Monday 27 November 2023

She held back for a moment, to let Lorraine McKnight get well ahead of her. Then she watched her cycle in the driving rain towards the entrance barrier to St James's Palace. A huddled figure in a flapping high-vis cape, and lit up from behind like a Christmas tree, Rose thought, complete with a flashing beacon on top of her helmet – instead of a fairy. Perfect. She was going to be able to spot her easily.

Rose never bothered too much with safety stuff. Sure, she wore a helmet and she had a red flashing light on the back of her heavy-duty e-bike, but she hadn't switched that on tonight – she wanted to remain as inconspicuous as possible. The reflector on the rear mudguard would at least enable any vehicle behind to see her. The bike's black colour was also perfect camouflage for her mission.

She knew the exact route Lorraine would take. They regularly cycled the first half mile or so together before she herself turned left, skirting the outside edge of Hyde Park Corner, before heading off through Belgravia, while Lorraine turned right, straight into the maelstrom of the full traffic nightmare of Hyde Park Corner, before escaping into the sanctuary of Hyde Park itself and crossing it diagonally, towards Paddington and Notting Hill.

Rose, who came a different way in the mornings, asked her once why she didn't dismount and go for the safety of the underpass. Lorraine had replied it was too much hassle and that Hyde

Park Corner was much easier to navigate on a bike than people realized – you just had to be aggressive. And, she had revealed, someone had tried to assault her late one night in that underpass. She felt a lot safer out on the road. And besides, the road didn't stink of piss.

One of the Royal Protection Officers stepped out of his booth, dutifully braving the rain to check, cursorily, that it was Lorraine, before raising the barrier. Thanking him, and waving him a cheery goodnight, she pedalled out.

Rose, her rucksack weighing heavily on her back, its contents safely bubble-wrapped, rode fast up to the barrier, where she was briefly checked by the same guard, who joked with her that she'd be better off in a kayak tonight. Then she joined the roar and the glaring headlights and tail-lights of the traffic, which was still heavy but now at this hour was moving well.

Lorraine's bike was a heavy old steed, and with the electric motor doing most of the work, Rose quickly caught up with her along Cleveland Row, before she turned right into St James's Street and down to the lights at The Mall. But she stayed a few yards behind and didn't announce herself. Carrying on in the darkness a short distance on, up Constitution Hill, she maintained a steady gap just behind her boss's rear wheel.

Just one sharp tap was all it would take.

And if it went wrong and miraculously Lorraine survived, she had the apology all prepared. *I'm so sorry, Lorraine, that idiot taxi caught my arm and shot me forward into you.*

Lorraine would ask her, later probably – again, only if she had miraculously survived – why she had followed her around Hyde Park Corner instead of turning off at the top of the hill and heading towards Putney. And again she had the answer ready. *I thought by following you, I could learn to cycle around there safely, too.*

She braked as Lorraine slowed, approaching Hyde Park Corner. One of the most hectic junctions in London, basically a huge oblong roundabout fed by six roads. Rose often wondered if perhaps it was *the* busiest – not that it mattered. Buses, lorries, taxis, cars, vans, motorbikes, and the occasional idiot on an e-scooter weaving in and out. And tonight, in the darkness and the rain, which was now coming down even more heavily, it was as busy and angry as ever.

But at least the traffic was flowing at a steady pace. Good. She did not want it jammed, did not want the traffic crawling at a snail's pace. Plan A would not work if that was the case.

Suddenly, catching Rose off-guard, Lorraine charged into the fray, pedalling through a narrowing gap between the front of a bus and the rear of a removal lorry.

Desperate not to lose her, Rose powered forward as the gap narrowed even further. *Shit*. She felt the glare of the bus's headlights, the heat from its radiator – *was the stupid bastard driver trying to crush her?* Then she was out, swung left into the gap between a taxi and the lorry, and saw Lorraine, a short distance ahead, slalom in front of another bus as she rounded the corner, then headed up towards the Lanesborough Hotel and the left turn into Knightsbridge. She was riding like a lunatic. Good. Rose followed. The traffic was moving faster here, but it took little effort to catch her quarry again.

And she had to make her move fast now. The move she had been planning since Lorraine had mentioned bringing in the police. At the top of the incline, Lorraine would be turning left, heading across six lanes of traffic towards the slip-road entrance into the park, just by Apsley House. This was the most dangerous part of her ride, where traffic entered at speed from the left, from Knightsbridge. Visibility was lousy tonight, which was perfect. Drivers of buses, taxis, everything, had to contend with blurry windscreens, dazzling lights, reflections on the wet tarmac, the approaching traffic from the right and trying to make the smart choice about which of the multiple lanes to be in.

Rose watched her boss hesitate, left arm sticking out, not that anyone was going to see it or take much notice even if they did. There was a bus – followed by another – thundering in from Knightsbridge at quite a speed. Was she going to try to beat it across?

Yes!

Just one tap. That was all she needed. Her heavy e-bike's sturdy front wheel would send her flying. Right into the path of the bus.

She could see Lorraine was hesitating – and now she was about to make a mad dash for it, right across the front of the first bus. Perfect! Her heart thumping, Rose accelerated, her front wheel now halfway alongside Lorraine McKnight's rear wheel.

Then, just as she braced, gripping her handlebars tightly, about to turn into that rear wheel, Rose felt a massive thump from behind. An instant later and she was launched helplessly over the handlebars of her e-bike. In the same instant it seemed the shiny black surface of the road was tumbling upwards towards her.

74

Monday 27 November 2023

Rose heard a massive bang. It sounded like a clap of thunder inside her head. Simultaneously she felt an agonizing jolt to her neck and a jarring thump in every bone in her body, like she'd belly-flopped from a great height onto concrete.

Dazed and winded, she lay still, with the smell of wet tarmac in her nostrils. She was dimly aware of vehicles all around, slithering tyres, brakes. An angry horn. Another. Aware she might be run over herself now – but beyond caring.

She heard the sound of a car door opening. Then another. Another.

Footsteps. Running. Splashing through water.

A female voice. Elderly. 'My dear, my dear, oh God I'm so sorry – I didn't see you. I just didn't see you.'

Another voice. Male. 'She's moving.'

Another. Female. Younger. 'I'm a nurse, let me check her. Can someone call for an ambulance?'

Another voice. Male. 'Yes, I have done it, just this second, an ambulance is coming.'

'I'm – I'm OK, I think,' Rose gasped.

'Don't move,' the nurse's voice said. 'I saw it, you landed on your head. Your helmet has split open. Let me check you.'

Rose struggled to get up onto her knees, the weight of her backpack making it even harder. 'I've got to – I've got—' she gasped, a sharp pain searing through the left side of her chest. A rib, she knew, bruised or busted – she'd done that before.

'Please don't move, wait for the ambulance. The traffic's stopped, you are safe here.'

Rose heard the faint doppler wail of a siren. Then another from a different direction. Both getting louder.

'Can you move your toes?' a voice asked, female, the nurse?

'I've – I've got – go to – get—'

Where was Lorraine? Rose knelt, shaking, pressing her right hand against her left rib cage. She was swaying. Giddy. The rucksack was pulling her over. She fought against it. The sirens were getting louder. There were people standing all around her. Concerned, chiaroscuro faces in the torrential rain and the glare of lights and the darkness. All looking down at her. Like she was some fucking Tracey Emin artwork. Or Damien Hirst, perhaps. Roadkill!

'I'm a doctor!' a woman said, pushing through. 'Are you OK?'

Do I look OK?

'I'm OK.'

'There's an ambulance coming.'

Anger was roiling inside her now. Fuelled by her failure. Lorraine McKnight had gone, pedalled on, oblivious, towards her home, her kids – and her threat to call the police tomorrow.

She pushed herself up onto her feet and stood unsteadily, wobbling, and almost fell over. Someone grabbed her shoulder, steadying her. 'Here, let me get this rucksack off you.'

She spun. Face to face with a man in his sixties, well-spoken, well-dressed, well-meaning, grey hair matted to his head by the rain. 'Don't touch my rucksack.'

She turned, looking for her bike. Saw it just a few feet away. It looked fine. She took a few, staggering steps towards it, still in shock. She knelt and lifted up the bike.

'Lady!' a male American voice called out. 'There's a paramedic just here . . .'

THE HAWK IS DEAD

She rounded on the voice – on the sea of faces and semicircle of people – and retorted, 'I was a soldier. I survived three tours in Afghanistan. I just fell off my bike, it's no big deal.'

Then she wheeled the machine through a space in the stopped traffic and mounted it. She turned the power to maximum, found a gap in the traffic streaming in from Knightsbridge and raced over towards the slip road. Seconds later she winced, as she jolted over the incline, then headed on into the darkness of Hyde Park, cursing the fact that she should have perhaps got Smoke to deal with McKnight but had thought she had it under control.

Now there was just darkness and the relentless rain. The occasional torch or bicycle headlamp. Hurting her more than the accident was her sense of failure.

75

Monday 27 November 2023

'I think I've got it!' Cleo called out in excitement, waking Roy, who had fallen asleep in front of the television. The news was on. She was sitting at the kitchen table, sheets of notepaper littering the surface, and balls of it on the floor either side of her.

'Got it?' He looked at her groggily, wondering for a moment what she was talking about.

'The puzzle – the first one! I think I may have solved it – well – at least – I have something that sort of makes sense. Possibly.'

'Amazing! Tell me?' He jumped up, excited, and walked over to her,

'I'm not one hundred per cent sure, but I think the encryption might be something that was used by Centurions to create a substituted alphabet – like a cipher. I've been on it for hours – most people would have given up by now. But I've got something that feels right.' She showed him a row of letters: A R B T T.

Grace looked at them, then said them aloud. 'A R B T T.' He thought for a moment, then said, 'Am I being thick? I'm none the wiser!'

'You're not being thick at all.'

'So what does ARBTT give us, my love?'

'Well, if we are going with cryptic, ARBTT could be the first letters of *A Rose Between Two Thorns*. Might that mean anything?'

76

Tuesday 28 November 2023

Greg Mosse, his lean frame sharply suited, and smelling like the fragrance department of Harvey Nichols, sat at one end of the long mahogany dining table, with a file folder and his Policy Book in front of him. The Detective Superintendent was giving the impression – or at least *trying* to give the impression, Roy Grace thought – that he was in his natural habitat, that this kind of place was normal for him.

There were imposing oil paintings on the walls, a mix of portraits of grand-looking people from past centuries and stormy seascapes, an ornate mirror above a beautiful marble fireplace and a brightly lit crystal chandelier overhead. One of the few things that looked out of period was a large free-standing monitor.

They were on the second floor of Buckingham Palace, and had a view through twin windows with gold curtains across the inner courtyard to the South Wing. Grace was again finding it hard to get his mind around that they really were here, in this iconic building, and that this wasn't the conference room of some swanky hotel with copies of famous paintings on the wall. Despite this being his third visit now, it still felt so surreal. He drank the cup of not great coffee from the pot Mosse had waiting for him and Glenn Branson.

'I believe your team used this room last week, Roy? For interviews?'

'Yes, they did.'

In addition to getting his mindset around being really here, in Buckingham Palace, despite Mosse's platitudes Grace was struggling to be friendly. This man reminded him, more than ever today, of his old adversary – and one-time jailbird – Cassian Pewe, former ACC of Sussex and the bane of his life for far too long. On top of that Mosse seemed displeased that he'd brought a colleague along, as if he'd been hoping for a cosy one-to-one bonding session. He'd almost totally ignored Branson, and Grace could tell that the DI was silently bristling, and seeing right through Mosse's phoney charm offensive.

Mosse smiled, his entire demeanour was one of polite superiority. 'You know, Roy and – er – I'm sorry, your name again?'

'Branson. Glenn. Detective Inspector.'

'Do forgive me, *Glenn*, of course. *Branson*, like the pickle, right?'

'The T isn't silent, Detective Superintendent,' Branson retorted. 'There isn't one.'

Mosse frowned for a moment, looking puzzled. 'Ah. Right. Yes.'

'It's *Branson*, as in the billionaire, Richard. *Richard Branson*.'

The Detective Superintendent laughed. 'Of course it is!' He turned back to Grace. 'So, what I was saying is that essentially we have here an original locked-room mystery. Just like those Golden Age crime whodunits, don't you think? One thousand, two hundred and fifty members of the Royal Household, including seven hundred employed by the Royal Collection Trust, and not forgetting members of the Buckingham Palace RaSPs. One of them must be Geoffrey Bailey's killer.'

Grace shot a glance at Branson, who was making copious notes, as well as recording the meeting – because Grace didn't trust what Mosse might report. 'I would say it is *likely* that one of them is the killer, but there have been security breaches in the past – one person even getting into the late Queen Elizabeth's bedroom. At this stage, I would keep an open mind on whether the offender is an insider or outsider.'

'Of course, good point, Roy. All the same, it's not often in a murder enquiry we can narrow the suspect list down to so few, is it?'

'If you exclude the possibility of an outsider.'

'Well yes, of course. Which I think for now we should. Exclude. Until we have eliminated all our locked-room suspects, don't you think?'

Grace let it slide. 'So what do you have so far, Greg?'

Mosse opened the folder with a flourish. 'Well, take a look.' He pushed a bunch of photographs across the polished surface of the table towards them. 'These are from the postmortem. There was a rather interesting object found rammed down the deceased's gullet.'

Grace looked at the first photograph, a close-up. It showed a medal, with Queen Elizabeth's face. The wording read, *For Long and Faithful Service*.

'Why would he have wanted to eat it?' Branson said, facetiously.

Ignoring him, Mosse asked, 'Can you shed any light on this, Roy?'

'I think actually we can.'

'Good, excellent.' He shot the cuffs of his suit jacket, making sure he revealed his expensive-looking watch, intertwined his fingers and leaned forward, expectantly.

Grace sipped some more coffee to give himself thinking time. Debating how much to share with Mosse at this stage. He had valuable information from the decoded diary that he had only so far shared with key members of his team, and hoped for more intel soon from Shannon Kendall. He didn't want Greg blundering around and alerting whoever the conspirators Sir Peregrine alluded to might be.

'Last week, when my team was conducting interviews with all members of the Household staff who had had contact with

Sir Peregrine Greaves, one of my detectives – DS Alexander – told me that a footman called Geoffrey Bailey had behaved strangely.'

'In what way?' Mosse made a show of producing a Mont Blanc pen from his pocket and unscrewing the silver cap, then wrote a note in his Policy Book.

'Well, DS Alexander felt that Bailey had used the opportunity of the interview to air a personal grievance. He reported that he seemed bitter that he had been passed over for The King's most recent award of medals to Royal Household staff, thanks to Sir Peregrine.'

'Well, that's highly significant, bearing in mind what was found in the man's throat,' Mosse said, and made another note. 'This is why it so important that we work together and share findings, don't you think?' he said, looking at Roy.

'Absolutely,' Branson said, emphatically, even though the question had been directed at his boss.

Grace looked back at Mosse. 'So, we have a footman aggrieved at being passed over for a medal. Then he's found dead inside the anaerobic digester – The King's recent energy-saving innovation – with a medal down his throat. What have you extrapolated from these facts, so far?'

Mosse looked momentarily lost. Then his face brightened. 'I think we need time to digest them. Haha!'

Grace forced a smile. 'In your opinion, do you think the murders of Sir Peregrine and Geoffrey Bailey might be linked?'

'I don't think either of us have enough information at this stage for an informed opinion. What do you think?'

'I agree not to rush to conclusions, but so far as I can ascertain, the last murder within the Royal Household was the poisoning of the poet Sir Thomas Overbury in 1613. So on that basis, given that murders in the Royal Household happen only once in over four hundred years, with two happening within a week of each other, it would seem there's quite a possibility that they might be connected.'

'But you don't know how?' Mosse said.

'I don't at this stage know how,' Grace replied to Mosse.

Grace was thinking again about the decoding of the diary in which Sir Peregrine admitted to some sort of inappropriate relationship with a colleague, and the fact that Jack Alexander had indicated Geoffrey Bailey was gay. Could Bailey have been that colleague?

But, he pondered, if Bailey had been angry because Greaves had passed him over for a medal, and had then ended up dead with a medal in his throat – over a week after the Private Secretary was killed – what could the connection be? Surely it couldn't all be just a big coincidence?

What was the link?

Blackmail?

Did the key lie in the five pieces of encryption, one of which Cleo had possibly solved last night. *A Rose Between Two Thorns*?

In the car on the way here, he and Glenn agreed that it was very possibly a reference to Rose Cadoret – but if so, why was it coded? Was he suspicious of her? Or was she an innocent trapped between two conspirators? Or was there some other reason? He made a note to talk quietly to Sir Tommy about her later.

He had also been thinking about all Sir Tommy had said about Greaves, as well as all his team had found out about him. Greaves lived well. In addition to his St James's Palace home – while grace but no favour these days, as Sir Tommy had put it, meaning he had to pay rent, albeit a reasonable one – he had a country pile in Wiltshire, with a retinue of servants, and generally lived pretty high off the hog.

Financial Investigator Emily Denyer had confirmed that prior to joining the Royal Household, Greaves had been in the Royal Navy. Both Sir Peregrine and Lady Margot had some considerable inherited wealth, giving them an income way above his relatively modest Royal Household salary. But had Sir Peregrine been further supplementing his income by stealing from the Royal Collection – while disingenuously trying to point a finger at others?

> And, in particular, I want to expose the ringleader of this sordid little group. Someone who is high up in Royal Service, who I have respected for very many years, and who I know is valued and trusted by both His Majesty King Charles and Her Majesty Queen Camilla.

Could one hypothesis be that Geoffrey Bailey had found out what Sir Peregrine had been up to – and been blackmailing him? Then, after the Private Secretary's death his co-conspirators had decided to silence Bailey? Or Bailey and Peregrine were working together to find out more information?

For the next twenty minutes, Mosse talked them through his team's actions to date, making frequent references to his notes. With the exception of ignoring the possibility of Bailey's murder being perpetrated by someone outside the Royal Household staff, he had covered pretty much everything and everyone that Grace would have done too, starting with a list of everyone who was on duty at the Palace over the weekend, including, importantly, overnight on Sunday.

A complication was there was no failsafe logging in of the Household staff, many of whom came and went as it suited them. Mosse had two officers interviewing the Palace guards who had been on duty during the period, as well as the Royal Protection Officers, for the names of everyone they could recall seeing on the premises during this time.

Mosse clearly wasn't a complete idiot, Grace thought – he just presented as one.

'And where is your team at currently, Roy, on the murder of Sir Peregrine?'

'We're making progress.'

'Any suspects?'

'Not yet but I think we may be getting close.'

'The coded diary you have – any luck breaking the code?'

'It's being worked on.'

'Good, you will keep me posted?'

'If you like – but email would be quicker,' Grace said light-heartedly.

Mosse looked at his deadpan expression, uncertain whether he was joking. 'Right, yes, haha, good point. So, is there anything else I can do for you today, anyone you'd like to see?'

'I'd like to read the pathologist's report.'

'I can – er – Pony Express that to you.'

Grace gave him a smile then glanced at his watch. 'We're meeting a colleague, Polly Sweeney, she's the Family Liaison Officer for Lady Greaves and she was going to see her this morning, to see if she could establish any connection between her husband and the deceased footman.'

'Perhaps I should come with you – or bring Polly Sweeney here, in the new spirit of our openness and working together,' Mosse said.

'Certainly,' Grace said. 'And the other thing is I need to use the bathroom.'

Grace was suddenly distracted by the ping of an incoming text. He nodded, looking down at his phone. It was from Shannon.

Call me as soon as you can. I have found something!

77

Tuesday 28 November 2023

In contrast to the classic stately home feel of the wing of Buckingham Palace they were in, the men's washroom was a surprise to Roy Grace. It looked like it belonged in a modern five-star hotel. A long row of oval basins, in a black-and-white veined marbled effect, and each with a gilded oval mirror above. Each had quality liquid-soap dispensers, free-standing, as if in the knowledge that only respectful people came here, and respectful people did not steal soap.

As the three detectives washed their hands, Mosse, busily looking at his reflection in the mirror and making tiny adjustments to his facial hair said, 'Roy, I'm glad of this opportunity to clear the air between us. Not just because cooperating is the sensible way forward, but I think you need to be aware of something.'

Grace frowned. 'I do?'

Mosse shot an irritated glance at Glenn Branson, as if wishing him out of the room. Then he lowered his voice. 'I've just been informed of an ACC vacancy coming up in Sussex Police. I'm going to apply for it and I've been told I've a good chance of getting it.'

'Really?' Grace tried to hide the dismay in his voice. 'Well, that would be great, Greg.'

'I was thinking, perhaps – if you wouldn't mind – you could put in a good word for me, with your Chief?'

'Of course, I'd be delighted.'

THE HAWK IS DEAD

Raising his voice above the whirr of the electric hand-dryer, Mosse said, 'I'm surprised you haven't applied for the role yourself.'

'It's because I love my job. My rank is the highest rank where it's still possible to be a hands-on detective. Go any higher and you become desk-bound. That's not what I joined up for.'

'You're not ambitious to become a Chief Constable one day?'

'No, I'm not. I'm ambitious to solve murders.'

'Well, maybe if I get the job, I could at some point trade roles with your current boss, ACC Nigel Downing. He might like to have a different responsibility from Major Crime – to broaden his portfolio and next promotion chances. Be fun if we worked together, don't you think?'

'I'm sure,' Grace tried to reply, quietly, but the two words were trapped, like a silver medal, in his gullet.

78

Tuesday 28 November 2023

Rose Cadoret shut the door to Sir Jason's office. The meeting with the Keeper of the Privy Purse had been short and to the point as he had to dash to the airport for his flight to Amsterdam. As she walked along the corridor and up the stairs, she recalled what she had told Jon Smoke – and only partly in jest – that the room she was now entering was the place she would want to be when the zombies attacked. It was from here that she would make her last stand against them.

The Indian Room. The domain of The King's Armourer. It was also the room from which the then recently abdicated Duke of Windsor – formerly King Edward VIII – watched the coronation of his brother, King George VI.

Located on the north-east corner of the Principal Corridor of Buckingham Palace, next to the Chinese Dining Room, the Indian Room had tall windows with crimson drapes, giving views across the front courtyard and Green Park, and a magnificent vaulted ceiling. The walls were lined with mostly empty, magnificent inlaid walnut display cases. These were currently in the process of being filled with over three hundred of the most beautiful, lethal and indestructible swords and daggers ever made.

All the blades were different. Some were curved, some wide, some narrow, some with serrated edges, and many with engraved inscriptions. All of them were ornately jewelled but that didn't detract, in Rose's view, from the purpose of each of these weapons – which was to kill other human beings in hand-to-hand combat. Many were designed to inflict even more catastrophic damage to the internal organs when being withdrawn from the human torso they had just penetrated, than the entry wound itself.

One of Rose's first tasks when she had joined the Royal Collection team was to help pack away the contents of the Indian Room into wooden boxes for safe keeping, while the entire floor underwent the renovations. Now she was helping to put everything back up, and ticking each of the six hundred items off on the inventory checklist she had commenced for Lorraine McKnight. And at the moment she was on her own in here.

That inventory was a job that would take the twenty members of the Royal Collection Trust to whom Lorraine had delegated the task many months. Rose would be long gone before then. Long before any of the items the three of them had taken were declared missing.

And besides, who would miss them, really, anyway? Just a relative handful of items worth a few dozen million pounds – a paltry sum when the entire Royal Collection was worth untold billions.

Four years ago, when she'd begun the task of packing up the swords, daggers and armour in here, she had gazed around the display cases, imagining how some of the items had been used, and the wounds they might have inflicted. Nothing in here was purely ornamental. Everything was for maiming and killing. Slicing off heads and limbs, filleting and disembowelling victims. All the fun of the fair!

Almost every single item here had been presented to the then Prince of Wales, later King Edward VII, during his 1875 tour of India. Swords and guns made a good diplomatic gift in those days – they showed off your nation's power and its technology. Back then the Indian nation was the world leader in sword and dagger technology, through the manufacturing technique of watered crucible steel. It made an Indian weapon the one you'd want to be holding in a sword-fight, because nothing was going to break it. Nothing. And it would be so sharp, you could have shaved with it.

She knelt close to a tiger skin on the carpet and lifted RCIN 11288 – a sword in its scabbard – out of a box. As she did so, she again winced in pain and had to take a break for a few seconds. Then she slid out the heavy, curved sword, with the blade engraved, and almost gasped out loud at its sheer beauty.

It had been a Coronation gift to King Edward VII from the Maharaja of Jaipur, and was decorated with over seven hundred diamonds, in gold settings backed with silver foil, with a total weight of two thousand carats. The scabbard and hilt were gold, enamelled in blue, green and red.

She ran her forefinger along the side of the blade, very carefully.

Rose had so many favourites in here. Among them a Katar, inventory number RCIN 11408, a punch dagger with a thickened armour-piercing tip and velvet hilt. But her favourite of all was RCIN 11289, the Ibrahim dagger. She knelt, stifling another jab of pain from her rib, and lifted it out of the box where it had been stored for the past four years. Then she removed the dagger from its scabbard and held it up. It made a distinct clack-clacking sound as she did so. She loved that sound.

And she loved the shape of this dagger. It flowed, like a jet fighter, a gleaming arc from the jewelled hilt, curving down then upwards to the armoured tip. It was utterly wonderful. And what she loved about it best of all was the groove, cut in sections along the centre of its blade, each containing rows of tiny pearls that rolled along, clack-clacking into each other. They were not just decorative, they were there for a sinister purpose. With good reason they were called 'The Tears of Allah' or 'The Tears of the Afflicted'.

She stood up in the empty room and slashed at an imaginary

THE HAWK IS DEAD

opponent, the pearls clack-clacking, unable to stop herself crying out, as her rib felt like it had just pierced her midriff. Then, her eyes watering from the pain, she looked at the blade. Imagined it slicing through an enemy's tunic and then his belly, with no resistance, like a hot knife through butter. She could see his eyes wide with shock and pain, hear his grunt as she twisted it, ripping through his liver and intestines. But most of all she loved the thought that, as he sagged to his knees in agony, haemorrhaging blood internally, light dimming in his eyes, he would be completely unaware that the priceless pearls that had just rolled through his guts and were not there solely for ornamental purposes were now ripping out parts of his vital organs as the dagger was withdrawn.

As she stepped forward and slashed again, she heard a polite cough, and spun round, to see the lean, elegantly suited figure of the humourless Deputy Keeper of the Privy Purse, Michael Innes, standing in the doorway. There was a distinctly disapproving expression on his face.

'Planning someone's demise, Rose? Don't you think we've had a high enough body count in the Royal Household for one week?' His snide voice really irritated her.

'With respect, sir, it is actually one week *and a day* ago.' She smiled, unable to hold back her cheeky reply.

'Not really a laughing matter, is it?'

'Not really, no, sir.'

'Their Majesties are extremely upset – and understandably worried. The Lord Chamberlain has suggested they decamp to Scotland where they can be away from all this and in safety.'

'That sounds a sensible decision, sir,' she said.

He nodded, then asked, 'Inventory check going all right?'

'It will be a long process.'

'Sir Jason is very concerned – he tells me he had a sleepless night. Lorraine McKnight phoned him late at his home and reported to him the number of items unaccounted for. Appalling – how can this have happened? You do realize quite how serious this is? We're not talking a couple of trinkets that have fallen through the cracks – this is part of our nation's heritage – and a significant part of its wealth.'

'I'm sure they will all turn up, Sir Michael. Things have been a bit chaotic. I don't think some of the workmen here quite appreciate the importance of all the items in the Royal Collection. The way some of them have been handled is frankly alarming.'

'It shouldn't be, Rose,' he said, coldly and levelly. 'The Royal Collection Trust team are paid to look after all the items. If any of the workmen here have mishandled them, this is your team's fault, not theirs. Perhaps if you took your job a little more seriously rather than playing with daggers, there might be fewer items missing.'

He spun on the heels of his black spit-and-polished Oxfords and strode off.

Rose gave him two fingers behind his back. 'Wanker!' she whispered under her breath.

Then she slid the knife back into its scabbard, lifted it up and placed it carefully back in its rightful position in the cabinet. Having done that, she stood back and looked around at the swords and daggers she'd returned to their places in the cabinets, so far. And smiled. Could there be any museum in the world that had a collection quite as beautiful as in here?

This room was truly a hymn to killing.

Smoke had told her she was weird. Maybe she was, but he was one to talk. Her wartime buddy who'd had her back. Friend. Co-conspirator. And now big problem. But conversations with her boss had cleared the way forward and she knew what she had to do.

Smoke and Lorraine McKnight. Two big problems. One would have been eliminated last night if . . .

THE HAWK IS DEAD

If she'd not screwed up.

If that stupid, blind old bat hadn't sent her flying.

She had planned to try again today. But when she'd woken this morning she felt still shaken up by the accident – cycling was out of the question today. Instead she'd gone to work by Uber, and she felt every damned pothole in the road, in that crappy little electric Prius.

She glanced at her watch. It was coming up to 2.20 p.m. For some days she had considered the unguarded lift entrance up on the footmen's floor to be the perfect way to get rid of a problem. But right now, she needed to sort two problems.

Both were threats. Smoke because he was a loose cannon. McKnight because of her insistence on an inventory check. Which Rose could manage for a while. But a limited while.

The lift could only be used once.

Which of the two did she need to get rid of the most urgently?

It boiled down to maths. She had to split all proceeds with the others. Smoke, with his erratic behaviour, posed a big risk. With Lorraine McKnight she just had to keep obfuscating until she disappeared – and the plans for that were all in place.

Smoke first was the best plan. Followed by a fast exit.

She ran a finger down the blade of the Maharaja of Jaipur's sword again. This time she drew blood, but only a small drop. She kissed it away.

You are right, Mr Smoke. Sorry, Lance Corporal Smoke. About what you said. About me being weird. Perhaps, you're just about to find out exactly how weird.

79

Tuesday 28 November 2023

'It's not going to happen, boss.' Glenn turned into Westbourne Villas in Hove and pulled into a parking bay. 'Cheer up!'

Grace glanced at his watch. It was 2.15 p.m. 'History repeats itself. Isn't that right? The lesson of history is that man does not learn the lesson of history,' he replied gloomily. He'd been brooding on his conversation with Greg Mosse for the past hour, while Branson drove them down from London. It was clouding his thoughts, preventing him from focusing fully on the case.

Branson shook his head. 'The man is not up to the job. ACC Downing is smart and so is the Chief.' He slowed and turned into a parking space, halted the car and switched off the engine. Then he put out an arm and gave Grace a reassuring pat on the shoulder. 'They'll see through him. It won't happen.'

'I wish I had your optimism.'

'Have as much of it as you like – help yourself, dig deep.'

Grace smiled. Then he frowned again as they climbed out of the car into a strong wind, and looked at the faded cream paintwork of the Regency corner building.

There were several steps up to a door that was long overdue a lick of dark blue paint. To its right was an entry-phone panel with a row of names. Branson pressed the one for 'S. Kendall' and a few moments later they heard her voice, no friendlier than it had been in the prison interview room yesterday.

'Yes?'

THE HAWK IS DEAD

They entered a messy communal hallway, illuminated by a meagre, bare lightbulb. The floor was covered in leaflets from local takeaways and food delivery companies, and two padlocked bicycles were propped against a flaking wall.

Moments later a door to their right opened, and Shannon Kendall summoned them in, barely uttering a word of greeting. She looked little different to yesterday, pale, wearing a faded jogging top, tracksuit bottoms and worn trainers. The flat was small and sparsely furnished, a large window with black vertical blinds looking out across the busy Kingsway towards the sea. The white paint on the walls looked reasonably fresh, and the flat felt inviting, compared to the dowdy common parts of the building, Grace thought.

She led the two detectives up a short staircase to a mezzanine, where there was a whole bank of monitors in front of a semi-circular desk. A rucksack was slung over the back of her chair, and a large plastic bottle of water was on the worktop beside her keypad. All the time she eyed them as if suspicious of their motives.

'How's it going, Shannon?' Grace said, trying to break the ice. 'Good to be home?'

'Do you know anything about miniatures, Detective Superintendent?' she asked, glancing equally at Glenn Branson.

'Miniatures?' Grace replied.

'Hans Holbein the Younger?'

He stared at her blankly.

'Wasn't he a painter?' Glenn Branson said.

'Didn't realize you were so cultured,' Roy ribbed.

'His name came up in a pub quiz a few weeks ago,' Branson retorted with a grin.

'OK, you guys know about the dark web,' Shannon said, 'so I won't bother giving you the kindergarten guide. You know it's also formed of layers that keep peeling away as you delve deeper into it. The first few layers take you into marketplaces. There are plenty of legitimate products on sale, but it's more about illegal ones – mostly drugs, counterfeit goods, weapons and stolen data. Then there's a whole layer for untraceable communications for the likes of whistle-blowers, political activists, and people living in countries where there is strong censorship or no freedom of speech.' She swigged from her water bottle before continuing.

'Then a whole section of forums and chat rooms – ranging from everything from basic hobbies to the really nefarious places you do not want to visit, like photos and videos of cannibalism, fatal accident victims and crime scenes. Another focuses on the dark side of sex in all its variants, one of which is sadomasochism, which gets increasingly dark and nasty. Then the full English of kiddy porn – I don't even want to think about that.'

For the first time since he had met her, Grace saw a flash of emotion in Shannon Kendall's face – it was revulsion.

'Then we have tools and services for hacking – such as malware and stolen IDs and other credentials. Buried even deeper beneath all this we find international arms dealing – at a nuclear level. Stuff like enriched uranium for sale. And down in the weeds, very cleverly concealed in the midst of all that shit, is what might interest you two detectives.'

'Which is, Shannon?' Grace asked.

'High-end stolen works of art. And I'm talking very high-end. Collectors happy to pay millions for works they know to be stolen and they know they can never display publicly or sell – at least not for a few generations.'

'We've come across people like that,' Glenn Branson said.

Shannon nodded. 'Oh yes. The thrill of ownership of some work of art of international interest – of knowing they are the only people in the world who can see it – to some people that's better than the best sex.' She smiled.

'OK,' Grace said.

'That's why I asked you about Hans Holbein. Well, to be correct, Hans Holbein *the Younger*.' She looked pointedly at Branson. 'Did "miniatures" ever come up in a pub quiz?'

He shook his head.

Becoming increasingly animated, Shannon said, 'The camera wasn't invented until the mid-1820s – and the internet a little bit later . . . Before then, if you wanted to know what someone you had never met looked like – and you had the money to pay for it – you would hire a miniaturist. They would paint a watercolour portrait of them and send it to you—'

'Is this art lesson necessary, Shannon?' Grace asked.

'Very,' she replied. 'With respect, please hear me out. In 1539, Henry VIII was anxious to strengthen England's position in Europe. An alliance with the Protestant German states, through a marriage with either Anne of Cleves or her sister, both related to the Duke of Cleves, would have been a smart move to counteract the power of the Catholic Hapsburgs, who were dominating much of central Europe at the time.' She took a swig from her water bottle, but did not offer either of them a drink. 'His third wife, Jane Seymour, had conveniently died and he was free to marry again. The Duchy of Cleves were totally on board, and commissioned Hans Holbein the Younger to paint miniatures of both Anne of Cleves and her sister. It also appears – although there is no hard evidence to prove it – that they encouraged Holbein to be somewhat flattering and he duly obliged – probably out of fear of being beheaded. The portrait Henry VIII subsequently received might, in today's idiom, be deemed to have been photoshopped. When The King actually saw her in the flesh for the first time, he felt deceived and was furious. He went ahead with the marriage, purely for political reasons, but history tells us the marriage was never consummated.'

'She was beheaded?' Branson asked.

Shannon shook her head. 'Henry wasn't a fool, he needed the

alliance. They divorced and had an amicable – almost brother-and-sister – relationship for the rest of her life. She actually outlived all his other wives, quite some feat.' She took another swig of her water and wiped her mouth with the back of her hand.

'One of the miniatures I've just described is in the Royal Collection; it's the only one of Anne of Cleves in existence and it's of incalculable value. The RCIN is 422297. It is also currently the subject of an international auction on the dark web. Bids have been invited from a known group of collectors around the world. So far there are four bidders. One in Georgia, one in Taiwan, one in the USA and one in Argentina. Because of its historical significance and provenance, it is likely to sell for well over £2 million, which is the current bid.'

Grace and Branson looked at her in astonishment. 'You know all this for certain, Shannon?' Grace asked.

'Do you think I'm making it up?' she demanded.

Grace shook his head. 'No. Are you able to establish who is actually selling it?'

'I'm working on that now,' she said. 'Whoever it is knows how to cover their tracks extremely well.'

'Shannon,' Branson asked, 'how computer savvy would someone need to be to access and navigate the dark web well enough to do what you've just told us?'

She looked pointedly at them. 'What do you guys think? To go as deep as whoever this is, you'd need to be able to write code, Roy.'

Grace frowned. 'Computer code?'

'Yes, you'd have to code – write – a program that would squirrel its way deep into the dark web. A coding language like Python, which is currently a popular one as it's relatively user-friendly.'

'Could anyone learn to do this?'

'You'd need an in-depth level of experience, and you'd also, if you are savvy enough, use AI to help you. But,' Shannon added, 'once it has been set up, anyone computer-literate could learn to navigate it pretty quickly.'

'So I could, or Glenn?'

'Pretty well anyone, Roy.'

'So what kind of people – by that I mean their background – would have the skills to do this?' Grace asked Shannon.

'A fairly wide number. There are plenty of trained computer programmers around the world who'd be able to. Some of them from military intelligence, too.'

'How exactly does this auction take place, Shannon?' Branson asked.

'The way it's been set up is using a forum called Dread – it's probably the only forum on the dark web that is trusted, in that you can rely on stuff that's on it. The Buckingham Palace thieves have posted a cryptic message on a Dread bulletin board, and clearly they've done this before, multiple times. Those who've been buyers before will recognize the message, and indicate if they want to register for the auction.'

'What was the cryptic message?' Branson asked.

'Baking banana, white chocolate and raspberry cake.'

'What?' Grace frowned.

Shannon smiled. 'It's totally innocuous and meaningless to anyone except those who actually know. It's a signal to potential bidders. On the assumption this isn't their first rodeo, they would already have user names and passwords issued, and the details of a Bitcoin account set up by the vendors, into which they would make part payment in the event of a winning bid, with the balance on delivery. Those interested would communicate with the vendors via an app called Telegram – which is end-to-end encrypted. As each bid comes in, it is invisible to all the others.

'It was developed by two Russians,' she added. 'Designed to be completely secure.'

'But not so secure that you couldn't penetrate it?' Grace quizzed.

She answered blithely, 'Nothing is too secure, if I'm given enough time.'

'I take it you think other items stolen from the Royal Collection have been sold this way?' Grace asked.

'Either by auction or straight sale, yes. For sure. Whoever is behind this doesn't think they're leaving any footprints, but they are. They are smart – very smart indeed. But I'm more up to date and, more importantly, I'm smarter!'

'And modest with it,' Branson said with a grin.

She gave him a strange look. 'I'm with Muhammad Ali when he said, *It's hard to be modest when you're as great as I am.*'

Branson was – for one of the few occasions in his life – left nonplussed and unsure how to respond. Grace came to his rescue.

'OK, Shannon, so you are brilliant. That's why you're here and not still in prison. Are you able to identify the four bidders in the auction?'

'Actually, there are now five bidders,' she retorted.

'Five? Where is the fifth one located?'

'You're looking at her.'

80

Tuesday 28 November 2023

As soon as they walked back out of the flat and towards the car, Roy Grace's mobile rang. It was Denton Scroope.

'Hi, Roy. Good news, I agree with your wife about the code – it is definitely a variation of a Caesar Cipher. I'm pretty confident I've cracked the cipher – Sir Peregrine has used his initials PG for the key, which is P equals G, and so on for each subsequent letter. I've got the first of the remaining four deciphered: S O T H.'

'S O T H?' Grace repeated. 'Have you worked out what that stands for, Denton?'

'It could be something like Sanctuary Of The Heart or Shadows Of The Horizon. But given Cleo's deciphering of A Rose Between Two Thorns, I favour either Song Of The Horseman? Or perhaps Son Of The Horseman?' Scroope told him.

'Neither means anything to me. Some allusion to the Four Horsemen of the Apocalypse, perhaps?' Grace suggested, wracking his brains but not coming up with anything.

'I'll have a good mull on it. Is there anyone one who rides, I wonder.'

'Or whose father rides?' Grace suggested.

'Indeed. The good news, Roy, is that having established the type of cipher, I should now be able to crack the remaining three.'

'Great work, Denton. Really great work,' Roy said. 'I appreciate anything you can do.'

Having reached the car, Roy then called Sir Tommy Magellan-Lacey's mobile before getting in. The Master of the Royal Household answered almost immediately, his voice charming and friendly as ever but sounding a little anxious.

'Roy! Everything all right? Any progress?'

Grace was tempted to ask him if he knew any horse riders in the Royal Household, but decided it would lead to too many questions from the Master.

'By the way, Roy, before I forget, I've arranged for you to see the box of Granny's Personal Chips where it's currently in storage, next time you're in the Palace.'

'Thank you.'

'How did it go with Superintendent Mosse?'

'Well, we're not exactly *besties*, but I think we've established a constructive working relationship, Sir Tommy,' he said, giving Branson a wink.

'Good, that's excellent news.'

'There is one name that has come up as a possible person of interest in our enquiries,' he said guardedly.

'Yes?' Tommy asked, eagerly.

'Rose.'

'First or last name?'

'It could be either. You have Rose Cadoret who was in Kabul with you?'

The Master nodded. 'Completely trustworthy. There's absolutely no way she would be involved in anything nefarious – well, it would be a complete surprise to me.'

'I'm afraid that as a police officer, nothing is ever a surprise to me, Sir – er – Tommy.'

'I'll make some discreet enquiries about Rose Cadoret. I don't recall anyone else with either the first or last name "Rose" in the Royal Household.'

'Thank you, I'd appreciate that.'

THE HAWK IS DEAD

'Are your Sussex enquiries taking us anywhere closer? Any leads, suspects? I'm due to see both Their Majesties later this afternoon to give them a full update. Of course, the big question they are going to be asking is whether the deaths of Sir Peregrine Greaves and Geoffrey Bailey are connected or not. I'm actually on my way to see Superintendent Mosse now – do you have anything I can pass on to them?'

'I've nothing new in terms of suspects, but we do have some intel that a very valuable miniature painting in the Royal Collection may have been stolen – or is about to be.'

'What?' the Master gasped, and Grace heard it. 'This is credible information, Roy?'

'Yes. I trust the source.'

'Which – which painting?'

'By Hans Holbein – Hans Holbein the Younger. It's a miniature of Anne of Cleves. I can give you the RCIN number.'

'No, don't worry, I'm pretty sure I know where the picture is – it was one of many taken down for safety during the renovations and it's in storage down in the vaults under the Palace. God, if you are right, this is unbelievable – outrageous.'

'I am right.'

'So on top of the murder of Sir Peregrine, which may or may not have been a failed assassination attempt on The Queen, then the brutal murder of a footman, we now have an art thief within the Royal Household? Where did you get this information from, Roy?'

'I'd prefer to tell you when I see you, I don't think it's sensible to tell you over an open phone line.'

'Yes, good thinking, very wise.' He was silent for a moment, then he asked, 'Roy, was your source able to say whether they think this is a one-off instance targeting this one picture – or are these buggers, whoever they are, going for others, too?'

Keeping his cards tight to his chest, Grace replied, lying, 'This is the only item I'm aware of.'

'I'll alert Lorraine McKnight, the Director of the Royal Collection, immediately. You say it may already have been stolen?'

'My source wasn't clear on this.'

'I'll get the guards to check all vehicles leaving the Palace, and all people carrying bags large enough to contain the painting – which isn't very large at all – as soon as I'm off this call – but—'

'Actually, Sir Tommy,' Grace interrupted him. 'I think we need to tread very carefully, and keep this information just entre nous. We don't want to tip anyone off that we know about the plans for the picture. If it is still in the Palace then you have a very good chance of catching the thieves red-handed. Just make a discreet or seemingly innocuous enquiry – come up with some pretext why you want to see the picture, so you don't raise any flags.'

'Good point, Roy. But one thing puzzles me.'

'Which is?'

'Well, I don't know how much the thieves have thought this through. The late Queen Elizabeth was particularly fond of this picture. It was she who made me aware of it, and of its significance. Hans Holbein the Younger's miniature of Anne of Cleves is, frankly, one of the best known and most important paintings in the world – particularly due to its political significance. Every auction house and art dealer on the planet would know it immediately – they wouldn't touch it with a barge pole, they'd know it was stolen from the Royal Collection. So I don't quite understand what's going on – unless these people think they are going to ransom it back to us.'

In the background, Grace heard a faint sound he recognized. He glanced at his watch: 3 p.m. exactly. 'I've had previous dealings with the criminal side of the art world,' he said. 'I don't fully share your view about everyone not touching it. But it would be

THE HAWK IS DEAD

very helpful if we could start by establishing if the painting is still at the Palace or has already been stolen. If you could find that out urgently.'

'And then set a trap if it's still here?' Sir Tommy said.

'That's exactly what I'm thinking.'

'Absolutely,' the Master replied. 'I'm on it.'

81

Tuesday 28 November 2023

Grace slipped his phone back in his pocket and filled Branson in on his conversation with Sir Tommy.

'Boss, why did you hold back and not tell him what Shannon said, that this isn't the first auction of items from the Royal Collection?'

'Sir Tommy's a nice guy, well-meaning and helpful. But at the moment we have to jump on whoever the thieves within the Royal Household are. Sir Tommy's not a detective and if he starts digging around for us, we risk the people we're after running for the hills.'

The DI nodded.

'We've got Shannon joining the bidding. Let's see what she comes up with. She's already said something extremely interesting that has got me thinking about Sir Peregrine in a different light.'

Clipping in his seatbelt, Branson said, 'Are you thinking what I'm thinking?'

'Code?'

He nodded, grimly. 'Shannon said that the skills required could come from someone with a Military Intelligence background. Sir Peregrine's military background was in Naval Intelligence, right?'

'That's what Lady Greaves told us.'

A lightbulb had popped on somewhere deep inside Grace's

brain in their meeting with Shannon Kendall. Not a searingly bright one, but a glimmer, nonetheless. And steadily getting brighter. 'Shit,' he said, then fell silent, deep in thought.

Branson looked at him, waiting for him to say something further, but the Detective Superintendent remained silent, his eyes closed.

'Shall I head on down to HQ, boss?' he asked.

There was no response.

Branson waited for some moments, then started the engine and reversed out of the parking space. As he did so, Grace suddenly raised a pointed finger. 'Could this shed new light on Sir Peregrine's death?'

'What's your line of thinking – although I think I've guessed it?'

'We already know Sir Peregrine was into ciphers – using his old military code in his diary. Let's hypothesize he was up to speed with modern computer code. Had he rumbled the conspiracy and was doing his own investigations on the dark web into who the conspirators were? And was that why he was murdered, to silence him? Or . . . ?' He looked questioningly at his colleague.

'Or was he one of them – one of the conspirators? Is that what you're saying?' Branson looked dubious.

'Up until now, we thought we had a clear motive for Sir Peregrine being the shooter's intended target, from his coded entry in his diary. Now we potentially have a second one.'

Branson drove in silence for some moments then he said, 'Peregrine on the trail of the conspirators, or Peregrine not quite the loyal household servant Their Majesties believed?'

'We've heard about his "proclivities", thanks to the decoding of his diary. But what else can we glean from what he wrote?' Grace glanced down at his phone, pulled up the decoded script and scanned through it, reading aloud various parts of significance to him.

'A group of conspirators – let's call them thieves . . . My source has discovered they are stealing high-value items belonging to the Royal Collection, which have been housed in the Palace. These items include ornaments, sculptures, paintings, small but rare pieces of furniture, and significant jewellery. An item on the target list is a priceless diamond of great historical significance from a collection known as "Granny's Personal Chips". My source told me they are planning to replace it with a fake that would be undetectable to the naked eye.'

He went on.

'If you are deciphering this it can mean only one thing, which is that The Hawk is dead . . . And, in particular, I want to expose the ringleader of this sordid little group. Someone who is high up in Royal Service . . .
  My source has given me this person's name, but I'm frightened to reveal it . . .'

'So who is this *source*? The Buckingham Palace Deep Throat?' Branson said. 'Or are we taking it all too much at face value?'
'I'm thinking, is this all a very clever double-blind? The diary is in code, so why hasn't he named either the *source* or this person *high up in Royal Service*? If he's speculating he might be murdered for delving into the conspiracy, why would he have shied from naming this person high up in Royal Service, so they got their comeuppance? Could it possibly be that the "source" doesn't exist and this person high up in Royal Service is actually himself?'
Branson frowned. 'But he must have been worried about being watched – and killed, to have written that diary entry in code. I don't get what he'd have to gain from that.'
'All part of clever obfuscation? Protecting his reputation, or

his family's inheritance in the event of his death, or perhaps both?'

'What do we know about his finances?'

'Financial Investigator Emily Denyer's looking into them. She's not found anything so far that raises a flag.'

'Does he have a Bitcoin or other cybercurrency account?'

'Aiden Gilbert's Digital Forensics team have his laptop and phone. If he's got a hidden account of any kind, they'll find it.'

As Branson drove on, Grace lapsed into brief silence again, deep in thought. Then he said, 'This case is a proper onion router situation itself. Layers and layers to peel away.'

'Exactly.'

'And the first layer is the death of Geoffrey Bailey so soon after Peregrine's. What we know so far is that the two of them were in some form of relationship that Peregrine felt was inappropriate, so he kept it hidden. We also know that Bailey desperately wanted a medal, which was in Sir Peregrine's gift to recommend to The King. Killing Sir Peregrine wasn't going to deliver him that medal, and from what we know of Bailey, he could never have planned the shooting. It was a proper military operation.'

'Sir Jason, as well as Sir Tommy, and others in the Palace are all ex-military.'

Grace smiled. 'Yes, it seems half the Household staff are.' He was silent again for some moments. 'I'm trying to think of what motive there could be for killing both Sir Peregrine and Geoffrey Bailey. We know there's the clandestine connection between them, so blackmail may be involved. That would be a neat fit. But killing both of them? Who has done that and what's the motive?'

'Lady Greaves would have something to gain. She learns about their secret meetings and kills them both.'

'Elegant theory but I don't see her as a modern-day Lady Macbeth,' Grace said with a wry smile. 'But she may be able to tell us something.' He called Polly Sweeney, who said she was at this moment on her way to have a cup of tea with Lady Greaves, her second visit in two days. He asked her if she could urgently, in her role as Family Liaison Officer, ask Sir Peregrine's widow if her husband had ever taken any refresher course in computer coding.

Ending the call, he turned to his colleague. 'Let's look at possible motives.'

'Jealousy, revenge, fear, anger and greed,' Branson replied glibly. 'Aren't these what you always say are the main motives for murder?'

'I don't just always say them, mate. I know them by heart. Over twenty years working on homicides has taught me a lot about human nature. So which of the five you've just reeled off are you going to bet your stack of chips on right now?'

'Greed,' Branson replied almost immediately.

'Greed is good,' Grace replied.

'Michael Douglas playing Gordon Gekko in the movie *Wall Street*. He said that. Famous line.'

'Is there any movie you haven't seen?'

'Yeah, actually. I've got a few on my bucket list. I've never seen *The Sound of Music*. Nor *Mary Poppins*. Not really my thing, musicals.'

Grace smiled. 'I actually wasn't quoting a movie when I said, *greed is good*. I actually think greed is a good hypothesis. Given the values of items in the Royal Collection, which we've had reinforced just now, greed has to be significant. Let's look at the death of Sir Peregrine first. Two potential hypotheses. First hypothesis, Sir Peregrine stumbled across the conspirators and needed to be silenced. Second hypothesis, Sir Peregrine was one of the conspirators – their ringleader? Let's go with the second for the moment, OK?'

Branson nodded, a tad dubiously.

THE HAWK IS DEAD

They were interrupted by Grace's phone ringing. 'Sir Tommy!' he answered.

The Master sounded distraught. 'Roy, I was so worried after our call I went straight from my office down to the vault. The miniature isn't there. I checked with Rose Cadoret, the Deputy Director of the Royal Collection. She is one of the few people who could authorize any item being moved somewhere different.'

'She doesn't know where it is? Is there anyone else who would have access to the store – apart from Lorraine McKnight of course?' Roy quizzed.

'There's Sir Jason Finch and also there's the Surveyor of The King's Pictures, Robert Randall – but they are both away on annual leave at the moment.'

'Conveniently?'

'Yes, could be these thieves have taken the opportunity of them being absent. I'll see if I can contact Robert Randall, but I very much doubt he would have moved it without notifying Rose. This is terrible, Roy.' The Master sounded near distraught. 'And I'll inform Sir Jason Finch right away even though I believe he's in Amsterdam with his wife. He's back next Monday, but I know he would want to be kept updated.'

'The Keeper of the Privy Purse?' Grace asked.

'Exactly. He will need to notify the Palace insurers right away. And he won't be at all happy about this.'

'Let me know if you hear anything more.'

'You're on my speed-dial.'

82

Tuesday 28 November 2023

Roy Grace remained silent until they drove past the barrier at HQ. Then, suddenly animated, he turned to Branson.

'OK! I have another possible hypothesis. So, Sir Peregrine Greaves, who has considerable internet skills from his background in Naval Intelligence, is the leader of a small group of Royal Household staff who are making a fortune, or planning to make a fortune, by stealing items from the Royal Collection that they think won't be missed until all the renovations have been completed. Let's say he's had a falling-out with Geoffrey Bailey, who has a crush on him. Bailey, bitter at not receiving a medal from Sir Peregrine, knows what he is up to and is threatening to expose him, which would blow apart the entire scam – with dire consequences for his co-conspirators. With me so far?'

'I am.'

'For reasons as yet unknown, Sir Peregrine is suddenly murdered by a person or persons unknown. Geoffrey Bailey is now left without the person who could have got him his medal and his deserved status. There are others in senior positions in the Royal Household who could put him forward for that coveted medal, and maybe Bailey thinks by naming the conspirators and preventing the theft of millions of pounds' worth of items, he will be awarded the medal. The conspirators as a group, worried about this loose cannon, decide the only way to guarantee his silence is to kill him.'

THE HAWK IS DEAD

'But why the medal down his throat?' Branson asked.

'To humiliate him?' Grace posited. 'Perhaps sending a message to anyone else he might have told who might try to blackmail them? And putting him in the digester – perhaps they hoped it would decompose most of his body – which it would have done in time. Or perhaps it was symbolic? That he was just a piece of compost?'

'You might be overthinking it,' Branson said as they drove uphill across the HQ campus towards the detectives' parking area. 'It might have just been a convenient place to dump his body.'

Grace smiled. 'You could well be right. The simplest solution, and all that. I'll leave this hypothesis off tomorrow's press briefing.'

'I think that would be smart, boss.'

As they pulled into a space a short distance behind his office, Grace asked, 'So, what do you make of Shannon's work so far?'

Branson nodded. 'Yeah, she's smart and she knows her way around the internet for sure. She's worked for some pretty big internet players, including Elon Musk, as well as a company funded by MI6. Sure, she wants to please us, to justify what we've done to get her out of jail, but I feel she does really know what she's doing. Evidenced by what Sir Tommy said a short while ago.'

Grace signalled he agreed, but his expression was uneasy.

83

Tuesday 28 November 2023

Moments later, Polly Sweeney rang. Grace switched to loudspeaker, and both of them listened.

'Roy, I'm sitting with Lady Greaves, and I just put the question to her that you asked: whether Sir Peregrine had recently taken any refresher course in computer coding. Lady Greaves just told me that he did an intense course quite recently, which finished a few months ago. But he wouldn't tell her why he was doing it.'

'Did he give a reason he wouldn't tell her?' Grace and Branson frowned at each other.

'Well – apparently, when she pressed him, all he would say was it was at the personal request of The King. That his boss was concerned about cyber-security and thought Sir Peregrine's military intelligence background might be helpful in establishing a firewall layer for the Royal Household network . . . Hang on a sec, Roy, Lady Greaves is saying something.'

They waited for a moment then heard her voice again. 'Lady Greaves has just told me that The King had asked him how up to speed with current internet technology he was, and when he told him that he didn't feel he was that much up to speed, The King suggested a fairly elaborate course he should enrol in – which he duly did. He had obviously researched it.'

'And that was a few months ago.'

'Hold on a second, sir.' There was another pause, then Polly

THE HAWK IS DEAD

Sweeney came back on the line. 'Lady Greaves says he finished the course in July.'

'Please thank her,' Grace said. 'This is very helpful.'

When the call ended, he turned to Branson and gave him a quizzical look.

'Interesting,' Branson said.

'Very. I guess there's one person who can verify whether Sir Peregrine was telling his wife the truth or not.'

'Who's that?'

Grace smiled.

84

Tuesday 28 November 2023

Precisely 4.40 p.m. That was the time Sir Tommy had given him, suggesting he dial in a couple of minutes before, as His Majesty was somewhat a stickler for punctuality and had a particularly rammed afternoon.

Despite all his professionalism kicking in, Roy Grace felt butterflies in his stomach, and his finger on the keypad wasn't as steady as usual. Although King Charles had been very friendly on their last meeting, he was nervous now all the same. He'd never actually phoned The King of England before.

The phone began ringing and a moment later he heard a female voice. 'Good afternoon, Buckingham Palace.'

Grace's voice came out sounding very small, he thought. 'Good afternoon, may I please speak to The King.'

'Your name, sir?'

'My name is Detective Superintendent Grace.'

'*Roy* Grace?'

'Correct.'

'He is expecting you. One moment please, Detective Superintendent, I'm putting you through.'

Grace took three deep breaths. A moment later he heard The King's now familiar voice. 'Detective Superintendent Grace, good afternoon, I gather you wanted to speak to me. How are you?'

'I'm – I'm fine, thank you, Your Majesty.'

'Good. Do you have some news? Good news, I hope?'

THE HAWK IS DEAD

His voice was warm but understandably tinged with anxiety, Grace thought. The King was not only Head of State and Head of the Commonwealth, but he also carried the normal burdens of any human being. Grace remembered a former Chief of the Met Police once saying that wearing a uniform does not protect you from trauma. The same could apply to The King – he might be head of the Royal Family and have all the privileges that went with it, but he was also just a human being, extremely worried about the safety of the woman he loved.

'We are making good progress, Your Majesty.'

'I'm pleased to hear it – I hope you can make sense of this terrible tragedy – well, two terrible tragedies now.'

'If I can give you any reassurance, Your Majesty, the further we get with our enquiries, the more certain I am that Her Majesty was not the intended target in this tragic shooting, and that her life is not under threat.'

'I would so much like to share your optimism, Detective Superintendent. I really would.'

There was such warmth and passion – and sadness – in those last words that Grace felt extremely moved. He wished desperately at this moment that he could say something that would put The King's mind completely at rest. All he could do was deliver what he knew was a rather lame-sounding platitude. 'I'm sure we will be able to give you something positive very soon, sir.'

'I do hope so.'

'I believe Sir Tommy has been keeping you up to speed, sir.'

'Yes, he has. So, what was it you wanted to ask me?'

'I know you are very busy, sir, it was just one quick question – regarding Sir Peregrine.'

'Yes, of course, fire away.'

'Can I ask, did you and Sir Peregrine have a conversation earlier this year or late last year about how up to speed he was with current internet technology?'

'Well, we talked daily about all matters.' There was a brief silence before he spoke again. 'How up to speed with internet technology, you said?'

'Yes, Sir.'

'Hmm. No, I don't recall talking about that specifically, no. But we may have discussed it at some point – we had issues with the Palace Wi-Fi a while back and Peregrine was fairly tech savvy, but it was Tommy who really knew the right people to bring in, not Peregrine.'

'What I need to know, Sir, is did you ever suggest to Sir Peregrine that he should enrol in a specialist course on internet technology?'

The King came back without hesitation. 'No. Never. Absolutely not. I'd remember that.'

'That's very helpful, Your Majesty. I won't take any more of your time.'

'You'll keep me updated, won't you, Detective Superintendent? Through Tommy is fine, but if there's anything really significant, always feel free to come through to me directly.'

Grace thanked him and ended the call.

Then he sat thinking hard for several minutes, before lifting his phone and asking Glenn Branson if he could come to his office.

Then, as he ended the call, his phone rang. He heard the dry, slightly smug voice of Denton Scroope. 'Roy, is this a convenient moment?'

'Absolutely.'

'I've deciphered another.'

'Excellent, what do you have, Denton?'

'Well, you gave me the letters R S Z K Y Z N K Z K S. Your man was using a numbers code with the code for each letter having to be deciphered separately. What I have for you is A B I T H I W T I T B.'

THE HAWK IS DEAD

'A B I T H I W T I T B?' Grace repeated.
'Correct.'
'I'm not sure I'm any the wiser.'
'Could it be A Bird In The Hand Is Worth Two In The Bush? Would that mean anything to you, Roy?'

Grace was silent for a moment, thinking. *A Bird In The Hand?*

What bird? Was any member of the Royal Household birdlike in some way? Or named after a bird?

Then he realized exactly who.

85

Tuesday 28 November 2023

Unfinished business. Rose Cadoret was losing her nerve. They all were. Since Smoke's botched shooting of Sir Peregrine and his insane killing of Geoffrey Bailey, things were unravelling. That astute Sussex detective, Roy Grace, was a real worry, and was making very dangerous assumptions.

Dangerous to them.

But she still had one piece of unfinished business. Actually, two pieces.

Detectives from the Met were crawling all over the Household staff following Bailey's death. If Smoke's misguided intention had been to silence the footman, it had catastrophically backfired. Dead men might not talk, as the saying went, but Geoffrey Bailey certainly had talked his head off in the days – hours even – before his death. He'd poured out his anger over the medal to anyone who would listen, but worse, Rose had heard, he had dropped very large hints that he knew about items that had been stolen.

If Smoke had simply put the frighteners on him, as he'd been instructed, it would have silenced the footman. Now, as the Met detectives interviewed his former work colleagues and were gathering disturbing information from them, it felt like Geoffrey Bailey was still shouting his head off from the grave.

Further, thanks to Detective Grace's meddling, unless the missing items from the Royal Collection were found, and quickly, Lorraine McKnight was poised to bring in the police to investigate their disappearance. And the items wouldn't be found, because they were no longer here.

The group had always known that the day would come when they would have to do a fast exit. They were rich beyond their wildest dreams from the items they'd already sold, and they had even greater riches stored in the unit conveniently near to London's Heathrow Airport. Their loot was in Bitcoins, shared out equally, into accounts each of them held, and they'd made two rules.

The first was never to cash in any of their Bitcoins until they were safely out of the country. It was drummed into them that the fastest way for a criminal to get caught was to start splashing unexplained cash around.

It was a rule she had broken. Not badly, she hadn't gone out and splurged on a Ferrari or anything daft like that. But even so she felt a little guilty, because she'd taken a risk. It was a tiny one – stupid, she knew. But it was something that as an only child she'd needed to do, while she was still here in England and able to.

She'd only cashed in a tiny fraction of the millions of pounds' worth of Bitcoins she had. It was to get her elderly, wheelchair-bound mother out of her damp council flat and into the beautiful care home in Bexhill, with a glorious sea-view room. It was expensive, costing £1,800 a week for her small suite, and a further £1,700 a week for her round-the-clock carers, and Rose had paid a year in advance.

It was just worth it for peace of mind. She was very aware that once she had left England she was unlikely ever to return or see her mother again. At least she now knew she was in good hands and in a place where she could live out her last years in a level of luxury she'd never before experienced. And probably could never have imagined.

Any guilt Rose might have had about stealing from the Royal Collection was more than assuaged by the knowledge that, at least, one under-privileged pensioner would benefit from the nation's treasures. Besides, how many of those treasures had been stolen or blagged in the first place?

And as for the rules, hey, soon they would be safely offshore. With different names, untouchable in a country with no extradition treaty with the UK. Each of them carrying on their phones and laptops a carefully backed-up string of thirty-five numbers and letters, some in uppercase, some lowercase, in electronic Bitcoin wallets. Untraceable funds she and the others could draw from, anywhere in the world, any time. Millions. She loved the sound of that word.

Millions!

And just the tiniest drop in the ocean for the Royal Collection.

The second rule they had made was for none of them to be too greedy. They had unanimously agreed that the moment the balloon looked like it was going up, they would be gone, accepting they would all be happy with what they already had. And they had a lot. A very great deal. They all had IDs, credit cards and passports in assumed names, ready for when Exeat, the code for Exit Day, came.

And before that they had work to do, covering their tracks as best they could. Tying up loose ends. She had two loose ends and she needed to move fast. The button had been pressed.

Exeat was in three days' time.

86

Tuesday 28 November 2023

'A bird in the hand is worth two in the bush.' Glenn Branson sat in front of Grace's desk the way he always did, spinning the chair round and straddling it as if it were a horse. He rested his arms on the back and leaned forward. 'Very smart. But Sir Jason Finch is away until next Monday, right?'

'In Amsterdam.'

'Is that significant? Like, Amsterdam?'

'I looked it up. It used to be one of the main hubs of the world diamond trade. Less so now, but still significant.'

'Confirming your original suspicions about him?'

'Not suspicions – let's just say *interest*. All the more so since Denton Scroope's deciphering. I'll look forward to interviewing him next week.'

Branson grinned. 'And in the meantime, get you! Detective Superintendent Roy Grace all cosied up to The King and Queen. How soon before it's Sir Roy? I'll have to start wearing a cap so I can doff it.'

'Very funny. Can we be serious?'

'Sorry, boss.'

'I'd hate to have to send you to the Tower.'

Branson grinned. 'So?'

'So you heard my conversation with Polly Sweeney, earlier, when she was with Lady Greaves. Lady Greaves was very definite that her husband – late husband – had enrolled in an advanced course on computer coding at the specific request of The King, right?'

'No question.'

'So I just had a conversation with The King.'

'As you do.'

Grace stifled a smile. 'He said he could not recall any such conversation.'

'What?'

'My thoughts exactly.'

'Hang on, this isn't making sense. Lady Greaves very distinctly said that His Maj was concerned about cyber-security and thought Sir Peregrine, with his intelligence background, might enrol in a course on computer coding, which could be helpful in establishing a secure network for the Royal Household. She said he'd mentioned about establishing a firewall.'

'She did,' Grace confirmed. 'This is not a conversation His Majesty was likely to have forgotten.'

'So someone hasn't been telling the truth?' Branson suggested.

'Either Sir Peregrine lied to his wife. Or Lady Greaves lied to Polly. Or—'

'Or your new bestie, The King, lied to you?'

Grace smiled. 'Shall we do a process of elimination? Top of my list to eliminate is The King.'

'Shame,' Branson said with a broad grin. 'Imagine the press coverage you'd get! *Top Sussex copper arrests King Charles III as prime suspect in murder case!* It would go viral. You'd instantly become the most famous detective in the world!'

'I'm not sure it would be the smartest career move.'

'Probably not.'

'So, Lady Greaves. What reason would she have to lie?'

'Trying to protect her late husband's reputation? Or were they both in it together?'

'In *what*, together?' Grace quizzed.

THE HAWK IS DEAD

'In whatever the hell's going on – the murder of Sir Peregrine, the murder of Geoffrey Bailey?'

He nodded, reflectively. 'That is a possibility, although I feel unlikely. Hopefully we'll get a clearer picture soon.'

'What do you think?' Branson asked. 'What's your gut telling you?'

'I think Lady Greaves was telling the truth. And The King was, too. Which means Sir Peregrine was lying.'

'Why?'

Grace thought for a moment. 'John Gotti, former head of the New York Gambino family, and a major player across the New York Mafia families, famously said: *I never lie because I don't fear anyone. You only lie when you're afraid*.'

'You think Sir Peregrine was afraid of something? Such as what, losing his life?'

'Let's consider the options. If he was one of the conspirators, he was afraid of getting caught. He wasn't going to risk telling his wife because he knew she wouldn't approve.' Grace raised his eyebrows.

'That's one possibility,' Branson conceded.

'Option Two. He was suspicious that something was going on with some members of the Royal Household on the dark web. He wanted to have a look for himself, but was nervous of telling his wife for some reason – perhaps that she might be a gossip.'

Branson nodded.

'Option Three – he'd discovered what was going on and was scared for his own life if he confronted the conspirators. So instead he decided to take a secret deep dive into their activities.'

Branson nodded again. 'All plausible. But we've heard about his inappropriate relationship. And about the strange torch signalling in Sir Peregrine's office late at night. We know the dark web is a place where you can get pretty much anything you want that you won't find on sale in your local high street, or Amazon.

Maybe he was just looking for company. Bailey had a crush on him, which was flattering, he didn't say no. And it's nothing to do with our enquiry. I mean, he's sure not going to have told his wife that, and making it up that he was improving his computer coding skills at The King's request would make it seem totally kosher.'

Before Branson could respond, Grace's phone rang. He didn't recognize the number, but answered. 'Detective Superintendent Grace.'

'It's Shannon,' she said. 'Are you free to talk?'

'Go ahead.' He put the phone on loudspeaker for Branson to hear.

'Do you have Rose Cadoret on your list of Persons of Interest?' she asked.

'Rose Cadoret, the Deputy Director of the Royal Collection?'

'Correct.'

'She is very much on my list, Shannon. I'm hoping to interview her on Thursday.'

'I'm working on getting more information, but from what I have so far, I would say definitely she's one to watch. I'll have more information for you by tomorrow.'

'What can you tell me about her now, Shannon?'

'I've only just come across her name, but it's unusual, I wanted to make sure.'

Grace spelled it out for her.

'Yup,' she said. 'That's her. Rose Cadoret.'

'OK,' Grace said, 'I have another name for your list, to check out, too.'

'Sure, who is it?'

'Sir Jason Finch.'

'Leave it with me.'

87

Wednesday 29 November 2023

Rose Cadoret had come in early. She wanted to be here when there weren't many people around, and before the workmen had started. Not that there would be any workmen in this part of the Palace, the south-west wing, today, nor for at least another month.

Her ribs were hurting less today than they had yesterday. Smoke had told her she should go and see the Palace doctor, but she knew there was nothing you could do about bruised ribs, you just had to ride the pain out, avoid coughing, sneezing and laughing. And sleep on your back – easier said than done.

She was tired and tetchy after a restless night and annoyed Smoke wasn't here. He was on the night shift, due to finish at 7 a.m., which was five minutes ago, and just perfect timing for her plan. She stood, high on a corner some feet below the former footmen's floor, on the steep, narrow wooden staircase, which she'd climbed two days ago with Smoke. It had been easier then, it hadn't been so uncomfortable.

She decided to go on, and wait for him higher up. She ducked under the strip of red and yellow tape carrying the warning sign *EXTREME DANGER – KEEP OUT!* Then she continued on to the top and stood, getting her breath back, sustained by the knowledge that in just two days' time she would be on a plane, that gorgeous Airbus 380, it was called. Smoke had told her that you got your own private cabin, and there was a shower room big enough to swing a substantial animal in.

Too bad he wouldn't be joining her.

She heard footsteps clumping up the stairs. Police boots. Then he came into view, all kitted up, with his weapons and his Kevlar vest and all the rest of his clobber. He was sweating and looked tired. Well, he had been up all night, and he'd told her many times that it wasn't the late hours that got you, it was the boredom that dulled your brain.

How dulled was it now? Very, she hoped.

'Hey babe!' His breath was rancid as he pecked her on the cheek. He smelled like unwashed laundry.

As they had on Monday, they stood in front of the jagged, unguarded opening that had been bashed through the wall of the light shaft, with the grimy ceiling above them. Rose turned away from him, placed her hands either side of the opening, leaned in, and looked down. Checking.

In the weak light, she could see at the very bottom the six thin steel spikes rising vertically several feet. The workmen from the lift company would be returning in a month or so when the renovations, under the guidance of Sir Tommy Magellan-Lacey, began in earnest on this wing.

Until then it was all sealed off. But not forgotten. Certainly not by Rose Cadoret.

'Why've you brought me up here again, babe?' He looked at her expectantly, signalling he remembered they'd had sex here two days previously. 'Cos you want me again?'

She stepped back. 'I read the highest distance onto a hard surface that a human can survive is a forty-foot drop,' she said.

'OK.' He gave her a puzzled frown.

'We have a big problem with Lorraine McKnight – as I've told you.'

'It's Exeat in two days. We'll all be gone. Larging it in the sun. Rum sours for lunch. G&Ts and Negronis at sunset. Lorraine McKnight will be history. It'll all be history. Their history, our future!'

THE HAWK IS DEAD

'You don't seriously think Lorraine McKnight is simply going to go away, Jon? You were happy enough to off Geoffrey Bailey, who was a minnow, now you're baulking at offing McKnight who is a Great White in comparison. Just tell me what you think – if I lured her up here and pushed her into the shaft, could we be one hundred per cent sure it would kill her? Like, is it high enough?' she said.

'Wouldn't killing her just compound our problems?'

'Like killing Geoffrey Bailey didn't?'

'Touché!'

'This isn't a fucking game, Jon, this is our future. All our futures. Which you've done your very best to screw.'

'Hey!'

'The footings for the lift shaft were done a month ago. It will be at least another month before work starts on the lift itself. If Lorraine were to *accidentally* plunge down it, there's a pretty good chance no one's going to find her for at least a week or two – by which time we'll be long, long gone.'

He looked at her.

'So tell me, Mr Crackshot Sniper. Tell me if you think the drop down the shaft is long enough to kill her – for sure?'

He turned and, just as she had done, placed a hand on each wall, leaned in and looked down. 'Difficult to see. Hang on.' He pushed himself upright, removed his phone from his pocket and switched on the torch, then leaned in again, holding on with one hand and shining the torch with the other.

'So you really think that drop would kill her?'

'It would kill anyone.'

'Good!' she said. Then she slammed the heel of her palm into the underside of his chin with all her strength, snatching his phone from his hand at the same time as he lurched sideways trying to grasp at anything. Her own cry of pain drowned out his feeble yelp of surprise as he tumbled into the void.

An instant later she heard a faint thud, like a sack of potatoes. Then she stood still for a moment, a little dizzy with surprise.

He was gone.

Actually gone.

She leaned in, cautiously, warily, just in case he was hanging on a few inches below the top and might grab her. But he wasn't.

She shone the torch down the shaft, and saw him.

He lay on his back at a strange angle. One of the steel spikes was sticking up through his neck, with blood pooling around. Another was through his right thigh.

He looked bloated, as if he had put on thirty or forty pounds since falling. Then she realized, one of the spikes must have pierced his midriff before coming up against his Kevlar vest, which it was raising, grotesquely.

He was still alive, she realized, to her horror. He was blinking, and his mouth was opening and closing, like a fish.

Then it closed and didn't open again.

His eyes stopped blinking. They remained open. And stayed open.

Silence. Beautiful silence.

Thanks for the ride, pal. It was fun, really it was.

She looked at his phone, which she held in her hand. She knew the code because she'd watched him, countless times, tapping it in. But far more importantly, inside the phone was his Bitcoin wallet app. And his thirty-five digit code inside that.

She smiled. In the past couple of minutes, she'd gotten rid of the group's liability. And massively increased her net worth.

What was not to like?

88

Wednesday 29 November 2023

Roy Grace had been at his desk in the Major Crime Team suite of Sussex Police HQ for just twenty minutes, preparing for yet another press briefing on Operation Asset. It was 7.25 a.m. Day ten since the shooting of Sir Peregrine Greaves, and he had nothing new to give to the press and media – well, nothing that he wanted to give out.

Exhaustive house-to-house calls in the surrounding area had been carried out. Ballistics tests had not yet given them the exact make of weapon the shooter had used, and it was unlikely they would. The motorcycle seen by the eyewitness Sarah Stratten was still not identified, and nor was whoever had subsequently threatened Stratten.

The murder of the royal footman, Geoffrey Bailey, gave him something fresh to talk about, and in today's briefing he would explain how they were looking to see what connections they could find between the two dead men.

After his call late yesterday afternoon with Shannon Kendall, he had googled Rose Cadoret, as well as asking ChatGPT-4 for any information it could come up with. But there wasn't a lot from either of them. An only child, Rose Cadoret had obtained a BA in Art History at the Courtauld Institute, but then in somewhat of a contrast she enlisted in the Army as a soldier – not even on an officer training course – and did three tours in Afghanistan. After leaving the Army five years ago, she had joined the Royal Collection team at Buckingham Palace, rising – rather quickly, he thought – to become its Deputy Director.

For much of the night he'd lain awake, fretting about the case, about what clues he might have missed. And just as importantly, who he could trust.

But for now he had a much more pressing issue. Shannon Kendall's rather cryptic choice of words about Rose Cadoret, yesterday.

She's one to watch.

What did she mean, precisely? Was this going to give them the answer to why Rose's name was coded in the diary?

And what was Shannon going to discover about Sir Jason Finch?

He didn't have long to wait to find out. His phone started ringing, and this time a name appeared on the display instead of just the number.

Shannon Kendall

89

Wednesday 29 November 2023

'Good morning, Shannon,' he answered.

'You ever play Monopoly?' she retorted, straight in.

'Monopoly? Yes, I did. Every Christmas in the evening with my family, when I was a kid. Why?'

'Good. So you'll understand what a Get Out of Jail Free card is?'

'I probably had a few in my time.' He found himself making a mental note that he and Cleo should get a Monopoly board, and teach Noah and one day Molly, and do the same, play it on Christmas evening, all engaging with each other instead of the usual thing of flopping in front of the television and falling asleep.

'Like, what I mean is, I think you're going to agree that this – what I'm about to tell you – is your vindication for springing me from prison.'

'It is? Tell me!'

'Rose Cadoret, right?'

'What have you found out about her?'

'She's a former soldier. Saw action in Kabul where she came under fire. She has a pretty impressive military background, which may or may not be significant, because that's how she ended up at Buckingham Palace – following a Royal Protection Officer she had an on-off relationship with, who was in the same regiment. Her former commanding officer in that regiment is now a senior member of the Royal Household, Sir Jason Finch.

All very cosy, the old-boy network and all that, not that there's anything necessarily suspicious in that. But here's where we cut to the chase. Everyone makes mistakes, that's human. Even the cleverest person. I'm sure you as a cop know that better than most, right?'

'Yep, very true.' Grace could think of dozens of examples. A pair of discarded surgical gloves found in a bin outside the home of a murder victim. The forensically aware offender thought he was clever, wearing those gloves. He hadn't realized his DNA was all over the insides of them.

Ronnie Biggs was identified by fingerprints on a bottle of Heinz ketchup on the kitchen table at Leatherslade Farm, the hideout of the Great Train Robbers. Timothy McVeigh, the Oklahoma City bomber, was stopped for driving without a licence plate. Ted Bundy's first arrest was because he'd forgotten to put his headlights on. The list was endless.

'I told you at my flat about the auction on the dark web?'

'The Anne of Cleves miniature – by Hans Holbein.'

'Hans Holbein *the Younger*,' she corrected.

He smiled. She said it like a teacher correcting an errant pupil. 'The *Younger*,' he repeated.

'OK, I've still not got to the bottom of whoever is actually running the auction, but I have made inroads. Someone very tech savvy is behind the way it's set up, but they've made one small mistake, through an IP – Internet Protocol – address. You'd have to be looking extremely hard to find it. And I mean *extremely*. It's buried deep beneath several firewall layers – which I've navigated through. That's part of what I do. Which not many people can.'

Grace listened intently.

'That IP address is for an internet account with an email address for someone called Gisella Standing. Gisella Standing is a real person, German-born from Dusseldorf, married to an Englishman and they live in Reigate in Surrey. She's a dentist and her husband is a maxillofacial surgeon. But Gisella Standing, almost certainly unaware of it, is an internet alias for Rose Cadoret, Deputy Director of the Royal Collection. Gisella might get the occasional email that makes no sense and she'd just bin it, assuming it was spam.'

'For what reason would Rose Cadoret use an alias?' Grace asked.

'There could be a number of reasons. A lot of people use aliases when surfing the net – particularly people looking at porn sites who don't want to take the risk of being entrapped by blackmailers. Or simply because they are well known and they want to be anonymous. That's a very plausible scenario for Rose Cadoret and nothing sinister about it. Her position as Deputy Director of the Royal Collection makes her a high-profile individual in the art world. If she wanted to make an acquisition on behalf of the Royal Collection, the moment she gives her name, the dealer's eyes are going to light up with pound signs. *Kerchingggggg!* The price has gone up twenty per cent before she opens negotiations.'

'I get that.'

'So far so good for Rose Cadoret. But then I went a little off-piste, and that's where it gets more interesting. I thought I'd take a look at her personal finances.'

'You hacked her bank account?'

'I didn't need to. I found out who she banks with – easy enough. OK, I told a bit of a fib – a white lie, right – to my lovely police Financial Investigator I was assigned to – Emily. I told her that Rose Cadoret was now a suspect in a major internet fraud scam, involving her bank and it was time critical. She spoke to her bank and, what do you know, I got all her account details through late last night.'

Grace smiled. 'Good work!' It had taken him a great deal of persuading the authorities to get Shannon released from prison, and there was a lot riding, reputational-wise, for him – on her delivering. His instincts had been right, and what he had just heard from Shannon was helping to confirm them. This information, together with Cadoret's name in the diary, felt like they were getting closer.

Shannon continued. 'Rose Cadoret's on a salary of £78k. She has an apartment in south-west London, in Putney, with a mortgage that costs her £24k per annum as well as an annual service charge of £6k. She gives her mother an annual £5k top-up on her state pension. She has an HP payment of £8k per annum on her Fiat 500 Abarth car. A raft of standing orders – a gym membership, magazines, a vitamin supplement supplier called Foodstate. All of these tot up to almost £3k per annum. She has total fixed outgoings, without food, travel, holidays, of around £40k. After tax of around £12k, her income is now down to below £20k. So she's not likely to be saving much, right?'

'Doesn't sound like it, no,' Grace replied. 'If anything at all.'

'She doesn't have a deposit account. Nor does she have any account with a stockbroker or wealth manager or IFA. What I'm saying by that is that she doesn't have a savings stash anywhere – at least not that I've been able to find, so far.'

'OK.'

'But unless she won on the lottery or won big at gambling somewhere – and nothing I've found so far indicates to me that she is a gambler – there's something I can't explain, and it needs explaining.'

'Tell me?'

'Five weeks ago an amount of £180k was deposited into her bank account. The source of the money has been well concealed.'

Grace considered this for a moment. Sir Jason Finch, as Keeper of the Privy Purse, had access to all the Royal Household's finances. *A Bird in the Hand?* 'Could the source of this be Sir Jason Finch, Shannon?'

THE HAWK IS DEAD

'Not that I've been able to find so far. Not a trace of any activity on the dark web, nor on the internet at all. He features in the Royal Household social media posts, but that's all – he's totally under the radar.'

'So he's either innocent,' Grace mused.

'Or very clever,' Shannon jumped in.

90

Wednesday 29 November 2023

At 9 a.m., Roy Grace stood in front of his Operation Asset team of fifty officers and civilian support staff, in the sectioned-off part of the room that had become his enquiry team's temporary domain. It was also where he would hold his next press conference in two hours' time, flanked by ACC Downing and one of the Comms team.

The only people in the room who knew about Shannon Kendall's findings were Glenn Branson, Emily Denyer and Luke Stanstead. All three were sworn to silence. At Grace's instigation, Emily had already spoken to Shannon this morning and would be taking a quiet, deep and secret dive into Sir Jason Finch's assets immediately.

Grace was well aware that among the faces in front of him were DCI Jacqueline Crawley from the Scotland Yard Counter Terrorism Unit, and Security Coordinator DS Russ Lewis from the RaSP unit. They would relay everything they heard that was of any significance directly back to Detective Superintendent Greg Mosse. If he announced Shannon's findings to the team, Mosse would be informed and would immediately want to take over questioning Rose Cadoret.

Grace knew what Mosse's argument would be. That Rose Cadoret was on his manor and there was no evidence to link her to the Op Asset enquiry. Grace felt otherwise, and had no confidence the Met Detective Superintendent would do anything other than make a total fist of handling someone who could be a crucial lead. It needed both a subtle approach and a highly tactical one.

Not only that, this was the first real lead they had. He wasn't going to squander it on that lightweight and let him take any glory that came from it. And Grace's gut instincts told him that a great deal of glory might come from it. Instead he made the briefing a short one. He gave a quick recap of where they were and asked if anyone had anything significant to report.

Only the British Transport Police detective had something. The CCTV cameras covering both Hassocks Station, to the north of Clayton Tunnel, and Preston Park Station, to the south, had only recorded up to 8 p.m. on Sunday 19 November, the night before the derailment. Their software had been tampered with – the system having been hacked was their best guess at this stage. This information didn't take the enquiry any further forward, but it was added confirmation to Grace of a conspiracy rather than a lone offender.

Grace hinted to the team that there were some promising developments through work being done by the Digital Investigation Support Unit and also at Digital Forensics, which was why neither Aiden Gilbert nor Jason Quigley were present, but beyond that he had nothing to report. He answered a number of questions about the murder of the footman, and an update on this was provided by DS Lewis from the RaSP unit, who said his team were looking closely for links between Geoffrey Bailey and Sir Peregrine.

As soon as the briefing ended, Grace hurried back to his office, closed the door and sat at his desk. He thought through his plan carefully again for a couple of minutes, and hoped to hell he wasn't making a bad tactical error. Then he raised his phone and hit a number that was now becoming very familiar.

91

Wednesday 29 November 2023

'Roy! Super to hear from you. Do you have some news?' Sir Tommy Magellan-Lacey sounded quieter than his normal, ebullient self and distinctly worried. 'Any developments? Their Majesties are very anxious for any news at all. This footman business has dreadfully upset them, on top of everything last week.'

'I want to ask you something in absolute confidence, Sir Tommy.'

'Yes, absolutely, anything you say goes no further than here, Roy. Always.'

'What more can you tell me about Rose Cadoret?'

'The Deputy Director of the Royal Collection?'

'Yes.'

'Well, gosh – what actually is it you'd like to know – about her?'

'You've known her a long time, right?'

'Absolutely. Many years, as you know she served in Afghanistan.'

'And you said there was a bit of an incident back then, involving her and another soldier now based at the palace, Jon Smoke?'

Magellan-Lacey sounded very uncomfortable suddenly, as if Grace had hit a raw nerve. 'Well, yes, Roy. There was. An unfortunate situation, as I explained. You've never been a soldier yourself, I believe?'

'No.' Grace was thinking hard. He asked, 'Did you have Smoke's whereabouts checked on the day Sir Peregrine was shot, Monday November the twentieth, Sir Tommy?'

THE HAWK IS DEAD

'My God, yes, he was the first person I checked after our conversation.'

'Really?'

'Well, he was one of the few people I could think of who had the skills to shoot accurately from the distance he did. He was a sniper attached to the Parachute Regiment. Both him and the fellow who was brutally killed behind Taliban lines. I was very relieved, I can tell you, when I checked the RaSPs' roster and saw he was in the Palace all that day.'

Smoke was a sniper? How had that not come up sooner? 'Can I get a copy of that roster?' Grace asked calmly, though his mind was whirring.

'Yes, no problem,' the Master replied. 'I'll make a note to get a copy and ping that over to you.'

'Thank you. So to go back to what you were saying, what then happened?'

'Well, Roy, some years later, Sir Jason Finch left the Army and joined the Royal Household, as Keeper of the Privy Purse, in 2016. It was soon after that he discovered Jon Smoke had joined the Met Police.'

Grace interrupted him. 'Sir Jason Finch, as their commanding officer back in Afghanistan, got Jon Smoke and Rose Cadoret out of a tight corner, didn't he?'

'He did and it cost him. He never got the recognition from the Army he felt he deserved.'

'Is he bitter about that?'

Magellan-Lacey hesitated. 'I think he probably is a bit bitter, still, yes.'

'And it was Sir Jason who helped Smoke become a RaSP?'

'Yes, Jason got in touch with me, as he thought Smoke would be a good man to have on the Palace team.'

'And Rose Cadoret.'

'Well, she is a very different animal. Very odd that she enlisted in the Army as a soldier, rather than doing officer training, because she was really overqualified.'

'A degree in Art History – from the Courtauld Institute.'

'You've done your research, Roy. So, you asked me what I could tell you about her. Well, look, this is a difficult one, but since we're on Chatham House Rules, as it were, and I can speak frankly, I've always thought there was something of the night about her.'

'Something of the night?'

'Do you understand what I mean by that? That she has a dark side. A real *dark* side.'

'In what sense, exactly?'

'You must have met plenty of them in your career, Roy. People who could kill with impunity – kill and feel nothing. She's on that spectrum for sure.'

'Which you saw in her in Afghanistan?'

'I did.'

'But you're comfortable with her in the senior and very responsible role she has in the Royal Collection team? And how quickly she got promoted to her high position?'

'I am, absolutely, but more importantly, so is Sir Jason Finch, the man who appointed her. She's made a few damned good acquisitions for the Collection and it's probably her ruthless streak that's helped her in the negotiations. Lorraine McKnight, the Director and her boss, has sung her praises to me many times.'

'I'd like to talk to her, as I've mentioned before,' Grace said.

'To Rose?'

'Yes.'

'About anything specific, Roy?'

'No, nothing specific, just background.'

'Of course, yes. When would you like to do this?'

'I was hoping tomorrow.'

'I'll find out where she is. She's not always here at Buckingham

THE HAWK IS DEAD

Palace – sometimes she's at Windsor Castle or one of the other royal residences – the Collection is spread over so many places. I'm sure I can sort it.'

Grace thanked him and ended the call. Then he sat lost in contemplation. Wondering if the Master of the Royal Household was still standing by his staff. Standing by that Bird In The Hand. And that Rose Between Two Thorns?

His thoughts were interrupted by his phone ringing. It was Denton Scroope.

'E J N W, Roy?' There was almost glee in his voice.

'E J N W? Have you cracked it, Denton?'

'N S W F. It's a short one but extremely hard to decipher. Do the letters mean anything to you?'

'N S W F?' Grace said the letters aloud again. Then it clicked. 'No Smoke Without Fire?'

'Bingo!' Scroope said.

92

Wednesday 29 November 2023

The media briefing at 11 a.m. went fine. Grace had informed Nigel Downing in advance that he felt close to a breakthrough, and the ACC had encouraged him to fully update the press with any information he could.

He'd barely sat back down in his office, when the first headline appeared, in the online *Argus*.

BREAKTHROUGH IN ROYAL MURDER PLOT IMMINENT

It was followed in minutes by similar but even more sensational headlines around the nation and the globe.

Der Bund's online edition boldly proclaimed:

ARREST OF QUEEN'S ASSASSIN IMMINENT!

But Grace wasn't smiling. His entire concentration was on the conversation he'd had earlier this morning with Sir Tommy Magellan-Lacey. There were two emails from the Master in his inbox.

The first said:

Roy, I've just spoken to Lorraine McKnight – Rose Cadoret's boss. Apparently Rose fell off her bike and has been sent by the Palace doctor for a chest X-ray for possible broken ribs. She'll be back at work tomorrow – likely to be in the Indian Room here at Buckingham Palace. But I'll confirm as soon as I know. I've also asked that Rose show you the box of Granny's Personal Chips.

The second said:

THE HAWK IS DEAD

> Attached is a scan of the duty roster for the Royal Protection team for Clarence House, Buckingham Palace and St James's Palace for Monday Nov 20th. As you can see, in answer to your very astute query about Royal Protection Officer Constable Jon Smoke, he was on duty at Buckingham Palace from 8 a.m. until 5 p.m.

Grace immediately opened the attachment. It showed, as Sir Tommy said, the duty roster for that day, and the shift hours of the Royal Protection Officers.

He focused on Jon Smoke's. Then zoomed in on it. And then zoomed in again.

Was it his imagination, or was the background a faintly different colour to the other names on the roster?

He tried to zoom further in, but the name and background became increasingly blurred.

He thought for a moment, then typed an email to James Stather at the Surrey and Sussex Police Forensic Recovery Unit.

> James, hope all's good. I've been sent this roster via email, showing Royal Protection Officers on duty on Monday Nov 20th – when Sir Peregrine Greaves, Private Secretary to Their Majesties, The King and Queen, was shot. I'm particularly interested in one of the names on this roster, Jon Smoke. I have a feeling, from trying to zoom in on it, that it may have been tampered with – by which I mean it is a false entry. I know you have highly sophisticated kit – could you, as a matter of extreme urgency, have your Imaging team run this through to see if they can tell whether the entire roster looks genuine or it if has been tampered with? Call me if you want any further information. In the meantime, I will obtain the original document. Best, Roy Grace.

Then he sent it.

93

Wednesday 29 November 2023

Grace, fed up with endless supermarket sandwiches, had started making himself a healthy lunch box. At a quarter past one, he popped open the lid and peered at the contents. A tuna, cucumber, tomato and avocado salad in one compartment, cottage cheese in another, a slice of buttered wholemeal sourdough in the third. In the fourth he found two Lindor chocolates – his guilty pleasure – added, without him knowing, by Cleo.

He smiled. It was the first time he had smiled in a while, he realized. And there was very little to smile about right now, as he read the email James Stather had just sent him. A little over an hour after his request to the Forensics expert.

> Roy, the Imaging team have had a good look at this. Can't say for sure – not enough to stand up in a court of law – but it looks to them as if there's been some surreptitious editing going on. Of course if they had the original, they would be able to tell with more certainty.

Grace replied to Stather that he should have the original tomorrow and thanked him. No sooner had he done that when an email from Sir Tommy pinged in. It confirmed that Rose Cadoret would be working on the restoration of the contents of the Indian Room all tomorrow. He also confirmed that Lorraine McKnight would be available to speak to Roy's team. He might be tied up himself in meetings with the damned building contractors, but the Deputy Master, Matthew Corbin, would give him all the help he might need. It would be helpful if Roy could give him an ETA.

Grace thought about that long and hard before composing his reply.

> Sir Tommy, there appears to be a possible anomaly with the copy of the rota you sent me. I need to see the original, not a photocopy or facsimile – who would I obtain that from? I will aim to come in to see Rose Cadoret at approximately 11 a.m. tomorrow – will be arriving by road.

The Master replied almost immediately.

> I will inform Deputy Master Matthew Corbin and Rose Cadoret to expect you for 11 a.m. tomorrow. If you arrive at the front gates, the guards will notify Matthew who will come out to meet you. He will direct you to a parking area and will then take you to Rose. Meantime, I'll arrange for her to have the original roster for Monday Nov 20th, which she will give you. Their Majesties would appreciate an update from you, but unfortunately they're not in London tomorrow – but perhaps we can set something up soon? All best and apologies if I don't see you personally tomorrow, but call me if you need anything. Tommy.

Grace typed back a brief thank-you.

94

Wednesday 29 November 2023

Just after 4 p.m., Shannon Kendall phoned Roy Grace. 'Roy,' she said, as he answered. 'I've got more information on Jon Smoke.'

'Tell me?' Roy said, full of energy.

'He has a Bitcoin account with the cybercurrency exchange, Coinbase. So far all I've been able to ascertain, with Emily Denyer's assistance, is that in July he made a deposit of a substantial cash amount, which was converted into Bitcoins.'

'What amount are we talking about, Shannon?'

'Three hundred and forty-three thousand pounds.'

He was silent for a moment. 'That seems quite a chunk of change for a police constable, even with London weighting.' He said it with a wry smile. 'Any idea where the money might have come from? An inheritance, a compensation payout?'

'Possibly. Or a big win at a casino. Sale of his house? Except Emily's checked on that one and he rents a one-bed apartment in Clapham. Then you have to question why he would put it into Bitcoins? Could be to speculate on the currency, but I'm thinking there's another reason.'

'Which is?'

'Cybercurrencies like Bitcoin are used by criminals to hide money. It's taken two days to find this – and I know my way around like very few other people.'

'Where do you think this amount of money might have come from? Is he dealing drugs?'

'That would be a pretty big drug deal, Roy. Not impossible. But here's the interesting thing. Using the portals I've opened, Emily has discovered two other deposits of an identical amount, three hundred and forty-three thousand pounds, made into Bitcoins through Coinbase, on exactly the same day this year. July the fifteenth, 2023.'

'By whom, Shannon?'

'So far we've identified one depositor, but not the second. We're working on that. But the first is our friend, Rose Cadoret.'

'Their Majesties pay big bonuses to people working in the Royal Household, do they?' Grace said.

'Yeah, right.'

'Good work. What else can you tell me? Any thoughts on who the third person might be?'

'Not yet. But Emily Denyer has identified a recent very substantial deposit into Sir Jason Finch's personal bank account – almost three quarters of a million pounds.'

'Three quarters of a million pounds?'

'Yes.'

'Do you know the source?'

'I'm working on it.'

Ending the call, Grace sat reflecting on what he had just heard. Jon Smoke and Rose Cadoret both receiving huge, identical amounts of cash. He was thinking about Sir Peregrine's coded diary entries.

Was Sir Jason Finch the third conspirator? Smoke and Cadoret had deposits to date totalling over a million pounds each. And Shannon reckoned these were just the latest in a series of deposits. Did these three all have their snouts in the royal trough?

In his experience there were people who killed business partners, loved ones and total strangers for a lot smaller amounts of money than this.

He called Glenn Branson. 'Polish your shoes, put on your least offensive suit and quietest tie – and bring your best handcuffs with you. We're going to Buck House in the morning.'

'Awwww, not the Palace again, you social gadfly, you. Living it up with your royal buddies?'

'If you're defrosting your fridge tomorrow, don't worry, I'll take Norman Potting.'

'The fridge can wait until Friday.'

95

Wednesday 29 November 2023

After his call with Glenn Branson, Roy Grace sat thinking the latest information through carefully.

Constable Jon Smoke of the Royal Protection team. A former army sniper. With his name on the duty roster for Monday 20 November looking like it might have been tampered with. Hopefully the original copy of the roster, which Rose Cadoret would have for him tomorrow, would provide the answer. But it was bothering him a lot.

He would interview Sir Jason Finch when he was back at work on Monday, and in the meantime his full focus was on Jon Smoke and Rose Cadoret. And the recent identical sums of £343,000 deposited into both of their individual cybercurrency accounts.

Huge amounts. And identical. That was what interested and concerned him the most. He knew that with the rise in property prices in recent years, some people inherited unexpectedly large sums, or made a killing selling properties. But £343,000, exactly. Deposited into both their accounts. And a third amount of exactly the same, deposited into another cybercurrency account. A third account. But not Sir Jason Finch's. Well, so far not that they knew.

So whose was it?

All those three identical transactions made on 15 July 2023.

Was there any significance in that date?

He used his latest research tool, which he was only just

starting to get familiar with, ChatGPT-4, to ask if any significant national events had happened on that date. But the only thing it came up with was that a fire broke out and destroyed the Royal Albion hotel on Brighton seafront. It was of no relevance.

Then he began thinking who that third person could possibly be. Of the thousand plus employees of the Royal Household he had only, so far, met a handful. Sir Tommy. His Deputy, Matthew Corbin. Her Majesty's Private Secretary, Jayne Bennett. Sir Peregrine's widow, Lady Greaves. He had not yet met Sir Jason Finch, nor the Lord Chamberlain.

If Shannon was right – and he believed she was – she had just corroborated what Sir Peregrine had said in code in his diary. That theft from the Royal Collection was taking place on a major scale. Everything he had learned from Shannon so far made Rose Cadoret and Jon Smoke prime suspects. Rose Cadoret, Deputy Director of the Royal Collection Trust, in the perfect position to remove items. Smoke, a member of the Royal Protection team, operating inside Buckingham Palace – was his value to the conspirators the killing of Greaves?

And Sir Jason Finch, in charge of all the Palace finances. How very convenient. How very tidy.

The finger at the moment certainly pointed to him. It made sense that the co-conspirators were three former military people from the same regiment, who had served out in Afghanistan together. Smoke, Cadoret and their saviour, Finch. Could that have been where they'd hatched their plot?

But was he overlooking anyone else who fitted that description of *high up in Royal Service*? Sir Tommy Magellan-Lacey, for instance?

But despite a few anomalies in the Master's behaviour in recent days, he struggled to believe Sir Tommy could be involved. He typed an email to him:

THE HAWK IS DEAD

Sir Tommy, I would like to speak to Sir Jason Finch urgently on his return, and to Constable Jon Smoke when I come to the Palace tomorrow. Best regards, Roy.

A few minutes after sending it, his phone rang. A now familiar number appeared.

Grace answered. 'Sir Tommy, good morning.'

'Ah, Roy, yes.' As before, the Master sounded uncharacteristically downbeat, and a little guarded. 'Thought it would be easier to speak – rather than pinging emails back and forth.'

'Sure, of course.'

'No problem at all about Sir Jason – he's definitely back on Monday and I've booked you in for 10 a.m. What is it you need to speak to Constable Smoke specifically about? Just so I can inform his Commander. Are you concerned about an irregularity of some kind?'

Grace hesitated for a moment. One of the key elements in interviewing any suspect was throwing something at them that caught them off-guard. 'It's just his name has popped up a couple of times on the list of people we're hoping to eliminate from our enquiries.'

'Ah, good.' The Master sounded genuinely relieved. 'I'll find out when he's on duty tomorrow and let you know soonest. I'll email you his shift rota.'

Grace thanked him, but as he ended the call, he felt again a slight shadow of doubt about Sir Tommy, but he wasn't sure exactly why. The Master was glib, he always had answers – and so far he had always delivered. Up to a point. Hopefully he would deliver everything he had requested Rose Cadoret to show him – the box of Granny's Personal Chips, and the original copy of the Royal Protection Officers' roster for Monday 20 November. And additionally, now, the shift rota for Jon Smoke?

As he considered this an email came in from Sir Tommy.

PETER JAMES

Roy, looks like Constable Smoke is on a rest day tomorrow and for the next two days.

Grace emailed him back.

Thanks. Could you let me have his home address and we will interview him there.

Of course – bear with me and I'll ping you it in a few minutes.

Good to his word, the Master sent Grace Jon Smoke's home address, in Clapham, ten minutes later.

Grace hesitated for a moment. Smoke was now definitely a person of interest and the potential sniper. He still needed more information before sending Sussex police officers to his address. So, since Greg Mosse had suggested they should work together, and mindful also that – *please not* – he might end up as his boss, Grace dialled his number.

96

Wednesday 29 November 2023

'Roy, good afternoon! What can I do for you? I hope you're calling in our new spirit of cooperation, perhaps?'

'Exactly that, Greg,' he replied. 'I have a Person of Interest who may shortly be elevated to a suspect. I need to know more about him, urgently.'

'A suspect? That would be extremely good optics for the media, Roy. And I think Their Majesties would like that, too. Can you tell me more?'

God, Grace shuddered, Mosse was using one of Cassian Pewe's favourite buzz words. *Optics*.

'I can't give you too much at this stage as we are still information gathering. But what I can tell you is that he's a constable in the Royal Protection team at Buckingham Palace. He's ex-military where he trained as a sniper, and there are – as yet unconfirmed – question marks over his whereabouts on Monday November the twentieth. His name is Jon Smoke.'

'Christ, Roy, sounds like he needs to be arrested right now. Bring him in for questioning – you've got more than enough to justify doing that. You do know the Treason act of 1351 is still in force, don't you?'

Grace did not, but wasn't going to admit it. 'Yes.'

'Well the shooter committed a prima facie act of treason. We should arrest this man, Smoke, immediately. Is that what you're calling to ask me to do?'

'No, Greg. It's possible he's the man who pulled the trigger, but if I'm right, from the intel I have so far, he's part of a major conspiracy. I want to make sure we nail the whole gang and don't send his colleagues running for the hills.'

'Seriously? A conspiracy? To do what?'

'I'll explain everything to you. Just trust me for now.'

'This Smoke might vamoose at any point.'

'I don't think so. We know who he is and he doesn't know that, which means he's not going anywhere soon – so far as we know.'

'So what is it you want from me?'

'I want surveillance put on him twenty-four-seven and his phones tapped.'

'You know, Roy, that's never an easy request. It requires the Home Secretary's approval.'

Grace resented Mosse's patronizing tone, speaking to him as if he was a fledgling cadet. 'Yes, I am aware of that. But given we are potentially talking treason the Home Secretary might be minded to look upon your request favourably.'

'Yes, of course, absolutely.'

'Wouldn't be good *optics* if it got out that she'd turned down your request and Smoke later took another pot shot at Her Majesty, would it?'

'No, indeed, you are right. Not good optics at all. Leave it with me.'

As soon as he ended the call, Grace dialled Shannon Kendall. He asked her to now focus all her attention on four specific names. To find out everything she could about them, by any means.

Grace then called Glenn Branson into his office. And briefed him for the morning.

97

Thursday 30 November 2023

Glenn Branson brought the unmarked Ford to a halt at the right-hand front gates of Buckingham Palace. A guard in red tunic and bearskin hat stood rigidly in his sentry box to his left.

'You know, I could get used to this,' Branson said.

Grace smiled. At this moment he wished so much his parents were still alive. How thrilled they would have been when he told them how he'd driven in through the front right-entrance gates of Buckingham Palace. How he had met The King and The Queen. And not just once.

How their *little boy* was running, as the *Daily Mail* had put it, THE MURDER ENQUIRY OF THE CENTURY!

If only he were here under less grim circumstances.

Grace and Branson showed their warrant cards to the Royal Protection Officers, who opened the gates. They waited while one of them phoned the Deputy Master. Then they were directed to drive through an archway.

Moments later, he recognized the tall figure of Matthew Corbin striding out of the side door to their right, with a broad smile. He stopped some distance away and like an aircraft marshal – but without illuminated batons – began a series of hand-signals to guide them over towards him and into a space amid a row of cars.

As they climbed out he said, with a welcoming smile, 'Good morning, Detective Superintendent Grace and DI Branson.

Matthew Corbin, Deputy Master – we have met before.' Grace could still not pin down his accent.

'We have indeed,' Grace replied, and Branson nodded.

'Sir Tommy sends his very deepest apologies – I believe he told you he has to accompany his wife to a medical clinic for a procedure, but he does hope to be back in time to catch you before you leave.'

Grace thanked him, but as he did so he frowned and shot a glance at Branson. This wasn't what Sir Tommy had told him yesterday. He'd said he would be in meetings all day but would try to find time to say hello. Perhaps his wife had suddenly become unwell? Although taking her for a 'procedure' sounded like something that had been booked for some while.

'You gentlemen have just driven up from Sussex?'

'We have,' Branson said.

'I'll take you up to Rose Cadoret, she's in the Indian Room. If you'd like any refreshments, tea or coffee, I can arrange that for you.'

'Coffee would be good, thank you,' Grace said and Branson nodded.

'I'll get that in hand.'

They followed him inside, into a rarefied smell of polish and antique furniture and up a short, well-kept staircase. Then along the now familiar corridor with a patterned red carpet and arched ceiling. On both sides of them were paintings, mirrors, vases, ornaments and clocks, most of them on shelves or plinths. It felt, as it had on his previous visits here, like walking through an utterly stunning museum. He clocked a bronze sculpture of a rider on a handsome horse.

They went up another flight of stairs, these longer, and came out into a corridor as equally plush as the one below. Corbin stopped outside a magnificent panelled wooden door. 'The Indian

Room,' he said with an almost reverent tone. Then he knocked on it.

A female voice on the other side called, 'Come in!'

He opened the door with a theatrical flourish, and ushered them through. 'Rose, these are the gentlemen I believe you are expecting?'

The room, with its low, vaulted ceiling, felt to Grace almost as if he had entered a secret inner sanctum. The walls were lined with exquisite walnut display cabinets, some empty, some partially filled with bejewelled swords and daggers. It smelled different in here, of fresh paint and a metallic polish.

A woman of around forty, with thick, wavy fair hair, smartly dressed in black trousers, a woven waistcoat over a white blouse and flat shoes was kneeling on the lush carpet, close to a tiger skin, unpacking what looked like carefully wrapped daggers from a wooden crate.

She turned her head, still kneeling. 'Detective Superintendent Grace and Detective Inspector Branson?'

'Yes,' Grace said.

'Sir Tommy said you would be coming.' She stood up, holding her midriff. 'I'm sorry,' she said. 'I fell off my bike and bruised my ribs. Painful. Especially if you cough, sneeze or laugh.'

'It is,' Grace said. 'I've been there. Very unfortunate for you.'

'Please excuse the state of this room, I'm slowly putting it all back together. We had to empty it completely for the renovations.' Her voice was less overtly posh-sounding than the other Royal Household staff he'd met so far. She was confident and radiated a tomboyish charm, Grace thought, and he could see the former soldier in her. She looked like someone who'd be more at home in jeans and a T-shirt or even in fatigues.

'It's magnificent,' Branson said.

'There are some quite fancy weapons,' Grace added, looking around with great interest.

She smiled, seizing on this. 'Back in the days of the Raj they knew how to kill people efficiently, in hand-to-hand combat. That was proper fighting.'

'Are all these *proper weapons*?' Branson asked.

'Oh yes, don't be fooled by their beauty. These were – no pun intended – the absolute cutting edge of hand-to-hand combat of their time. You wouldn't want to mess with someone holding any of the blades in this room.'

There was something about the way she said it, and a look that came into her dark brown eyes, that disturbed Grace. *There's something of the night about her*, Sir Tommy had said. He felt he could see that now.

'Do you have a favourite?' Glenn Branson asked.

She smiled and Grace saw that look in her eyes again. 'Oh yes, if I could take one home with me it would be this.' She reached up to a cabinet, wincing in pain again as she did so. The glass door was open and inside was a display of daggers in their scabbards, in a criss-cross pattern. There were several empty spaces. She stretched up, letting out a small breath and removed a dagger with a very finely jewelled handle.

She pulled the dagger out of its scabbard and held it up. It made a clack-clacking sound as she did so. Almost with the pride of a zealot she announced, 'The Ibrahim dagger!'

Branson let out a gasp. 'Wow, it's so sleek. It's like the shape of Concorde.'

'It is,' she agreed. 'So modern. But it's actually over a hundred and fifty years old.'

'May I feel it?' Grace asked.

She held the blade and passed it to him. He took it by the handle and peered at the dagger closely. In particular at the rows of pearls down the centre of the glinting blade, which all rolled, clacking again as he moved the heavy, stunningly beautiful weapon. 'These are real pearls?'

'Of course.'

'For decoration?'

'Oh no, Detective Superintendent. They're not there for decoration. They are purely functional – elegant, but functional.'

'And their function is?' he asked, tilting the blade. The pearls went clack-clack again.

She smiled and again he saw that look in her eyes that increasingly unsettled him. 'Evisceration!'

In answer to his and Branson's frowns she said, 'It's one thing to simply stab an enemy. In and out with a normal dagger will leave a nasty wound but not necessarily fatal. But these pearls, as the stabber withdraws the dagger from the victim, will rip out anything in their way. And should the stabber twist the dagger after it has entered the human torso, the pearls will add enormously to the internal damage. If you can rip through part of the bowel – not difficult – then without instant surgery, the victim will die of what we now know as sepsis. And it's a slow, agonizing death.'

He handed her back the dagger, courteously holding the blade, and she re-sheathed it then knelt, with another gasp of pain, and placed it on the floor beside the box in which, Grace noticed, was an unsheathed curved sword. He glanced at Branson, wondering if he was picking up the same vibes from this woman. But the DI was looking around the room in almost a state of rapture.

Then, remaining on her knees, Rose Cadoret said, 'But, much though I would be happy to talk about swords and daggers all day, I don't imagine that's actually what you've come here to talk about, is it, gentlemen?'

Grace smiled, but it was an uneasy smile. 'No, we have a few things we'd like to ask you, Ms Cadoret.'

'*Rose* is fine. I don't do the whole *Miz* thing.'

'OK, Rose, thank you. The first question I wanted to ask you is whether there are any cuckoo clocks in Buckingham Palace?'

'Cuckoo clocks?'

'Yes.' Grace ignored the *WTF, have you gone nuts* look Branson was giving him. But noted that his partner was strategically blocking the doorway. Smart.

98

Thursday 30 November 2023

'Cuckoo clocks?' Rose Cadoret shook her head in amusement. 'You've driven all the way here from Brighton to ask me about cuckoo clocks?'

'It's one of my questions, yes,' Grace replied, calmly.

'We do actually have just three cuckoo clocks in the Royal Collection. My favourite is a particularly beautiful one acquired by Queen Mary. It features a unique gilt bronze chapter ring and cuckoo striking mechanism with a circular pendulum. There is another in the Collection with moon-shaped hands and a painted face, which also has a unique mechanism. But none are here in Buckingham Palace. One is at Sandringham, one is in the Lodge on the Balmoral estate. I'm not actually sure where the third one is – but I can find out for you. If you are interested, I could introduce you to the Keeper of the Clocks. There are over one thousand clocks spread across the Royal Palaces and five full-time clock winders.'

Grace nodded. 'Another time perhaps.' Then he looked hard at her. 'Do you have the duty roster for PC Jon Smoke, showing Monday November the twentieth for me?'

'Pardon?'

'Sir Tommy Magellan-Lacey said he was going to give you the original copy of the duty roster of PC Smoke, which included that day, to hand to me.'

She looked puzzled. 'No, I – he – didn't say anything about it. I do apologize. I'm sure I can get it for you quite easily.'

'When we've finished, thank you, I need to see it,' Grace said. 'He also told me you were going to let me see the box of Granny's Personal Chips. Where is that kept?'

She looked hesitant. Her eyes darted around wildly for a moment and, just fleetingly, her face had a strange, almost feral expression. It reminded him of something but before he could think what, it morphed into a friendly smile. She said, 'Yes, yes, of course, yes! It's down in the vault, I'll take you there. Do you want to go now?'

He raised a placatory hand. A call was coming through on his mobile phone. He saw it was from Shannon and stepped to one side, taking the call, but said nothing in response to the information he was given, just a 'Thank you, goodbye.'

He turned back his attention to Cadoret. 'Just a couple more questions before we go to the vault, please.' He took a moment before continuing, watching her face very carefully now. 'Rose, there's something I wonder if you can tell us. I understand you recently paid a company in Bexhill, in East Sussex, called Silversands Residential, a substantial sum of money. I understand this is a very high-end care home for the elderly. Can I ask you where that money came from?'

She hesitated again, her eyes looked wildly around once more and that feral expression fleetingly returned. 'It was actually one hundred and eighty-two thousand, five hundred pounds and ninety-two pence, if you want it exactly, Detective Superintendent.' Her eyes shot from Grace to Branson and back to Grace. 'And what the hell business of yours is it, no disrespect, where that money came from?'

'It's very much my business,' Grace replied, still calm. 'I'm conducting a murder enquiry into the death of Sir Peregrine Greaves, and I'm looking at everyone with whom he had connections.'

'And just what does my paying money to a care home have to do with Sir Peregrine's very tragic death?'

THE HAWK IS DEAD

'I would be grateful if you would answer my question, Rose,' he said, with a sharper edge to his voice now. 'I asked you where did the money come from?'

'From my savings,' she answered with an insolent expression. 'Is it illegal to have savings?'

Again her eyes roamed the room and that expression returned; suddenly Grace realized what it reminded him of. It was a trapped animal. A desperate, trapped animal.

99

Thursday 30 November 2023

There was a long silence. Grace, increasingly wary, watched Rose Cadoret's eyes moving from him to Branson and back to him.

'Actually,' she said, 'no, I don't want to tell you where the money came from.'

'In which case, Rosemary Catherine Cadoret, I'm arresting you on suspicion of theft and on suspicion of conspiracy to murder.' As he spoke, he dug his hand into his right pocket to pull out his handcuffs. 'You do not have to say—'

She was faster than he imagined she could possibly be, especially with the pain she seemed to be suffering, and caught him totally by surprise. Within what felt like a nanosecond she was on her feet, holding in her right hand the unsheathed and clacking Ibrahim dagger, and in her left the long, curved sword. And lunging at Grace.

He stepped back.

'Stay away from me!' she shrieked. She lunged again and he stepped back again. Then out of the corner of his eye he saw Branson moving towards her. But as he did so, she suddenly spun on her own axis, launching a spinning back kick to the DI's stomach, sending him tumbling backwards with a grunt of pain as the wind was taken out of him.

Then she was gone through the door.

100

Thursday 30 November 2023

Grace glanced at Branson, who was trying to get to his feet, all the while struggling to get his wind back. 'You OK?'

'Get her!' Branson gasped, hauling himself up. 'I'm right behind you.'

Grace sprinted to the door, looked left then right and saw her, some distance away, sprinting along an eau-de-nil-coloured corridor lined with marble busts and huge vases, the walls hung with paintings.

As he raced after her, a footman emerged from a door at the far end of the corridor and she ran in through it. Grace followed her in half a minute later. And found himself in a large and very grand, formal drawing room. There was a Persian carpet covering most of the floor, a wide oil painting of the Colosseum, flanked on each side by portraits of two rather self-important-looking men in frock coats and grey wigs. Elegant chairs and sofas were arranged around a fine white marble fireplace. One entire wall was floor-to-ceiling bookcases lined with red and green leather volumes.

No Rose Cadoret.

She had vanished into thin air.

The tall windows with swagged curtains were all shut. Where the hell was she?

Branson came limping into the room and looked briefly around, frowning.

'She came in here, I saw her,' Grace said.

'Didn't Sir Tommy say something about a room – was it the *White* Drawing Room? A sitting room where there was a secret corridor that let the monarch move from the state apartments to the more public reception rooms without being seen?'

Grace nodded. It was ringing a bell. He looked at the floor-to-ceiling library shelves at one end of the room. One did not look properly aligned. He hurried across, grabbed it and, wary she might be standing behind it, pulled it open and stood well back. He considered raising the alarm, but was worried about who could be trusted. The secret door revealed a dark space beyond. He switched on his phone's torch. A long dark corridor swallowed most of the dim light. He sprinted down it. At the far end, he came out through an open door into a small, elegant sitting room. Another open door on the far side led him into a musty-smelling bedroom, with a two-poster bed that was sealed in polythene, as were all the rest of the soft furnishings. It felt like a mausoleum. A door was ajar on the far side.

Rushing through it, still holding his phone, he caught sight of Rose almost at the end of another corridor. He ran flat out after her, wishing he was wearing a stab vest. Light from a chandelier glinted off the blades of her knives as she disappeared around a corner, past a photocopier and a long-case clock. As he rounded, he almost barrelled straight into two very smartly dressed women who emerged from a side door.

Blurting an apology he ran on, into a magnificent gallery, the walls lined with white pilasters. On either side of the red carpet were huge marble statues on columns and plinths, interspersed with equally enormous, finely decorated vases and urns. At the far end was a sofa beneath a tapestry that almost filled the wall. Rose dashed to the left and went out of sight. He heard a door bang shut. And as he rounded the same corner, and saw her ahead, he heard footsteps behind him. He turned and saw it was Branson, limping. 'Careful,' Grace cautioned.

'We're going to get her, boss,' he gasped.

'Stay behind me,' Grace said firmly as he ran on, as fast as he could, as she threw a backwards glance then disappeared around another corner.

Moments later he found himself in a long, narrow corridor with double doors at the far end. Rose Cadoret hurtled through them but as Grace reached them, several seconds later, they opened towards him and he barged headlong into a liveried footman, sending him flying into a wall and his loaded tray of coffee, cups, milk and biscuits crashing to the floor. And Grace very nearly with them.

Gasping an apology he ran on, gulping down air, wondering who he could call for backup, and suddenly realized he no longer had his phone in his hand. Must have dropped it just now, he realized, but there was no way he was going to stop the chase to go back for it.

He caught another glimpse of her, then another, as he ran, increasingly breathless, along corridor after corridor, lined with paintings, fine furniture, display cases filled with jewellery, ornaments, chinaware. Then he passed an ancient-looking brass and steel lift cage, with rickety wooden doors, the whole thing looking like it belonged in a hotel from another era.

She turned into a corridor with bare walls and large rectangular shadows on them where paintings had been hung. It was lined with statues and chairs all trussed-up with white dust sheets. They looked eerie, like ghosts, he thought as he sprinted past them. Ahead, she darted through a door with a warning sign, and he followed her, onto bare floorboards, with internal scaffolding above him. There was a strong chemical stench and a loud mechanical whine. He fleetingly glanced up and saw two masked men in hard hats with spray paint guns.

For a moment he thought he was gaining on the woman. Then she ducked through a side door and when he reached it and went through he found himself on a spiral staircase, with temporary wiring in bright red insulating tape snaking up it. There was a deafeningly loud sound of drilling. For an instant he wasn't sure whether she'd gone up or down. A small framed sign in blue on the wall read, *SILVER PANTRY – BASEMENT – BLUE ROUTE.*

He looked behind him, hoping to see Glenn so they could cover both directions, but there was no sign of him. The drilling suddenly stopped and he heard what sounded like a door slam below him, and decided to chance it. He ran down, pushed through the door at the bottom and found himself in a vast basement. The bare floor was outlined with red and white hazard markings around the edges, temporary-looking plywood partitions, more overhead scaffolding and warning notices everywhere. It felt more like he was in the bowels of a hospital than a palace.

There was no sign of her. He looked frantically around, breathing heavily, his chest aching. There was a door marked *SWIMMING POOL.* He tried the handle but it was locked. Where? Where the hell was she?

There was a grinding din from a drilling machine – a worker in a hard hat and ear defenders was cutting into an exposed wall. He saw a large yellow sharps bin, a moveable red barrier with a sign, *STAIRWELL CLOSED.* Then what looked like the boarded-up entrance to a lift shaft with the sign in large red and white letters: *WARNING – DEEP EXCAVATION BEHIND DOOR. STRICTLY NO ADMITTANCE.*

There were huge wooden boxes and plastic containers everywhere. The faint smell of hot electrics and freshly sawn wood. He saw a trip hazard notice. Then a map, highlighted with an arrow. *BASEMENT FLOOR – RED ROUTE. You are here.*

Then, at the far end, a good hundred yards or so away, he spotted her. She ran out from behind a partition, blades glinting, and then shot off to the right. As he reached the far end he saw her, at the end of a wide corridor, where four workmen in hard hats were preoccupied trying to lift a huge insulation panel into place with the aid of a mechanical hoist. She was pulling the handle of a tall, very old-looking door. Pulling desperately. Still with both weapons in her hands.

A sign above the door read, *TUNNEL ENTRANCE. HARD HATS MUST BE WORN*.

He raced towards her, his hopes up. If he could get to her before she heard him—

She spun, brandishing the sword and the dagger, with a clack-clacking sound from the dagger. That feral look he'd seen on her face in the Indian Room had returned, with real ferocity. 'Get back,' she yelled. 'Fucking get back!' She lunged at him and he stepped back, smartly. She lunged again, then again. *Clack-clack . . . clack-clack . . . clack-clack . . .* She looked crazy enough to kill him. Then she seemed to leap up in the air, throwing out a foot, and an instant later it felt like he had been hit in the stomach by a sledgehammer as he was propelled, winded, onto his back.

101

Thursday 30 November 2023

Roy Grace got back onto his feet, panting heavily, his stomach hurting badly, but he didn't care. He looked around, everywhere. Where was she? She hadn't run past him and she hadn't gone into the tunnel. Then he noticed a narrow doorway with a small sign, white on black, with an arrow pointing upwards, saying *FOOTMEN'S FLOOR.*

Taking several deep breaths he hurried towards it, running on adrenaline now, then began climbing the steep, narrow, wooden staircase. As he reached the first floor, where there was a door out into the corridor, he stopped and listened. And heard the sound of footsteps on the treads, faintly, above him.

He began sprinting up the stairs, taking them two at a time, stopping again at the next door briefly to listen. Again he heard footsteps above him. As he reached the third floor, he saw the stairs from this point had been sealed off with red and yellow tape, and there was a sign reading: *EXTREME DANGER – KEEP OUT!*

The tapes were torn. He ran through them and on up, past what looked like the entrance to an elevator, covered in polythene sheeting, securely taped and with another sign warning, *DANGER – DEEP SHAFT.* Then he felt a cold blast of air on his face and looked directly up, to see daylight through an open hatch. Blue sky. The steps up from here were extremely narrow, gridded metal, like a fire escape.

THE HAWK IS DEAD

He climbed rapidly, then stopped a few feet below the hatch, wishing he had something to defend himself with against the blades of the sword and dagger. Was she waiting to jump him when he went up through the hatch, or had she an escape plan up here?

Taking a deep breath, he raced up the last few steps as fast as he could and peered at a view of the rooftops of the Palace, and part of the skyline of London beyond. A stiff breeze was blowing as he clambered out onto lead roofing, and stood upright, looking around in all directions. He could see the gardens a long way below, the acres of lawn, the lake, the skeletal framework of a marquee that was being dismantled, a gardener on a ride-on mower, too far away to hear more than a faint sound.

The rooftop was on several levels, all covered in ribbed strips of lead and with metal-grille walkways and stone balustrading around the edges. CCTV cameras were dotted along, pointing downwards, covering the grounds. There was a fine copper dome, turned green, with a curved balustrade in front of it, almost directly beneath him. Where the hell was she?

Though never good with heights, today Grace didn't care; he was going to get her, whatever it took. She had to be up here somewhere.

There were gridded metal steps ascending steeply to another roof level across the far side. Had she gone up there? Gripping the rails with both hands he hauled himself up and onto a narrow viewing platform. The wind was even stronger here. But he could see no sign of her as he looked around and then down. Just acres of lead, skylights, chimneys, scaffolding and plastic sheeting in some parts.

Was she hiding behind the sheeting? There was one area that resembled the edge of a tent and could easily conceal someone.

He clambered down, hurried across the roof, careful not to trip on the lead ribs, and reached the stone balustrading. Keeping one steadying hand on the flat stone rail atop the balustrading, to his right. He tried to avoid looking down at the sheer drop of one hundred feet or more on the far side of it, down onto lawn or gravel – he couldn't see which. He reached the sheeting, but it was sealed tight. He was about to turn round when he heard a sound behind him.

Clack . . . clack.

102

Thursday 30 November 2023

An icy gust swirled deep inside him. His brain swirled with it. He silently cursed his stupidity. *Jesus. How—*

'Raise your hands in the air. If you do not, or if you try anything silly, I will kill you, unpleasantly and with very great pleasure.'

He raised his hands slowly, thinking hard. And wary he was precariously close to the balustrading.

'Turn around, do it very slowly.'

He began turning; she yelled out, 'Stop there!'

He stopped. And realized he was now backed up against the hard stone of the balustrade.

She brandished the dagger and the sword, feinting stabs at him with each in turn. Each time the dagger repeating the *clack-clack . . . clack-clack* sound.

Rose Cadoret had a completely crazed look on her face. Was it the same look she'd had when she'd killed the Taliban patrol? 'Rose,' he said calmly. 'This is not going to help you.'

'Is that the best you can come up with, Detective Superintendent Grace? What would actually help me would be a first-class air ticket to a country with no extradition treaty with the UK.'

A pigeon flew close overhead. He heard the faint wail of a siren but it wasn't coming here, it was moving away into the further distance.

'Is that what you want, Rose?'

'Of course. But I'm not going to get that, am I? Instead I want to talk.'

'So, talk.'

'Move around,' she commanded. 'Move away from the balustrade.' She still held both weapons out towards him at arm's length and threateningly.

They executed a kind of clumsy dancers' shuffle, Grace not taking his eyes from her face, until she was now the one with her back to the balustrade.

At that instant, Grace heard a shout, a really loud bellow.

'DROP YOUR WEAPONS. THIS IS THE POLICE. DROP YOUR WEAPONS.'

She didn't flinch.

Grace glanced fleetingly back and saw to his relief Glenn Branson and three Royal Protection Officers – two of them with their automatic rifles braced. Then he focused hard on Rose, waiting to see what she did and to seize his moment. To his relief, she let her weapons fall to the ground. He heard the clatter.

His relief was short-lived.

Before he had any time to react, she jumped upwards and back, landing on the narrow, flat, balustrade rail. She wobbled, flailing her arms, and for a horrified instant he thought she was going over backwards. But as he lunged forward to try to grab her, she shot a leg out into his chest and shoved him backwards so hard he almost lost his balance.

Then she stood, calmly, like an acrobat or a gymnast, on top of the balustrade, in her black trousers, woven waistcoat and white trainers, wavy hair blowing in the wind. She was hardly swaying at all now and had her balance, but it looked to Grace a very precarious balance. He was scared that at any second she would topple backwards.

Suddenly looking past him, she yelled out at the top of her voice, 'Stay back, don't come any nearer or I'll jump.'

THE HAWK IS DEAD

Grace shot a glance over his shoulder. Branson and the three RaSPs stood still. Both rifles were still trained on Rose. He turned back to the woman. 'Rose, come down, please.'

'Why?'

'So we can talk.'

'I can talk here. But do we have anything to talk about?'

Roy Grace had once been trained as a suicide negotiator and had been called out on four occasions to try to talk people out of taking their lives. One had doused herself in petrol. One was standing on a parapet at the top of a multi-storey car park – much like Rose was standing now. One had a gun to his head. And one was threatening to drive his car over a cliff. Somehow, he had managed to talk each one of them out of it. But it had been a long time ago. He was trying very hard to remember all the key points from his training now.

'Tell me about yourself, Rose.'

'What?'

'Tell me about yourself. I want to try to help you.'

'Seriously?' she said with a derisory tone. 'You don't want to help me, you've just nicked me. That's why you're here. Well,' she said, with a sudden big smile and an expression on her face as if all her cares in the world had gone. 'I'm not going to let you do that, Detective Superintendent Roy Grace. Nice knowing you. Bye!' She raised a hand, waved and toppled backwards.

103

Thursday 30 November 2023

As Rose started to fall, Grace lunged at her, somehow just managing to grab her legs below her knees. But his hands got barely any grip on the shiny material of her trousers, and slid down to her ankles. Then her trainers. Which were laced tightly.

She stopped with such a sharp jolt it almost pulled him over the top of the balustrade, and he bashed his chin painfully on the rough surface. In this position she was a dead weight, and he was holding her with all his strength. But she was pulling him over. He stared down in horror at the very long drop to the gravel path, way beneath them.

Suddenly he felt his feet leave the ground.

Oh shit, no.

He was going to fall.

The tails of his suit jacket flapped over his head and he heard the jangle of coins and other items tumbling out.

Is this how it ends? he wondered, bleakly, suddenly. Thoughts were flashing through his mind. *Not that long ago I said goodbye to my first-born son for ever, and now this. Never see my family again.*

An instant later he felt hands, like iron clamps, gripping each of his legs and the reassuring voice of Glenn Branson. 'Gotcha!'

Way below he saw three people walking along, all in hard hats, one holding a clipboard. Totally oblivious to him above them.

The woman was kicking out, struggling like a hooked fish,

trying to break free of his own grip. And her weight felt like it was pulling his arms out of their sockets.

He shot a glance up, just as the wind blew his jacket tail clear, and saw Glenn Branson peering anxiously down at him, leaning over the balustrade with a burly officer either side of him doing the same.

'You're a heavy bastard, aren't you?' Branson said.

'This is probably not a good time for me to argue with you,' Grace replied, feeling sick with relief as the strain of Rose Cadoret was relieved by the RaSPs.

Branson hauled him up and over the balustrade and back onto the roof. He stood giddily for some moments, swaying as the blood rushed from his head, and his colleague gripped his arm firmly to stop him from falling.

Grace saw the third officer had Rose on the ground, and was cuffing her hands behind her back.

'You bastards!' she shouted. 'You know how much that hurts?'

The officer hauled her to her feet, keeping a tight hold on her, and she stood, arched, glaring at them all.

Grace took some deep breaths then looked directly at her. 'As I was saying before we got interrupted a little earlier, Rosemary Catherine Cadoret, I'm arresting you on suspicion of theft and on suspicion of conspiracy to murder. I'm now adding to that assaulting two police officers and attempting to murder another police officer. You do not have to say anything. But it may harm your defence if you do not mention when questioned, something you later rely on in court. Anything you do say may be given in evidence. Your arrest is necessary to prevent injury or harm to a person, prevent your disappearance, and for the prompt and effective investigation of your conduct in this matter.'

'I want to say something,' she retorted, sullenly.

'Go ahead,' Grace said.

'It's not me you want, Detective Superintendent Grace. I'm

just a minion. It's Sir Tommy. He's the man you want. He's the mastermind. He just forced us into this, Jon Smoke and me, because he had some evidence from Afghanistan on us.'

'Yes, I had come to the same conclusion,' Grace replied.

'Go talk to him. If you can catch him in time.'

'How do you mean?'

'He may already have gone.'

'Gone where?'

She said nothing.

'Gone where, Rose?'

She gave him that feral look again. 'You're the detective. You figure it out.'

104

Thursday 30 November 2023

Roy Grace turned to the officer who was holding Rose Cadoret's arm, his stomach and chest hurting from where she had kicked him, although at the moment he barely noticed. 'I suggest two of you escort her to custody – she's got quite a line in fancy footwork.'

'Very funny,' she said, almost spitting at him.

He turned away, then patted his pockets, checking what was missing. His wallet, handcuffs, house keys had all fallen out. He'd have to worry about retrieving them later. Glenn Branson reached out an arm and handed him his phone. 'Think you dropped this, boss.'

'Brilliant! Good work, thanks.' He ushered Branson away. As he did so, one of the officers called out, alarmed.

'Sir! You've blood on your face – your chin.'

Grace stroked it with his hand. It was sticky. He looked at the palm and saw streaks of blood. But right at this moment he didn't care, adrenaline was coursing through him.

Branson took a good look. 'You might need stitches, boss.'

'We need to find Sir Tommy and see if Rose is bullshitting, or right.'

'And your feeling is?'

'That she's right.' He turned to the third police officer, a man-mountain with a thick beard. 'Can you take us to Sir Tommy Magellan-Lacey's office right away.'

Last night Grace had obtained a search warrant for Tommy's office and home. It was in his pocket if he needed it.

'Yes, sir. You sure you're all right and don't need to see the doctor?'

'What's your name?' Grace asked him.

'PC Beckett, sir.'

'OK, thanks, PC Beckett. I don't need a doctor, I need to see Sir Tommy very, very urgently.'

The two detectives followed Beckett, racing down the stairs all the way to the first floor, then along a maze of corridors, some of which now looked familiar to Grace, until they were back in one that was very definitely familiar, at the top of the short staircase. PC Beckett stopped outside a door and knocked. He knocked again. There was no response. He turned to Grace. 'Doesn't seem like he's in, sir.'

Grace opened the door and peered into a spacious, very traditionally furnished office with fine paintings on the wall and a window overlooking the gardens. There was nothing on the mahogany desk at all, other than a leather blotter, an antique silver calendar, a computer terminal and keyboard. It looked more like a desk in a vacant hotel suite than a working office. Like it had been cleaned out of everything.

He turned back to the officer, Rose Cadoret's words ringing in his ears.

He may already have gone.

'You know where Sir Tommy Magellan-Lacey lives, in St James's Palace?' he asked Beckett.

'Yes, I do, sir, I've been on guard there many times.'

'Can you take me the fastest route there. We need to run.'

They ran. Along the corridor, down the stairs and into the courtyard, through the archway and across the parade ground. Another Protection Officer opened the gates for them, barking at the crowd to clear a pathway.

THE HAWK IS DEAD

They sprinted across Constitution Hill and Green Park, and on, past the elegant white facade of Clarence House, the RaSP nodding at two of his colleagues at the entrance, around the side and up to the front door of Sir Tommy's residence, directly across from the two RaSPs who were part of the team permanently stationed in the hut by the entrance barrier.

Grace knocked on the door, hard, and rang the doorbell.

Then heard a voice behind him.

One of the Royal Protection Officers, with a jovial, quite bucolic face, was walking towards him. 'Sir, if it's Sir Tommy you're after, he and his missus have just gone on holiday.'

'Holiday?' Grace demanded. 'Seriously?'

'They left in a black cab – what – about an hour and a half ago.' He turned to his colleague, who had now joined him, for confirmation. 'We helped them with their bags. They had a lot of luggage. Travelling like Royalty, they were.'

His colleague, much younger, a tall, alert-looking woman, nodded in agreement.

'A black cab?' Grace asked. 'Do you know the company?'

Both officers shook their heads.

'Did either Sir Tommy or his wife tell you where they were going?'

Again they shook their heads.

'Do you have CCTV here?' Branson asked.

'We do, yes, sir,' the female RaSP said and the man nodded.

Five minutes later, Grace and Branson, crammed into the small hut with the two officers, watched the CCTV replay. On Grace's watch, the time was currently 13.10.

The colour footage was scrolling forward from 10.30 a.m. At 11.32 a.m. a black taxi came into view and the red and white barrier was raised. It pulled up outside the Magellan-Laceys' front door. The number plate was clearly visible.

Grace memorized it and immediately dialled Greg Mosse's mobile phone.

The Detective Superintendent answered on the second ring. 'Roy, good to hear from you! How's it going, any developments?'

'I'll give you the full download, but this is really urgent, Greg. A black cab picked up the Magellan-Laceys from their St James's residence at 11.32 a.m. today. I have the cab's licence plate. I need you to find out which cab picked them up and where the driver was taking them.'

'Am I missing something here, Roy?'

'Possibly, Greg. I'll update you, but first can you do this, as a matter of the greatest urgency – in our new spirit of cooperation?'

'Absolutely, Roy. Consider it done! I'm on it, like a car bonnet!'

Promising to call Mosse back to explain, Grace ended the call and turned back to the RaSPs. 'Do you have a bosher?'

'You mean a big red key, sir?'

'Exactly.'

'What do you need that for, sir?'

'To get into the Magellan-Laceys' house.'

'You don't need a bosher, sir. They never lock the door. It's not like they're going to get burgled, with us standing fifty feet away, twenty-four-seven, is it?'

105

Thursday 30 November 2023

Roy Grace and Glenn Branson entered the Magellan-Laceys' London residence, which was starting to feel familiar, Grace thought. Although it had a strangely empty atmosphere now. But maybe that was his imagination?

As before, it felt to him extremely homely, more like being in a family farmhouse than a palatial residence. They both heard a plaintive miaow. Grace looked around and saw the couple's dark brown cat sitting halfway up the staircase.

'Hello, cat!' Branson said. Then he turned to Grace. 'Can you remember its name?'

'George,' Grace said.

'Hello, George!' Branson called.

The cat miaowed again, louder and more pitifully.

'Sounds like he's hungry.'

Lost in thought, Grace barely heard him. He was very mindful that Rose Cadoret could have been lying. But it was more than just mildly suspicious that, in the middle of all that was going on, Sir Tommy and his wife had gone off on holiday without mentioning a word about it to him.

And that they had a lot of luggage with them, too. *Travelling like royalty*, the RaSP had just said. A *lot* of luggage?

As they entered the kitchen, Branson said, 'What the hell?'

'That wasn't here before,' Grace said.

'It sure wasn't.'

Out in the hallway was a shrill, 'Cuckoo'. But they barely noticed it as they stared at the tall, black machine standing beside the wooden kitchen table. It looked like an industrial-size photocopier. But both detectives instantly recognized it as a paper shredder. The bin tray was open, showing it was full to the brim.

Alongside a ceramic bowl of bananas and apples on the table was a tall stack of A4 paper, all with printing on. It looked like someone had been interrupted in the middle of shredding it.

Grace and Branson looked at the top sheet. But couldn't make any sense of what they saw.

```
/
@app.route('/')
def index():
return render_template('index.html')
@app.route('/login', methods=['POST'])
def login():
submitted_key = request.form['key'].encode('utf-8')

if submitted_key == b'correct_key': # Simulate
key checking return "Invalid Key. Access
Denied."
```

The next page contained more of the same. As did the next, and the one after. And reams more.

Grace looked at Branson, frowning. 'Recognize the language?'

'I'm guessing it's *computer*,' the DI replied. 'Code, algorithms, some kind of software program.'

Grace took a photograph of several sheets. 'I know someone who'll be able to tell us.' Then he emailed them with a note to Shannon, asking her to call him as an absolute priority the moment she received this. He glanced at his watch, and decided he would give her five minutes.

THE HAWK IS DEAD

But she needed less than two. He stared at her emailed reply.

A little basic, I'd have done it differently. It's software code for an online auction site – on the dark web.

106

Thursday 30 November 2023

'It looks like the very charming Rose Cadoret might be right,' Grace said.

Branson nodded, pensively.

'I think we—' Grace was interrupted by his phone ringing. He answered. It was Greg Mosse.

'Is this fast enough for you, Roy? I've got what you need.'

'Already? Nice work, tell me?'

'The black cab that picked up Sir Tommy and Lady Fiona was booked yesterday afternoon at 5.24 p.m., for a pickup at 11.20 this morning.'

Grace thought back. That was shortly after he'd been in communication with Sir Tommy about interviewing Rose Cadoret, and the whereabouts of Jon Smoke. 'Where did it take them, Greg?'

'To London Heathrow Airport – Terminal 5.'

'Did they talk to the driver at all, about where they were going?'

'No, I'm afraid not. My officer spoke to the driver, but the driver said they hadn't spoken – but they paid him and gave him an extremely good tip, in cash. What's going on, Roy?'

'It looks like Sir Tommy is doing a runner.'

'A runner?'

'Let me explain it all later. We need to find them, stop them getting on a plane.'

'Them?'

THE HAWK IS DEAD

'Him and his wife. I'll call you back, I'm going to be needing your help.'

'I'm here!'

As he ended the call, Grace looked at his watch. It was now almost 1.15 p.m. The drive from here to Terminal 5 would take around forty minutes. Sir Tommy and his wife would have reached it at about midday. Given that airlines, particularly if you had check-in baggage, required you to be there a minimum of two hours ahead, it was likely their flight wouldn't be until 2 p.m. at the earliest. One of dozens taking off every hour. Which gave the police at the airport a possible window of only forty-five minutes to find the couple.

He turned to Branson. 'Where the hell have they gone?'

'What was it Rose Cadoret said? *You're the detective, you figure it out.*'

Grace studied Branson's face for a moment, as if the answer was written on it. 'I'm the detective, figure it out,' he murmured. 'So let's imagine he has so much luggage because it's full of loot – stolen items. And he knows the police are after him. Where's he going to go?' He looked quizzically at his colleague.

From out in the hallway they heard a sharp, 'Cuckoo!'

It startled them both.

'It would drive me nuts to have that going off every fifteen minutes in my house!' Branson said.

'They have their uses.' Grace gave a knowing smile, which Branson didn't pick up on.

'Cuckoo clocks? Yeah, well, each to their own.'

Grace clapped his hands. 'OK, let's focus on where Sir Tommy and Lady Magellan-Lacey might be going.'

'Somewhere that doesn't have an extradition treaty with the UK?'

'Move to the top of the class.'

'Where do we find out which countries those are?'

'I know them,' Grace said. 'There aren't many. Currently, Russia, China, North Korea, the United Arab Emirates and Saudi Arabia. There may be a few more that I can't think of.'

'So we're going to have to find out all the flights leaving this afternoon to all those countries?'

'No, we haven't time, we're going to need to eliminate some. North Korea for starters. Tell me, which would be your country of preference, if you were heading off with a big stash?'

Branson shrugged. 'The Emirates would be top of my list. Sunshine and bling – what's not to like?'

'Mine too,' Grace agreed, glancing at his watch again. 'But if we are right about Sir Tommy – and I'm increasingly sure we are – I don't think he'd be dumb enough to travel with his wife under their real names.'

'I agree.'

The cat prowled into the room and miaowed again.

'Maybe we can narrow it down,' Grace said.

'How?'

Grace locked eyes with him. 'You need a new ID, fake passport, fake everything. You're going to go for a common surname and not one that sticks out, right?'

'You mean like Smith or Jones or Williams or Brown or—'

Grace looked pointedly down at the cat.

Branson's eyes widened. 'George? Is that what you're suggesting?'

Grace shrugged. 'Good as any and it's right under your nose. We have to start somewhere.' He picked up the phone and called Luke Stanstead. When the researcher answered, Grace gave him his instructions: to extremely urgently get onto the London Heathrow Terminal 5 police, and request the passenger lists for all flights leaving this afternoon for Dubai, and any parts of Russia, China and Saudi Arabia. He was to look in particular for common surnames, and he was to call him back immediately if there was

THE HAWK IS DEAD

a Mr and Mrs George booked on any flight. Also, just in case the Magellan-Laceys were travelling under their real names, he told Luke to check for those too.

As he ended the call, the cat miaowed again, very plaintively.

'Let's find some food for him,' Grace said. 'You never know, he might just have earned himself a slap-up dinner.'

Branson knelt and began opening cupboard doors.

107

Thursday 30 November 2023

Tommy Magellan-Lacey was feeling pretty damned pleased with himself. A couple of glasses of the perfectly acceptable pink champagne British Airways provided in their Gold lounge had added to his well-being. And equally importantly to his wife's.

'Cheers, my darling! To our rather rosy – or should I say *rosé* – future.' He lay back in his comfortable seat and clinked glasses with his wife.

'A rosy future, indeed!' Fiona replied.

They were both so pleasantly woozy.

With all the money they had, as well as the treasures in their luggage, for which he already had buyers lined up, he was never going to have to work a day in his life, ever again. Nor Fiona.

He kept a watchful eye on the flight departure board. Theirs was still showing on time. The sooner they were away the better. He wouldn't fully relax until they were in the air. But he was chilled enough now. That rather beady detective, Roy Grace, would be focusing his attentions on Rose Cadoret – and Tommy had enough on her to ensure her ongoing silence. And thanks to the crazy bitch's actions, he was guaranteed Smoke's silence. That thought made him smile.

Happy days!

And if the balloon did go up – well, hey – by then he and Fiona would have long left Dubai and be safely ensconced in beautiful Georgia where he had a couple of very interested buyers for some of the merchandise they had stored in their warehouse. It was another country that had no extradition treaty with the UK. But also a very nice place to live. Until they decided where, in the world that was now their oyster, to buy their forever home.

He stood up, a little unsteadily, clutching his and Fiona's glasses, and topped them up again. As he did so he felt a sudden burst of exuberance like nothing he'd ever experienced before.

I'm a millionaire! He felt like shouting it out across the packed lounge. *I'm a millionaire! No, correction! I'm a MULTI-MILLIONAIRE!*

It was all in his phone. In Bitcoins.

Oh my God!

He handed Fiona her glass. Then clinked his against hers. 'To the future, my darling!'

'To our future!' she said.

'Indeed!'

Champagne spilled over the rim of his glass as he sat – almost falling – back down, the seat lower than he had remembered. Instantly he felt a damp sensation on his lap and he peered down, seeing a dark patch. It looked like he had peed himself.

'Bugger,' he said.

Then he saw the change on the Departures screen to *Boarding. Gate B14.*

Clutching his very precious briefcase, he said, 'We should go, darling.'

'Let's finish our champagne,' she said. 'They're not going to take off without us, not with all the luggage we have on board!'

He grinned. 'Good point.'

Five minutes later they rode the escalator down. He was now a totally different persona to the old Sir Tommy Magellan-Lacey, Master of the Royal Household, who was always attired in a Huntsman suit, Hilditch and Key shirt and conservative old Marlburian or Athenaeum Club tie. Now he wore a Panama hat at a jaunty angle, Ray-Ban sunglasses, a white Paul Smith jacket over a pink linen shirt, his damp-lapped chinos and, sockless, Todd loafers.

Fiona too looked pretty different to her past twinset and pearls persona. Her brown hair bunched up inside a blonde wig, to match her new passport, she wore an emerald Versace trouser suit and Prada sandals.

The pair strode, a little light-headedly and somewhat unsteadily, against what seemed an endless tide of travellers flowing towards them. They negotiated, in their boozed-up care-free haze of happiness, the oncoming barrage of wheely bags, wheelchairs, mobile phoners, loose children and dodderers, passing some of the fancy shops – nothing in the windows out of their price range now – and then another escalator down to the shuttle platform.

A few minutes later they emerged from the train and took the two long escalators up. Tommy held his beloved wife's hand as they walked on, at the top, towards Gate B14, their flight to Dubai, towards freedom and the start of their new life.

He felt so incredibly excited. It had worked! They'd done it, got away with it! They were rich beyond their wildest dreams!

And beyond the reach of the British law!

Gate B14 was ahead. The electronic sign said, BA 2971 Dubai.

Just a few more minutes!

They joined the Priority Boarding queue.

An announcement was made. Boarding had started for all passengers with a 0 or a 1 on their boarding cards. They had a 1 on theirs, of course!

A few people in wheelchairs were pushed through. Then a bunch of parents with annoyingly shouty sprogs. Then he and Fiona held their printed cards as they approached the automatic gate. A man in front was struggling with his boarding card on his phone, which the machine didn't seem to want to accept. He was about to turn away when it finally went green and the gates opened. The light went red, then green again and Fiona went through. And a few moments later he was through too.

Then two police officers, in full airport protection kit and holding sub-machine guns, stepped into their path. They were apologetic and very polite.

'Mr and Mrs George?' one of them, a clean-shaven male, in his early thirties, asked.

Tommy gave them his most charming smile, practised to pitch-perfect on monarchs and their acolytes over the past decade. 'Yes, can I help you?'

'We'd like you to come with us, please.'

Tommy and Fiona exchanged a nervous glance. 'What is this about exactly, officers?' he asked.

'We'd like you to come with us, sir,' the officer repeated, a little firmer and a little colder.

Tommy looked around, suddenly feeling bewildered. All the feel-good from the booze suddenly drained away. 'I'm terribly sorry,' he said. 'My wife and I have a flight to catch.'

'I'm aware of that, sir. But I need you to come with me.'

Tommy shook his head. 'No, I'm sorry, we are boarding.'

'Sir,' the officer said, even more insistently now. 'If you don't agree to come with us voluntarily, then we will have no option but to arrest you and your wife, here in front of everyone.'

The officer's colleague was a robust-looking woman, with an equally robust expression.

'Nicholas,' Fiona said. 'There's clearly a mix-up of some kind. We should go with them – and we'll get it sorted out.'

Tommy jabbed the air with his finger. 'Officer, you are making a terrible mistake.'

108

Thursday 30 November 2023

'And no mistake,' Grace said with a wide grin as he sat in the passenger seat of the Ford, staring at the photographs of *Mr Nicholas and Mrs Virginia George* that had been sent through to his phone.

Glenn Branson was driving on blue lights along the M4 towards Heathrow Airport, following closely behind the escort of two police motorcyclists that Greg Mosse had arranged, to help them cut through the traffic. 'You are sure, boss?'

'Bet my life on it. It's him, and I recognize her from the photos in their kitchen.'

'When did you suspect?'

'Only in the past few days, for sure. He's been very clever at covering his tracks.'

'He's so charming. So damned charming.'

'Ted Bundy was charming, too. A lot of the women giving evidence against him in court thought he must be an attorney – either for the defence or prosecution. It was his charm that enabled him to get away with it for so long. He was executed in 1989 for the rape and murder of two college students, and the attempted murder of a twelve-year-old girl. He eventually confessed to the FBI officer who arrested him to twenty-nine rapes and killings. But the FBI believe his total tally was around one hundred. Dr Harold Shipman was charming too. He despatched two hundred and fifty patients, who all adored him.'

THE HAWK IS DEAD

He continued. 'A great mentor of mine, way back when I first became a detective, told me that the essence of being a good detective is not so much what you know already, but knowing the questions to ask. Do you know the questions you are going to ask Mr and Mrs George?'

Branson nodded. 'I do. The first one is, where the hell do they keep their cat food?'

109

Thursday 30 November 2023

Gregg Mosse was standing outside the front entrance of the Arrivals Hall of Terminal 5, as Glenn Branson pulled the car up.

As they climbed out, Grace strode up to him, holding out his hand. 'The great man himself!'

Missing entirely the subtle innuendo, Mosse almost simpered. 'Well, thank you, Roy – and nice to see you, Detective Inspector Ronson.'

'It's Branson.'

'Ah right, yes, like the pickle!'

'Yeah, the T is silent,' Branson retorted for the second time.

Mosse briefly frowned, clearly not getting this jibe, either. 'Ah.' He turned back to Grace. 'Well, Roy, I was not going to miss this big moment.'

Grace thought: *Of course not, of course you wouldn't want to miss the opportunity of claiming the glory of this for yourself.*

Mosse doled out a badge on a lanyard to each of them. 'I've got you both airside passes. I'm afraid we still have to go through damned security.'

They followed Mosse, and an armed airport police officer they weren't introduced to, through a lane marked *Fast Track*, all four of them depositing their phones in a tray, and their jackets, belts and boots in another, and walked in turn through the screener. Dressed again, the four of them walked along a corridor, up two flights of stairs, and then into a small, windowless room.

THE HAWK IS DEAD

Two armed officers stood at the back of the room. Behind the couple who sat in front of them, at a bare metal table.

It was a slight shock for Grace, for a moment, to see the normally very conservatively dressed Sir Tommy looking so louche, in his white jacket, and pink shirt. And wearing an expression that was somewhere between defiant and sheepish.

Fiona looked very different to her photographs in the house. In those, she had brown hair. She was now a glamorous blonde. And with a look on her face that was anything but glamorous at this moment.

Over the years, Roy Grace had learned to read the expressions of arrested suspects. In particular how so many transitioned from one of defiance to one of defeat. He saw the latter in their faces now.

'Mr and Mrs *George*!' Grace said. 'How very nice to meet you. Mr George, you remind me so much of someone I know.'

'OK, Roy, well done. I misjudged you,' the Master said.

Grace stood for a moment, silently, sizing him up and then his wife.

'Sir Thomas Burnett Julian Magellan-Lacey, I'm arresting you on suspicion of conspiracy to murder and conspiracy to commit theft.' He read him the rest of his rights, then addressed his wife. 'Lady Fiona Ariane Susan Magellan-Lacey, I'm arresting you on conspiracy to commit theft. You do not have to say anything. But it may harm your defence if you do not mention when questioned, something you later rely on in court. Anything you do say may be given in evidence.'

She stared back at him coldly and without any hint of emotion.

Then Glenn Branson, unable to restrain himself, spoke up. 'Sir Tommy, I think maybe you'll now agree that I've made a better job of this investigation than I did of dunking my biscuit?'

110

Friday 15 December 2023

'Cuckoo clock?' The Queen said.

'Cuckoo clock?' The King repeated, frowning amiably.

Roy Grace sat on a sofa facing them across an elegant coffee table, on which was the delicate china teacup and saucer he had been handed by the butler. Grace had put it down because he was shaking, nervous again in their company and terrified of spilling any on the carpet.

They were in Their Majesties' private drawing room in Clarence House, which had a comfortable, lived-in feel. Everything felt on a smaller scale than the grand formality of Buckingham Palace. Even the paintings and ornaments seemed smaller, and there were personal touches, Grace noticed, which included framed family photographs dotted around, Christmas cards and invites on the mantelpiece above the welcoming roaring fire, and a water bowl for the dogs on the floor.

The King was dressed the way Grace had always seen him, in a conservative suit and tie, shoes polished to within an inch of some valet's life. The Queen wore a powder-blue two-piece, buttoned high up. Her two Jack Russells sat nuzzled up to her legs.

Grace had come at their invitation. The now Acting Master, Matthew Corbin, had phoned him to say they wanted to thank him personally.

'I'll explain, Your Majesties!' Grace said.

THE HAWK IS DEAD

'Please do.' The King smiled warmly. 'We are most intrigued!'

'Well, it was three weeks ago, my colleague, Detective Inspector Branson and I had just left Buckingham Palace and were driving back down to Sussex. I called Sir Tommy – it was just coming up to 3 p.m. I told him that from information I had received, the Holbein the Younger miniature of Anne of Cleves might be missing. Sir Tommy expressed great concern and said he would get back to me. While we were speaking I heard a cuckoo clock in the background calling 3 p.m.'

The Queen raised her eyebrows.

Grace smiled. 'Indeed, Ma'am. Sir Tommy then rang me back, just five minutes later, and sounded quite distraught. He told me he had gone straight from his office and down to the vault, where the miniature was being stored during the renovations, and that it wasn't there.'

'Five minutes?' The King said, with scepticism in his voice. 'He rang you back in five minutes?' His brow furrowed. 'But that's impossible. The cuckoo clock sounding 3 p.m. puts him in his home at St James's Palace. It would take all of five minutes, going at quite a pace, to get from there to the front of Buckingham Palace, let alone down to the vaults. I doubt even Usain Bolt could have done it in that time.'

Grace smiled again. 'My point exactly. You should have been a detective, Sir.'

The King replied with a laugh. 'No, that would be my darling wife, she'd make a great one, with all the crime novels she reads!'

The Queen nodded thoughtfully. 'So, clearly Tommy wasn't in his office on that first call, he was at home?'

'Exactly, Your Majesty. It was the cuckoo clock that told me. Sir Tommy didn't go running over to Buckingham Palace and down to the vaults, because he didn't need to. He knew the picture wasn't there – because he had it in his house all along – and latterly in a suitcase. Just to be sure, I did check whether there are any cuckoo clocks in Buckingham Palace. There are three in the Royal Collection, but they are all in other locations.'

The Queen nodded. 'Yes, they are. One of them is extremely pretty and unusual.'

'What an absolute scoundrel!' The King said. 'To think my mama put so much trust in Tommy, as we have done too.' He looked at his wife and she nodded agreement. 'As for those other two – Cadoret and Smoke—'

'Three, actually, Sir,' Grace interrupted.

'Three?' The Queen quizzed. 'You're not going to tell us dear Perry was part of this too, are you?'

'No, absolutely not,' Grace replied.

'Then who? Was it Geoffrey Bailey, the footman?'

'No, Ma'am, we think Bailey was just trying to blackmail the group into getting Sir Tommy to give him the medal he wanted. It would seem that Sir Peregrine, who was increasingly suspicious of Tommy and his colleagues, may have indiscreetly told Geoffrey Bailey a few things and perhaps they started working together building evidence of the thefts.'

'Pillow talk?' The Queen suggested, with a wry smile.

'Possibly, although we don't believe the relationship had gone very far.'

'So, Detective Superintendent,' The King asked, 'if not Geoffrey Bailey, who is this fourth person you are referring to?'

'Fiona Magellan-Lacey, Sir,' Grace said.

'As a willing accomplice?'

'I would say more than that. She has a First in mathematics from Oxford University, and a number of impressive computing sciences qualifications. From the laptops we've seized from them both, it would appear she was the mastermind behind all their work on the dark web.'

THE HAWK IS DEAD

The King looked puzzled. 'Tommy always told me she worked in an art gallery – a part-time job that she enjoyed.'

'Sir Tommy told a lot of people a lot of lies,' Grace replied.

Both Their Majesties nodded, a little ruefully.

'But he had all the charm in the world,' Grace went on. 'We were completely taken in by him, for a long time.'

'I think I do owe you an apology,' King Charles said. 'I believe I was a bit short with you the first time we met.'

'Understandably, Sir, you were concerned about Her Majesty.'

'I was – I clearly underestimated your abilities. Not only were you right in your original assessment of the situation, you've done a remarkable job since then – and you have saved countless treasures that are part of our nation's heritage. I don't know how you detectives do it, or your thought processes, but my wife and I want to thank you from the bottom of our hearts.'

'I appreciate that, Sir. I'm just glad my team has got the result it has.'

The King then looked bemused, and slowly shook his head from side to side. He raised his hands in the air and then lowered them again, as if unsure how to express what he wanted to say. 'It's – as if – you've had to put together the pieces of a gigantic puzzle.'

'Exactly,' Grace replied. 'Almost all major crimes are exactly that: big and often complex puzzles that we have to try to solve.'

The King frowned again and his voice came out a little tighter and more strained than before. 'What I still just don't fully understand in all this, is why poor Peregrine was shot. Presumably to silence him, but there would have been a lot of easier ways, surely?'

'I agree,' The Queen said. 'That is what is baffling me, too.'

'I think I can explain,' Grace replied. 'Rose Cadoret has already told us quite a lot – she is, as the expression goes, *singing like a canary*, in the hope of a reduced sentence. What seems to be the case is that the plan the conspirators made was an extremely dangerous one, based around the classic distraction technique favoured by magicians, but on a far grander scale.'

'A conjuring trick?' The King queried.

'Not a conjuring trick, no, Sir. She told us that she was the one who pushed the length of track onto the line to derail the train. The set-up with the derailing was to make the shooting look like a failed conspiracy to assassinate Her Majesty. By doing it on this scale they felt it would appear the work of either an anti-monarchy group or some terrorist organization wanting to make a very big public statement through their actions. What went wrong, for them, was the sniper's shot.'

'Very fortunately,' The King said.

'Well, the intention was always to kill Sir Peregrine. The plan was for the sniper to take his shot when Sir Peregrine and Her Majesty were just inches apart. But for whatever reason, he didn't get that chance, and fired anyway. If there had been only a few inches between Her Majesty and Sir Peregrine, then the obvious assumption would have been that the shooter had missed. But to throw our investigation he fired a second shot to give the impression he was still trying to kill Her Majesty. In which case, our investigation would have been very different and we wouldn't have been looking anything like so hard into Sir Peregrine's background. All our energies would have been focused in a different direction.'

'And you are pretty certain, Detective Superintendent,' The King asked, 'that the sniper is the fellow found dead at the bottom of the lift shaft?'

'Yes, PC Jon Smoke and Rose Cadoret were responsible for the murders. We recovered Smoke's private phone hidden in Ms Cadoret's flat in Putney. There's a possible legitimate reason for it being there, because we know they did have an on-off relationship.

THE HAWK IS DEAD

But GPS triangulation puts Smoke's phone in Buckingham Palace, and in that part of the Palace where the lift shaft is, at around the estimated time of his death. From there it travelled back to Ms Cadoret's apartment.'

'All on its own?' The Queen said with a sardonic smile.

'It puts a whole new meaning to *teleporting*,' Grace said.

Both Their Majesties laughed. 'Straight out of *Dr Who*?' King Charles suggested.

'Indeed, Sir.'

'It seems from what you've told us that technology has played quite a major role in this investigation,' The King said.

'Yes, Sir, but so have some good old-fashioned investigation techniques. We were lucky to have somebody who was able to crack the cryptic codes in the diary and the names of those involved, who Sir Peregrine knew all had unrestricted access to the Royal Collection.'

'In addition to your wife, Cleo?' The King said, with a smile.

'Indeed, Sir. She was weaned on puzzles! The last name was the hardest to crack and that, of course, was Sir Tommy who had us all fooled.'

'How does that proverb go?' The King asked. 'Fool me once, shame on you. Fool me twice, shame on me.'

Grace smiled and nodded. 'Sir Jason Finch was for a time very much a POI, as we say.'

King Charles frowned. 'POI?'

'A Person of Interest, Your Majesty.'

'Ah.'

'For some while, Sir Jason Finch met a lot of the criteria for a suspect. Pretty much up to the deciphering of the code for Sir Tommy – which was WGFTGIGFTG: What's Good For The Goose Is Good For The Gander. The key to the cryptic clue is the goose – the Magellan goose.'

Queen Camilla smiled, then said, 'He certainly did have us all fooled. It was very smart of dear Perry to have kept all this information secret in his diary – what a clever Hawk he was!'

'It *was* smart, Ma'am. As you say, modern technology also played a major part. As in most investigations these days. Whenever we use any modern technology – or even travel in a modern car – we are leaving electronic footprints everywhere. Villains know that, but fortunately for us, sometimes they're forgetful, as all humans can be. PC Smoke failed to switch off his phone when he went to take up his position near the south portal of Clayton Tunnel. It puts him clearly there at the time of the shooting. And we subsequently found the sniper rifle he used concealed under floorboards at his house. We also found a motocross motorcycle matching one seen by a witness, in his garage. Traces of mud on the tyres and on the chassis of the machine also match the soil type at the scene of the shooting.'

'So you are very confident it was Smoke?' The Queen said.

'Very, Ma'am.'

'Remarkable,' The King said.

'Detective Superintendent,' The Queen said, 'I noticed you seemed to take quite an interest in some of the art in Buckingham Palace.'

'I did indeed, Ma'am, yes.'

'How about as a small thank-you, one day in the coming weeks I give you a private tour? And if your wife would like to join us, she would be most welcome.'

Grace could imagine Cleo's face, and he beamed in delight. 'I would love that, Your Majesty. I know Cleo would, too!' He thought for an instant. 'I also know my colleague Detective Inspector Branson, who played a very big part in the investigation, would really love that, too. Would it be possible for him to join us?'

'Yes, of course,' she said. 'With great pleasure. Now, is there anything in particular that you would like to see?'

'No,' he said. 'I would be more than honoured to leave it to

THE HAWK IS DEAD

you, Ma'am, as my tour guide.' Then he smiled. 'Well, maybe there's just one part of the Palace we don't need to worry about.'

'And which is that?'

'The roof, Your Majesty. I think I've seen enough of that.'

111

Sunday 17 December 2023

'Get you, tea with your new besties!' Cleo, lounging back on the sofa, teased. 'Cucumber sarnies with the crusts cut off? Scones and cream? Victoria sponge?'

'Just Earl Grey tea, that was all.'

'Served in the finest china tea set, by the butler of course?'

He smiled. 'Of course.'

'You know that bone china is made from real bones, don't you?'

'Seriously? I've never thought about that before. You mean *animal* bones, I hope?'

'Rather than human ones?'

They were squashed together, book-ended by Humphrey leaning against Grace and Kyla against Cleo. The kids were settled and Grace was enjoying his first proper drink in a month. He was holding a very stiff and cold vodka Martini, and Cleo a large glass of wine.

'I'm sure there are plenty of unscrupulous cemetery operators,' she said. 'Half the components of fine bone china is ground-up cremated bone. It's what gives it the translucency.'

'Hmm, thanks, that might come under *too much information*! Think I'll stick to a plastic mug in future.' He put down his glass and stroked Humphrey on the nape of his neck. 'So, how come you know so much about fine china? You got a side-hustle on the go – supplying the potteries with bone ash?'

THE HAWK IS DEAD

Cleo grinned. 'Hang around a mortuary for long enough and you'll learn everything you never needed to know!'

Grace picked up his glass and clinked hers. 'I'll drink to that,' he said.

'Your first vodka Martini in a long time. Another influence from your royal buddies?'

'Influence?'

'I read that His Maj is rather partial to a Martini, too. But he has it made with gin, rather than vodka.' She gave him a cheeky glance. 'Clearly that's the posh way to do it.'

'So I'm a pleb, having it with vodka?'

'Just saying . . .'

They had spent a happy weekend with the children, decorating the house and the Christmas tree. Noah had proudly displayed the angel on top of the tree that he had made at school. Molly had brought home a cardboard snowman from pre-school. Earlier they had both sat at the kitchen table, with Noah at one end constructing his Lego models and Molly, at the other, putting together a Duplo unicorn figure, loving seeing how focused both children were on their tasks.

'Did you ever solve the last of the five cryptic ciphers you were given?' Cleo asked, suddenly. 'The one about the Horseman? Song of the Horseman or Son of the Horseman?'

Grace nodded. 'Sorry, I should have told you. Have you still been trying to work it out?'

'It's been keeping me awake night after night.'

He looked at her and saw the teasing smile on her face.

'But I have been mulling on it,' she added.

'Denton Scroope finally figured it out. Each of the five clues was someone who had easy access to the Royal Collection – but not necessarily a suspect. It's Lorraine McKnight, Director of the Royal Collection. McKnight is of Irish origin. In Gaelic it means, *son of the horseman*.'

'Sir Peregrine sounds like he had quite an intellect,' Cleo said.

Grace nodded. 'You don't get to be high up in the Royal Household by being a dimwit. Sir Tommy was pretty smart, also.'

'Just not smart enough?' she quizzed.

'Or maybe too smart,' he replied. 'He nearly got away with it, so very nearly.'

On the coffee table in front of them, next to a pile of Christmas cards they had opened and read, was a tall stack of pages from newspapers, over the past month, which Cleo had carefully cut out and kept in place with a glass paperweight. It was for posterity, she'd said. A big scrapbook for their children, and one day their grandchildren, to see how famous their dad or grandad – or maybe even great-grandad – had been. The most recent one, from the *Telegraph*, lay on the top.

The headline read: MURDER IN THE ROYAL HOUSEHOLD – THREE DENIED BAIL.

Cleo shot a glance at the stack. 'So are your royal besties going to be called on to give evidence at the trial?'

'I hope not. Rose is going to plead guilty as part of her bargaining, and I would hope Sir Tommy and Fiona, villains though they may be, will have the decency not to expose Their Majesties to that. I mean, they are totally bang to rights and it would only involve The Queen – but I very much doubt that will happen. The evidence against them is strong and three of their five suitcases we pulled off the plane to Dubai were full of pretty much priceless items from the Royal Collection. Including the missing Vermeer, Holbein's miniature portrait of Anne of Cleves and the entire rest of Granny's Personal Chips.'

'Minus the one fake?'

He nodded. 'Yep. Minus the one that got away and one that didn't.'

'People do pack things by mistake, don't they, my love?'

He shrugged. 'It happens.'

THE HAWK IS DEAD

'Like the fleece gilet you packed last year when we went to Corfu in August?'

'Exactly! We also struck lucky with the information that Rose Cadoret gave us about a storage unit in a warehouse near Heathrow Airport. There were two packing cases full of items from the Royal Collection, including pictures, jade ornaments, sculptures and small items of furniture. They were due to be shipped to the Magellan-Laceys' new address in Dubai, labelled as "personal items".'

They looked at each other and both burst out laughing. 'It's surreal,' she said. 'This whole thing.'

'It is.'

'But what is brilliant is how much stuff you've recovered.'

'Much of that was thanks to Rose Cadoret singing.'

'And you recovered most of the money they received from what they had sold and delivered?'

'We got all their Bitcoin wallets, where the money was hidden, off their phones. Sir Tommy's code was cracked by one of our brainboxes in Digital Forensics – Charlotte Mckee. The code was a combination of his and his wife's initials and the date they joined the Palace.'

'And Rose Cadoret gave you hers?'

'And Jon Smoke's. So all the cash they made has been returned to the Keeper of the Privy Purse.'

'Sir Jason Finch?'

'Yes. One of my prime suspects, originally. Even more so when we heard he was away with his wife in Amsterdam. We thought they might be selling diamonds, but it turns out one of their daughters has opened a restaurant there with her partner, and they'd gone to the launch to support the couple. Then our suspicions deepened when our Financial Investigator discovered a cash deposit of three quarters of a million pounds into his bank account. But that turned out to be legitimate. They were in the process of selling a number of paintings Sir Jason had inherited. One of them was by Landseer – he had a picture by him that was very similar to one in the Royal Collection.'

Humphrey turned his head and licked Grace's hand. The dog's tongue felt like wet sandpaper.

'Humphrey loves you!' Cleo said. 'He loved you from the moment he first saw you, remember?'

'Just like you did!'

Cleo punched him. 'Don't get *too* big-headed or you'll need a larger hat. Tell me more about the diamond you've just said was missing and the fake.'

'Good old technology again,' he said, a tad smugly. 'Triangulation on Fiona Magellan-Lacey's phone put her in Hatton Garden. A building where there are five major players in the diamond industry. Thanks to the woman I got released from prison on licence, we know who she has been doing business with.'

'The woman released from prison – you mean Shannon Kendall?'

He nodded. 'She's delivered everything we could have wanted – and more.' He gave his wife a big smile. 'It didn't take long for Nick and EJ to work out from that triangulation, that Fiona had met one of the diamond dealers in that location on several occasions. She made the mistake of having lunch at a nearby restaurant with him on one of those visits, enabling the team to identify him. His name is Gary van Damm. When he was arrested, about to board a flight to Mumbai, he had one of the diamonds from the famous collection of Granny's Personal Chips in his jacket pocket.'

Cleo leaned forward and picked up her glass of Rioja. 'I read in the *Daily Mail* that in addition to Charles liking his Martini, Camilla likes red wine – Pomerol is her favourite. So we don't quite match Their Majesties.'

'We're a little less regal?' Roy Grace suggested.

She nodded in agreement. 'But no less charming! You are my

THE HAWK IS DEAD

Prince Charming, and that's as regal as you need to be!' She hesitated. 'God that sounds cheesy!'

'Cheesy is good!'

She grinned. 'Did Sir Tommy – and all of them – seriously think they would get away with it?'

Humphrey licked his hand again. 'You know, I actually think they were big-headed enough to think they would. And the Magellan-Laceys very nearly did.'

'But they hadn't reckoned with my very smart husband.'

'Those are kind words, my darling. I don't know how much is down to me, and how much is down to the mistakes they made.' He paused. 'I don't know who said it, but it's very apt: *The walls of a prison aren't just made of concrete and steel, they are also built from the lost hopes and the silenced dreams of those within.*'

'But we get a behind-the-scenes tour of Buckingham Palace, by Her Majesty The Queen out of it? That's not rubbish, is it?'

'Not complete rubbish, no.'

'I do actually think, on rare occasions, this is one, that being married to a homicide detective isn't all bad.'

Grace raised his glass. 'Nor is being married to someone who spends her days with dead people!'

They clinked glasses again. Grace ate the last of the four olives in his Martini and sipped from the glass. 'This is a seriously good one,' he announced, with a big, contented smile.

'Dead for a ducat,' Cleo said.

'Dead for a *what*?' Grace responded.

'Hamlet.' She blew him a kiss. 'I know Shakespeare's not your thing.'

'Dead for a what? Tell me?'

'It's a line by Hamlet. No one is quite sure of the meaning. A ducat was a gold coin – worth a fortune at the time. It could mean that killing Polonius was worth it. Maybe the modern equivalent would be, dead for a diamond.'

'Three people dead – for a diamond? Or a bit more besides just a diamond or two . . .' Grace added.

'A bit more, yes.'

'But never enough.'

'Can you ever have enough diamonds?'

'You know what Gandhi said?'

Cleo frowned: 'About what?'

'It was something along the lines of the world can provide enough for everyone's needs, but not for everyone's greed. I think that deserves another drink,' Roy Grace added.

Cleo smiled. 'I'm with you. And I really don't think that's being greedy.'

'Not at all!'

She looked at him for some moments, with a big smile, 'I think that's why I love you.'

'So it's not my good looks, my charm, my skills as a detective?'

Cleo shook her head. 'I'm afraid not, my love. It's because sometimes, just sometimes, you like being naughty too!'

He raised his Martini. 'I'll drink to that!'

The moment they clinked glasses, there was a cry from Molly on the baby monitor. Cleo jumped up. 'I'll check on her.'

As she walked out of the room, Grace noticed an unopened envelope on the floor. He put his glass on the table, leaned down and picked it up, then tore it open and removed the card inside.

It was a cheap Christmas card, Santa and his reindeer. Inside, above the message of goodwill, was a handwritten one. It read:

'You might not remember me. But I remember you. Enjoy your last Christmas.'

AFTERWORD

The question every author is probably asked most often is: 'Where do you get your ideas from?'

When I began my writing career, the answer I never thought I'd be giving in a million years would have been: 'Well, for this book, my ideas are from Her Majesty The Queen, actually.'

But it's true. I'm fortunate enough to count Queen Camilla as my number one fan. In 2019, as the then-Duchess of Cornwall, she wrote me a letter asking if my next Roy Grace novel might be centred in London. As history tells us, things have not ended well for people who have displeased any former Queen of England – just look back to Elizabeth I, who had 100 or so men hanged, drawn and quartered, or to 'Bloody' Mary, who turned some 300 souls into human bonfires.

Not relishing such prospects, I instead thought: *What better place in London than Buckingham Palace?* At least for a key part of the story. I mulled it over for the next four years, as I always do when I'm planning and plotting, trying to think how a detective based in Sussex could become involved in a major crime in the Royal Household.

Then I read in a newspaper article that all 775 rooms of Buckingham Palace were undergoing major renovation, taking place over the course of several years. There were concerns for the security and safety of more than a million highly valuable items housed in the Royal Collection during that period – items such as paintings and sculptures by some of the greatest artists of the past, rare ornaments, jewellery, furniture, silverware, glassware and more. Almost all of incalculable value.

This gave me the meat I needed for the bones of my idea! I wrote a brief outline about Queen Camilla travelling on the Royal Train to Sussex, where, on arrival, a senior member of the Royal Household is murdered. As this is Roy Grace's manor and he is the on-call SIO, he takes charge of the case. His enquiries lead him to Buckingham Palace, where he uncovers the true hornets' nest: a conspiracy to steal items from the Royal Collection and sell them on the dark web. And the ruthless conspirators – trusted members of the Royal Household staff – are willing to murder anyone who gets in their way . . .

Soon after starting my serious research, I learned something I have learned many times before: so often the truth can be much stranger than fiction! In 2021, a Buckingham Palace footman was arrested and subsequently found guilty of stealing items of royal memorabilia, which he sold on the internet. Less sophisticated than the villains in my novel, he was caught through recognition of the pattern of the counterpane on his bed, on which he had laid out the items to photograph . . .

This novel has been the most brilliant and amazing adventure for me. I've had wonderful insights into the workings of the Royal Household, seen what goes on deep inside Buckingham Palace and, as a totally unexpected bonus, achieved my boyhood dream of driving a train.

A key scene very early in the novel is when the Royal Train, carrying Queen Camila and her entourage, is derailed in a tunnel just north of the city of Brighton and Hove. I wanted to introduce a character who is the proud driver of this train. There are a few drivers who are trained to drive the Royal Train – but, for security reasons, none of them knows if they are to be chosen to drive the train that day until the day itself. And, as the train is rarely used, some drivers never get the chance to drive a Principal in their entire career. So, on this occasion, for my character Stan Briggs, approaching retirement, this is the pinnacle of his professional life, driving the train from London Victoria to Brighton. Little does he know that disaster lies ahead.

I was fortunate to receive enthusiastic help from Network Rail, who allowed me in the cab, alongside the driver, on a journey from Brighton to London and its return route. Additionally, I had a lesson on a very realistic simulator. I learned that there is so much more to driving a train than I had ever imagined and this is described in the scenes of the book. The responsibility of driving any passenger train is massive, often transporting far more passengers than an airline pilot would, and the driver has to be aware of so much, all the time. Not to mention it can take a mile to bring a full train of eight-to-twelve carriages to a stop. I asked my instructor – who is both a train driver and the senior instructor for Network Rail – if he had ever forgotten to stop at a station. He admitted he had once forgotten to stop at Gatwick Airport, resulting in many people missing their flights. 'You only forget to stop once!' he told me with a wry smile. I came away with tremendous respect for these drivers.

I hope that, as much as you enjoy the story itself, you will find the inner workings of the Royal Household fascinating too, whether or not you consider yourself a royalist. I also hope that you will have as much fun delving behind the scenes of Buckingham Palace – which is more than just a globally iconic building, it is an enduring symbol of the British nation – as I had writing this novel.

GLOSSARY

ANPR – Automatic Number Plate Recognition. Roadside or mobile cameras that automatically capture the registration number of all cars that pass. It can be used to historically track which cars went past a certain camera, and can also create a signal for cars which are stolen, have no insurance or have an alert attached to them.

CID – Criminal Investigation Department. Usually refers to the divisional detectives rather than the specialist squads.

CPS – Crown Prosecution Service.

CSI – Crime Scene Investigators. Formerly SOCO (Scenes of Crime Officers). They are the people who attend crime scenes to search for fingerprints, DNA samples etc.

DIGITAL FORENSICS – The unit which examines and investigates computers and other digital devices.

FLO – Family Liaison Officer.

MO – Modus Operandi (method of operation). The manner by which the offender has committed the offence. Often this can reveal unique features which allow crimes to be linked or suspects to be identified.

RaSP – Royalty and Specialist Protection (officer/team).

PETER JAMES

SIO – Senior Investigating Officer. Usually a Detective Chief Inspector who is in overall charge of the investigation of a major crime such as murder, kidnap or rape.

CHART OF POLICE RANKS

Police ranks are consistent across all disciplines and the addition of prefixes such as 'detective' (e.g. detective constable) does not affect seniority relative to others of the same rank (e.g. police constable).

Police Constable	Police Sergeant	Inspector	Chief Inspector

Superintendent	Chief Superintendent	Assistant Chief Constable	Deputy Chief Constable	Chief Constable

ACKNOWLEDGEMENTS

Every novel I write is special to me, both for what I learn during my research and for the characters I encounter during the journey from the first line to the final words. But, of all the novels I have written, this one feels the most special – and not just because I learned to drive a train as part of my research! I have so many people to thank.

Firstly, to all at Buckingham Palace who have helped me: I can never thank you enough. While I've tried to be as accurate as possible, I have taken some small fictional licence, both within the Palace and with some items of the Royal Collection.

To so many members of the police, with firstly a very special mention to Detective Superintendent Andy Wolstenholme, who has, as ever, given the most incredibly detailed feedback to help me get all aspects of policing in this novel accurate.

Thanks to: Police and Crime Commissioner Katy Bourne OBE; Chief Constable Jo Shiner KPM; Divisional Commander of Brighton & Hove, Chief Superintendent Rachel Carr; Chief Superintendent James Collis; Financial Investigator Emily Denyer; ACC Allan Gregory, British Transport Police; Sergeant Rebecca Cohen, British Transport Police; Robin Smith, Chief of Police, Jersey States Police; PC Jonathan Jackson, Met Police; James Stather, Forensic Investigations; Aiden Gilbert and Jason Quigley, Digital Forensics; Polly Sweeney, Major Crime Team; Beth Durham, Suzanne Heard, Jill Pedersen and Katie Perkins of Sussex Police Corporate Communications; Paul Holmes, Firearms Technical Support Unit; and Dave Hutton, former RaSP.

Also to my invaluable team on the railways: train-driving instructor Simon Willard, Driver Competence Assurance Manager for Thameslink Railway, who I managed to scare even on the simulator before we got on the track; Tom Guiney, Area Operations Manager, Southern Railway; Steve Butcher, Southern Railway train driver; Chris New, Network Rail; and Jon Bennion-Jones for all the introductions.

Big thank-yous are due for all other areas of research help to: Nicky Curry of Pangdean Farm; Sean Didcott; Geoff Duffield; Rebecca English; Gary Monnickendam; Russ Phillips; Suzy Pinel; Derek Pratt MBE; Amy Robinson; two individuals who inspire some of my very young characters, Kit Robinson and Molly Robinson; and pathologist Dr David Wright.

Thank you to my honest, open and trusted early readers, Martin Diplock, Jane Diplock, Lyn Gaylor, James Hodge, Rob Kempson and Dr Georgina Maclean.

A special mention to my ever-vigilant and lovely mother-in-law, who publicizes my work far and wide and is the first to alert me to press clippings – Margaret Duncton (I'd like to call her hawk-eyed, too, but in a good way!).

A massive thank-you to my amazing team at Pan Macmillan, both here and overseas, headed up by Joanna Prior. Specifically, I want to mention my brilliant commissioning editor, Francesca Pathak, as well as Jonathan Atkins, Melissa Bond, Lara Borlenghi, Emily Bromfield, Claire Bush, Tom Clancy, Sian Chilvers, Alex Coward, Raphaella Demetris, Stuart Dwyer, Claire Evans, Lucy Hale, Daniel Jenkins, Andy Joannou, Christine Jones, Rebecca Kellaway, Ellie Kyrke-Smith, Neil Lang, Rebecca Lloyd, Sara Lloyd, James Long, Poppy North, Rory O'Brien, Guy Raphael, Grace Rhodes, Katie Roden, Laura Sherlock, Emily Sumner, Charlotte

Williams and Leanne Williams. Plus my meticulous freelancers, Susan Opie and Nicole Foster.

Massive thanks, as always, to my tireless literary agent, Isobel Dixon, and to everyone at my UK literary agency, Blake Friedmann: Sian Ellis-Martin, Nicole Etherington, Julian Friedmann, James Pusey, Tabitha Topping, Conrad Williams, Daisy Way, Alexander Falkenberg. And to my UK PR team at FMcM – Emma Mitchell and Kealey Ridgen – and my US PR team – Emi Battaglia and Tina Joell – thanks also.

The image many have of an author is that of someone toiling away at their keyboard, perhaps in an attic or a shed, all alone. But I prefer to work as part of a team and I am blessed to have Team James helping me. I'm so grateful for: Danielle Brown and the team at Out of Office – Megan Webster and Alex Goncalves – who run our social media and communications; Emma Gallichan, our wonderful PA; Sarah Middle, who keeps us solvent; Mark Tuckwell, who drives us about tirelessly; and Chris Diplock and Chris Webb, who both make sure our IT systems run as smoothly as IT systems ever will!

Within Team James, there are two utterly indispensable members: my wife, Lara, and former Detective Chief Superintendent David Gaylor. These two help plot, plan and line-edit all my work and are vital to my daily writing.

The first time I met him, back in 1997, David Gaylor was a Detective Inspector in Sussex. In 2002, after being promoted to Detective Chief Superintendent, he happily became my role model for Roy Grace and we have worked together closely on every novel, television screenplay and stage script ever since. David guides me not only on how Roy Grace and the other police officers in my scenarios would think and act, but also on just about every creative aspect of my work. He is an endless font of knowledge, wisdom and creativity, and each of my novels is immeasurably richer for his input.

My most special thanks of all are to Lara, who somehow – in

PETER JAMES

between her marathon training, managing our business and tending to all our wonderful animals – keeps on top of every word I write and adds wisdom and brilliant creative thinking to every novel, television screenplay and stage script, too. Lara brings so many vital dimensions to each story, and one of the most important of all is her understanding of how people think and behave. Her grasp of human nature is incredibly perceptive and she constantly makes me aware of things that I simply wouldn't have known if I had been writing in isolation. That's because she is super smart and totally in tune with the zeitgeist of our times. And, like David, she is incredibly hard-working and has an eye for detail far sharper than any hawk. If you have enjoyed this book, so much credit is due to Lara, as well as David.

Lastly, thank you to all the creatures in our ever-expanding menagerie – a big welcome to our gorgeous rescue rabbit Ryan, who we have taken in and rehomed through the wonderful JSPCA. Ryan came with an ASBO and is now a delight! When I hunker down to write, I'll always have one of our dogs under my feet and another keeping a watchful eye from another chair, making sure I stick to my word count, while one of our cats will be prowling around, too, just checking on me . . .

And thank you, dear readers, for all your amazing support. Do keep your messages coming through any of the channels below.

Above all, stay safe and well.

Peter James

contact@peterjames.com
www.peterjames.com
 @peterjamesuk
 @peterjames.roygrace
 @peterjamesuk
 @thejerseyhomestead
 @mickeymagicandfriends
 @PeterJamesPJTV
 @peterjamesauthor

THE HAWK IS DEAD –
READING GROUP QUESTIONS
FOR DISCUSSION

1. What three words would you use to describe *The Hawk Is Dead* and why?

2. Did you know the story of Granny's Chips before reading *The Hawk Is Dead*? Is there anything else new about the Royal Family or Buckingham Palace that you've learned from reading this book?

3. Did you get a strong sense of place from Peter James's description of Buckingham Palace? When Grace chases Rose through the Palace, how did the setting impact the scene?

4. How accurately do you think King Charles and Queen Camilla were portrayed by Peter James?

5. In this instalment, we see Cleo helping Roy to crack the case by decoding Peregrine Greaves' diary. Did you like seeing husband and wife team up?

6. What did you think of the tension between Grace and Mosse? What do you think will happen if Mosse joins the Sussex Police in future books?

7. We met Shannon Kendall in *One of Us Is Dead*. How do you feel about her character making a return?

8. Rose Cadoret uses funds from the royal art theft operation to pay for her mother's care home. Does this make her character more relatable to you? What would you do in her position?

9. Did you always suspect that Sir Tommy (and his wife) were the masterminds behind the operation or did your suspicions shift to and from different characters throughout the story?

10. Who do you think sent the mysterious Christmas card to Grace at the end of the book?

11. Look back at the three words you chose at the beginning of this discussion. Have they changed? Why or why not?

Read on for more information on the brilliant charities mentioned in this book . . .

THE QUEEN'S READING ROOM

The Queen's Reading Room, launched by Her Majesty Queen Camilla in 2023, is a charity championing literature in the UK and beyond.

Through groundbreaking neuroscientific research, it seeks to discover and celebrate the unique power of books to improve brain health, mental health and social connection. Its first study using brain scans and skin conductance tests found that just five minutes of reading fiction both reduces stress by 20 per cent and improves the brain's capacity to manage stress, all while boosting concentration and focus and reducing feelings of loneliness.

The charity seeks to promote the accessibility and joy of stories and storytelling and it reaches more than 12 million people in 174 countries around the world each year with its free, educational book-based content, as well as staging major festivals and events across the UK and internationally. The charity was born from an Instagram book club launched during the 2021 lockdown.

The Queen's Reading Room is proud to partner with a range of charities to help bring books, authors and stories to everyone. Because books make life better.

For more information, visit queensreadingroom.co.uk

@thequeensreadingroom

BOOK AID INTERNATIONAL

Book Aid International

Book Aid International is a UK registered charity that shares the power of books and helps create a more equal world.

Access to books enriches lives. Books open doors to a lifetime of learning, light up imaginations, fire ambitions and help us see the world in new ways. Yet millions of people globally have few books or no books at all.

Book Aid International's vision is a world in which everyone has the opportunity to read. Every year the charity provides more than a million brand-new books to thousands of communities in which people need books. It also works with its partners to create hundreds of warm and welcoming reading spaces in schools, libraries and communities.

Each book the charity sends is carefully selected in response to partner requests. All of the books provided from the UK are donated by publishers. Book Aid International also funds the purchase of thousands of locally published books every year.

In an average year, more than 21 million people have the chance to read thanks to the charity's work.

Book Aid International receives no government grants or support and relies entirely on the generosity of book lovers like you to reach readers around the world. It costs just £2 to send the next brand-new book.

To find out more or to get involved, visit bookaid.org

Book Aid International is a registered charity in England and Wales. Charity number 313869 and company number 880754

SAFELIVES

Ending domestic abuse

For too many people, home isn't a safe place: the people who are meant to love them hurt them instead. Whether it's physical or psychological, abuse can happen to anyone, no matter where they live, how old they are or what sort of lifestyle they lead.

Thousands of survivors from all across the country have bravely shared their stories with SafeLives. Their experiences tell us everything about the warning signs and the consequences of inaction. And their insight shows what works to keep victims and their families safe.

Together with survivors, SafeLives is transforming the response to domestic abuse and abusive relationships so that those being harmed are made safer sooner while those doing the harming are held accountable.

If this has happened to you or to a friend or family member, please know that you are not alone. There is help and support for you.

If you'd like to support SafeLives, please find more information at safelives.org.uk/support-us

Domestic abuse helplines:
England and Wales 0808 2000 247
Scotland 0800 027 1234
Northern Ireland 0808 802 1414

Charity number 1106864

ST WILFRID'S HOSPICE EASTBOURNE

St Wilfrid's Hospice

St Wilfrid's Hospice provides high-quality care and support for people with life-limiting illnesses across Eastbourne, Seaford, Hailsham, Uckfield, Heathfield and all points between. Support is offered at the hospice, in patients' own homes and in care homes across the area.

Our expert teams support the physical, emotional, psychological, spiritual and practical needs of patients and their families and carers. We provide nursing, medical care and therapies in patients' homes, in care homes, in our Inpatient Unit and through our Living Well Hub, as well as on our telephone advice line. The hospice also provides pre- and post-bereavement support for the family and carers of patients.

As a registered charity, we receive only a small proportion of our running costs from the NHS. We count on the generosity of our supporters to help us with the rest, meaning that every donation or gift left in a will makes a difference to the support we can offer patients and their families.

Website: www.stwhospice.org
Email: hospice@stwhospice.org
Telephone: 01323 434200
Address: 1 Broadwater Way, Eastbourne, East Sussex, BN22 9PZ

Charity number 283686

SOUTHERN HOSPICE GROUP

This book mentions Queen Camilla's visit to the real Sussex hospices Martlets and Chestnut Tree House.

From fundraising and volunteering to gifts in wills, both hospices rely on the generosity of the local community to keep on caring.

Martlets and Chestnut Tree House, along with St Barnabas House adults' hospice in Worthing, form the Southern Hospice Group, a charity providing palliative and end-of-life care on-site, in the community and in people's homes.

Martlets

Martlets provides essential services to adults affected by terminal illness in Brighton and Hove and the surrounding areas. Their expert teams offer the very best hospice care and support, helping patients and their loved ones make the most of the precious time they have together.

martlets.org.uk

Chestnut Tree House

Chestnut Tree House is the children's hospice for Sussex and south-east Hampshire. Thanks to support from the local community, children and families who know they don't have long together have the chance to live life to the fullest and say goodbye in the way that is right for them.

chestnut.org.uk

'Peter James is one of the best crime writers in the business'

KARIN SLAUGHTER

Some will know how it begins . . .

Her name is Sandy. You might know her as the loving wife of Detective Superintendent Roy Grace. But there's more to her than meets the eye. A woman with a dubious past, a complicated present and an uncertain future. Then she was gone . . .

Some will know how it ends . . .

Her disappearance caused a nationwide search. Even the best detective on the force couldn't find her. They thought she was dead.

But nobody knows this . . .

Where did she go? Why did she run? What would cause a woman to leave her whole life behind and simply vanish?

AVAILABLE NOW

NOW A MAJOR ITV SERIES

Peter James's first twelve books in the Detective Superintendent Roy Grace series have been adapted for television and star John Simm as Roy Grace.

Discover Peter James's books at peterjames.com

'Another stonking story from the master of the craft'
EXPRESS

THE NUMBER ONE BESTSELLER
PETER JAMES
I FOLLOW YOU
...UNTIL YOU ARE MINE

To the outside world, charming doctor Marcus Valentine has it all: a loving wife, three kids and a great job. But there's something missing.

Driving to work one morning, his mind elsewhere and not on the road, he almost mows down a female jogger who is the spitting image of his first love, the girl who got away.

Despite all his attempts to resist, his thoughts are consumed by this woman. And when events take a tragically unexpected turn, his obsession threatens to destroy both their worlds...

AVAILABLE NOW IN PAPERBACK, EBOOK AND AUDIOBOOK

'So horrifyingly scary that I was unable to sleep'
THE MAIL ON SUNDAY

THE NUMBER ONE BESTSELLER
PETER JAMES
PERFECT PEOPLE
WHAT LIES BEHIND PERFECTION?

WITH A NEW FOREWORD FROM PETER JAMES

John and Naomi Klaesson desperately want another child but fear passing on the genetic disease that killed their first son.

Then they hear about Dr Leo Dettore. He has methods that can spare them the heartache of ever losing another child. But his clinic is where their nightmare begins.

They should have realized something was wrong when they saw the list. Choices of eye colour, hair, sporting abilities. But now it's too late to turn back. Naomi is pregnant and already something is badly wrong . . .

AVAILABLE NOW IN HARDBACK, PAPERBACK, EBOOK AND AUDIOBOOK

'Sensational – the best what-if thriller since *The Da Vinci Code*'
LEE CHILD

THE NUMBER ONE BESTSELLER

PETER JAMES

ABSOLUTE PROOF

Investigative reporter Ross Hunter nearly didn't answer the call that would change his life – and possibly the world – for ever.

'I'd just like to assure you I'm not a nutcase, Mr Hunter. My name is Dr Harry F. Cook. I know this is going to sound strange, but I've recently been given absolute proof of God's existence – and I've been advised there is a writer, a respected journalist called Ross Hunter, who could help me to get taken seriously.'

What would it take to prove the existence of God?
And what would be the consequences?

AVAILABLE NOW IN PAPERBACK, EBOOK AND AUDIOBOOK

'Impeccable'
SUNDAY TIMES

17 MILLION COPIES SOLD

PETER JAMES
THE HOUSE ON COLD HILL

EVIL ISN'T BORN,
IT'S BUILT...

Ollie and Caro Harcourt and their twelve-year-old daughter Jade are thrilled with their move to Cold Hill House – a huge, dilapidated Georgian mansion – and the countryside surrounding it.

But within days of moving in, it becomes apparent that the Harcourt family aren't the only residents of the house . . .

AVAILABLE NOW IN PAPERBACK, EBOOK AND AUDIOBOOK